Waldenstei

Waldenstein

a novel by
Rosalie Osmond

Seraphim
EDITIONS

The publisher gratefully acknowledges the financial assistance of the Canada Council for the Arts.

 Canada Council **Conseil des Arts**
for the Arts **du Canada**

Library and Arhives Canada Cataloguing in Publication

Osmond, Rosalie, 1942-, author

    Waldenstein : a novel / by Rosalie Osmond.

ISBN 978-1-927079-19-5 (pbk.)

    I. Title.

PS8629.S547W34 2013   C813'.6   C2013-905049-3

Editor: Kathryn McKeen
Design and Typography: Julie McNeill, McNeill Design Arts

Published in 2013 by
Seraphim Editions
54 Bay Street
Woodstock, ON
Canada N4S 3K9

Printed and bound in Canada

For the grandparents I never knew.

Contents

Prelude | 9

Aaron's Kingdom
Millers and Wentzells | 16
Fractures | 36
Varieties of Death | 44

Erika
Season of Discontent | 56
Winter at the Camp | 68
Truth | 88
Consequences | 95
Flight | 104
Aftermath | 124

A Shaking of Certainties
Rose | 142
Another Country | 161
Enlightenment | 175
Madness | 195

The New Generation
Skirting Sex | 218
Moving On | 227
Absence | 253

Knowledge
Adam | 262
Search for a Father | 271
Coming Home | 289
Endings and Beginnings | 308

Acknowledgements | 327

Prelude

1912

Emma and Virtue woke as one. A soft, pale light filled their bedroom silvering the coarse, white cotton of the wool-bed cover and the pillow cases where their small heads lay. The window glass was covered by frost that stole inside to coat the frame as well. It must have snowed during the night, but under the covers it was warm and cozy. The young sisters shifted comfortably, savouring the contrast between the warmth and the cold. They were about to lapse back into sleep when they were struck by a feeling that something was wrong. Perhaps they had not been awakened by the snowy light alone. Through the round iron grating in the floor came a flickering red light that bounced on the silver walls and threw up alarming, changing shadows. Then there were cries. They did not sound like human cries; they were inarticulate, high, piercing wails that resolved into something that sounded like "No, no, nooo." A word, it seemed. So maybe the cries were human after all.

The two small sisters glanced at one another. Then, barefooted and white-gowned, they leapt out of bed and ran downstairs. There, lying on the kitchen floor, screaming and writhing, was their elder sister, Flora. Mama and Papa were trying to hold her down, but she was fighting them off with all her might. Suddenly her mouth contorted like a picture of the damned in hell they had seen in their Sunday School leaflet. The two girls stopped short, terrified. What was happening? What could Flora have done to deserve such a terrible punishment?

Mama glanced up. She did not seem surprised to see Emma and Virtue standing there; she did not tell them to go back to bed. Instead she said abruptly, "Run across to the Conrads and get them to come over here; Papa will give Ebenezer the horse and sleigh to go for the doctor."

For a moment they stood still, uncomprehending. They were only eight and six years old. "Across" was not across the street but across the lake or, even farther, around it. They were never allowed to play alone by the lake even in the daytime. And now it was the middle of the night and snowing.

"Go!" Mama shouted at them. Then dragging her attention momentarily from Flora, she added, "Put on your coats and boots, and take the lantern. Hurry!" And a few seconds later as they were struggling to put on their coats over their nightdresses, "Best not go across the lake. It might not be solid yet. Go around."

Soon they were outside the house, running through the snow, trying to find the path around the lake, too frightened to speak to one another. When they were both out of breath they stopped, and Emma looked around. "It's pretty," she said. And indeed it was. The snow flurry had ended, and the moon was just coming out once more from behind some clouds. A soft radiance shrouded everything. Ahead of them the lake gleamed, flat and white. All around were tall spruce trees, bent low with the heavy snow. Remembering their mother's admonition, they turned to the right and walked where they thought the shore path must be.

It was hard work, pulling their small feet out of the depth of snow that they sank into with each step. Yet, in spite of this, slowly Emma began to feel a sense of exhilaration. "We're on a *mission!*" she exclaimed to Virtue. Whatever terrible thing it was that had sent them out on this midnight ramble was bringing Emma some small pleasure. Virtue thought about being cold; she thought about how annoying Emma could be, always making things up, always using big words. "A mission," she snorted. "Mama doesn't care if we die or not. It'll be like one of those fairy tales. We might be eaten."

"It's too cold for anything to be out eating us," Emma replied.

"Well, we're out, aren't we? Other things might be too. You don't know everything."

Emma felt snubbed. Anyway, she was too out of breath to argue. But it was beautiful. Was it wrong to see that, even when something awful was happening at home?

Eventually they reached the Conrad house. Everything was dark. Even the path to the back door was only a shallow indentation under the new fallen snow. The dog began to bark. Now it was Emma who quailed. "He's shut up in the barn for the night," said Virtue. "They always do that."

They banged on the door. After a while Mr. Conrad appeared, dressed in a white nightgown doubtless made from bleached flour sacks, just like theirs. "What in the name of...?" He stood astonished, seeing the two tiny girls. "What are you doing here at this time of night?"

"Mama sent us," Virtue began, asserting her status as the elder. "Something's wrong at home – with Flora. Mama said would you please come over as fast as you can and go for the doctor. Papa will give you the horse and sleigh. And would Martha please come too."

Virtue considered that she had discharged her duty adequately. But Emma felt her account somewhat lacking in colour. "They're holding Flora on the floor, and she's screaming. It woke us up. I think even Mama and Papa are scared."

"Well, come in, come in. If Agnes and Aaron need help, I'll be there. I'll get a fire going."

"No you mustn't do that. Mama said to hurry, hurry."

Just then Martha came down the stairs, and decisions were made. Ebenezer would set off at once, and Martha and the girls would follow when they had warmed up and had a hot drink.

The journey back, Emma felt, was not as much fun as going out had been. The moon had disappeared again, and every so often there was another snow flurry. And Martha kept asking questions – questions they couldn't answer. "What exactly was wrong? Why did they

11

need the doctor? Was Flora sick? When did it start?" And on and on. As they approached the house, Emma felt a knot of fear harden in her stomach. The barn door was open, so Ebenezer and Josh, the horse, must have started on the twenty-four-mile round trip for the doctor.

Virtue found herself suddenly shaking, and not just from the cold. She thought maybe she might throw up, right there in the snow. "What do you think…?" she began.

"Do we have to go in?" Emma finished.

"Flora…" Was she still the Flora who bossed them and played with them? Or had that person disappeared, slipped down some incline where the screaming came from and left them for good?

It was little Joan, only two and a half, who was crying when they entered the kitchen, her dark hair damp and stuck in small clusters against her forehead, her little hands pushing it back in vain against the flood of tears that streamed down her face. Flora was sitting inert in an armchair by the stove, her head hanging limply, saying nothing. Was she still alive? Mama was trying to comfort Joan, and Papa was kneeling in front of Flora. When they came in Mama stood up, gave Joan to Papa, and said to Martha simply, "Come." The two women disappeared into the parlour.

Emma and Virtue, now mere bystanders in the unfolding drama, stood wet and dripping, as near to the fire as they could without getting close to Flora, who was not their sister anymore but a strange, fearful being for whom doctors were being sought and to whom potions were offered. Perhaps she was a witch, Emma thought.

Only when Agnes and Martha returned from the parlour did Mama seem to notice her two children, still in their outdoor coats and hats. She glanced briefly at them and said in a voice nearly breaking with tears, "What brave girls! Take off your coats and boots and warm up. You can go back to bed. There's nothing more you can do." Thus Agnes, still preoccupied, dismissed them.

They took off their boots and coats, and Martha wrapped them in warm blankets, but they had no intention of going back to bed. They sat on the bench that ran along one side of the kitchen and waited.

And waited. Silence enveloped everything. No one seemed to know they were there.

After a long time there came the sound of sleigh bells; Dr. Carter had arrived. He was a small man, thin, with an upturned moustache and keen blue eyes. Aaron led him to Flora, but when the doctor bent over her, as if on cue, she threw her head back, twisted her face and began to scream again. "See, she is a witch," whispered Emma. There were things like this in the Bible. She regretted that Papa had no pigs. If he had, everything might have been solved easily.

"Don't be so stupid." Virtue was having none of it. Doctors could cure things; they could cure anything.

After a bit, Dr. Carter straightened up and put his stethoscope away. "It looks like epilepsy," he pronounced after some time. "Epilepsy!" What a word. Anyone who knew a word like that could cure anything. Virtue nudged Emma as if to say, "I told you so."

"We need lots of hot water and two large tubs. Can you provide those?"

Mama was uncertain. "We've got the tin bath, that's one."

Aaron intervened. "I can get another." He went out to the barn and reappeared with a huge, filthy pan. "It'll have to do. Can you clean it, Agnes?" So she took the old, appalling pan over to the sink and pumped water into it and swooshed it around, scrubbing it with a brush and soap. But you could barely hear the swooshing of the water because of the awful noise Flora was still making.

At last the two pans of water sat beside one another on the wooden floor, one steaming, one ice cold. Then Flora, who had gone limp again, was undressed all except for her bloomers, and Papa and the doctor lifted her first into the cold water, then into the hot, then back into the cold again, over and over. As they moved her, Emma concentrated on Flora's hair, brown and wavy, floating down behind her, shining in the lamplight, its ends dipping gently in the water. No one had hair like Flora, or so her mother said. So she kept her attention riveted on the hair to cut out everything else. For if Flora had screamed before, it was as nothing to the sounds she emitted now – sounds Emma

13

and Virtue had never heard come from a human being, high-pitched and disembodied. With Mama, Papa and Martha, the girls stood in a circle around Flora and the tubs, the red firelight glowing out through the cracks in the iron stove, the only other light a dim oil lamp on the kitchen table. No matter what else you tried to think of, you couldn't get rid of the terrible noise. Maybe this was what hell was like, Emma thought. But neither she nor Virtue could move. They stood riveted by the scene. They would never forget it.

Aaron's Kingdom

Millers and Wentzells

1896

Midsummer in Waldenstein: heat gently rising from the grass, swirling in soft puffs around the leaves of apple trees, the lulling drone of cicadas everywhere. In the midst of this soporific landscape, Aaron Miller stood alert and purposeful, holding a map. It was a map of the whole county, but he had folded it so that Waldenstein, this tiny community of ragged farmland, woods and lakes spread over about six square miles, was uppermost. He was studying it intently.

The house at the farther edge of the orchard where he stood was deserted now; Aaron's father was long dead, and his half-sisters gone to "the States," that inscrutable country to the south. But the orchard, in some measure, survived – gnarled, scrubby, insect-ridden. The tiny apples, he noted, were marred with black spots. Some of the leaves were already browning and dropping to the ground. He tried an apple and spat it out. But Aaron was young, just twenty-one, and not easily discouraged by surroundings, such as the orchard, that manifestly belonged to his past. What he felt here was a certain comfort, a tranquility that flowed out from him to the fields and low hills beyond. In this orchard he felt he belonged – but in Waldenstein?

He knew he was still called the "Englishman" behind his back. His ancestors, as far as he knew, had been "New England Planters" who had moved into the province of Nova Scotia from the eastern seacoast of America to fill the fertile lands in the Annapolis Valley from which the French had been forcibly evicted. Why Aaron's father, old Joseph Miller, had made the journey from the Valley to the unpromising soil of Waldenstein no one, including Aaron, was certain. Joseph had had bad luck – or made bad choices. It was not just his own mother who had died, Aaron reflected. Three other wives had vacated their office successively and permanently, one by one. Not that anyone suspected foul play – they all died in perfectly legitimate ways: three in childbirth, one of pneumonia. And it wasn't just the wives who died. Even this orchard that Joseph had planted on a piece of scrubland behind his house failed to flourish.

None of this deterred Aaron. He stood defying the dying trees, firmly holding the map. He was planning his future.

To be sure, the map, like the orchard, did not present an encouraging picture. The first thing Aaron noticed was that it was full of little tracks and roads that trailed off spider-like and came to an abrupt end. Naturally, he was aware of this as he travelled about Waldenstein, but the map somehow emphasized the discontinuity. These roads didn't end because they came to bigger tracks or roads, or natural obstacles like lakes or rivers, he observed. They just ended. Someone became exhausted and stopped and built a house. Someone cut timber as far as he was allowed. Someone ran out of time or money – or died. And the names that were imprinted on the map! Misery Lake, Skull Lake, Grandmother Head Lake (why on earth that?) Moose Snare Lake, Beck's Shoals, Ben Wentzell's Big Rocks. But none of this seemed a portent that had anything to do with him. He gazed beyond the orchard at the rolling treed hills and the valleys studded with lakes. Someday it would all be his; he was invincible.

Then he looked up and saw that he was not alone. A young girl, still in her apron, was wandering through the deformed trees. Ah, it must be Agnes Kraus. She lived nearby with her parents and two brothers and, by all accounts, was kept pretty busy by her mother who had been heard to say it was "good training for a girl; teaches her what to expect out of life." She was probably fifteen, Aaron guessed. She was not strikingly beautiful but pretty in a petite, demure way, with clear skin, and large dark eyes. She must have walked the half mile along what was now little more than a track to the old house and orchard in an afternoon break between cleaning up after dinner and getting ready for supper. As she came nearer, Aaron could see that she looked pensive, head down, lost in her own thoughts and feelings, whatever they might be. It was a fine day, and she was young and healthy as far as he knew. So why did she look so sad? Then she raised her head and noticed Aaron.

They knew one another, of course; everyone in Waldenstein knew everyone else. They had met at church and at general social events such as weddings, funerals, maple sugaring and communal building projects where the whole community joined together to raise the frame of a house or barn, church or school. Still, he could not recall ever actually speaking to her. She was a child; he owned a mill and now employed half the men in Waldenstein.

She walked up to him as he stood there, tall and impassive, leaning against the tree, folding up his map. She seemed tentative, uncertain how to begin, yet wanting to stay.

"It's lovely weather. Good for haying my Father says."

"Yes, indeed. I saw the Conrads out with the oxen hauling some that had dried back to the barn this morning," Aaron agreed, smiling down at her, wondering how to put her at ease, how to keep her there. But she showed no inclination to bolt.

"You don't have any hay to make, do you?" she said.

"No, just logs to saw into lumber. Winter, when we're cutting in the woods, is the busiest time for me."

"What's it like out there, cuttin' down trees all winter?"

"Well, sometimes it's hard when it's stormy, and it's always cold. But there are lots of us, and we keep each other good company. In the evening we sit around the fire and play games. Not for money," he added hastily.

"My brothers work for you, and they seem cheerful enough – at least they're always jokin' and laughin' when they're home – but they never tell me what it's really like back at the camp."

"I'm glad they're happy. They're good workers." It sounded stilted, wrong as soon as he said it.

There was a pause. She seemed about to go. But then she looked up at him again and said, "So you own the mill…" (Was there an implied rebuke – "while my brothers only work for you"?)

So, instinctively, he replied to what she had left unspoken. "I guess I was just lucky. Josiah adopted me because he had no sons, and then when he bought a lot of woodland and built the mill he got me involved in running it." Now that he had begun, the whole narrative wanted to tumble out in front of this tiny girl-woman. "And when I was only fourteen he gave me fifty acres of land for my very own to sort of pay for the help I'd given him up to then. From then on he paid me proper wages as well, so by the time I was sixteen I could buy a hundred acres more. Then, three years ago, when I was eighteen, he died, and I was left running the mill and the winter lumber camp on my own. I still miss him, but getting the mill and all that land has certainly given me a good start."

If Agnes was impressed, she knew better than to show it. She looked at the map in his hand. "Why do you have a map?"

"Well I…actually I was just looking at what land might come vacant to buy in the next year or so." He faltered. Perhaps Agnes would think him greedy. But if so, she made no comment. She just returned abruptly to her own life.

"We work all the time, my mother and me. Winter or summer, it doesn't matter. And…and we don't play games in the evening, either. There's socks to knit or darn or somethin'. Always somethin'. "

Was this a complaint? What did she expect from him in return? She had pulled a leaf from a low-hanging tree branch and now looked down again as she wound it round and round her finger. The sun glistened through the leaves onto her dark hair.

"You must be a great comfort to your family," he finally said. Inane, not the right thing, he told himself again. But it only seemed to spur Agnes on.

"Maybe. Most of the time they don't seem to care whether I'm there or not. I'm just help; not even hired."

"Oh." What else could he say?

There was a long pause while she twisted the leaf to extinction. Suddenly she threw it down, turned and left, not looking back.

The next evening Aaron went to visit her.

ॐ

Down the hill from the old Miller farm, in a fertile dip in the landscape, Jacob Wentzell walked determinedly to his barn to yoke the oxen. There was a sense of entitlement in his very step. He was, after all, the fourth generation of his family in the New World. He knew their story, had been told it from his cradle. There had been Jacob Wentzell the first, whose father, Michael, had been born amidst the bustling creation of Karlsruhe, that German Versailles where his father, Johann, had been one of the Archduke's outriders. To Jacob, listening as a child, this had sounded unbelievably wonderful. They had lived in a small house near the stables, built on the outer circumference of the grand circle that was the Royal estate. They were loosely attached to the court, but they had no land; they could not read nor write. So at eighteen, Michael Wentzell put his X on the shipping list and allowed himself to be transported in a foul vessel called the *Pearl* to the shores of the New World. Through disease and hunger, he had persevered and founded a family. Jacob, his great-great-grandson, hadn't been lucky to marry the prettiest girl in Waldenstein; he had deserved her.

Jacob knew that he, like his horse-riding great-great-great grandfather, was handsome, with the same large Teutonic blue eyes, dark wavy hair and tall presence that had perhaps drawn his ancestor to the attention of the Archduke. So of course he had married the beautiful Frederika, a second cousin with fair skin, light brown curls and, most important of all, good child-bearing hips. And those hips were at this very moment supporting their first child, due to be born later in the month.

Jacob ruminated on all this as he left the house for the barn. It was a beautiful morning in early July. The sky was cobalt behind the frail green of the apple trees. He sang as he began to harness the oxen.

Old farmer John from his work came home
One summer afternoon
And sat him down 'neath a maple tree
And sang himself a tune.

After the song, he turned the team towards the road and talked to the animals in a friendly sort of way, treating them more or less as equals in the struggle for survival. "Come on, lads, we've got a bit of excitement today." Indeed they were going on a small adventure, hauling the winter's cutting of wood down to the ship in Mahone Bay that would carry it to Liverpool. He would have no company on this journey (his brother, Ben – he of the Big Rocks – declined to go with him). But it was a fine summer day, and he was happy to travel alone.

He went into the house to say good-bye to Frederika. "I'm on my way." One day down, one day back; he would not return until the following night. He kissed her and stroked the swollen belly. "I won't stay a minute longer than I have to," he promised.

"You'd better not. This little fellow is kicking as if he wants out soon."

The ox cart lumbered slowly out of Waldenstein. The first cross-roads, the centre, insofar as there was one, of the community was marked by the cemetery. Here Jacob turned left, calling out "Haw". Past the tiny school and the single white church (Lutheran, of course) they rumbled. Again a left turning, and again "Haw". Then it was straight along a road with only woodland on either side for thirty miles.

The sun shone warmly down on his head, his bare arms, his rolled-up trousers. The lumber made a gentle bouncing clunk-clunk as he travelled over the dirt road. Leaves on the tree branches created dancing, dappled shadows on the cart. He began to hum a song he had just learned at the sight-singing classes an itinerant musician was offering weekly at the school: "Was ist Sylvia?" He belonged to the last generation who could still speak German, and he moved between it and English with ease. What was Sylvia, indeed? He saw a girl with light brown curls, fair skin and blue eyes. Not flirtatious, given to housewifery. Rather like Frederika.

He didn't think about happiness; it simply surrounded him. Until eventually a slight wisp of something, a faint shadow clouded his song. What was it? There was something deep down that was scratching away at the all-encompassing perfection of the day, a tiny feeling of unease. Ah yes, it was Aaron, Aaron Miller. Now that he had the mill he would soon own them all. "Not thinking of selling any of your land, are you Jacob?" he had asked him the other day.

"No, what makes you think I would?"

"Just wonderin'."

And he had swung off smartly on his horse and wagon with a flick of the whip. "Just wonderin'." As if all the land in Waldenstein, even that in Jacob's own family for a hundred years, was just sitting there, waiting for Aaron to buy it. Still, it was good to have the mill to get your lumber sawed, and a chance to get some wages for cutting wood in winter. And at least the wages he paid were fair. But where had he come from? If old Josiah had not taken a fancy to the boy and left him the mill, he would have been nothing, nothing.

Still, what was the use of working himself up over it? He went back to Sylvia and music. Gradually the singing changed to humming, then stopped. His head drooped. After a minute he jerked sharply up, took the whip in his hands and waved it a bit in the air as if to re-establish control. The oxen lumbered on, gently switching their tails to keep the flies away. Soon his head drooped again, and he was fast asleep.

The next thing he felt was a violent swaying, a listing to one side, the whole cart tipping over, himself thrown out of his seat to the ground, and then the excruciating pain of the lumber falling on his legs. Where was his head? It seemed to be almost upside down, leaning sharply into an incline of fern and grass. He tried to move; he tried

22

to lift his head to see better exactly what the problem was. But with his legs pinned down at the top of what he now perceived to be the ditch, and his head a foot below at the bottom, this was hopeless. Anyway, every exertion gave him so much pain that he soon ceased to struggle. He waited.

Frederika. What was she doing now? The baby would be coming soon. He had promised her. He struggled a bit more, gave up as sweat poured from his forehead. It was inconceivable that someone should not come along the road soon, he reasoned.

But the day passed, the shadows lengthened, and he was still alone. When he turned his head he could just see the oxen, tethered to the fallen cart, moving as far as they could towards the ditch and eating what grass they could reach. They had the advantage of him, he reflected; he had nothing to eat or drink, and soon he was overtaken by a raging thirst. Night fell, and still no one came. It was midsummer, and most farmers, he knew, were not travelling the road but making hay or weeding vegetable crops. The only reason he had decided to bring this load to town now was to get the extra money before Frederika had the baby.

The pain wasn't too bad if he didn't move. With his one free arm he managed to reach a few tufts of moss to put under his head, still hanging at a most precarious angle. Then, at last, he slept. And he dreamed. He was thirsty, intolerably thirsty, and he was crawling, crawling ever so slowly towards a tiny pond of water. Just as he was about to reach it he saw Aaron, standing in front of the water, and smiling down at him as he moved to block his path. "This water is not for you," he said enigmatically. There was a woman beside him as well. She had a rounded figure and wavy, light-brown hair. Who was she? Aaron had his arm around her shoulder, and she turned and smiled at him. Jacob seemed invisible to her.

He woke in the pitch dark, shivering from the cold. Nothing he could do would warm him. And it was all his own fault. He had fallen asleep, and the oxen had veered off one side of the road. No "Gee" or "Haw" would help until someone else arrived. His thirst grew even more insistent. As it began to get light, he saw a bottle of water he had brought for the journey lying in the ditch, just out of reach. He stretched and wriggled until finally his fingertips touched it and rolled it farther away.

Another day he waited – and another night. He no longer thought of anything – not even Frederika. What time was it? How long had he been by the side of the road? Finally, on the third day, he heard the rattling of another ox cart. It was his brother, Ben.

*

"What on earth!" Ben had known something must have happened when Jacob didn't return as planned – but this!

"I fell asleep." No excuses, no self-justification, just the blunt truth.

Ben was a practical man who didn't waste time on pity. First, he gave Jacob the water bottle. Then, methodically, he began to pull the timber off his legs, sliding it along the bank and down into the ditch. When Jacob was free, Ben pulled him up and moved him, groaning with pain, onto his own cart. One leg seemed more or less intact; the other dragged helplessly. There was no way Ben could right the broken cart on his own, so he unyoked the oxen to forage and left the cart on its side. Then they began the slow journey home. There were no recriminations on Ben's part, and little spoken gratitude on Jacob's. Wentzells knew that talking about such things was a waste of time. Jacob had been careless, but his brother had come and rescued him. These things happened.

When they reached the crossing by the cemetery, Jacob noticed that they were not turning; they were going straight on. Through the fog of pain, it occurred to him for a brief moment that maybe Ben was about to enter the cemetery and bury him. Anticipating Jacob's confusion, Ben said, "We've got to go to the doctor in New Germany."

"But Frederika?" Now the thought of her came back to him with longing.

"We've got to go to the doctor. Your leg's broken. You ain't no good to Frederika or anyone else like this."

So off they lumbered for twelve more miles, every jolt of the cart an agonizing stab of pain.

As they were passing through Barss Corner, there came the clattering of a horse's hooves behind them. It could only be one person. Aaron swept up to the ox cart and stopped. Reluctantly, Ben stopped as well.

"What's goin' on?"

Jacob was past speaking, so it was Ben who replied, "Jacob's broke his leg. We're on our way to the doctor."

"How'd that happen?"

"Ox team went off the road and overturned the cart on the way to Mahone Bay with a load of wood."

"But how on earth…?"

Ben wanted to lie; he wanted to say that one of the oxen had gone mad and left the road in a wild frenzy. But he couldn't; the habit of truth was too deeply ingrained. "Seems he probably fell asleep, and the oxen strayed into the ditch."

"Too bad." They could feel the scorn. Aaron never fell asleep – possibly not even in his own bed at night. He was up at dawn, planning till midnight, working, working, working – and making money.

Now, having heard the story, he flicked his horse gently with his whip and was gone, calling out as he left, "Hope you're better soon, Jacob. I'll need you for the winter cutting."

Even in his pain, Jacob felt a sharp anger rising. "Drat him, drat him," he muttered. He and Ben, *their* ancestors were the ones who had cleared the land, who had done the early planting and building of houses. Who was this upstart? The humiliation of being seen by him like this, lying helpless on the cart, and having his stupidity, his falling asleep, exposed!

Ben reached back and put a hand on his arm. "Don't mind him. Pride goeth before a fall." Jacob sank back and closed his eyes.

Eventually he raised his head and saw a few houses dotting the roadside. They must have reached New Germany, a well-established little village with fifty families, a tiny grocery store with a curious ceiling made of interlocking bits of corrugated cardboard salvaged from fruit boxes, and a doctor. Ben knocked at the surgery door, and a large woman with red hair, the doctor's wife, appeared. "He's out. Someone way back and beyond's having a baby."

Jacob heard Ben saying, "But it's my brother; he needs help real bad. He's broken his leg and been by the side of the road three days and nights."

"Well, you can bring him in, but I've got no idea when he'll get seen by the doctor. Sometimes these women take forever to have a baby, you know."

In agony, Jacob, with Ben's help, got down from the cart and hopped into the doctor's house. There he slumped in a chair and sat staring at an elaborately patterned carpet, the like of which he had never seen before, for half an hour.

When the doctor appeared, he was bouncing with enthusiasm over the successful birth he had just attended. "Absolutely beautiful, mother and baby both. No problems. Just pushed it out as if she'd done it a hundred times. But the poor thing had no husband around – said he'd gone to Mahone Bay with a load of lumber three days ago and not been seen since. I wonder. Well, some men can't take these things. A great pity, though. She was very brave – and pretty. What an oaf her husband must be."

Jacob, hearing all this, roused himself. "Was the baby a boy or a girl?"

"A little girl, pretty as her mother."

"And where…where do they live?"

"Ever so far back. Twelve miles from here on the most deserted road in Waldenstein. Why people moved there at all, what with the rocky soil and the loneliness, I can't imagine."

"I think – I think mebbe it's my baby." And with that, as the doctor began to set his leg, Jacob became mercifully unconscious.

26

The following May a wedding took place in the old orchard. Agnes and Aaron stood under the gnarled apple trees and vowed to love one another forever. They had chosen to be married here where they had first spoken almost two years before.

Spring favoured the orchard; the dead and stunted branches and the twisted trunks were hidden by pale, pink blossoms. New grass grew underfoot, pale mayflowers lurked beside some of the trees.

Aaron had bought a suit – his first – from the Eaton's catalogue. He was painfully aware that it didn't fit perfectly; indeed the sleeves were about an inch too short, but the shiny dark blue jacket and trousers, the white shirt and the tie subtly figured with small flowers that echoed the blossoms on the trees showed a height of dress sense never before attained in Waldenstein.

Agnes' dress was both more usual and more elaborate. Dresses were more easily made at home than suits, although she hadn't had much to do with this one herself. Muriel, her mother, had taken making this as her duty and privilege. Cut from fine cotton, elaborately tucked and gathered, with a high cream lace collar that circled Agnes' tiny neck and a further extravaganza of lace that overlaid the entire bodice, it was a wonder to behold. Most marvellous of all was her tiny waist, grasped firmly by numerous tucks and folds that then expanded into a lavishly flared skirt, also of lace. The whole effect made Agnes look like a tiny doll, a pretend bride, playing at getting married. Aaron looked in amazement. Could he really take this fearful and acquiescent being as his wife? It seemed an act of violation almost, of cruelty. Yet, he would do it. He would promise to love her forever. What would that mean? How could anyone promise that? Agnes' parents had, and as far as he could tell, it had turned out to be a lie.

Friends and family stood around, and a group of the men who attended the sight-singing class broke into an impromptu rendition of "Was ist Sylvia" when the short ceremony was over. Then they all walked back to Agnes' family home where they ate cold chicken, potato salad, fresh rolls, cakes and preserved fruit; the wild strawberries had not yet ripened.

ঙ

Frederika watched it all. She sat with Jacob at one of the tables that had been set up outdoors, while little Erika laughed and played in the grass. Frederika looked enviously at Agnes' tiny form. How could she help it? She had once been considered the prettiest girl in Waldenstein, but now her figure had thickened, and even her features, she thought when she looked into the mirror, seemed larger and coarser. Her nose was still straight, her skin fine and unlined, but there was a thickness about her neck, a lack of definition to her cheekbones.

She glanced at Jacob. Yes, he was definitely better looking than Aaron, who had straight black hair and tiny grey-blue eyes so sharp they pricked you like pins when he looked at you. This was reassuring. But there was something about Aaron – the way he carried himself, the confidence with which he even laughed. And then she glanced down at Jacob's leg; their eyes met. She saw that he followed her glance and her thoughts and was flooded with guilt. But how could she help it? The accident had changed him. Now he had a tiny limp – not noticeable most of the time, only there when he carried back the full, heavy milk pails in the evening – but bound to get worse as he got older. She stopped thinking and ate a piece of cake.

Then there was fiddling by Jim Corkum and square dancing on the lawn. "Let's go home," Jacob said. "Erika needs to go to bed." He picked the child up and sat her on his shoulder. "Home we go!" Erika bounced on her perch and laughed.

Frederika gathered up her cloak and followed. Only once did she look back at the dancing couples.

❧

Eventually everyone else went home as well, and Agnes and Aaron stood alone on the deserted lawn. From inside they could hear the rattle of dishes being washed up. Aaron gently put his arm around Agnes and drew her into the house. He could feel her body tensing.

"I've heard that some couples 'go away,' after they get married. For a vacation, sort of," Agnes murmured. "But not people here, I guess. Where would we go? How on earth would we get there? By ox-cart?" And she laughed wistfully. "We don't even have our own home yet."

"No, but we will, we will. I swear we won't be here with your parents for more than a year. The land I've got by the little lake – I'll start building there tomorrow. The front of the house will face the rising moon as it comes up over the water. Just you wait."

The kitchen, as they entered it, could not have been a greater contrast to the scene Aaron was conjuring up. Muriel, Agnes' mother, ran around clearing up plates while her two older brothers sprawled nonchalantly on the wooden bench that sat under the kitchen window. Zachariah, Agnes' father, was nowhere in sight.

"You can run along now, if you want to," said Muriel.

"Wohin?" asked Agnes. "Where to?" In times of stress she sometimes still spoke German. She looked at Aaron; he cast his eyes down and did not meet her gaze. He could see that she was afraid; she did not want to go anywhere, certainly not up to the bedroom that had been newly decorated for them. But he also knew that she was a good girl who had given all her life so far to doing her duty. He turned and smiled at her. He took her hand, and slowly they went upstairs.

Slowly, slowly she undressed. Aaron had deft fingers, and he helped to free the tiny buttons from their little loops. She stepped out of the dress, put on her white nightgown and slipped under the covers. Aaron looked down on her face. In it he saw pure terror. Her eyes were wide, her lips drawn in a straight line as she lay still and silent. For a moment, he pitied her. Then, gently, he drew back the sheet.

৯

Their first child, Rose, was born the next summer. She was a beautiful baby, with her mother's large dark eyes and her father's white skin. They were delighted. And so, naturally, was Muriel. It was, after all, her first grandchild.

At first Agnes was grateful for her mother's help. Just seventeen, what did she know of looking after an infant? Her two brothers were older, and there had never been any close neighbours with young children that she might have practised on. She fed Rose, and then gave her up willingly to be changed and rocked back to sleep by her grandmother. When the child began to sit up and play, the two of them sat on the floor, one on either side of Rose, taking turns rolling a ball to her, playing pat-a-cake, or pointing out the pictures in a simple book that Aaron had drawn and painted for her.

Agnes had occasionally walked down the hill to visit with Frederika and little Erika. The little girl, now two, seemed to be delighted to have a baby to play with. But Frederika, while always polite, seemed to close up some inner door of her being when Agnes arrived.

"Do you ever find it hard to look after Erika, running around after her all day?" Agnes ventured, tentatively.

"Not really. I'm used to hard work." There was a pause. Agnes didn't know how to respond to this. So Frederika went on. "And I don't have a mother to look after my child either."

Agnes murmured something about being lucky. It seemed to be the expected response.

"And then too, there's the farm chores. Jacob can't be expected to do it all. The hens and milking – that's my job."

"Oh yes. How is Jacob's leg?" Agnes thought maybe this was what Frederika was getting at.

"Jacob's leg is fine – just fine." And Frederika thumped the iron down on the shirt she was pressing.

After a few more fruitless attempts at befriending Frederika, Agnes gave up on the only other young mother within miles and retreated home to Muriel.

Zachariah largely ignored little Rose, as indeed he ignored Muriel – had done so for years. And Agnes' brothers, Rose's two uncles, were either working in the woods or at Aaron's mill or, in the summer evenings, "out wenching." Aaron was always busy, leaving at sunrise and returning, exhausted, at seven in the evening, just in time to see Rose put to bed. So they mothered together, the two women, and Agnes drew closer to her own mother than she had ever been since she herself was little.

Still, there were moments that filled Agnes with trepidation and made her long for her own home.

"What are you doing to that child?" Muriel exclaimed once when Rose had a small choke while being fed. "You're stuffing it in too fast. No wonder the poor thing can't swallow it." And she came and took the spoon roughly out of Agnes' hand and took over the chair she had been sitting in. "There, there. Grandma knows how to feed little girls, doesn't she?" Agnes felt her eyes fill with tears.

If Rose bumped herself as she began to toddle, that too was Agnes' fault. "You must hold her hand, not just let her roam around and bump into things all over the place."

"But she wants to be free. She doesn't want me holding her hand all the time. She wants to explore."

"Well she may explore to her own sorrow – and yours too."

ॐ

This time she told Aaron. To him it was nothing new. For a year now he had watched his wife and child being eaten up by the possessive Muriel. They seemed to be in a conspiracy, and he was shut out.

The remedy, however, was at hand. The house by the lake had been proceeding slowly because Aaron had to divide his time between building it and running the mill, but once the baby was born, he began to work on it with renewed enthusiasm. Now he was doing it not only for Agnes but for Rose as well. He imagined her playing on the freshly laid and polished kitchen floor, sleeping in the little cot with limber, bouncy wooden slats that he was building for her.

It took a second year, but by the following summer, when Agnes was again pregnant, the house was finally finished. One Friday evening in early August, he walked in for a final look at his creation before moving his family. Aaron surveyed his completed work with pride.

Built entirely of wood, it bore a remarkable similarity to most of the other houses in Waldenstein. The front door, which, like all front doors, was for show only, opened onto a short narrow hallway, half of which was taken up by stairs. On either side of the hall there were two rooms, the back ones considerably smaller than the front and accessible only through the latter. He turned to the first door on the left. Here was the parlour, reserved for Christmas, weddings, christenings and funerals – and any other occasions when the minister might turn up – a spacious room with windows on the front and side. Behind this was a small spare bedroom, likewise reserved for the minister or possibly an elderly relative who could not climb stairs. Then he went back to the hallway and across it into a second large room. This would be the family's sitting room. Everything would happen in this room – conversation, schoolwork, reading, sewing, knitting, and maybe later (because Rose was very beautiful), courting. Behind it was a dining room where the whole family – even the large family Aaron anticipated – could eat together. Next he went upstairs and surveyed the bedrooms – four of equal size, one for him and Agnes, one for the boy-children, one for the girls and an extra one for any overflow. Finally he went back down the stairs and into the large, one-storey "ell" jutting out from one side. Here all the family meals would be cooked on the huge cast iron wood stove, newborn babies would be placed in a basket before the open oven door to be warmed in their first hours in a cold world, a shiny new pump and sink in the corner would give water from the freshly dug well. Along one wall ran a smooth wooden bench for sitting – if ever there was time to sit. In the middle of the room stood a wooden table he had made and six newly carved wooden chairs. It was a light and airy space, with windows on both sides so that you could see across the meadow down to the lake and back to the woodland behind the house all at once.

There was little decoration, but then Agnes would provide that, not only with her person but also with embroidered cushions, cross-stitched wall hangings, maybe a picture or two that her mother would give her.

On the 9th of August, Aaron swept the house inside and mowed the grass around it. Tomorrow they would move in. He had never had a home of his own, and this place that, except for the cellar and frame, he had built largely with his own hands was a source of immense pride. He knew that providing a home for his family was the first thing a man was expected to do in Waldenstein, and he had accomplished it.

At six o'clock he left the house; by six-thirty he had reached the home of Agnes' parents. He heard one of her brothers laughing raucously in the yard and reflected that this was the last night he would have to come home to such a noisy household. Inside Muriel was busy cooking a chicken stew for supper, dropping the white dumpling dough on top of the bubbling chicken, potato and carrots. She kept her eyes down, concentrating on the task.

"Where's Agnes?" Usually at this time she would be bathing Rose in the enamel bowl in the middle of the warm kitchen.

"Upstairs." Still she did not look at him.

He ran up the stairs to the room that had been their home for the first two years of their married life. And there indeed was Agnes, weeping as he had never seen her weep before and holding Rose so tightly to her that the child was struggling to escape.

"What on earth is going on?"

"She won't let her go." Agnes was cryptic, not daring to face him.

33

"Won't let who go?"

"Rose. She won't let us take her with us."

The language was foreign to him. People in Waldenstein no longer told him what he could and could not do. "Don't be silly. Rose is ours."

But Agnes went on relentlessly. "She says not. She says this is the only home Rose has ever known and she shouldn't have to be upset by moving to another place."

Now for the first time he felt fear. "But that's absurd. It's us she knows and loves, not the house, not your mother." Though he was not at all certain about the latter.

This only produced a further tearful flow from Agnes. "And then she says – she says that soon we'll have another one, which is true, and so we won't mind so much not having Rose. And she has no one anymore. I'm gone and the boys are off working in the woods most of the time, and Papa – well, she didn't say anything about him, but we know how things are between them, don't we?"

"That's no reason for her to take our child." Fear was turning to anger.

"She thinks it is," Agnes replied implacably.

"She can't make us." He stood up, towering over Agnes and the child. "What's wrong with you? If you can't stand up to her I certainly will!"

"No, no. You musn't do that. Oh, you don't understand what it's like, you have no idea!" And Agnes sobbed more violently, so that even Rose curled up her face and began to cry.

"What has she said to you?"

But on this Agnes remained silent. She said simply, "God says we are to honour our Father and Mother."

"Well, thank God I never had any then, if this is what it comes to." Muriel must have used Agnes' obedient trust and fear of God in some way to subdue her like this, he thought.

"Oh Aaron." She tried to reach out for his understanding that, for the first time, she sensed was not there.

"It's the silence," she said after a while. "She goes away into some awful place where I can't find her." And he knew he was defeated. Not because they couldn't take Rose with them – of course they could, if they wished – but because Agnes was still more a child than a mother herself, and she was caught now in a web of fear and doubt so strong that nothing he said – and not even her love for Rose – could counter it.

Aaron left Agnes and went down to the kitchen. Muriel was still attending to the stew. "You're a wicked woman."

"And aren't you grateful for two years' free board and lodging?" she retorted, snapping her head up sharply.

"I didn't plan to give my first child as payment for it." And he walked out the door.

That night Aaron, Rose and Agnes, all three, slept together in the big double bed. In the morning Aaron and Agnes left alone for their new house. Agnes could not look back as Rose waved cheerily from Muriel's arms.

Fractures

1899

Agnes' second child was born in November. Muriel, more in her role as community midwife than as mother and prospective grandmother, came to help. Since she had taken Rose, Agnes had had only the most formal of dealings with her mother; Aaron could barely be brought to speak to her. But here she was now, unfolding the clean cloths, arranging the cot, making strange clucking noises rather like a mother hen, Agnes thought.

At last, after the agony, there was a moment of complete joy. The baby was a little boy, and Aaron was summoned to see his son. But before he could run up the stairs, the baby, after a few feeble whimpers, fell silent. As he entered the room, Muriel was slapping the infant's feet in panic, then reaching into his tiny mouth to remove any mucous. As Aaron stared in disbelief, she took the tiny form and wrapped it in a warm blanket, shaking it slightly as if this might evoke some sound, some movement. But there was nothing.

"Is he…?"

"Yes, I think so," said Muriel.

He saw stark horror on the faces of both the women. Agnes began to scream. At first it was inarticulate, but then it resolved into words, pleading, furious, "Give me Rose; give me back Rose."

"You're in no fit state to be looking after any child," was Muriel's reply.

"Get out of this house. Get out of this house now!" And Aaron pushed her towards the stairs. She went without looking back.

There were other children, of course. Of course, because what were women in Waldenstein for but to bear babies and look after them?

Flora was next. She was indeed "fairest of flowers" with eyes that were large like her mother's but the grey-green hue of her father's. When at last it appeared, her thick and wavy hair was the colour of honey. She was almost as precocious and beautiful as Rose, Agnes thought.

Muriel was not allowed near any of the subsequent birthings. Instead, Aaron brought a midwife up from Mahone Bay on each occasion to help deliver them. She was competent and unattractive; the first quality satisfied Aaron and the second Agnes. But she could not bring them the luck of a son. All these babies were girls – Virtue, Emma, Hannah, Joan.

"Another girl, I'm afraid, Mr. Miller," the apologetic nurse would say, twisting her round face into a wry smile.

"Why are you afraid woman?" Aaron finally retorted after the birth of Joan. "Do you think I imagine you're castrating them at birth?"

After that nurse Anna said she would come no more; Mr Miller "wasn't a nice man at all." She pinched her thick lips tightly together when she said this, giving the impression that if she were to release them ever so slightly she could say much, much more.

At least having all girls made the sleeping arrangements easy, Aaron reflected. And as they grew, they were good girls, fun girls to be around. He jostled them on his knee in the evenings; he read them stories. Virtue was all dark seriousness, "Mama's little helper." Emma was given to fits of giggling – sometimes giggling at her older sister.

But strangest of all were the questions she sometimes asked. You had to think hard even to understand the questions, never mind figure out the answers – if you knew them. Like the day they were riding in the horse cart when, as they were passing a row of pale birch tree trunks, the remnants of dead trees, she suddenly asked, "Papa, why don't the numbers stop?"

"Huh?"

"Why don't they stop?"

Aaron thought she must be counting the interminable birch trunks. "Well, there must have been something – maybe some kind of bug – that killed the trees a while ago, and now there are lots of these trunks just standing here."

Emma was impatient, "No, no, I don't mean the tree trunks. I mean the numbers. You know, you go 'one, two, three, four, five, six, seven, eight, nine, ten'. Why don't they stop?"

With a shock, Aaron understood what she was asking. He had not spent much of his life contemplating the mysteries of infinity. He could only say, "I don't think I know that, Sweetheart."

Emma was surprised into silence. Her father didn't know everything, it seemed.

❦

1912

Aaron heard it first – a faint whimper from across the hall. "Go back to sleep," he muttered, partly to himself, partly to the child. "Go back to sleep."

Sleep…sleeping children…five of them now, all girls. He sighed. There had been John. It was the whimper that made him think of John, the child that Muriel had confidently promised them in place of the abducted Rose. But John had whimpered only once and then disappeared back into the silence from which he had come – perfect, waxen, still. Mustn't think of that. Then came the girls, one after the other, fine, healthy, mostly good-looking.

Another whimper, the sound of sheets tossing, then a full-blown scream, high and inarticulate. "Aah, aah, aeee!" It must be Flora; it could not be one of the two little ones with whom she shared a room, the voice was more mature, a child's voice, not that of a baby.

By this time Agnes was awake as well, and they both rushed across the hallway.

"Flora, hush, what's the matter? You'll wake your sisters."

A winter moon lit the room dimly, so they could see that Flora's whole body was contorted, her head thrown back, unearthly sounds emitting from her stretched mouth. With one movement Aaron picked her up, put her, struggling and screaming, on his shoulder, and started down the stairs. Agnes grabbed two blankets, one for herself and one for Flora, and followed him. The stove had just enough spark to be revived, and Agnes rapidly fed it some wood.

"Flora, Flora, wake up; it's only a dream!" But Flora continued to writhe in his arms as he sat on the bench under the window. Her eyes rolled wildly, her mouth twisted and uttered high piercing shrieks. Aaron laid her on a blanket on the floor and tried to stop her limbs from thrashing. If he could just keep her still, perhaps the sound would stop. *The sound must be stopped.*

Then he saw two little figures, white-gowned and open-mouthed. Emma and Virtue stood, silently witnessing the horror.

"Go back to bed," he instinctively said.

But Agnes intervened. "Go to the Conrad's, girls. Tell them we need them to come and help while Papa goes for the doctor."

Still they stood, motionless, uncomprehending.

"Run!"

Then they moved, running in night dresses towards the door.

"No, put your coats and boots on first!"

"But Mama…"

"Go around the lake, not across it; it's not frozen solid yet."

Aaron looked up momentarily as they went. What had Agnes done? Sent an eight and six-year-old around the lake, one mile or more, to fetch the neighbours. What else *could* she do?

Suddenly Flora went limp and lay pale and still on the blanket.

Agnes looked at Aaron. "Is it too late? Is she…?"

"No, she's still breathing. But Agnes – this is not just a bad dream. Something awful has happened to her."

"God is punishing us."

"What for?"

Then Flora began to scream and writhe anew.

At last Ebenezer Conrad arrived. Going out to harness the horses in the bitter cold was a positive relief for Aaron. The animals, surprised to be roused at this time of night, shivered as he led them out of the barn, twitched nervously and pawed the snow.

"There, there. You're just going on a little adventure with Ebenezer. It'll be all right." He stood for a moment or two after Ebenezer had left, looking around at the innocence of the snowy scene. How could this be happening? That joyous afternoon when he had cleaned the house for his family had led all too swiftly into the dreadful moment of the actual move, childless, into what suddenly was a large, empty space. The boy baby that Agnes had been carrying that fateful day had died at birth. Now his third child, Flora, had effectively been taken from him as well. Maybe it was Fate…or God. But why? He was a good man, a responsible father and provider. Then he forced himself back into the house.

By the time Ebenezer and the doctor arrived, Mrs. Conrad, Virtue, Emma and even baby Joan were all standing around watching the scene which became even more spectacular as Flora, at Dr. Carter's instruction, was moved between hot and cold tubs like some noisy vegetable that needed to be cooked and then blanched, over and over again. For a moment all compassion left Aaron, and he thought of running away – just to be rid of that sound, that cascade of shrieking. Then he looked at Agnes, and continued moving Flora as Dr. Carter instructed.

Eventually Flora's periods of limp silence lengthened, and finally the doctor said he could do no more, and Flora, or what remained of her, was dried, clad in a clean nightgown and returned to bed.

The other children followed, slowly. Only Hannah had slept through it all.

For the first few days Flora lay limp in her bed, scarcely bothering to eat the food her mother and sisters brought her.

"Look, Flora, here's a lovely bowl of chicken broth – your favourite. Don't you want just a little sip?" And Agnes, having wrapped a clean napkin under Flora's chin, tried to raise her up and prise her lips apart with the spoon. But Flora's lips remained firmly closed, and she let her full weight fall back on her mother's arm.

On the third day she allowed herself to be propped up with pillows and sucked the tiny strips of apple that Virtue conscientiously brought out of the cold cellar and cut up for her. By the fifth day she sat in a cushioned chair, brought upstairs especially for her. All this time she was silent. Perhaps her voice had been all used up in that one terrible night, Emma decided. But when she suggested this to Virtue, her older sister, as usual, told her she was being silly. Voices didn't get used up. "You talk enough," she retorted to Emma. "And still you can talk!"

Then, on the sixth day, she was brought downstairs, and after she had eaten a whole cinnamon bun that Agnes had made particularly for her, she said, "Tank."

"Tank?" Aaron came in as Agnes was fighting back tears. "It's not that she *won't* talk; she *can't* talk anymore."

Aaron looked at Flora, his once beautiful daughter, and saw other things that he didn't dare whisper to Agnes. Had her eyes always been so carelessly aligned? Was she just pouting, or did her lower lip now always hang low and slack? And what about the small clump of hair he had surreptitiously gathered up from her pillow as he picked her up that morning to carry her downstairs?

After a week, Aaron returned to the logging camp. He had simply been home for the weekend, as luck would have it, when Flora became ill, and at Agnes' entreaty he had stayed for a week afterwards. He had left Jacob Wentzell in charge of the camp. A good worker, a sensible man and, after his one daughter, blessed with three sons, Aaron reflected somewhat bitterly. Yet sometimes he had caught Jacob looking at him with a kind of hooded hostility. Why? Of course he was the boss and Jacob the hired worker, but he had always treated him right. So why? Why was everyone always against him?

What had he done wrong? Why was he being punished? From an unpromising start, up to now, he had been so lucky. After his father died when he was seven (his mother had died even earlier, when he was two) and his two older half-sisters had gone off to the United States, he was completely alone. He remembered crying himself to sleep in the spare bedrooms of Waldenstein as he was passed about from family to family, a small package of itinerant child labour.

If it had not been for Josiah Kaulbach – and if Josiah himself had had a son.... But, like himself, Josiah had had only daughters, so he had taken him in, a surrogate son. His wife, Rebecca, had been less convinced of his merits. One night he had overheard his future being discussed. "He's a bright lad; maybe we ought to send him to school." Josiah's voice sounded tentative, testing cautiously what Rebecca might feel about the matter.

There was no doubt in her strong voice that ascended through the heat grating in the ceiling to the bedroom where Aaron lay. "Go to school? Don't be foolish. The lad's ten years old. He's got to earn his keep – else why did we take him in? Anyway, he can read already; sneaks away with a book or paper whenever you're not after him. What more learning does he need?"

Still, from that beginning he had risen to be the owner of a mill and a logging camp that, summer and winter, employed most of the other men in Waldenstein. So great was the change in his life that he had come to believe that he was favoured by the Almighty, a chosen man – his wife, Agnes, and his family "chosen people."

Now this. Flora's head thrown back in agony, her screams echoing all night across the snowy landscape. Instinctively, he lapsed into Biblical language. "Oh Lord, let me know what I have done to displease Thee, so that I may repent, so that my child may be healed."

He pushed through the snow, relishing its resistance, the immense effort it took to pull his boots out of the two-foot drifts with each step. When he looked up, the logging camp was in sight. His pace quickened.

Varieties of Death

Summary, 1915

Sunday morning. The gravel yard in front of the little white church held four ox carts and one horse-drawn wagon. The wagon, naturally, was Aaron's. His girls fluttered down from it in their starched white full-skirted dresses – Virtue, Emma, Hannah and Joan. Their hair was light brown, flowing freely now in kinky waves, released from the plaits that held it tidily all week.

The four ox carts held only the elderly and those from distant parts. Anyone less than two miles away walked. Among the walkers were Jacob and his family, now grown to a brood of four – one girl and three boys. Erika had turned into a young woman with the blond hair of her mother and the dark blue eyes of her father. Some unkindly remarked that she had the beginnings of the buxom figure of her mother as well. But she was an assured and attractive young woman. Maybe she laughed a bit too loudly at times, but then why shouldn't a young girl be allowed to laugh and swing her hips a little if she wanted? The middle boy, Obadiah, was chubby and laughing like his sister, but his elder brother, Hibbert, and Nathan, still the baby at eight, were tall for their age and slender, with their father's dark wavy hair and deep blue eyes.

Hibbert, a recluse at twelve, hid shyly behind his mother, but Nathan stood transfixed by the spectacle of the white, frilly girls descending from the wagon. One in particular caught his eye; she jumped from the wagon with both grace and determination. It was Emma. She did not smile, but Nathan felt she knew he was watching, that the whole world was watching her as she jumped from the wagon on this Sunday in July.

Another girl, much older and larger, also jumped, but no one watched her do so – or if they did they turned away in grief or embarrassment. In truth, she could barely see to jump. Her eyes were crossed, she had no hair and her lower lip turned down in a perpetual pout. This was Flora. She tried to keep up with her sisters, but it was no use. They dashed before her into the church and filled the family pew while she stumbled behind. Agnes took her by the hand, but even her own mother did not look at her.

Rose, verging on womanhood, was there as well, dressed in wool even on this warm summer day lest she catch cold. And indeed, she did have the remains of a nasty cough that she tried to hide behind a perfectly starched handkerchief. She didn't run to her sisters, and they scarcely seemed to notice she was there. Her grandparents escorted her quickly into the church, where she sat, safe from contamination of any sort, wedged between the two of them.

By eleven o'clock the church had filled. The minister rode up on his grey horse, robed himself in black, and the service began. A small girl, barely into her teens, stood at the front and began to sing – Ophelia, the song starter, Ben's only daughter and Nathan's first cousin. Her dress was plain white with a modest blue sash; her hair was tied back at the nape of her neck with another piece of blue ribbon. Nothing in her diminutive appearance and ordinary features prepared one for that voice. From the age of nine, her voice had rung out in the church, certain of pitch and rhythm. Now she began clearly, her tone strong and radiant. They all followed, joining in, their voices rising to the wooden beams of the church and flooding out of the open windows to the woods beyond:

Liebster Jesu, wir sind hier
Dich und dein Wort anzuhoren
Lenke Sinnen und Begier,
Auf die sussen Himmels lehren.
Dass die Herzen von der Erden
Ganz zu dir gezogen werden.

"Dearest Jesus," they sang, simply and with unquestioning faith. "We are here to hear you and your Word. Turn away sin and greed through sweet Heaven's teaching, that our hearts may be drawn from Earth, wholly to you."

Naively, sweetly, with their whole hearts they sang. Here they were all children, simple and certain that God did indeed see them as they met to sing his praise. They might have built a cathedral if they could, but instead they had settled for a small white clapboard structure, oriented correctly however, and with gothic pointed windows and a tall, tapering spire.

Often they sang in German, but the preaching was always in English. They must be encouraged to forget the old ways. Today the text was Ecclesiastes 7.1: "A good name is better than a precious ointment; and the day of death than the day of one's birth." The first part they understood. In a tiny community like this, how easy it was to lose your good name – a whisper, a small indiscretion – everyone knew. Your neighbours, your help in time of trouble, would vilify you, given half a chance, as quickly as they would help pull your ox out of a pit should it, in true Biblical fashion, stumble into one.

The second half of the verse was, admittedly, more problematic. Why should death be better than life? Certainly once you were dead, there was no chance of losing your good name unless skeletons came falling out of closets even then, so you were safe, they supposed. And of course there was Heaven. But Heaven, though sincerely believed in, remained a bit hazy, like the blue mist that quivered on the edge of the fields at sunrise.

The Pastor ended with an injunction against over-much mirth, against foolishness. "Here you may feel yourselves alone, out in the field, mowing or cultivating your vegetables, you may think yourself unseen, away from all prying eyes. Then is the time for a discreet meeting, a fleeting kiss that the world will never see. But I tell you, God sees. Don't be foolish; remember the end you will come to, and the end of all things. Be ready for this time, so that the day of your death may indeed prove better than the day of your birth. Amen."

The authority of the preacher was absolute; how could they question it? Still, as they stumbled out into the hot sunshine, the green spruce trees, the sweet juniper underfoot, the very smell of the earth spoke of life. Tanned and supple, bred to the hard life they led, they looked forward to getting on with the summer's work. They spoke to one another of the weather and haying. On Sunday they would not work, but at times Sunday seemed chiefly an interruption in the rhythm of their lives; and their lives were about keeping themselves and their families alive, not dying.

Freed at last from the confines of the service, Aaron's children ran round and round in some peculiar game of chase with rules of their own invention. Nathan wanted to follow, but held back, shy, aware even now of the differences between a family that had an ox cart and one that had a horse and wagon. "Go on, why don't you play with them?" Frederika urged. She worried that Nathan might be a loner, "queer," like his older brother Hibbert. But Jacob said, "No. Why tell 'em to go and run like crazy with that bunch of stuck-up girls?"

So Nathan remained clinging to his mother and looking for Obadiah, who was busy with a few other older boys torturing with a stick a frog they found in the marsh.

"Don't do that," he implored. But Obadiah and another boy kept on.

Gradually people began to drift away. Aaron hoisted his family up into the wagon. Jacob and Frederika started to walk the long, dusty road back to their house, children in tow.

"Why did you do that?" Nathan asked Obadiah as they walked along.

"Don't know. It just seemed fun." And then, with a sly grin, he added, "Maybe the day of the frog's death was better than that of its birth."

Nathan skinned the rabbits. He didn't like doing this; he couldn't help imagining what the rabbits felt or would feel if they were still alive. But it had to be done. How else would he have the money to go on the merry-go-round and buy sweets at the picnic? So his small hands wielded the knife with precision. They were good skins, shiny and brown with darker flecks to set them off. Ebenezer, who sold such things to people in the town, would give him at least ten cents each for them, which came to sixty cents in all. With that he could do everything he wanted at the picnic. And, he reasoned, when the rabbits ran into the trap and it went "snap," it was quick, over in a second. His father and brothers would laugh at him if they knew he thought like this. Animals were there to provide people with fur and food. To think otherwise was womanish and foolish. There was some point to skinning the rabbits, so it was different from Obadiah torturing the frog. He took the soft, burnished skins the two miles across the little lake to Ebenezer who said, "Ah…good…lovely," and gave him the money.

Now he could think of the picnic without feeling sorry for the rabbits. And what a picnic it would be! It was held on the shores of a lake about ten miles from Waldenstein, and not just the families from their own church but all the churches within a radius of twenty miles came to it. The lake was surrounded by a large grassy field on one side, and there was a small sandy beach for swimming. Even the great outside world took note of the picnic, such that one small company from Halifax always sent a merry-go-round, stalls with games of chance and a few exotic animals and birds such as monkeys and parrots. You could buy exotic foods as well, if you had the money – oranges and bananas, some years even pineapples. And of course there was candy – peppermint and caramel, chocolate and vanilla fudge – piled up in enticing heaps at the stalls with exuberant striped awnings.

At eight, Nathan was capable of the most acute anticipation. Days before, whenever he was left alone for a moment, he could see the merry-go-round, hear the tunes cranked out by the mechanism in the centre, see horses whirling, whirling round and up and down. The night before the picnic, he fell asleep late beside Obadiah and dreamt of wooden horses and candy.

He woke up abruptly, convinced that it was day. Everything was still in darkness, and he could hear Obadiah's soft breathing on the other side of the bed, but he knew that if he didn't get up at once he and his whole family would miss it all, and the rabbits would have died in vain. So he jumped out of bed and made his way through the black hallway towards his parents' room. The upstairs walls of the house were still not finished on the inside, so the posts and beams were all exposed. As he ran along the corridor something hit him very hard on the head. The darkness intensified; he fell to the floor and knew nothing.

Then gradually he felt himself very cold. His head throbbed unbearably. From somewhere a pale grey light seemed to shine. But now, in contrast to his certainty earlier, he felt it could not really be morning; morning might never come. He crawled quietly back to bed where he fell into a troubled sleep.

Obadiah shook him awake – violently, it seemed. His head was still dull with pain.

"What on earth happened to you?" Obadiah whistled in astonishment at the large cut and lump on Nathan's forehead. "Did you go out and have a fight with a bear?"

"Ran into the pillar in the hall." He could still talk; he even remembered, more or less, what had happened. This, he reasoned, was good.

"Get up. It's the picnic." Obadiah already had his pants and socks on.

Nathan rolled over. "I know. That's why I ran into the pillar."

This made no sense at all to Obadiah, so he just said again, "Come on. Get up. Or we'll go without you."

Gingerly Nathan tried sitting on the edge of the bed. The world gradually came into focus. He moved slowly towards the chair his clothes were hanging on. They looked strange, but they seemed to remember his body when he put them on. Once downstairs, he met with more horrified exclamations from Frederika and Jacob. "But you can't possibly go to the picnic. Go back to bed!"

"No, I'm goin'. I'll be all right."

The very thought of breakfast made him sick, but he climbed up onto the cart and set off gamely with his family, who made certain that he was kept abreast of every subtle change as the wound spread purple down around his eye. He sat glumly, feeling still quite determined but sorry for himself as well.

At last they came over a small rise and there it all was, spread out before him – the lake shining in the sun, the merry-go-round, the brightly coloured wooden horses spinning and reeling to the music. All the booths with their striped awnings seemed to dance in rows on the lawn. Lots of men and women and girls in fancy dresses were walking around with baskets, looking for the best places to claim for their picnic. Emma must be among them somewhere. But in the excitement of the moment, he couldn't stop to search; he would find her later. He jumped down from the cart, paid his ten cents and grabbed a dappled white and black horse that had a shiny red saddle. Round and round he went, holding on dizzily, and as the music churned out of the gramophone he forgot the pain, forgot everything in the joy of the motion and the music. He had never been so happy.

Autumn came. Agnes struggled heavily up the outside stairs from the basement. Another child was pulling down at her belly as she raised and lowered the heavy wooden doors that closed off the stairway.

"Have you got the pails ready for the meat yet?" Aaron's voice cut sharply. It was the killing time of year. She could smell the scent of death in the leaves that were piled up and burned; the animals could smell it too. They gathered close for warmth in the fading sunlight

50

slanting across the mown and golden fields. Agnes gave Aaron the pails she had brought from the basement and then, delinquent, went over to the fence to stroke her favorite milk cow.

"Can you come back here, Agnes? I need your help."

She turned. "I don't want to help with the killing."

"For goodness sake, woman, we go through this every year. Do you want to eat this winter? Who else will help if you don't? The girls are still too little."

"And there is no son," she knew he thought but would not quite say. What was she carrying now? Another girl, probably.

"Why don't you hire Ebenezer?"

"Because he's as busy with his own work as I am with mine. Now please."

"So what do you want me to do?"

"You know perfectly well. Hold the heifer and keep it calm while I come up from behind to stun it. Then, once it is dead, it would be awfully good to have some help with getting it hung up to drain the blood, if not with the skinning."

So Agnes, accomplice, deceiver, stood beside the heifer and stroked it while Aaron came up from behind with the large hammer. One quick blow and the animal dropped. Then Aaron came round with the knife to "bleed it." If the term suggested a quaint medical procedure, what actually happened was both simple and violent. He slit the throat of the heifer and watched the blood flow into the dusty soil. Agnes had no choice but to watch as well. Nausea rose and overcame her. She ran to the house.

"Where are you going now?"

"I'm sick."

"Oh for goodness sake, I thought you were farther along than that."

But it wasn't the pregnancy alone. It was the terrible revulsion against watching life drain away; the animal had trusted her until its last moment, and it had been wrong, fatally wrong for it to do so. But of course Aaron was right; they had to have food for the winter. How else could they survive? Inside she concentrated on preparing the pails of salt water that would preserve the meat. Still, if Aaron was right, he was also hard; he didn't even think of the animal's desire to survive. And what of her? Did he even care for her anymore, or was she just another animal, a part of the whole cycle of reproduction and death?

When the action moved to the pig pen she did not have to take part in the slaughter, but she did have to clean the intestines and grind up the meat with spices and herbs to make sausages and pudding that were then forced back spoonful by spoonful, a foreign mixture, into the pigs' very own guts.

During these weeks, the sun shone golden and perverse upon the sadistic rites. Each evening the land was burnished with fire as it set in a red, death-like frenzy. How could she bear to look?

March, 1916

Winter came to an end with the making of the maple syrup. The warm days and the freezing nights of March encouraged the sap to rise, moving secretly between the wood and the bark of the trees, swelling their buds. At last, a season of hope and joyfulness! And Aaron had his son. Agnes, spent with the effort of everything, gave a sigh of relief.

Ben Wentzell, Jacob's brother, had a fine stand of sugar maple trees behind his house down by the river. At the beginning of the month, Ben cut a small slit into the trunk of every tree and from a few nails inserted above the slit hung a pail to catch the sap as it bled from the tree. Every day the pails were emptied into a large vat, and by the evening of March 30, Ben decided that the time had come to begin the boiling down. It would take days of boiling until it became syrup, and even longer until it became delectable, sugary candy, but the beginning of the process was always a kind of celebration, an occasion for an impromptu party. So Frederika and Jacob were there with their family, and Emma and Virtue had been allowed to come on their own; Agnes stayed home with the new baby. Rose, too, arrived and stood on the sidelines, neither child nor quite yet woman. Muriel and Zachariah themselves were not given to celebration.

Once the huge fire had been lit under the pot, still others, seeing the flames, turned up for a jolly. They told jokes, drank apple cider and imagined that the coming summer would be the perfect one – rain and sun in just the right measure and strictly rotated as needed. No one would fall off the hay cart and break a limb, no one would suffer from sunstroke while making hay, no one would become sick at the crucial times of planting or harvest.

The children played in the shadows cast by the fire among the trees. They ran in and out, uncertain whether it was hide and seek or Settlers and Indians. It was running and laughing madly until they couldn't run anymore – running because they were up later than usual, and it was a celebration, and they felt like it.

In the midst of all this, Ophelia, Ben's only daughter and the "song-starter" at church, detached herself from the group and began to sing – first old folk songs that everyone knew and joined in. Then she branched out into a melody no one could follow, low at first and then higher and faster, and with it she started to dance around the fire. Slowly she circled, then as her excitement rose and the music gathered momentum she went faster and faster until she was almost running but still singing her new, enchanting song.

"Careful, Ophelia," someone called.

Of course she didn't hear. How could she hear a warning like that when she was singing songs dictated to her by a spirit?

Afterwards, no one could say quite how it happened. Perhaps she grew dizzy from circling the fire; perhaps a large spark flew out and caught her dress, perhaps….

Suddenly the music turned to a scream, then a chorus of screams. "Her dress is on fire."

"Get a blanket to beat it out."

"Put her on the ground and smother it."

"Take her to the river."

But they were frozen with horror; and for a moment no one stirred while the flames encased her like a shroud. Then Ben himself dashed to grab her as she fell, and on the cool, damp grass they rolled and writhed together.

Meanwhile her mother, Sophia, who had at first stood transfixed along with everyone else, began to scream as if she too were burning in the flames of hell. "No, no! Save her, save her! Ophelia! Ophelia!"

"Hush, hush, Mother. It ain't no good screamin'. Father's doin' all he can." Dilphin, her elder son, held her in his grasp. But she broke free, creating more pandemonium as she ran crying to the house and came back, still hysterical, carrying an empty bucket.

"Take her to the river," again someone called. And carefully, now that the flames had been beaten out, her father carried Ophelia down and cradled her in the cool water. She was scarcely breathing.

After a time they took her back into the house, cut the clothes that remained from her charred body, and laid her on her bed. Soon she became conscious and began to scream. Her voice could be heard for more than a mile, it was said afterwards. It followed Emma and Virtue as they ran the entire way across the rocky fields and woodland path back to their home with the dreadful news. It pounded at the closed bedroom window only two hundred yards away from Ben's house where Nathan lay in bed beside Obadiah, covering his ears. All night she screamed, and when morning came, and the screaming stopped, she was dead.

Erika

Season of Discontent

June, 1916

Frederika was baking bread. This was not unusual; she baked bread every second day. Today she was making two extra loaves for Ben's wife, Sophia. Sophia would not be making bread today, she feared. Indeed, she would not be doing any of the things that made life possible in Waldenstein. She would not be cutting out and sewing clothes, cultivating vegetables, eking out the last of the winter's salt meat, feeding the pigs, the hens, collecting the eggs. And she most certainly would not be making bread. She would be sitting – maybe dressed, maybe not – just sitting on her rocking chair looking out the window at the river. What was she thinking of? What *could* she be thinking? Of Ophelia, almost certainly, but what of her duty as a mother, as a wife? She clearly was not thinking of those things. And while Frederika sympathized with the "terrible thing" that had happened, she could not imagine a woman forgetting her duties – duties ingrained into her from her earliest years. One did not sit on a rocking chair, one just did not, unless one was darning socks. Even then a straight chair was better. Life must go on, as she had told Sophia a hundred times. Life must go on, no matter what. To which Sophia had replied, "Why?" To which Frederika had no answer.

It had been three months now, for heaven's sake. The house was a disgrace – cobwebs everywhere, dust in the corners, the fire unmade, towels smelling of mildew, dirt from men's boots covering the floor. Ben couldn't do it all. As for their son, little Benjamin, he had stopped going to school and just hung about with his father. He was only ten and more of a nuisance than help. But then whom was he supposed to talk to? Not his mother, that was certain. She wouldn't give him the time of day. Frederika supposed she ought to look after him. But why? She gave the dough an extra hard thump. She had children of her own. Everyone had troubles. Sophia's just happened to have been more showy and public than most. Having your child burn up before your very eyes was unusual, to say the least. Wasn't it burning they used for heretics, because it was the most terrible death? But they all had lost children. Agnes' second child, a boy, died almost as soon as he was born, but did Agnes sit down in a rocking chair? No, she just got up and had some more – all girls, admittedly, but that was hardly her fault.

And then there was the whole business with Flora. She'd never be right again. Imagine having a child like that! She looked so ugly, apart from anything else – no hair, crossed eyes, and that terrible turned down lower lip that made her look as if she was always pouting. Even she, Frederika, had had her share of sorrow. The child she was carrying at Agnes' wedding had been stillborn, and then there were no more until Hibbert, five years later. And just because a child was alive didn't mean everything was fine. Hibbert now, he was a bit queer to be sure – he wasn't what you'd call sociable, and recently Nathan and Obadiah said he wasn't going to school either. So where was he? He'd lag behind them on the road and then disappear altogether, they said. Once they'd found him hiding in a ditch. When they confronted him, he'd screamed and run away into the woods. She sighed. But he'd sort himself out. He was a good help to his father with the animals already, and in the end what did school matter?

As for Erika – she smiled as she thought of Erika. So like herself at that age – beautiful, with curls and glowing skin and large blue eyes – almost grown up, ready for her own life and family. She had taken Ophelia's death hard – although they were four years apart in age, since they lived so near to one another, the cousins had played together a lot as children. But she would be fine. They had sent her away to New Hanover to help a distant relative who had just had twins. Of course she would be fine. All she needed was for some young man.... The trouble was, she was fussy. Naturally, she could be, endowed as she was. Frederika had been fussy herself. But you had to know when to stop looking and settle down. When she came back, she must have a word with Erika.

At last the dough was finished, smooth and elastic under her hands. She thumped it one last time, rolled it into a huge ball, patted the top, and settled it into a dish under a tea towel to rise.

ฅ

July

Nathan was out helping to make hay in the rough land. He stood tall and strong for his almost ten years, and now, for the first time, he was expected to wield a scythe. In the last few weeks the summer had turned hot and dry, which was good for the haying. Everywhere in Waldenstein, on every open field, groups of men and boys were swinging their scythes, scattering the hidden birds' nests, taking time out to eat a few late wild strawberries that they uncovered. They mowed the easy, open fields first. Then they mowed the rough land, the fields that still had granite boulders sticking up everywhere. Here you had to be careful not to strike the scythe against a hidden rock. It would damage the scythe, certainly, but worse, it might bounce back and give you a nasty cut. So Nathan moved slowly and cautiously. He didn't mind the rocks so much, but he was not looking forward to moving on to the heavy swamp grass, which they always left for the last. The ground was muddy, and the grass itself had sharp cutting edges so that even in the hottest weather you had to wear long trousers.

Indoors, Erika was busy making pies. She had returned from looking after the twins to help her mother feed the extra hired men during the haying. The trip seemed to have done her no good. Indeed, if truth be told, Frederika was beginning to feel that Erika was a bit odd. Not odd like Hibbert, who was just quiet and unsociable. Erika, in her unhappiness (if that's what it was) struck outwards.

Frederika had indeed tried to talk to her. It was an awkward business. She really had no idea how to begin. "You're all finished school now, aren't you?" This, the most glaring of platitudes, implying the "what now?" did not go down well.

"Yes." (Somewhat sullenly)

"So…did you enjoy your time with the twins?"

"It was all right. They cried a lot. I think maybe Dora didn't have enough milk for them."

"Most girls like babies." (Hopefully)

"They're all right." And Erika turned her head away.

This didn't seem like a wholehearted endorsement of marriage and parenthood. "Oh. Only all right?"

"Look Mum, do you want me to go out and work full time in someone else's house? Is that what this is all about?"

"No, I wasn't thinking of that. I was thinking that maybe you'd want to be having some babies of your own soon." Yet even as she said this, she thought, "Who would be a mother – or at least a mother of such a stubborn and withholding daughter?"

"And who did you have in mind for the father?" (Aggressively)

"Oh, no one in particular. There's lots of nice young men around. What about Ben's oldest boy, Dilphin? He's a good worker and not bad looking." Privately, Frederika felt that someone was going to have to move in soon to look after Ben and the boys if Sophia didn't pull herself together, and if Erika was that person – well, it would be one problem solved.

But Erika was having none of it. "He smells. He smells of hay and cow dung, plus his own disgusting odour." And she walked out of the room. Frederika decided she had better bake two cakes for dessert – one for her own family, and the other for the unfortunate, smelly family down the hill.

Meanwhile Erika sat in her room in a state of quiet fury. At least she had a room to retreat to – which was more than her younger brothers had. She was angry about many things. Most of all, she was angry about her name, which was clearly a diminution of her mother's. Everything else that she was angry about flowed from the simple fact of the name. All the expectations about her were inherent in it. That was what she was supposed to be – a diminished Frederika. She was supposed to be skilled at all things domestic, indoors and out – an excellent cook, an immaculate housekeeper, a milker of cows, feeder of pigs and weeder of vegetable gardens. Of course she was not expected to be quite as good as her mother at these things or, heaven forbid, to surpass her. That would be "uppity."

To make things worse, she was horribly aware that she looked like her mother. She was pretty. Not beautiful, but pretty. Golden curls, fair complexion, decent features, blue eyes. How terribly boring. Nevertheless, she knew that with these attributes she could probably have any young man in Waldenstein – not that that cast the net very wide.

Outside her bedroom window the tiny green apples in the orchard were beginning to swell. Beyond them the vegetable garden waved in neat rows, surrounded by the tidy fields where she could see Nathan, Obadiah and her father mowing. Her father moved more slowly than he used to and limped as he progressed with his scythe in a straight path towards the woods. Everywhere, the enveloping woods that the feeble scythes would run up against. And beyond the woods? Who knew?

Erika fidgeted in the low, handmade chair. She knew what she didn't want. She didn't want a life like her mother's. So predictable, so safe. But she didn't know what she did want. She merely felt that it was out there somewhere, beyond Waldenstein, beyond the woods.

Inside her head something was screaming, "I won't, I won't, I won't!" But what would she not? Sometimes she yelled about the trivial things she had been asked to do. Then she was reprimanded – severely. First by Frederika, and then, after her mother had talked to Jacob, by him as well. "A big girl like you, talking to your mother like that. Why can't you help her out more? You're not doing anything else, are you?"

So she retreated into sullenness again.

ॐ

September

"Where are you going?" Agnes, as she rubbed innumerable bits of underwear on the scrubbing board, saw Flora edging towards the kitchen door. Always, she had to keep an eye on Flora. You never knew what she might get up to.

"Out. To see the kittens."

"Well, take someone else with you. Emma or Virtue."

Flora pouted – really pouted, not just the perpetual downturned lip. "Emma's readin', and Virtue don't want to go. She just said so."

Flora disappeared. Agnes was uneasy about letting her outside alone. She might just wander off, or she might have another fit, although there hadn't been anymore since that terrible night three years ago. Perhaps the thing that caused the fits had died within her, Agnes thought. Certainly enough else had. What would become of her? She went to school faithfully, trotting along with her sisters, but she seemed to learn nothing. She could write her name and even knew that it meant flower. Bringing in a bouquet of wild roses, she would say, while proffering it, "Flora pick flowers." But she read very little. Before her "accident" she could read anything.

Still more than her lack of intellectual progress, Agnes mourned her appearance. Flora had indeed been a flower, a beautiful flower, with white skin, hair that had darkened to chestnut, and large grey-green eyes, all her features small and regular. Now she was grotesque – curled lip, no hair, and eyes that no longer focused properly. She was getting fat as well, because eating was her chief pleasure.

Agnes dried her hands on the roller towel and went up to the girls' room. "Emma, Flora's gone out, and I'd like you to go with her."

Emma didn't move. "I'm sick of following her around. She just mopes; she won't play anything. And you can see I'm reading."

Agnes respected reading. With her, as Emma knew, it could be used as an excuse for getting out of almost anything. But this time she was having none of it. "You go."

"But she's older than I am – a lot. Why must I go? Send Virtue."

And in the end it was Virtue who, mumbling about the selfishness of others, went out to the barn to find Flora and the kittens. Flora was kneeling down in the hay nuzzling the newborns. Indeed, she was talking to them. "Don't worry, kitties, I know you can't see now 'cause your eyes is shut, but soon they'll open, and then it'll be all pretty. Nice barn, nice hay, lovely smell. Flora loves the barn and hay smell. Away from the horrible ones." Then she heard Virtue's step. "Go away, you horrible one. Go away."

"Mama sent me." Thus Virtue presented her credentials.

Flora nuzzled the kittens closer. "Don't care. Mama is horrible too. Just Flora and the kittens alone. Nice kittens."

Virtue turned on her heel and went back to the house.

"She doesn't want me. She called me horrible and told me to go away. She's just out there talking to the kittens like a crazy."

"Don't you dare call her that again!"

"Well she called me horrible."

Wearily, Agnes left the washing, picked up one-year-old Harry who was playing on the kitchen floor, and went out to the barn.

Upstairs, Emma was still reading. She had barely heard what it was her mother had asked her to do. In fact, she was not in Waldenstein at all, but in 16th century England where Henry VIII had just decided to get rid of his Queen to marry the beautiful but evil (anyone who would take the place of a man's wife must, by definition, be evil) Anne Boleyn. She, Emma, was a lady-in-waiting to Catherine, poor deserted Queen, consoling her, reading to her, maybe even praying with her – though here the scripting left something to be desired.

Suddenly there was Virtue, rushing like a whirlwind into the room, grabbing the little red-covered history book and hurling it across the room. A single leaf fluttered out between the covers.

"What are you doing? My book, my book! You've broken it!"

"It's only a story book."

"It's not; it's history."

"That's all you care about. Your selfish self and people who died centuries ago. You don't care about Flora, or Mama, or…"

Now Emma did finally sit up. "That's not true! I do care about Flora, but there's nothing to be done about her. She's just how she is, and she's going to be like that till the end of time. Just like we're going to be like ourselves till the end of time. And all the people in the history books are still like they were, and you've ruined my history book, and I'll never forgive you – not till the end of time." In the midst of her fury, still the symmetry of her accusation pleased Emma, and on this apocalyptic note, she stormed out of the room.

An hour later, Emma was in the kitchen peeling the carrots for supper. The latch rattled, and Aaron came in, smelling of pine and hemlock. He breathed deeply, taking in the cooking smells, the tidiness of the kitchen with the evening light slanting across the scrubbed floor, his son – yes, at last, his son – playing on the floor, Agnes herself, too thin and perhaps a bit tired looking, but still desirable, her slender waist defined by the tightly tied apron band. She pushed back her still-dark hair and turned to him. "A good day?"

"Yes, a very good day. We got the big job of sawing done for Abe Creaser. It can go out tomorrow. Then, if I'm really lucky, he might pay me." He laughed, and for an instant she saw the man she loved and married twenty years ago. He was still tall and athletic, arms strengthened by cutting down trees, getting them on the ox cart, carrying them to the river, supervising the men as they sent the logs cascading down stream to the mill. This was his life. She worried sometimes, but on the whole she sighed and accepted it; this was his job.

Aaron looked across at Emma, still industriously peeling vegetables. She was his favourite girl, not because she was prettier than the others – though with her dark blonde hair, her flawless skin, and perfect profile, she was – but because she was the brightest. This evening, before she went to bed, he would take her on his lap, and they would read together. Or she would tell him what she was learning in school, all about the Reformation and King Harry, after whom his son and heir, little Harry, had been named. He had thought of naming him Laurier, after the great Prime Minister whose picture hung on the living room wall, but Emma felt that Henry, being more ancient, must augur even greater things. And he had listened to his nine-year-old daughter, so his son was Henry Laurier. Just now this heir of English and French Canadian expectations was having an intense battle with his mug, throwing it across the room, crawling to retrieve it, then punishing it again by banging it against the floor.

What Aaron did not look at was Flora. Her presence impinged all too frightfully without any active attention. As she sat clasping her knees and rocking back and forth on the wooden bench that ran under the kitchen window she looked lost, deserted. Her very presence seemed a reproach. After all, what had she done? But then, what had they done? Yet guilt hung around her like black gauze, translucent but all-enveloping. If they could go back…if they could all just go back three years, erase the anguish, be a whole family again.

Admittedly, they did a pretty good job of pretending. An hour later, if you had stood at the dining room door as they all sat eating the chicken stew with carrots and parsnips, sliced turnips and potatoes, everything flavoured with the summer savoury herbs that Mama dried in the autumn, they looked the perfect family. But if you came closer, you might see that Flora had dribbled some of the juice down the front of her dress, that Virtue was trying not to notice, that in a minute Emma would say something tactless about it, and that the corners of Mama's smile were tense and forced as she said, "Go more slowly Flora, go more slowly. It won't go away before you have finished." And then Aaron sighed, not really knowing he had sighed, and Agnes looked even more anxiously around the table feeling that, despite the good meal, something was amiss, amiss, amiss.

At last it was night. All the children were asleep – Flora in a small room of her own, Emma and Virtue in the large bedroom sharing a big bed with another bed against the opposite wall for Joan and Hannah, Harry in a cot in his parents' room. And Rose – well, Rose was with her grandparents, as she had been always since her first year. Agnes thought of her every night as she went around to kiss the sleeping children – Rose alone with her grandparents who were barely on speaking terms with one another, Rose undressing slowly in her silent room, Rose kneeling to say her prayers with no mother to bid her goodnight.

Aaron and Agnes undressed by the light of one flickering candle that shone on the white sheets and made strange shadows among the rafters. "Come over here," Aaron said, holding out his arms. For a moment Agnes hesitated. Her white nightgown fluttered as she made one step forward.

Then she did something she had never done before. She said "No."

Aaron could scarcely believe his ears. "No? What's the matter then?" Even so, he did not say "Love" or "Dearest" or any such thing. It wouldn't have occurred to him.

"Nothing's the matter. I'm just tired, and I don't want another baby." There, she had said it.

"But why? Another good gift from God." In Aaron's world, theology could justify almost anything, sex included. And he wanted another baby. It might even be a second son.

"You've got your boy at last. Surely that's enough." And Agnes turned away to tuck the covers more tightly around Harry.

"But anything might happen to him; you know that. He might have an accident, or get diphtheria, or even die of whooping cough like the Wamboldts' child down in the Bay."

"I'll take good care of him, and if anything happens, well then it must be God's will." She could use God for her case as well!

And with that she kissed sleeping Harry and got into bed.

Aaron stood looking out the window. It was a beautiful autumn night, with a new moon just setting behind the lake. A light breeze stirred the papery, dying leaves on the trees silhouetted against the dim light. It brought with it a faint whiff of something acrid, sharp as desire. What on earth had gotten into Agnes? Maybe she really was tired. How could a woman, who stayed indoors all day, just cooking food and mending clothes and minding children, tire herself out like that? But now, as if to prove her point, Agnes was already asleep. He turned from the window, blew out the candle and lay down to sleep himself.

ॐ

October

"The harvest is past, the summer is ended, and we are not saved." Emma rolled the words over her tongue. What exactly did they mean? Who was not saved and why? But unlike Virtue who, if she did not understand, would have dismissed the words as nonsense, Emma loved the sound and the rhythm for its own sake. Desolation poured out like a wave from these words, and as she walked to school, crackling through the fallen leaves on Monday morning, the text from Sunday kept rolling over and over in her head like a tune she couldn't forget. Its eloquent misery made her inexplicably happy. Virtue was walking beside her, talking about "Papa" and "losses" and "no good, lazy cooks," and Emma said nothing. In fact, she wasn't even listening until Virtue grabbed her by the sleeve and cried, "Don't you even care?"

She stopped short. Virtue was always accusing her of not caring about something. She thought she did care, but often her caring got muddled up with bigger things, like summer ending and being "not saved" (whatever that meant) and so it didn't come across to Virtue as caring. Virtue knew all the facts and now spread them out in front of Emma like her very own carpet of rotting leaves.

"It's really serious. Papa may have to lay off all the men who come to the camp every winter to cut the trees. And if they don't cut the trees in winter they can't go down the river to get sawn into lumber in the spring. And if they can't get sawn into lumber and sold, then we won't have any money and we'll starve. It's all Jeremiah Schwartz's fault, Papa says. He had a fight with Jimmy Kaulbach last spring, just before they closed the camp up, and now Jeremiah won't come back this year. And Papa says he's looked everywhere for a new cook, but no one will even give it a try. So what's he to do? He can't hire men to go back in the woods and starve."

Emma scuffled in the leaves some more. Perhaps it would be romantic to be poor and starving. She had just discovered a novel by Dickens. There were lots of poor and starving people there, and it all came right in the end. But she didn't mention this to Virtue. Virtue would just sniff. Virtue had developed a habit of sniffing that got on Emma's nerves – the sharp intake of breath through the nostrils that drew up the ever-present snot in a gesture of disdain. So Emma said nothing.

Winter at the Camp

1916–1917

"I've got a job," said Erika one morning. Frederika stopped scrubbing the floor in midswipe.

"What job? I thought you said you weren't going to go out and help with housework anymore."

"I'm not."

"So what are you going to do then? Go out and milk cows?" She resumed scrubbing more vigorously than ever.

"No. I'm going to go and cook for Aaron and his men." She looked furtively at her mother for some reaction.

Frederika sat up on her haunches like a surprised animal, her scrub cloth in mid-air. "He'll never have you. What do you know about cooking for a whole bunch of hungry men? And living way back there, the only woman, all on your own. That'll be a fine story for the neighbours. Soon you won't be able to get out even one day a week, what with the snow and ice."

Erika struck home. "Look, you can't have it both ways. Either I stay here and live off you and Papa or I go out and work. And he will have me. He's said so."

"I'd heard he was desperate."

"Thanks."

Then, accepting the inevitable, Frederika asked, "When do you start?"

"On Monday. He's told all the men the camp is opening up for the winter then."

And there seemed nothing more to say.

Erika had heard her father talking about the problems at the camp; if he couldn't go and cut trees for Aaron in the winter, how would they manage to survive? Farming gave them food, but there was no money at all – not even to buy the wool Frederika knit into socks, the cloth she sewed into coats and dresses. Her parents wanted her to work; well, she would try.

So the next morning she had walked the two miles to the sawmill to see Aaron (or Mr. Miller, as she had been taught to call him). As she turned at the shanty corner and walked past the cemetery down the road to the river, she seemed to have trouble moving; she realized she was shaking with fear. Not only did he own everything as far as the eye could see, but there was something about his height and the very way he carried himself that was intimidating. Even his good looks seemed intimidating. They were not just normal good looks but severe, sharp-featured, eyes boring through you. He didn't shake her hand when she came tentatively up to him that morning, just looked up with surprise from the log he was cutting into lumber.

"Hello…Erika." She noted he appeared to think a moment before he remembered her name. "What can I do for you?"

She took a deep breath. "Well…Mr. Miller…I…I wondered… I heard that you needed a cook." Why was this so difficult? Why wouldn't her hands stop shaking?

"Why yes, I do. Do you know of someone?" He wasn't making it any easier.

"Uh, yes. Well, I was thinking that maybe I could try to do the job."

Now he did look at her – hard. "You?" He didn't say it with scorn or anything, just more total surprise at the idea that a woman could maybe cook for anyone other than her family.

"Well, yes. I've never cooked for quite so many men, but I've always done most of the cooking for the help at haying and things like that, and I think I could do it if…if you wanted me."

"Hmm." At first she thought he was going to say no, desperate as he was. But instead he said, "What about your parents? Would they let you do it?" She stopped for a moment. No one knew better than she how her father felt about Aaron – yet he worked for him himself.

"They want me to go out and work, I know that." This at least was the truth.

"But to do this job?"

"I don't think they'd object." This was not wholly the truth. Of course she knew they would, but she also knew that in the end they'd let her go.

"Well," he conceded, "if they're willing for you to do it, we'll give it a try."

And then he did shake her hand, as if sealing the deal.

🦋

If Frederika had been less than enthusiastic about Erika's plan, Jacob was furious.

"Go and work for that stuck-up slave-driver? My daughter?"

"But you work for him yourself."

"That's different."

"How?"

"It just is." But in the end he didn't forbid her to go.

"Anyway," Erika reasoned with him, "you'll be there as well to see nothing awful happens to me."

But, as it happened, Jacob wasn't. Two days before they were due to start at the camp, while rounding up the oxen that had been put out to pasture, Jacob fell and twisted the leg that had been wounded so severely years ago. There could be no question of him going to work in the woods, at least at the beginning of the season. This made it even more necessary that Erika should go out and earn some money.

So on a grey Monday morning in the middle of November, Erika rose early and put her belongings in an old leather suitcase – two dresses she had made herself, two thick sweaters knit by Frederika, two white flannel petticoats and bodices, two nightgowns, also flannel, heavy stockings, a spare pair of shoes and, of course, the "unmention-ables." Then she walked the three miles to the camp. The lake had not yet frozen solid, so she had to go around it.

When she arrived, the men stared but said nothing. Their liveli-hood depended on her cooking skills. Aaron took charge and showed her to a small bed in a corner around which he had hooked up a primi-tive cotton curtain. He had even nailed a shelf on the wall and a small piece of tin for a mirror. She was impressed. No one else had ever done anything to make her feel special – except sometimes Nathan, who would bring her wild flowers to put in her hair. But he was only a baby and her brother.

The camp itself was built entirely of logs and quite generous in size. Four bunk beds lined each of the walls on the side, with three single beds across the end. One of the end beds was the single oc-cupied by Erika. The other end wall was the cooking area. This Erika busily began to examine. In the centre stood a huge stove with piles of logs stacked neatly beside it. In one corner there was a pump and sink, in the other a large rough table for preparing food. On shelves above the table were piled plates, mugs, soup dishes and cooking bowls, tin pie plates and wooden mixing spoons. A large bin full of flour opened out from under the shelves and another smaller bin lined with tin held sugar. The middle of the room was taken up by a huge wood trestle table with rough-hewn chairs around its sides. There were two oil lamps, one at either end of the table, and more lamps hanging over the cooking area. It looked a thoroughly delightful little kingdom with herself as queen of it.

Now, what should she cook? It was ten in the morning, and on this first day the men would probably be busy setting up their gear until after dinner, making sure the saws and axes were sharp and ready, the oxen and carts both in good working order. Dinner, she had been told, was at twelve noon sharp; supper at five or six depending on when the light failed and the day's work was over. It seemed doubly important to have a good meal to set them up for their first afternoon's work, and she had only two hours.

She saw that Aaron had brought in enough bread for the first day, and there was a huge crock of baked beans (made by Agnes?) as well. The stock of meat consisted mainly of salt beef and salt pork, all marinating in large pails. There would not be time to soak out the excess salt and cook any of it today. But then she saw the sausages hanging in delectable links from the rafters. Sausages with beans and bread and molasses. What could be better? But what for dessert? Molasses cookies, of course. She got out the flour and butter, sugar and molasses, and even (perhaps Aaron would think this extravagant) some raisins. When noon came, everything was ready, and she scurried about, setting up the table and serving with pride. The men did not complain. They didn't compliment her or thank her either. Men didn't. If they simply tipped back their chairs with their hands behind their heads and went on talking after the meal, you knew you had done well.

After a minute or two, they got up and went out into the woods without a word to her. She was left alone to clear up the mess and prepare the next meal.

She gathered up the dishes, piled them on a large wooden tray, carried them to the counter beside the sink, then came back for another load – on and on it seemed. She boiled water on the stove and carried it back to the large round metal dishpan in the sink. She scrubbed and scrubbed. Periodically she stopped off to dry and put away. When she was finished, the sun was slanting down towards the horizon. It was three o'clock already – time to prepare supper. What now?

There were mysterious barrels sitting on the floor under the counter, so she started to explore. A strong bitter smell that she knew well came up when she opened the cover of the first one – sauerkraut. That, with some salt pork, would do for dinner tomorrow. But now? The second barrel held apples, tidily arranged in layers. Apple pie, that would be splendid for dessert. So she set about peeling and chopping until a large pile sat on the counter. Then she found a big bowl, poured in lots of flour and looked around for butter and Crisco. Butter she found, but Crisco there was none – only greasy lard. This must be what they used. So she cut in lard and butter, mixing it up with cold water,

72

rolled out the pastry, and soon the pie was in the oven. Dessert was all very well, and what the men cared about most, if truth be known, but they would expect a main course as well. It was half past four already, and she could see the men who were working out in the yard looking hungrily towards the cabin windows. Pancakes! Pancakes with maple syrup could be cooked on a griddle while they ate. Flour again, salt, sugar, soda and cream of tartar, eggs and milk. In it all went, and soon the pancakes were cooking, puffy and golden, on the griddle. She had made it through the first day.

Supper was met with the same lack of comment as dinner. At the end of the meal they began to smoke, then got out the cards and played Auction 45 by the light of two oil lamps. They did not play for money (Aaron would not allow it), but simply for the prestige of playing a hand well. Erika sat in a chair apart and watched them, eating her pancakes the while – the cards flicking down on the table, the smoke curling gently up to the rafters, the "I got you there" of a momentary triumph. It was a strange world, just these companionable men and herself, the only woman in the place, sitting on the periphery of their play. This time, since they were not going back to work, they brought their plates over to the sink, and while they gossiped she stood at the sink washing and drying them. Sometimes there was a quiet remark, then a burst of laughter, and one dug another in the ribs as they exchanged knowing looks. Would they have spoken louder if she were not there?

They were still at their card game when she finished clearing up, so she sat down again, this time in a rocking chair, the wicker bottom alarmingly frayed, and took up some knitting she had brought. This, she felt, was what they might expect a woman to do. She drew herself up to sustain the role – the role of "woman," surrogate wife, for this group of men, all of whom had known her individually from childhood, but all of whom now ignored her totally as a personality, as, indeed, she did them. She was the cook; they lumbermen.

Half an hour later she was struck by a horrifying thought – making two meals today had occupied her fully, but most days had three

73

meals in them. There would be breakfast as well tomorrow. Was there enough bread left? She got up to check. Just about.

"When," she asked tentatively, "what time do you usually have breakfast?"

Aaron answered, "We want to be out at work as soon as it's light enough. That'll be about eight, so we should have breakfast around seven." He had not joined the other men in their game but sat back from the table, just near enough so that he could get a bit of light from the oil lamps to shine on the book he was reading.

"So – seven o'clock." Seven o'clock! She had better go to bed. She would have to be up at five to start the fire and get everything ready.

She went into her curtained cubicle, stored her few essentials on the shelf above the bed and hung her clothes on the three hooks provided. She set the primitive alarm clock with two big bells on top that her mother had lent her. When she had on her long flannel nightgown, she remembered she had neither washed her face nor brushed her teeth, so she ventured out to the pump in the eyes of all to do these things. Then she retreated. No one said goodnight.

For a long time she lay in the dark listening to the muted voices and laughter, the gentle slap of the cards on the table. Eventually she heard the scraping of chairs, the working of the pump, the sound of shoes dropping on the floor and beds creaking. As if she had finally been given permission, she fell asleep.

She woke up several times during the night, worrying that she might have slept through the alarm. At last the clock detonated; she pushed back the wool-bed and got up in the cold darkness. Aaron was already dressed and walking around with a candle checking on things. He nodded to her but did not speak. "Is everything all right?" she ventured.

"Yes, yes, of course. Everything fine with you?"

"Yes, only…could you get me some Crisco the next time you get supplies?"

"Crisco! Crisco? Agnes don't use Crisco." Was this a rebuke, a refusal, or a mere statement of surprise?

Then he pulled on his boots and disappeared into the frosty world outside the cabin. Why did these men seem suddenly deprived of speech in her presence?

His bed must be the one beside hers. It also had no upper bunk and was surrounded by a curtain, now pulled back.

For an hour she worked on her own, rinsing the pork that she had put in to soak the night before, laying the table, cooking porridge, bacon, toasting bread, on and on. Gradually the world came to life around her. Sighing and groaning the men prepared for their first full day of work in the woods. They spoke briefly to one another about the weather, their homes left so recently, their children.

"Looks like it'll be a fine day."

"Yeah. Cold though."

"How did you leave the Missus?"

"All right. One kid's down with the croup already though."

"Give 'em steam, lots of steam from boiling water, I say. Only thing that helps."

"Once Jimmy had it so bad we had to call the doctor."

"And what did he do?"

"Nuthin'. Just got that listenin' thing out and shook his head and left a bottle of useless pink stuff that the kid wouldn't swallow. And charged a fortune. Kid got better anyway."

"Yeah. That's the way. They're pretty useless, doctors."

She listened to them talking back and forth across the room, each adding his voice to the general din, while she, efficient, invisible, cooked and served and took plates away. This was her life now. Not once did it occur to her that she might give up or leave. One didn't give up or leave in Waldenstein. One's fate was as ingrained as the granite rocks in the fields.

৯

Agnes looked out at the snow. It was falling softly now, covering everything, the bare trees, the dead grass, the frozen lake. It was quiet and comforting, the snow, like a great duvet you could curl up in, be silent and never wake up. If you lay down in the snow you need never cook another meal, wash another floor, darn another sock. You would be both confined and free at the same time.

She was more or less alone as she thought these things. The older children were in school, Harry was having his nap, and Joan was playing quietly with her dolls. Aaron, of course, was nowhere around. He would be back at the camp till Christmas, home for a few days, then gone again until the spring melt. He had asked them all to come and have dinner on Saturday. Often she ignored these invitations: to get the children ready, harness the horse and sled, drive them through the forest road and across the lake – so much effort, and for what? For a carelessly cooked meal prepared by a bored cook, and very little or no time alone with Aaron. But this time she felt a certain desire to go. The children were eager, of course. Beyond this, however, she wondered about what the camp was like now that Erika was doing the cooking. How was she coping? Was she any good? And, unacknowledged, pricking at the back of her mind, should she have spurned Aaron again on his last night at home? She was perfectly right in not wanting more children, she told herself. "Yes, but will you carry on spurning him forever?" a little voice nagged. "And just what do you expect to happen if you do?"

There was still a thick snow cover on Saturday so riding in the sleigh would be no problem. "Come early," Aaron had said, "come early or you'll miss dinner." So she dressed all the children in their warmest clothes, scarves, mittens, and woolly hats, and piled them into the sleigh. The horse shivered with anticipation – or cold – and off they went, bells jingling.

They arrived just as the men were coming back to the camp from felling trees. What smells wafted out the door to greet them! A rabbit stew rich with carrots and turnips and onions bubbled in a huge pot on the stove, and Erika was just taking the cover off to put in the dough boys – flour and soda, butter and water all flavoured with dried summer savoury – by spoonfuls into the pot. Then she closed the lid tightly so that they would puff up as they cooked, white and fluffy as clouds on top and succulent with rabbit gravy on the bottom. "My, that smells wonderful, Erika. Worth travelling miles in the freezing cold for."

Erika smiled at her. "Thanks, Mrs. Miller." Agnes glanced at her briefly. Why this reticence? And "Mrs. Miller"?

Just then Aaron himself came in and scooped up Harry and Joan in a big hug. He kissed her of course – or at least she felt that "of course" was tagged onto the kiss. Then everyone was talking and laughing, while she and the children were sat in their places at the especially extended table. The meal was good, there was no question about that. "Why can't we have rabbit stew like Erika makes?" asked Emma.

"Because there's no one to trap the rabbits when Papa's away." Did Emma prefer Erika's food to hers? Dessert was apple pie with the flakiest, most scrumptious pastry anyone had ever eaten. Everyone said so. Erika had got her Crisco.

Then the children played outside in the snow, and some of the men joined in, helping to build a huge snow fort and then fighting snowball battles once it was erected. Agnes and Aaron sat inside talking, mostly about practical things, while Erika busied herself washing the dishes and tidying up.

Yes, she was managing. Didn't she always? Yes, of course Flora was difficult, but that was no change. Naturally she was looking forward to Christmas. What should she get the children? How much could they afford to order from the Eaton's catalogue? Was Harry, at not yet two, old enough for a little tricycle she had seen? Aaron was certain he was. Already, Agnes knew, he could deny Harry nothing.

He said nothing to her that he might not have said to a maid, she reflected. Was this because Erika was still there in the corner, taking as much time to wash up as if she were inventing the process from first principles? Or was it because…?

And then it was three-o'clock, time to go if they were to get home before dark. "Erika's doing well," Agnes said, half hoping for some signal – she knew not what. Aaron's face gave nothing away. "Yes, she's fine. The men find it a bit strange, having a woman around, but they're getting used to it. And she certainly excelled herself today." Another "of course" kiss, and they were gone. She looked back and saw Erika, a dark shadow in the doorway, watching them.

🦅

"How's it going back there with all them men?" Frederika was using the Christmas break to pump Erika, but Erika was having none of it.

"All right. It's a lot of work, but I can manage."

"Bet they eat a lot." Frederika really did want to know what life was like for Erika, but how to discover this escaped her.

"Yup. They cut down trees all day, so why shouldn't they eat a lot?"

"What do you do in your spare time?"

Erika stiffened, "What spare time?"

Frederika gave up.

In fact, now that she had got into the swing of things, Erika did have some spare time. And what she did in it was either take a walk in the woods, which were surprisingly beautiful in the snow, or read some of the books Aaron lent her. Then, sometimes, after supper, they would sit together and talk about them while the rest of the men played cards. These books were by people she had never heard of – Dickens, Jane Austen, even poetry by someone called Tennyson, who definitely had it all over Longfellow. "Did you read these books with Agnes?" she once asked, tentatively.

Aaron did not seem to feel the question impertinent. "No, she never had time," he said matter-of-factly.

And suddenly Erika felt a surge of pity for Agnes, who had looked so small and lost among all those children the day they came to visit the camp. "She never had time…."

"Emma, now. She reads a lot," Aaron went on. "Understands it all too. She's a real bright girl."

But, Erika reflected, Emma must have time as well as intelligence to read.

The return after Christmas seemed almost like coming home. The winter days went by in a routine of cooking, baking, washing up, going for walks, and reading – a not unpleasant life. Gradually the men began to talk to her, only in jokes at first, but then she started to register as a real human being in their eyes. Sometimes they even asked her to join in a card game. In truth, she rather fascinated them – one of their own, but yet apart, the most capable and efficient cook the camp had ever had. Still, they were watching her. She knew that. They would see nothing.

Before she knew it, the end of March had come. The snow was melting, and the logs were being rolled into the lake for the beginning of their journey to the mill. Erika watched in fascination. A large "boom" of logs was in place, and once as many logs as it could contain had been rolled down the still-icy bank, the boom was closed so that the logs were completely encircled by a string of larger logs, all fastened strongly together with thick rope. Then the boom was fastened to the "headworks" – a strong raft-like structure that housed a windlass. An enormous piece of rope was attached to the windlass at one end and to an anchor at the other. She watched as a small boat took the rope to the extent of its length, dropped the anchor, and then six men on the headworks began to winch the rope and the boom of logs gradually towards the anchor. Thus slowly, laboriously, the logs were carried along.

It took days to move everything that had been cut during the winter, and during this time Erika was still on duty in the camp. Things seemed to be going well until the very last day when Erika heard the men out on the lake yelling. "She's stuck. Try moving her a little that way if you can." Then, after a while, "No good. Someone's going to have to go out and move her."

Erika ran to the shore to look. There was a cry, "I'll do it," and she saw Dilphin, her cousin and Ben's oldest son, start out from the boat and walk precariously across the sea of logs until he reached the large boom log on the end. He held a pike, both for balance and to move the logs, and he looked large and confident as he balanced on the rolling logs in the icy water. Briefly, she recalled that her mother had suggested she marry him.

Then, as he reached out to grapple with the recalcitrant boom log, something seemed to snag his foot, and he wobbled slightly to one side. "Rock," they thought they heard him yell. "She's stuck on a rock."

He appeared to recover and pushed again. Suddenly the boom log gave way, knocking the log he was standing on sideways. He tried to balance with the pike. For a frantic second or two he seemed suspended over the water, logs and ice, flailing violently. Then the pike dropped, and he fell, still flailing, into the icy water. The watching men, horrified, yelled out. Several started themselves across the logs to where he had disappeared. But nowhere was there anything solid, just floating, rocking logs. "Bring the boat, bring the boat." And the boat was cut free from the anchor and the boom, and slowly, oh so slowly, it seemed, moved around the edge of the boom, away to the back where Dilphin had fallen. They looked through the logs and the floating ice; they saw the rock that had snagged the logs, but Dilphin was nowhere to be seen.

Just as they were about to leave for the shore, someone yelled, "There." Bobbing uncertainly under the logs was a pile of soaked clothing and the form of a man. They reached out with the pike and caught it on his jacket. Slowly they swung it up, until two of them could stretch out of the boat and pull him in. They laid him on the bottom of the boat and rowed back to the camp.

"Didn't want to learn to swim, said he'd sooner go quick, not struggle."

"Well, that he did."

"Get the girl out of the way," someone ordered.

"Find Aaron," barked another.

But there was no possibility of getting Erika out of the way; she had watched the whole scene unfold from the shore. Now, as Dilphin's body was carried in and laid on the table she felt overwhelmingly sick and went outside. It was the first time; probably just the shock of the dead body. But her own body…why would it not bleed? She pushed the thought aside; how could she consider this when her cousin lay dead not fifty feet away? She went back inside to help the men.

"Who's going to tell his mother?"

That was a question indeed. First Ophelia, now Dilphin. Fire and water.

Just then Aaron arrived and took charge. He would tell Sophia, of course. Or he would tell Ben, who would break it to Sophia. It was his duty.

Erika packed up her clothes and headed home with a heavy heart. She had got used to the camaraderie of the camp, the sense of being useful, appreciated, good at what she was doing. Now what? Who would she be when she stepped back into her family home?

Her arrival was completely overshadowed by grief at Dilphin's drowning. Her mother and father were not even at home – probably down the hill with Ben and Sophia. She had no desire to go down to join them, so she climbed the stairs with her belongings to her small room and lay down on the bed. She looked at the faded wallpaper with the little sprays of pink flowers that she had picked out when she was ten. Now she saw it through a vague nausea that might be physical or might not. Everything was so familiar, yet so much had happened she felt a stranger. Could she be? No, no! It didn't happen that way, not just once. God couldn't be so cruel. And she hadn't meant it, not really. It just somehow came to be. And lying on her bed she rehearsed the scene, not for the first time.

It was three weeks before the end of the logging season – just three short weeks ago. She and Aaron had been reading and discussing Richardson's *Clarissa* together. (He did manage to get the most amazing books. Where had this dog-eared copy come from?) By the time they stopped reading, all the men had gone to bed. She went into her little cubicle as usual to undress. He was busy about the large room, checking the fire, making sure the door was locked. When she came out to wash at the pump he was still standing there, watching her. She felt uneasy under his gaze. What was he waiting for, what did he want?

"Erika."

"Yes?"

"Are you happy here?" It was not just a formal question; it was tender, caring.

"Yes, I think so." And so she did think – independent and happy for almost the first time in her life.

"I should hate to believe this job had made you unhappy. Not an easy thing for you to do. I am so grateful." And she sensed that beneath the caring there was stiffness, almost embarrassment in his speech.

"It was hard at first, but now I think I've come to enjoy it."

She knew it was he who was unhappy, but she couldn't imagine why, unless it had something to do with Agnes, who always seemed sad and withdrawn.

Now he moved slightly closer to her and put a hand on her shoulder. So comforting. Until that moment, she had not realized how alone she had felt. She wanted his approval and affection so much – more than anything else. But now the hand was doing things she thought maybe it shouldn't be doing. (How lovely and relaxing it felt, though.) And now she was in her little cubicle and the curtains were being softly closed, and the hand was still there, in the cubicle with her. It enticed her, held her captive, till she was lulled into a kind of trance, broken only by the sharp pain of penetration.

What was this? How had it happened? Was this what her mother had warned her about? "Never, never, never should a girl give herself up without a ring." But she hadn't "given herself up." She had simply been taken to her bed, as it might have been by her father, and cuddled, only then something strange and inexplicable had happened. It hadn't seemed to be connected with an act of will at all.

Aaron, meanwhile, was distraught. "I didn't mean. Oh my God! How could I? I'm so sorry." All this in a panicked whisper. And then, "Go, wash yourself. It'll be all right. I promise. It'll be all right. " No one will ever know. I swear I'll never again…"

She got up, sore and bleeding. She went to the pump, washed herself thoroughly with a rag, tied another rag around herself as if she were having a period, then burned the first rag in the dying stove fire like a criminal destroying evidence.

"It'll be all right." His words swam on the ceiling now as she lay on her bed reliving the scene. But suppose – suppose it wasn't all right. Aaron was a married man. It struck her that were Dilphin still alive she could play the dutiful daughter and marry him. Then no one would ever know. In her near-hysterical state this somehow struck her as funny. And then she thought of the cousin she had played and fought with, and of how he never could have any children of his own now, and she began to weep – for him, for herself, for the whole mess life was.

Eventually she heard noises downstairs. She must get up and let them know she was home. Frederika rushed to embrace her as she came slowly down the stairs. "Isn't this just terrible, terrible. What more can happen to poor Sophia?" And then, without a pause, as if it were part of the inevitable pattern of grief, "Erika, can you make some muffins to take down the hill to them. There's nothing in the house; I looked."

And as Erika wearily got out the flour, she added, "And when you take the muffins down, you might just dust and tidy a bit. All kinds of people are coming in; the minister'll soon be there; and I don't want him to see a relative's house in that kind of mess. There's stuff strewn everywhere. And Sophia just sittin' on that chair, rockin'."

Erika made bran muffins with large, juicy raisins in them. While they were still warm she wrapped them in a tea towel, took a large pat of butter out of the cool cellar and walked across the road and down over the field. By now a huge crowd had gathered. The women were in the kitchen surrounding Sophia, who seemed scarcely to notice their presence. On the kitchen table sat enough food – pies, cakes, bread, roast chicken – to feed the Wentzells for a month. Some women actually appeared to be making more food in the kitchen itself. Cups of tea were handed round, pieces of fruit cake, Erika's own muffins, still warm and steaming when broken in half. Sophia took no interest in the tea or cakes. Indeed, she seemed to be the unwitting hostess of a party she had neither planned nor desired. Erika remembered her mother's injunction to tidy and dust. But others were already busy at this task, and anyway there were few surfaces left to clean; everything was covered by either food or people.

"How did you make out back there with all them men?" someone enquired, sniggering slightly.

"You look pretty good on it, I must say," another replied. Then she laughed too. What was so funny?

It was warm in the little room, what with the crowd and the fire in the stove. Things began to revolve slowly, the voices became dim...

Someone was lifting her up to lay her on the bench that ran under the window. "Go get some of the men to take her back home," another said. The men were in the barn, naturally, enjoying the solace that in this temperance community was reserved for them alone. Every wife swore that her husband couldn't be found consuming liquor, but nevertheless, he would go out to look at the cattle with his friends. Who could blame him for that? Right now it was strong apple cider that was circulating in the barn. The men were focused on guilt – who could have saved Dilphin, and how. Ben sat on a windowsill, almost as inert as his wife in the house. Of all the men there, he alone did not have a glass in his hand. "Such a good boy," he muttered over and over. "Such a good boy. Always did what he was told."

He didn't even stir when Muriel burst in and said some of them were needed up at the house to take Erika home. Neither, more remarkably, did Aaron.

Half an hour later Erika was lying on her bed again with Frederika flapping around, half concerned, half annoyed with her it seemed.

"What did you have to go and make a spectacle of yourself for? They've got trouble enough down there. And you're not the fainting type. I've never fainted in my life." Meanwhile she fluffed up the pillows, got a glass of cool water from the pump downstairs and generally did her best to make Erika comfortable.

Eventually she went downstairs leaving Erika to contemplate what was becoming a horrible possibility. What would she do? She couldn't appeal to Aaron for help; she mustn't let anyone know whose it was. She had no idea how she might get rid of it. All the suggestions she had half overheard seemed nothing short of outlandish. There was something about knitting needles – what did you do with them? Stick them randomly up your insides? She had also heard that if you drank a lot – but how could she do that? The only drink was out in the barn, and anyway her parents couldn't fail to notice if she were drunk. A hot bath. Where did people live who thought up these crazy schemes? The only place for a bath in Waldenstein was in a large tub in the kitchen, Saturday night only, please, and since all the water had to be heated on the stove the chances of getting it super hot were non-existent. Finally, one could, she supposed, throw oneself down the stairs. But the effects of this were bound to be imprecise. Anyway, at heart she was a young and healthy woman, and the idea of deliberately harming herself was repugnant. After a while she managed to get up and go downstairs where Hibbert, Obadiah and Nathan were already eating heartily.

She was not allowed to go to the funeral. She might create a scene as she had the day he died. There would be drama enough without that. So she stayed at home and spent the time wandering randomly through the orchard and woods in back of her house. What would she do? What *could* she do? She could go away somewhere to do housework until the baby was born, but what would that solve? Everyone would know, and where would she and the child go afterwards? For in the course of a few days the object growing inside her had changed from "it" to "baby." Giving him up no longer occurred to her.

❦

Meanwhile the minister was doing his best to assure them that the state of bliss Dilphin was now enjoying was so superior to life here on earth that mourning should be superfluous. No more would he wade knee deep in the freezing water of swollen lakes, no longer would he get up in the frosty dark and put on damp trousers that had frozen to the wall next to his bunk. The general tenor of his message seemed to be that life was a vale of tears and Dilphin was well out of it. Nathan watched in bewilderment as everyone sat silent, heads lowered, apparently assenting. He thought briefly of the earlier sermon in which the day of one's death was said to be better than that of one's birth. Could this really be true?

Only at the graveside was decorum shatteringly broken. Sophia, who had been in a catatonic state up to this point suddenly said as the coffin was lowered, "Is that Dilphin?" Ben, holding her tightly, said "Yes, it's Dilphin, my love." And then she howled, drowning out the words of committal, drowning out the creaking of the ropes. "How did you get there, Dilphin, how did you get there? They've shut you up forever. You wanted to live, didn't you Dilphin, you wanted to marry Erika and have babies."

"Shh, shh," Ben soothed her. Others were horrified. No sense of dignity and solemnity, and dragging poor Erika (thank heavens her parents had not let her come) into it as well. Eventually Ben and little Benjamin took her away, one on either side. Everyone else followed and went straight home.

❧

"I don't believe that." It was Emma, walking beside Virtue back to their lakeside home, who uttered the rebellion felt by many who watched the young Dilphin buried.

"Don't believe what?" Did Emma expect her to be clairvoyant?

"That life's all awful and you're better off dead. Do you?"

"No, I don't think so." Pressed, Virtue didn't think she believed this, but if the minister said so....

"Well that's what Pastor Rasmussen was saying, wasn't he? And the only reason he has to make us believe it is so we don't think it was awful that Dilphin was drowned. We know what being alive is like – and being dead might be like anything. How does he know anyway?"

"He's a minister; he's studied lots of stuff." Virtue could see that Emma, as usual, was treading on dangerous ground.

"I don't care. If I die, don't you dare let him say anything like that at my funeral."

Truth

1917

Erika was excused from the haying. Everyone knew now, so she was relegated to the status of cook for the men in the fields. At least she had had practice.

When the awful day of confrontation with her mother had come, she had said nothing. Denial was useless. Contrition would get her nowhere. The sin was beyond forgiveness.

"It's true, isn't it? You're havin' a baby." It was an accusation.

Erika nodded her head.

"I might've known this would happen when you went back in the woods to stay alone with all them men."

"I was working, Mama."

"Yes, working by day and other things at night." Frederika sniffed.

"It wasn't like that. Really. You've got to believe me."

"Well, what was it like exactly?" Was her mother capable of sarcasm?

Silence.

"Who's the father then?"

More silence.

"We've got to know so he can help support the child."

"That's not possible," she said quietly but firmly.

"Why? Even if he's married…"

"No."

Then a thought struck both mother and daughter simultaneously – for one it was an extenuating possibility, for the other a known falsehood that could exonerate her – sort of. What if the child were Dilphin's? Then she would have the glory of bearing a child for the dead man, of giving him a posthumous heir. Perhaps they had been secretly engaged. And her fainting at his death and inability to go to the funeral would be explicable to everyone.

Frederika gave her the chance to use this escape. "Is it…could it be…Dilphin's?"

But she could not. It would be a deception too far. She remained silent, her head lowered.

"Well then, let me know when you're ready. You know your father will have to be told – if he hasn't noticed already – and the boys."

Yet Erika knew her mother's kindness would win out over her judgment. In the end, Erika and her baby would be looked after, even loved. Often she had envied Aaron's daughters. Now, unexpectedly, she thought of what Agnes would be like as a mother in similar circumstances. Her daughters could expect no mercy. Nor could she expect mercy from Agnes if she ever discovered that Erika's child was half-sibling to her own. She must never let slip the truth to anyone. How could they guess? She had been at the camp for five months with fifteen men. It could be any of them – including Dilphin.

ॐ

Rumours spread fast in Waldenstein. "Erika is having a baby" – the general view being that she had been asking for it, living back there with all those men. But then the speculation moved on naturally as to whom the father could be, and the rumour that it was Dilphin seemed to arise spontaneously, out of the ether. There was something profoundly satisfying about the idea, quite romantic, in fact. The idea that he should have conceived a child and never even known about it had an irresistible appeal. For some weeks this remained the generally held view.

But then nastier, more cynical rumours surfaced. It was not Dilphin's after all. Why? Because if it were, Erika would confirm it, and anyway, while their mothers were busy match-making, Erika and

Dilphin had never shown any marked liking for each other. They heard that Aaron and Erika read books together by candlelight. Reading for pleasure – reading that was anything other than the Bible – was a pursuit most believed dangerous, akin to witchcraft. The words on the page enticed and drew you in. They had never heard of Paolo and Francesca, but they knew reading could be godless and lead to foolishness. Aaron always had been a bit of a mystery to them, and Agnes was rather a stick now, after all that childbearing. It all made a lot of sense.

Aaron, meanwhile, kept out of the way. He was busy at the mill. No, he knew nothing about Erika and her affairs. Hadn't noticed her being particularly close to anyone during the winter. A good girl, did her job well. Pity about the trouble she was in. Naturally, if it had happened during his employment of her, he'd do what he could to help.

But Agnes knew. How did she know? By a thousand signs and intuitions, unconscious signals. At times Aaron seemed distracted. When she indicated that she had reversed her position on conjugal relations he merely sighed. Then, desperate, she confronted him directly. "You are the father, are you not?"

He affected not to understand; it gave him a few seconds of time. "Father of whom?"

"Don't pretend not to know what all Waldenstein is talking about. The father of Erika's baby."

How could he lie to her? How could he *not* lie to her?

"People have dirty gossiping minds. I know nothing about Erika's baby." He spoke and turned away.

She didn't believe him.

🐦

December 6, 1917

Everything was still dark when Erika inexplicably awoke. For a while she lay there, heavy and unwieldy, reluctant to throw off the wool-bed that cocooned her. In some way she couldn't quite define, she was uncomfortable. So with a sigh she heaved herself up and out onto the braided rug by her bed. Suddenly there was water everywhere – on her thighs, on the rug, trickling off onto the floor. At the same time a small, distant throb of pain, a mere intimation of pain, stroked her abdomen. So it was to be today, then.

She called her mother and went back to bed. It felt safe there. But then the pain found her, even under the wool-bed, and seized her more intimately and roughly. She had willed none of this. Causation seemed entirely outside her, but sensation was just as surely inside her, pain taking her body and shaping it according to its will.

There was no reason to call a doctor – a strong, healthy girl like her. Frederika did send Obadiah to get Muriel, who acted as a kind of unofficial midwife to other women's children, now that she had been banished from delivering her daughter's brood. She came with Rose, who at nineteen was thought old enough to know about and even assist at such an occasion. Rose arrived muffled in a large coat, two sweaters, a hat and big rubber boots. But once she divested herself of all these clothes she set to work with a will, warming the room with a small brazier brought from their home for the purpose, getting out the baby's clothes and basket and setting them up at the foot of the bed, smoothing back Erika's hair, wiping her perspiring face and uttering words of comfort. Deep within her stirred the sense that maybe this vicarious birthing was all that she herself could ever hope for. Could she envy even disgraced, agonized Erika?

Gradually a weak sun pushed itself up over the frosty trees. Inside the little bedroom things were moving swiftly. By nine o'clock, there was barely time for Erika to catch her breath between contractions, and she was sure she was going to die. But then the bottom of the wool-bed was rolled up, she felt an urgent need to push, and fifteen minutes later a dark-haired little boy emerged. He was chubby, red, and enraged. Quickly Frederika bathed him in the warm water, patted him dry and gave him to Erika.

"There now. We can't say he looks like his Pa, but he certainly ain't really light like you." She lay him on the bed on top of Erika and watched. He snuffled a bit more, then latched onto Erika's swollen breast with a vicious determination. She had never been so happy.

Just then the earth began to rock. At first they all thought they must be imagining it. But the next minute they heard the sound of dishes crashing to the floor in the dining room under them.

"What in the name of...?" Muriel sat down heavily on the floor beside the baby's basket.

Frederika took charge. "An earthquake. Must be. Stay in bed, Erika." And she went downstairs to investigate. Half the china on the open sideboard shelves was in pieces, but apart from that, things seemed to be holding together. After a minute or so everything was quiet again, and Frederika returned upstairs. She thought, though she did not say, "A sign." On entering the room, she knelt for a moment, and Muriel and Rose followed her example. Everything meant something. The whole world was planned by God like a giant crossword puzzle where you just had to work out the clues, and the meaning became plain. Unlike an ordinary crossword, however, God's crossword wasn't just random words but a whole interconnected pattern. Of course no one had ever completed the crossword and seen the pattern, but that didn't mean it didn't exist.

So if this were a sign, what might it mean, Frederika mused. The child himself seemed healthy and whole. Was the secret conceiving of a child a curse or a blessing? Or did it mean something else altogether?

She rose from her knees and, with Muriel and Rose, helped to clean Erika's room and settle the baby in his basket. Then Muriel and Rose left to see what damage might await them in their own home, but Frederika stayed with Erika, holding her hand until both she and the new baby were asleep.

When she finally went downstairs and looked out the window, she saw clusters of neighbours, Jacob and her own boys among them, talking animatedly about the earthquake. But it hadn't felt like an earthquake, Jacob was pointing out; it was one big shudder, with nothing before or after it. And if you were outside, he swore, you could hear a distant "bang."

"Maybe it's the war," Obadiah suggested helpfully.

"Don't be silly. How are the Germans goin' to get this far? They ain't even invaded England yet," Jacob replied.

So they talked and speculated until, in the evening, news came. It was the war, after all, but not in the way anyone had expected. After dark, Aaron, riding on his horse, came dashing along the road. He dismounted quickly in obvious agitation. He had been in Mahone Bay earlier that day where the noise and shaking had been much worse. Then two hours later someone had come riding down from Halifax as if the devil were after him. There had been an explosion – two ships, one Belgian and one French – had collided in the harbour. But here was the terrible thing. The French ship was packed with munitions going to Europe for the war. It exploded, with flames a mile high, and half the city was destroyed. As he recounted this he seemed to become the maddened messenger from the city himself.

His voice rose in histrionic tones. "Thousands are dead, no one knows how many. The north part of the city just isn't there anymore, they say, and everything's burning. They need help real bad – people to fight the fires, tents for the homeless, blankets, food. It's winter, for God's sake; they'll all die, even those who have been spared, if they don't get shelter. A lot of people in Mahone Bay just dropped what they were doing at once and started up then and there to help. I'd 've gone myself, except that I promised Agnes and the children I'd be back tonight and how would they know what had happened if I didn't come?"

At last he paused. The men and boys around him were silent, stunned. The war that had seemed so far off was now marching across their own snowy fields, scattering blood and limbs in its wake. Tragedy in Waldenstein usually came singly, to Ophelias and Dilphins. There was time to absorb its impact. But this was unimaginable horror. "'Thousands killed,' did you say?" Jacob asked, numbly.

"Yes, thousands. That's what the man from the city said. And he looked wild enough, I believed him."

Indoors, Frederika was wrestling with a more intimate dilemma. Should she tell Aaron that Erika had had her baby? It would be only neighbourly, and he'd discover soon enough anyway. Besides, if she didn't tell him it would look as if…well, as if she believed certain rumours. So she went out to the men, who told her all about the explosion.

Then she said, "Well, somethin' good has happened today anyway. Erika's had her baby – a beautiful boy."

Frederika watched Aaron. Did he tense at the news? Did he show any emotion at all?

At first he simply said, "Oh, I knew it must be soon." Then hesitantly, he added, "Would it be all right if I had a peek at it, or would I be disturbing her?"

How could she refuse? "Certainly, you can see the baby. He's gorgeous – pink and fat and hungry. He has dark hair."

"Dark hair. I see."

So he went up, followed by Frederika. Erika was just awake. "Here's Aaron, come to see your baby."

She looked up. In the dim lamp light neither of their faces gave anything away. Aaron looked down at his son, who, as if at a signal, or maybe it was the lamplight, began to whimper. Frederika picked him up. "A fine boy, isn't he?" Frederika prompted.

"Yes, a fine boy indeed."

He looked at the child, squirming and nuzzling. *My* fine boy. But he said nothing more.

Consequences

February, 1918

Erika insisted on calling the baby Adam. He was the first, un-questionably – and what would come afterwards was all ob-scure. Sometimes she saw him as a child of promise and ex-pectation, wandering blissfully through a green landscape of meadow and forest, a Waldenstein perfected; then she looked again on him and was filled with pity, seeing him as an already fallen Adam, doomed by the accident of his conception, cast out from human society. Just now, he certainly was leading an Eden-like existence. He fed, slept, and babbled at will. He smiled at his mother and grandmother and anyone else who came within range. He moved his hands and played with the shadows they made when the winter sun slanted through the window onto his bed.

But when he left the cocoon of his home, it was different. The minister said it would be better for him not to be baptized at a Sunday morning service. At least he didn't refuse to baptize him altogether! So on the first Sunday in February, Erika, Jacob and the three boys crept in after the regular service for the baptism ceremony. Adam was angelic throughout and didn't cry even when the water was poured on his head.

As they left the church, a few stragglers from the Sunday service were still hanging around. They stared in curiosity at Erika and her new baby. Some whispered, and a few young people giggled; others gave her pitying looks. Holding Adam close to her, she strode out to-wards the ox cart. But before she reached it, Agnes and Aaron came up to her, ostensibly to show that they at least would not ostracize the child and his mother but really, on Agnes' part, to satisfy curiosity.

"A beautiful boy," she said. But what she actually saw was the image of Harry, fleshed out and rosier perhaps, but with the same dark hair and inquisitive eyes.

Aaron stood stiffly by. "Yes, indeed. And so alert."

Emma was running around excitedly. "Let me see. I want to see the baby too."

So Erika bent down to show her the bundle in the shawl.

"He looks just like Harry did when he was little." Immediately she sensed it had been the wrong thing to say – though she had no idea why. She added lamely, "But perhaps all little babies look like that."

Then they all went their separate ways, Aaron and his family in the horse wagon, and Jacob and his newly enlarged one in the ox cart.

🐦

Suddenly the war was everywhere. Some of the younger people in Waldenstein had gone to Halifax to help after the explosion and came back with tales of horror. There were people with only one leg, one arm. Children with no parents, parents looking for their children. And there were some people, they swore, who seemed to have gone crazy. They were just wandering around, doing nothing, saying nothing. When you spoke to them, they just looked right through you and didn't reply. If you offered them food, they might eat it but in an absent-minded way as if they didn't notice they were doing so. The young of Waldenstein had never seen anything like it. They mostly stayed for a week or less and then fled, it was so eerie.

And now there was a rumour that the Germans were going to put on one big, final push. Billy Veinot, who was the one person from Waldenstein to have joined up at the beginning of the war, was long since dead – a heroic death, his mother claimed, but there were rumours that suggested otherwise – pneumonia after sitting in the trench mud for months on end, gangrene from a small wound he didn't have the sense to get treated or, most slanderous of all, shot for cowardice when he refused to go over the top. The idea of Billy as a hero just didn't fit with what they knew of him, so they created the Billy they wanted.

But by now Billy was no longer the only person from Waldenstein to have gone to war. With conscription, only those young men actively engaged in farming could be excused. That meant that most were exempt, since even those who logged in winter farmed in summer. Still, there were exceptions.

Young Cornelius Oickle went down to Mahone Bay in March to apprentice as an electrician. Two weeks later an officer turned up at his boarding place. "You Mr. Oickle?"

"Yes."

"Yes Sir. What is your present occupation?"

"I'm...I'm training to be an electrician...Sir."

"Not farming anymore?"

"No, Sir." (By now the "Sir" was beginning to feel almost natural.)

"I think you need to come with me to fill out some papers, Cornelius."

And so he was sucked into the war machine, vacuumed up and blown to France, whether he wanted to be or not.

Through his pain, his father made judgment. "If you'd stayed at home and helped me like I wanted, you wouldn't be in this mess." Gradually, even Waldenstein was coming to see the horror and futility of the war.

Even the weather seemed to be in mourning. It was April, but there was no sign of spring. Two weeks before Easter the remains of snowdrifts, now coloured a dirty brown, clogged the fields and ditches.

"Imagine living in that kind of mud and wet all the time and being scared as well that any minute you'd be shot," Emma said to Virtue as they lay in bed one night.

"They don't send girls," was Virtue's reply. So that was that.

ॐ

The next morning, after the children had gone to school, Agnes stood looking out across the patches of exposed dead grass, brown and matted, towards the lake. It was open, but small cakes of ice still floated on the surface and piled up on the rocks by the shore. Harry, too young for school, was off with Aaron on an expedition to buy groceries in New Germany. They would be gone most of the day. Rebecca, the oldest daughter of the Conrads from across the lake, was doing the laundry. This was new. Just a month ago Aaron had looked at Agnes and seen the sunken cheeks, the bent shoulders, the tendency to fall asleep as soon as she sat down. And she was still in her thirties, he realized with a shock. So Rebecca was hired to help out three mornings a week.

But Agnes herself saw this sudden concern for her well-being as further proof of what she not only suspected but now felt she knew. How could Aaron, living in one open room in the camp with all the other men (and Erika in the bed next to his) not know who the father of her child was? And if he did know, why would he not tell her? There could be only one explanation. And that explanation was corroborated by what she had seen of the child. Emma was right; he might have been Harry. And all babies did not look alike, as Emma had tactfully tried to suggest.

She left the kitchen to Rebecca and the washtub and wandered through the family sitting room, across the narrow front hall and into the parlour. This was where the family pictures were, hanging against the greying wallpaper or standing on the narrow, white mantel. She sat down on the thinly upholstered sofa and looked around. Their marriage certificate hung in pride of place over the reed organ – an elaborate affair, with little cherubs holding ribbons that floated over the written evidence that Aaron Miller and Agnes Kraus were married in Waldenstein by the Reverend Ernest Rasmussen on May 5, 1897. On another wall, each of their baptism certificates, similarly elaborate, similarly framed, hung side by side, evidence that they were both members of the true Church. There, on the mantel, was a picture of Aaron himself (though not looking much like himself) taken just after they were married. His dress and pose were formal. He stood ramrod stiff in a three piece suit, a watch chain (that must have been lent by the photographer, because to Agnes' certain knowledge he had never owned one) dangling elegantly across his chest, one hand on the back of a chair, face squarely looking towards the camera. You couldn't distrust a man who looked like that! And then there was a picture of her, similarly formal, except that she was sitting in a high-backed chair in a dress tight around the neck and wrists, with a lace collar and cuffs. She too was looking straight at the camera, but there was a heaviness to her eyelids, a solemnity that said, "All this is inexplicable; I want it to go away."

Now she looked back at the picture of Aaron. And then, as she continued to stare at it, something strange happened. That trustworthy, solemn figure, still standing behind the chair, winked. Only once. But he had winked, she would swear it. He had winked as perhaps he had winked at Erika – once. He was unfaithful. Perhaps he had loved her at some time in the past, but he didn't love her anymore, and who would love her with the lines beginning to run down from the corners of her mouth to her chin, her eyelids even more drooping now, her figure erased to a flat cardboard surface by the bearing and caring for children? She was as insubstantial as the cut-out dolls that the girls pinned paper dresses on, she thought. To be insubstantial…to vanish.

She got up and went back into the kitchen. Rebecca was making good progress; some of the clothes were already out on the line. She picked up a small sharp knife and a shriveled, last-season's apple (in case picking up a knife on its own might seem odd) and went upstairs to the bedroom. It was completely clean and tidy, and amidst the turmoil in her mind lurked a tiny corner of regret that she was going to mess it up. She put the apple down on the white wool-bed cover. It was in the old apple orchard that she had first met Aaron. That day she could see nothing in her life but the drudgery of being the only daughter in a family of boys, and then, all at once, there was Aaron standing under the tree. He came into her life and everything changed. The things she did had not changed much, but the purpose for which she did them had, and that made all the difference. Now he had left her. She hated him. Even her children seemed just part of the intolerable burden of her life: Rose, who had been snatched from her as a baby; John, barely alive at all; Flora, a perpetual care and worry; Virtue, self-righteous and bossy; Emma, outspoken and precocious; Hannah, so large for her age and so riotous that she didn't seem to fit into the family; Joan, who was – well, just Joan; and Harry, who was scarcely her child at all, Aaron having taken full proprietary rights over his one surviving son.

She looked at the knife and experimentally slid the blade across her wrist. Aaron insisted on keeping the knives sharp, so even this tentative scrape drew a small ribbon of blood. Fascinating. She tried again, harder this time. Now the ribbon became a rivulet, falling down on the white bedclothes. This was more like it. A third stroke, and the blood came out in pulsing leaps, dripping onto the bedside carpet. Well, she had done it. There was no going back, not in Waldenstein.

Just then she heard Rebecca calling, "Mrs. Miller, Mrs. Miller."

She felt a surge of annoyance; could she not even be allowed to die in peace?

The blood jumped and flowed in small rivers. "Mrs. Miller."

Rebecca was searching the house downstairs for her. The voice vibrated louder and then softer as she crossed the hallway into the parlour and back again. Agnes was getting dizzy; she wanted to lie down, but still the voice persisted. Now there were footsteps on the stairs. "Mrs. Miller." Even this presumptuous girl wouldn't come into her closed bedroom, surely. But then she saw that she hadn't shut the door. Rebecca was at the top of the stairs now; she was turning towards her bedroom at the front of the house, and soon Agnes heard faint screams of alarm. Then she heard nothing.

Rebecca couldn't quite decide what she was seeing. Was it a horrible accident or deliberate? But then, being a practical girl, she knew it didn't matter – not at the moment. What she had to do was to stop the blood. People in Waldenstein all knew something about first aid; they had to, what with the innumerable accidents that happened on a farm: cuts from scythes, cuts from farm machinery and from carving up the carcasses of animals, falls from haylofts, broken limbs of all sorts when working in the woods, and worst of all, injuries from having a tree fall on you – the latter usually beyond all skill. So Rebecca did what she knew how to do. She tore up the bed sheet and made a tourniquet to stop the blood. Then she bandaged the wound itself. Finally, she bathed Agnes' face gently to see if she could be roused.

"Go away." Faint, but unmistakable. "Leave me alone. I want to be alone."

"But you've hurt yourself; you need help. I'll stay with you until someone else comes, and then we can get the doctor."

"No, no!" Slightly louder and alarmed this time.

Gradually it was dawning on Agnes that if there was one thing worse than committing suicide in Waldenstein, it was failing to commit suicide. Everyone would know; worse, they would guess why. She stayed lying on top of the bed where she had fallen and hoped she would never have to move. After what seemed a long time (Rebecca did not try to make conversation), she heard the horse and wagon come into the yard. Then Harry's tiny footsteps were bouncing up the stairs. But Rebecca intercepted him, saying that Mummy was feeling a bit sick and maybe the two of them could go and find Papa. Harry turned obediently, and they went down the stairs together.

Agnes tried to sit up and look for the knife. But of course Rebecca had had sense enough to take it with her. She fell back on the bed, defeated.

When Aaron came in she could not look at him. He was simultaneously tender with remorse and defiant with guilt. "What have you been doing to yourself?" And he bent down and kissed her. "You know how much I love you."

But that was just what she didn't know. He hesitated. He saw that Rebecca had left the room, so he went on in a whisper, "What I know you suspect….What does it mean anyway?"

She could barely move her lips, but she had to get it out, "You read books with her they say; you spent time with her like you never spend it with me."

And then she knew that she was more jealous of those hours Aaron and Erika had spent reading novels and poetry than she was of whatever had happened behind the curtains of the bed. He had betrayed her doubly – a betrayal of mind and body.

Naturally she did not explain this to Aaron nor would he have understood it if she had.

"Am I not allowed to read with or talk to other people?" On the face of it, Agnes' remarks seemed crazy. "She was there, she was eager to learn, so I read a few books with her."

Agnes turned on the bed so that she no longer faced him. He could not understand the despair she felt; he would neither admit what he had done nor deny it. That was how it must be.

"Don't do anything silly like this again, Agnes. Suppose Harry had found you. Or one of the girls."

How could she explain to him that she was past caring about trivial things like who might find her? If she had succeeded in dying, she wouldn't even have known.

"Now you get into bed properly and rest. I expect Rebecca's gone for the doctor."

When the doctor came, Aaron told him that Agnes had had a nasty accident while cutting up a chicken for a stew. She was cutting through the backbone when the knife slipped – lucky the girl who did the washing was around. He didn't really expect to be believed – there was more than one wound on the wrist – but it prevented questions. The doctor bound the wrist expertly and said nothing. He had seen many things in his country practice – this by no means the worst.

Whatever the doctor may or may not have believed, the chicken story didn't go down very well in Waldenstein. Anyway, there was another version – Rebecca's. And she had actually been there. What more proof was needed of Erika's son's parentage?

Flight

1918

Erika was furious. And the person she was most furious with was Agnes. She had wronged her, of course, and she had been genuinely sorry. But now Agnes had paid her back a hundredfold. Wherever she went with Adam she felt people were talking, gossiping. She was not only an adulteress (whore, she had even overheard once), she was a murderess as well. Poor Agnes, driven to such a state!

Erika found herself in quite a state as well, but no one seemed to notice that. Well, she wasn't going to kill herself at least. She had Adam to think of, and unlike Agnes, she took her child and his needs seriously. He needed a mother even if it seemed Agnes had decided her children didn't. But life in Waldenstein was impossible. She knew that with her cooking and housekeeping skills she could get a live-in job anywhere in the County. This was the course Frederika favoured. "Jacob and I are happy to have you here as long as you want to stay, but I can see things are pretty hard for you. Why don't you go down to the Bay and look for work? There's plenty of people would love to have you, I'm sure."

Erika grunted, which meant that she had heard what her mother had said and was unimpressed. Anywhere she went in the County word would leak out; she would be followed by rumour and innuendo.

Evenings she sat by the oil lamp sewing or knitting the little things Adam needed and thinking of escape. Eventually she was struck by an idea that amazed even her. Why didn't she go away – not just to Mahone Bay, but really away – like to Halifax at least. Or maybe….

A few weeks later, as if he had read her thoughts, Aaron gave her some money. No acknowledgement of paternity, no reason at all, just a few bills in a brown envelope he slipped surreptitiously to her one Sunday after church. "Thought you might be needin' some money for the baby."

She was so astonished she took it. Ten dollars. A lot of money! Then after a while she became angry and thought, why should she humiliate herself by accepting his help? The baby was hers! Hers alone! And then, after a further while, she thought, why should she not accept it? She did need things for the baby; her own parents were providing food and shelter, surely that was enough. And still later, it occurred to her, with a rush of excitement that yes, now at last she could get away. She could take the money and start a new life.

The first step, and the most difficult, was to get to Mahone Bay. She couldn't walk, not with Adam and all the things she would need to take for him. And there wasn't exactly any public transport. She would have to pretend to be going only to Mahone Bay to get someone to take her down with a load of lumber or vegetables. Then, once she was there, she could do what she wished.

So she went back to Frederika and told her she agreed that going to the Bay for work would be the best idea. Now Frederika was not so sure. She would miss Adam horribly. "You'll need to make certain you have a good place for the baby as well as yourself."

"Of course, Mama. You know that would be what I'd think of first."

And even Jacob worried. He'd like to horsewhip that Aaron! Just because he had more money than the rest of them he thought he could get away with anything. But of course Aaron, being the only person in Waldenstein with a horse, was also the only one with a horsewhip. In any case, he owed his winter employment to Aaron, and with three boys coming along to start working in the woods as well, he would probably soon be even more indebted to him for his daily bread.

So in the end it was arranged that Erika should go.

Ebenezer Conrad was taking a load of lumber down to the Bay on Friday, and she and Adam could go with him. He'd be glad of the company.

Between the Monday when these things were decided and the following Friday, Frederika and Erika were frantically busy. Clothes must be sewn and packed, food parcels to tide her over prepared, a trunk brought down from the attic and dusted off. And there were presents. Once it was known Erika was leaving, everyone seemed to love her. A clip for her hair, endless pairs of booties for Adam, and finally, as she was leaving, Nathan came with a small wooden bird he had carved and painted, "so that Adam will remember me."

Then she was gone, jostling down the road where her father had fallen asleep two days before she had been born.

She had never seen a town in her life. Hibbert and Obadiah – and sometimes even Nathan – had been taken on trips with the ox cart hauling lumber down to the port, but she was a girl. Why would they take her? It had rained the night before, and the streets of Mahone Bay were muddy with puddles here and there. The houses were so big. And they had all kinds of unnecessary things on them – like verandas with turned railings and bay windows surrounded by wooden ginger-bread, porches with mock columns also made of wood, flower gardens, tidy stone walkways up to the front door. She stared in amazement. What was the use of stuff like that? What kind of grand people must live in houses like that?

Ebenezer had been selling eggs to certain regular customers as well as delivering lumber for some years, and he had a plan. He head-ed straight away for the house of Mrs. Meisner, a widow of about sixty who, he thought, might be interested in having a young girl who was smart, could clean and cook, and would only want room and board and pin money. Besides, he knew she loved babies. And indeed, it all worked out as he had thought it would.

"Oh, what a little darling," she exclaimed when Adam was un-wrapped from his blankets. "She looks like a good, wholesome girl," she remarked to Ebenezer, "even though...."

"Not really her fault, probably…well, not much her fault." Mrs. Meisner nodded. It had happened, and she would not ask too many questions. So Ebenezer sold her the eggs, and then unloaded the possessions of Erika and Adam into Mrs. Meisner's front hall. Her house was not one of the very grandest in the town, Erika observed, but it was smart enough – white clapboard with green trim, a large veranda where, it was pointed out, Adam could nap in the fresh air and be sheltered from the rain, an enormous front hall with a staircase running up on the left, two front rooms, one on either side of the hallway, and everywhere oak polished floors. She and Adam would have a large room at the back overlooking the garden, and next to her room, wonder of wonders, was a bathroom with running water, a toilet and a large enameled bathtub. Ebenezer shook hands with Mrs. Meisner, pecked Erika on the cheek and took his leave.

Suddenly Erika found her needs were important. Mrs. Meisner discovered a crib and an old pram in the attic that she cleaned and polished for Adam. Erika's duties in the house were not onerous. She shopped in the local store for food, cooked it, and cleaned and polished everything once a week. Learning how to turn the tarnished silver and brass into objects of shining beauty was a positive joy. Like the trimmed houses themselves, she saw that these objects were not necessary to life; they were an ornament to it. She had never before encountered the idea of wanting or possessing something simply because it was beautiful and because it made life itself that bit more beautiful. The very dishes they ate off – the patterned china brought in from England and hand-painted with flowers and pheasants – were designed to please, to make you feel that eating was a small ceremony, not a quick refueling so that you could get on with your chores. She began to read as well. In the evenings when Adam was asleep, Mrs. Meisner (who had been a schoolteacher) would sit in the best parlour and read and encouraged Erika to join her. There were hundreds of books in the house – not just stories like she had read with Aaron, but books about real things, like how the earth was formed, oceans and volcanoes and mountains, books about different kinds of birds and animals, history books that told you how and why your ancestors had ended up where they had, and even some books about mathematics. These Erika ignored until one evening Mrs. Meisner took one up and began to explain some geometry to her. Then, fascinated by the wonderful process of its logic, she became absorbed in theorems and problems.

"Are you happy here, Erika?" Mrs Meisner asked one evening as they were finishing their dinner. The sun was setting behind the house, and the whole Bay to the east was suffused with a pale pink reflected glow.

"Oh yes." And then she added, "I think…I think maybe I have never been so happy before." Moving any farther than this was, for the time being, forgotten.

The summer passed; September came. It was a fine crisp day, and she hummed to herself as she wheeled Adam down to the grocery store. She glanced in the window as she approached the door and stopped short. Aaron. The familiar horse and wagon were tied up outside, and he was standing idly, gazing out the window, with a small bundle of purchases in his hands. Had he been waiting for her?

She wanted to flee, to turn around with her pram and run back to Mrs. Meisner, but she had a shopping list to fill, and anyway it was clear that Aaron had seen her. If she left he would know she was running away. She pushed the pram into the shop.

"How nice to see you again, Erika."

She tried to smile; she felt her lips cracking, turning upwards in pretence. She could think of nothing to say.

"May I see Adam?"

"Of course. There he is." And there he was, indeed, sitting bolt upright in the pram, his chubby face – rosy-cheeked, blue-eyed, and framed by the anomalous dark hair – looking around at everything and now focusing on this strange man who was peering at him with keen attention. How could he know it was his father?

"He's a lovely baby – happy and healthy-looking too." Well might he say so, she thought, for all the part he had played in bringing this about. But still she said nothing. Then he added, "Are you happy here?" The same question Mrs. Meisner had asked her on the summer night a few short days ago.

This time Erika thought about her reply more carefully. Yes, she supposed she was happy or had been until five minutes ago. "Yes. Mrs. Meisner is very kind; I have everything I could hope for." Hope for…well, everything she could hope for now, her circumstances being what they were.

"That's good. I'm pleased. You always were a good worker."

So – a good worker. That was how he remembered and commended her. She turned away and began to consult her shopping list. He also turned partly away and seemed about to leave. Then, so softly she barely heard him (did she hear him?) he said "I'm sorry." He pressed another envelope into her hand and was gone, the horse and wagon rattling along the road.

Erika was shaking. She stuck the envelope into her pocket and tried to concentrate on the shopping list. She stood in front of the counter and managed to read it out to Mr. Spidel, the shopkeeper. He wrapped the goods up in a parcel she could tuck under the pram as he always did and put the amount owing on Mrs. Meisner's account. She was free to go. For an hour she walked with Adam, who always enjoyed being in motion, up and down the dusty streets, out of the town to the top of a hill where she could look out over the boats and harbour to the open sea. She could not stay here any longer; she had been found and had just endured the encounter she most wished to avoid.

"We've got to go on a big trip, you and me, Adam. Who knows where we'll end up?"

At least she had some time. Aaron never came down to the Bay more than once a month. And even in her paranoid state she didn't imagine that the whole of Waldenstein would immediately descend out of sheer curiosity to see her. But it was already the end of September, and if she wished to go anywhere, she had better do it before winter. Carefully, fearfully, she opened the envelope. No note. But this time two crisp ten dollar bills. And she still had five dollars from what he had given her before. She had twenty-five dollars! She had never seen so much money in her life.

Two weeks later, she had made her plans – insofar as this was possible without knowing what the options might really be – and was ready to set out. It was a Wednesday afternoon, and from two to five Mrs. Meisner was out at the Ladies' Aid meeting in the church. She had decided she needed to take the pram; she didn't think Mrs. Meisner would mind. It was not as if she had been using it for anything else before Adam took it over. Into this she managed to pile all Adam's things, including his favourite toys. He sat on top like a chubby little monarch. Her own belongings she fitted into a large laundry bag that she slung over her back. Lastly, she put her note propped up by the dog and cat salt and pepper shakers on the kitchen table.

> *Dear Mrs. Meisner,*
>
> *I'm truly sorry to leave in this way after all your kindness to me and Adam, but you must understand that I've got to go. Someone I left Waldenstein so as not to have to see again came down here and talked to me in the store a few days ago. I know if I stay he will come again, and I can't bear to see him. Thank you so much for all the things you've taught me and for being so nice to Adam. I'll look after him as best as I can.*
>
> *Erika*
>
> *P.S. I'm sorry I've taken the pram. I hope you don't mind.*

It seemed short and even a little brutal when she reread it, but what else could she say? She didn't want to be followed, and anyway she didn't know quite where she might be going.

She walked with Adam in the pram past the three churches (Anglican, Methodist, and Lutheran), past the last house and out onto the main road to Halifax. Just as she was beginning to climb the steep hill up from the harbour, a small black truck slowed and stopped.

"Would ya' like a lift?" It was a middle-aged man with short-cut red hair and freckled arms.

Erika was inherently cautious, particularly now with Adam, but a lift sounded awfully welcome. "Maybe. Where are you going?"

"The big city itself."

She hesitated for a moment. He didn't smile, but he seemed well-intentioned and trustworthy insofar as one could judge these things. Then, "Yes, if you have room, I'd be glad of a lift."

"Hop in then. I'll put the pram on the back." Then, as an after-thought, he added, "I'm Ned."

And so, with Adam in her arms, they set out for the ruined city.

It was a silent journey. Her benefactor didn't seem to have much of a flow of small talk, and Erika was eager to avoid interrogation: "Where are you going? Why? What about the baby?" Better taciturn silence.

After about thirty miles she got up the courage to ask, "Why are you going to Halifax? Do you work there?"

"Sort of. I sell stuff. You know. Rawleigh's. They need lots of stuff in Halifax right now. Don't always have the money to pay for it though."

"Oh." Yes, she did know Rawleigh's; Jack, a cousin of her father's, sold it too, but he did so from a horse cart. Wonderful stuff. Jack would turn up about twice a year, open the cart, and there was everything you had ever wanted – sweet-smelling soap, powder, shampoo, hair brushes, even cooking things – lemon pie mix, vanilla flavouring, all kinds of wonders. So all these amazing things must be what was in the back of the truck under Adam's pram.

After this brief conversation, silence again descended until they finally arrived at half past six in the evening. The September sun was low in the sky. Despite her fear and exhaustion, the city, at first glance, presented itself as a marvel to Erika – first a cove of sparkling water, pale pink in the evening light, small boats bobbing up and down. Then large houses, painted all shades of the rainbow and streets shaded by trees with leaves just beginning to turn. She had thought the city was destroyed, but here neat lawns with small flower beds lined the streets. It was like fifty Mahone Bays lined up in rows. "South End," Ned volunteered. "Not much damage here." Then, as they moved farther into the city, he asked, quietly, almost as if it were an intrusion into her private life, "Where d'you want to be let off? Where d'you plan to spend the night?"

"I'm not sure, but I've got some money; I can pay for a room for the night."

"Good girl. Smart idea to have money. Don't always succeed myself. I tell you what, if you don't mind taking my advice, I know a nice little place back there in the south end where the lady'll fix you up good for a dollar."

So they drove up to a large Georgian house, somewhat shabbier than the ones lining the street that she had seen earlier, but still imposing. Her newfound friend rang the bell for her, and soon a large matron in a white apron appeared. Yes, she had a nice big room at the back; no she didn't mind the baby. The room wasn't near anyone else so it wouldn't matter if he cried.

"But he doesn't cry," Erika broke in. And to prove the point, Adam gave a large smile.

So it was fixed. Ned slipped a small bottle of Rawleigh's perfume into her hand and unloaded the pram. Then he disappeared from her life as quickly as he had entered it. After a generous supper for both herself and Adam, they were shown to a large clean bedroom where they slept soundly until morning.

After breakfast, she began to explore the city, or what was left of it. She had thought that perhaps things would have been cleaned up, but as soon as she left the leafy green of the south end and ventured further north, she saw utter desolation everywhere. A huge hill with something that looked as if it might once have been a fort was still strewn with rubbish – broken trees, boards and shingles from houses, great quantities of glass – as if the explosion had happened yesterday. And there were people in rags – yes, rags – roaming about the rubble, some scavenging, others wandering apparently pointlessly.

"Awful, ain't it?" one middle-aged woman said to Erika as she stopped to cross a street.

"Why haven't they cleared it up? I thought this all happened nine months ago."

"Not enough men. Half o' them are away gettin' killed in Europe, and the other half 'ave been killed here at home. Then there's those that'll never work again." And she pointed meaningfully to her head. "Lots of folks 've gone queer with it all."

Erika pondered this as she continued to walk, and thought of Ben's wife and how she had gone "queer" after Ophelia's death. But in Waldenstein there was always someone who would see you had food, someone who would come to clean out your house if you couldn't. She had thought cities were wonderful and exciting, but this was neither. This was the face of hell.

She knew she couldn't stay here. What kind of child would Adam become, growing up in this moonlike landscape after the fields and trees of Waldenstein and the tidy white houses of Mahone Bay? She would have to put into operation her other more drastic plan.

So she made her way down to the harbour, her own desperation somehow minimized in the context of the desperation of those around her. The ships were clustered at the outer end of the peninsula since all the docks farther in had been destroyed. She stood and looked at them – large, square-masted vessels, even larger ones powered by steam, smaller boats with sails more like the boats in Mahone Bay, only bigger. How did you pick a ship? At one level, she knew what she was doing was crazy. At another, she felt it was perfectly logical. She wanted to get away. This would get her away, all right.

After a while she gained the courage to speak to a man who was rolling barrels of something up a gangplank of a large steamship. She had never seen such a ship before. "Excuse me, but can you tell me where this boat is going to?"

"Liverpool."

Liverpool. She had heard of a Liverpool farther down the coast from Mahone Bay. Could that be it?

"You mean Liverpool just down the coast?"

"No. I mean the real Liverpool in England. If there's one down the coast it must have been named after this one."

"Oh. I didn't know there was one in England. Is it a nice place?"

"It's fine for the likes of me. I ain't too fussy. At least it's not blowed to bits like this place."

Then, tentatively, she asked, "Do you ever take passengers on your ship?"

"Well yes, we used to take a few, but then we stopped because it was too dangerous in the war. But now that the war's nearly over, or so everyone says, the captain might start again."

"Would he consider taking me – and my baby?"

"You!" He stared, incredulous.

Erika pulled herself up. "I have money. I can pay my passage. At least I think I can. I have twenty dollars."

"Twenty dollars!"

"And I can cook. I can cook for a lot of people. I've had experience."

What could he say to this rush of enthusiasm behind which he sensed a kind of desperation? "Well, I'll talk to the captain. We're leavin' tomorrow at daybreak."

And so it came about that on the 20th of September, 1918, Erika and Adam Wentzell left by steamship for England.

🐦

The tremors from this momentous event did not reach Waldenstein. No one, certainly not her parents, knew that Erika was not in Mahone Bay. Jacob had gone to visit her on the one trip he had made down that way since she was living with Mrs. Meisner, and came back reporting that she was happy and living in a style to which the rest of them would never be accustomed. No one knew Aaron had seen her.

But in late October, just before he would be moving back to the camp in the woods for the winter, Aaron made another trip to the

Bay. He did his business of selling the timber, saw it unloaded from his wagon onto the wharf and then moved towards the grocery store. You could get things here you couldn't get in New Germany; perhaps he could find a treat to please Agnes. And, of course, he had another agenda as well. He finished his own shopping and then tried to invent excuses for hanging around outside. He played with the harness on the horse; he adjusted the wagon seat; he studied the ships lined up by the wharves. Finally, he gave up and went home.

However, two days later, he found that he had forgotten an essential supply for the camp that could not be bought nearer than Mahone Bay. Very stupid of him! He didn't think Agnes was fooled, but the compulsion to see his son was too much for him. So he went back, waited as long as he decently could at the store and then walked the streets, circling particularly the area where he knew Mrs. Meisner lived. He could ring the bell and ask Mrs. Meisner directly if he might see Erika – but what conclusion might she draw from that? The correct one, obviously. No, that wouldn't do. He went back to the store. A gaggle of old men were standing outside smoking pipes and talking; he moved towards them cautiously. "There was a girl come here a few months ago from up the country somewhere. I think she worked for a Mrs. Meisner. You don't happen to know if she's still around, do you?" They wanted to laugh – a middle-aged man asking so earnestly for the pretty young thing with the baby – but Aaron was an imposing figure, and they didn't quite dare.

"Oh, she's been gone quite a long time – six weeks or so, I guess. Mrs. Meisner thinks she went to Halifax, but I'm not sure even she knows for certain."

Aaron could barely conceal his shock. "But why would she leave? Wasn't she happy with Mrs. Meisner?"

A shrug, a sigh. "Who knows? Young people today, they like to move around."

So once more, Aaron went back to Waldenstein.

"Did you see her?" Agnes was not going to let him think she had been fooled about the reason for the second journey.

"No." At least he could tell her the truth, whether she believed it or not.

Now he had a dilemma. He had reason to believe that Erika was not where her parents thought she was. It seemed he had a duty to tell them this. But how could he do so without letting them know or guess that he had been trying to see her?

A few evenings later he walked the mile and a half to the Wentzells' house and knocked on the door. This was all about making sure that Jacob would be able and willing to start work in the woods in two weeks' time. Was his leg good enough this year? And what about Hibbert, Aaron continued. He was no longer going to school – insofar as he ever had – so was it time for him to begin work in earnest?

Jacob, who felt like hitting Aaron every time he saw him, controlled himself and managed to say that yes, this year he was fine to work. And what about Hibbert, Aaron pressed. He was a big boy now; did he want to come as well? So Hibbert was called and agreed that, yes, he would go with his father this year. When everything was settled, and Aaron had his hand on the door latch, he hesitated, and then said casually, "Ever hear from Erika?"

Then Jacob boiled over. "What right have you to ask or care. You think you own everything around here – even her." And to his own and Aaron's astonishment, he began to weep. Aaron left as fast as he could.

Jacob was mortified. He had given that wretched man the satisfaction of seeing just how much he had hurt him. At the same time, he thought maybe he should go down once more before winter to see how Erika was doing. So the following day he set off with his oxen.

He, at least, had no scruples about going directly to Mrs. Meisner's house. After all, he was her father, not her illicit lover. Mrs. Meisner was visibly distressed to see him. "Do come in, but I'm afraid Erika isn't here anymore."

"Not here! But where is she?" This was impossible, he thought, and leant against the doorframe for support. Why would Erika leave a place like this?

"The truth is, I don't really know. All I have is a note she put on the kitchen table when she left. I can show it to you."

Jacob read the enigmatic note. "It was Aaron then; he must've been followin' her."

"I don't know. No one ever came to the house to see her."

"No. Aaron's too smart for that. Probably waited at the store for her."

"It sounds…I think…she's probably gone to Halifax." Mrs. Meisner felt herself in the wrong. "I guess I should have got word to you right away, but I thought she'd let you know herself. I'm so sorry. And I'm sorry she's gone for my own sake. She was a great help to me and good company besides."

"I'm pleased to hear that, Ma'am. I know she's good company. We miss her a lot at home." As he said this he was aware of how much more she would be missed now that she was in the inaccessible city.

"I'm sure you do," and she smiled in sympathy.

She made Jacob some tea and brought in some little cakes and cookies. He ate them awkwardly, feeling he had strayed into a foreign land where there was hand-painted china, a silver teapot and cakes bought in a store. Then sheer worry brought him back to his own life and its troubles. What should he do? Even as he framed the question, he knew the answer. He must go to Halifax and look for her. But how could he let Frederika know? Pondering these things, he thanked Mrs. Meisner for everything and wandered out to the street where his oxen were waiting patiently. It would take two days to get there and two more to get back, not counting the days it might take to find her. The oxen would need food, and he had little money to buy hay. But there was no doubt in his mind; the journey had to be made.

He had one initial stroke of good luck. As he was driving the oxen along the harbour road, he saw a neighbour, Ephraim Zwicker, with his team stopped by one of the wharves. With a loud "whoa" he brought the oxen to a halt, jumped down and hailed Ephraim.

"Listen, Ephr'm, do me a favour, will you? I got to go to Halifax to look for Erika. She ain't here with Mrs. Meisner no more. Tell

Frederika where I've gone, will you, and why I won't be back tomor-row like I planned. And tell Aaron I may not be there in time to start the cuttin' after all." The thought of inconveniencing Aaron gave him a small, momentary satisfaction even in the midst of his distress.

Ephraim agreed to tell Frederika and privately decided he might tell Aaron more than the message he had been charged with. Just be-cause he had a horse, did he think he could treat any woman like his filly?

☙

Sonny Hermann was out driving, "taking a spin." His car, the first one in Mahone Bay, really belonged to his father, Jason Hermann, who owned most of the waterfront and a good many of the boats that tied up there. But he didn't mind Sonny taking the car out for a little lim-bering up now and again. He regarded it rather like the horse it had replaced; it needed exercise to perform at its peak.

Sonny, going nowhere in particular, got down as far as Martin's River on the Halifax road when he saw an unusual sight – a team of oxen pulling a cart with no load on it and a tall, sober-faced man driv-ing them. He had never seen the man before, and that was curious too. So he pulled up beside him. "Hey, where you going?"

If Jacob was surprised at being thus accosted, he didn't show it; by this time Jacob was beyond surprise. "Halifax," he replied laconically.

"Halifax!" Sonny was incredulous. "With those critters? All the way to Halifax? It's more than fifty miles!"

"Yup."

"But why?" People like Jacob didn't go to Halifax at all in Son-ny's experience, and if they did, they certainly didn't do it with a team of oxen.

"My daughter. She's missin'." What more could he say?

Sonny was good-natured at heart, and, apart from altruism, it sud-denly occurred to him that he might have an excuse for driving all the way to Halifax. His father couldn't possibly object when he told him he had been helping out an old man who had lost his daughter.

"Hey, I'll drive you."

The idea was so improbable that Jacob didn't take it in. "Drive my oxen? No, they don't like strangers handlin' them. Makes them nervous."

"No, no. I mean leave the oxen here and I'll drive you in my car."

"I never been in a car." Jacob still couldn't quite grasp the idea.

"Doesn't matter. It's good fun. Cheer you up. Make you forget your troubles."

"But what would I do with the oxen?"

Sonny seemed to have an answer for everything. "Leave them with a farmer I know just up the road." And in truth Sonny did know a farmer up the road, and most of them down the road as well. In this town he functioned as a kind of minor royalty who knew and was known by everyone. Indeed, he was now beginning to wonder whether the missing daughter was the girl with the baby that he had seen walking about the town with some frequency a few months ago. Damn pretty, if that's who she was.

So Sonny led the way to the Smeltzers' farm where the oxen were unyoked and promised food and water until Jacob returned. And then they set off for the city.

Sonny was like no one Jacob had ever seen. Light curly hair cut short, freshly-shaven face, alert blue eyes and a manner that seemed to say he was utterly certain that whatever he did would be the right thing. Mr. Smeltzer couldn't possibly have refused to take in Jacob's oxen, because if Sonny asked him to do it, it must of course be the most reasonable request in the world that only an utter churl would deny. If he hadn't been preoccupied with finding Erika, Jacob would have been scared out of his wits. He had never travelled so fast in his life. On the straight he reckoned they must be doing about thirty miles an hour at least. He couldn't think of anything to say, and indeed speech seemed incompatible with such speed, all thought needing to be directed to holding on to the seat. But Sonny talked for both of them.

"I guess I've been real lucky in life so far. My Dad's pretty rich – well not really rich, but rich for these parts – and I'm going away in the autumn to Boston to go to school. Harvard. Pictures look pretty good, at least. There'll be lots of hard work, but I guess I'll manage to have some fun as well." The idea of having fun struck Jacob as original, but he could see that, if anyone could, yes, Sonny would manage to have fun.

Then he began to talk about Halifax and the explosion. "Your daughter couldn't have been in Halifax at that time, could she?"

"No, she was still home with us then."

"That's good. Because if she was in Halifax then, the chances she's dead would be as good as those that she's alive."

"No. The woman where she boarded said she's only been gone about six weeks."

"Aha," Sonny thought, "so I am right about who she is."

"Do you have any idea where she might be staying in Halifax? Did she know anyone there?"

"No."

"That's not good. The city's some mess now. Lots of people are still living in tents on the Commons – and winter coming. I hope she's found somewhere good to live. Why would she go there anyway?"

"Don't know." Jacob was rigid with terror. Sonny's words opened for Jacob the awful prospect of Erika and Adam wandering the city alone, having nowhere to stay, nothing to eat. Why did she ever have to leave Waldenstein? Suddenly he felt completely exhausted, even sitting in the leather seats of the roadster.

There was silence for a time. Then he added, "Maybe she's not in Halifax at all."

Sonny was so startled he let his foot slip off the accelerator. "Really? Why are you going there to look for her then?"

"Because I got to go somewhere; I got to find her."

There was a long pause until Sonny added, partly to lighten the mood, "Maybe she's run away to England on a boat."

"Naw. She'd never do that."

But now Jacob felt a new panic within him. How did he know any longer what Erika might or might not do?

They arrived at the outskirts of the city and drove down, down, towards the back harbour on the undamaged southwest side of the city. Jacob had never seen so many houses and people in his life – large houses with big windows and verandas looking out over the pleasure boats in the water. He saw luxury beyond belief; at the same time he was repelled by the closeness of the houses, the tiny plots of land, the crowds of people cluttering up the sidewalks. Madness, he thought. What could Erika have been thinking of coming to a place like this?

Then it got worse. As they drove farther into the centre of the city, they began to see signs of devastation everywhere. First there were windows boarded up where the glass had broken and not yet been replaced, then there were roofs with shingles gone, and still farther in, there were houses with no roofs at all, and walls tilting at crazy angles. The surface of the road had huge holes as well, and Sonny had to steer carefully to avoid damaging the car. Eventually he stopped by a large junction where five roads met.

"Sorry, but I daren't go any farther. The roads get even worse, and I might break an axle. Then Daddy would be really furious. But listen, how long do you want? Two days? It's Monday now, say I come back on Thursday to pick you up. I'll meet you right here at two o'clock. You can remember this place, can't you? Anyway, if you forget, you can ask someone. It's called the 'willow tree'." And Jacob then noticed that there was, indeed, a scraggly willow tree growing out of a bit of poor soil in the middle of the junction. So Sonny left him there, calling back, "Remember, Thursday at two. Willow tree. Good luck." He waved his hand and was gone.

Now what should he do? Deciding to go to Halifax to look for Erika was one thing. But he had had no idea it would be so big. Where to start? And where to sleep and eat? He had one dollar that he had planned to give to Erika. But what would it buy him here?

First things first. He must get a map of the place in his mind and then systematically cover every street. The explosion had worked in his favour in one respect; half the city no longer existed. And since the whole was built on a peninsula, it was possible to work out a kind of grid system moving from one end to the other, always excluding the northern half that was flattened. So he began to walk. He looked for pretty young girls with vivid blue eyes; he looked for prams with dark-haired babies in them. Sometimes, if he met someone who looked sympathetic, he would stop them and ask for Erika. But no one had seen or heard of her.

The first night, just when he thought he might have to sleep on a park bench, he saw a small sign advertising a night's lodging for thirty-five cents. He knocked and was admitted by a large, middle-aged woman. Yes, she had a bed for the night. Then Jacob became bold and asked if he could have three nights' lodging for a dollar. She thought for a moment. Jacob looked honest at least, if dusty from his travels. "Oh all right, then."

This gave him lodging but nothing left over for food. Luckily, breakfast seemed to be included in his landlady's deal, and he also found that there were churches serving hot meals at lunch time to people still homeless from the explosion. So he survived. For two days he walked through scenes of utter desolation. Every street in the city he walked, looking studiously for any sign betraying Erika. The cry of a child brought him to a halt until he decided, with a kind of perfect pitch, that it was not his grandson. Where the streets ran down to the front harbour, he paid particular attention to the boats and engaged some of the men in conversation. "Would it be possible, now, for someone, say, to get a passage on one of these cargo vessels?"

"Might be, if you had some money. Or if you had a skill…like carpentry or…"

"Cooking?"

"Yes, maybe cooking." He paused. "Come to think of it, we had a young girl come here a month or two ago who said she was a real good cook, and they took her on the Northern Star."

"What did she look like?"

"Oh, reasonably pretty. Only remarkable thing, really, was that she had a baby with her."

"What kind of baby?"

"What kind of baby? Well, just a baby. Good looking, like its mother. A boy, I think from the way she dressed it. Looked as if it was big enough to crawl."

Jacob heard no more. Huge tears welled up in his eyes, and he began to cry in great sobs.

"Hey, old man, what's the matter?" And he put his hand on Jacob's shoulder.

"My daughter. It must have been my daughter."

⚘

On Thursday at two o'clock Jacob was standing by the willow tree when Sonny rattled up. He got in silently without even expressing gratitude for Sonny's prompt arrival.

"Well, did you find her?"

"No."

"Too bad. I'm really sorry, old chap."

"But I think I know where she's gone." Jacob knew he could not look at a sympathetic face without weeping, so he stared straight ahead.

"Oh? Where?"

"I think mebbe she's gone to England."

Aftermath

1919

Within twenty-four hours of Jacob's return from Halifax, everyone in Waldenstein knew that Erika had fled not just the place where she grew up, but the country. The immensity of it was hard for people, who rarely ever went more than twelve miles from where they had been born, to grasp. Little groups knotted together at the mill or after church, talking quietly to one another, falling silent and slowly dispersing if Aaron came into view.

As for Aaron, he had never felt so isolated in his life. Before, he might not have belonged, but his separation had, in some ways, seemed a badge of superiority. Now he moved through a dark fog that enveloped him wherever he went. Even the air he breathed was glutinous. He had betrayed both wife and mistress. His wife had attempted to kill herself. Erika, younger and hardier, had run away with his son. One simple lapse – the fallout seemed quite disproportionate. Naturally, no one believed it had been one lapse only, but that, he would swear at the church altar, it had been. Once! He had been foolish, indiscreet, led by passion, what you would, but he was not a philanderer. Would it have been better if he had owned up immediately and offered to support Erika and the child? Better or worse? And for whom? For him? For Agnes? For Erika? He didn't know. Events had unfolded with a kind of horrible inevitability, the way they did in novels. And it had been reading novels with Erika that got him into this mess in the first place, he reflected.

All winter he thought incessantly about these things, while he ran the logging camp and went back to see Agnes every weekend. He owed her this, at least.

"Why does Papa come back every weekend now?" Emma asked, innocently, one evening.

Agnes bit her lip and disdained to reply. But Flora piped up, "To keep Mama company because she had a bad accident with the knife."

"Hush, Flora, you don't know anything." Agnes rebuked her sharply. Flora rocked her body back and forth in the chair and began to cry softly.

⚘

One Friday evening in February, as Aaron set out for home, it began to snow. At first the flakes danced down gently, and he rather enjoyed their mellow descent in the gathering dusk. Then, as he ventured out onto the lake, it began to storm in earnest – wild, swirling blasts of snow sweeping across his face, curling down inside his turned-up collar. The world disappeared in a white blaze, flames of ice dancing, burning, cutting the tender flesh. All this he had experienced before and survived, but this time, travelling home in the evening as he had never done in previous winters, he found a more frightening difficulty – crossing the lake he lost his way. Terrible stories of other like travellers filled his mind – men who went out to feed their cattle in a blizzard, could not find their way from the barn to their own back door and died fifty feet from their kitchen fire. And now that he was out on the lake, which was more than a mile across, there were absolutely no landmarks to guide him. He had left his compass back at the camp, never thinking it would be needed. If he should turn accidentally and walk down the lake instead of diagonally across, he would inevitably fall into the narrows, the passage that joined lake to river and never froze – or never froze reliably. Turning back, however, was not an option. It would be almost as dangerous, and besides, Agnes was expecting him. Indeed, at some deep level, he felt the danger and suffering were just, a fit punishment for his infidelity. "The gods are just…" No, he didn't think it was the Bible, though the Bible did say many similar things; it must have been something in one of the older children's school books. Maybe the storm was deliberate, sent by God particularly to test or destroy him, Aaron Miller, once first citizen of Waldenstein. This idea sent a new fear surging through him, colder than the storm. If it was all intended, then there was no hope, no point in struggling.

At the same time, the woodsman in him was automatically calculating how to go straight, how to keep the wind always on the same side of him. "But what if the wind changes direction?" a tiny voice said. On and on he walked, spurred by naked terror. To rest in the snow would be fatal, he knew. Then finally, when he was convinced that he must be walking in the wrong direction because otherwise he should have reached the shore by now, his foot hit a stone and the trees of the shore rose up before him like grey guardians against the black sky. Another mile or more he walked through the woods, which at least sheltered him from the worst of the wind, and then finally he was out into the meadow just above the much smaller lake beside which his house was built. There was a single light in one window. It must be very late, the children all in bed.

And so it was. Agnes was sitting alone with a single lamp, mending a child's sweater. He stood before her, his snow-covered figure mutely showing forth his sacrifice as clearly as if he were holding it in his hand. Seeing him standing there, silent, unable to speak, she saw what he would never say, that he was truly sorry, and she was finally able to accept it, to put behind her the terrible thing that had happened. She got up and kissed his icy face. "I thought you'd never come."

"It was bad weather on the lake; I was afraid I might lose my way."

"You lose your way? Not very likely." She would not give him the satisfaction of knowing how worried she had been.

No one missed Erika more acutely than Nathan. Eleven years older than himself, she had helped to bring him up – changed his nappies, played with him and, when he was older, helped him with his schoolwork. Even more than Erika, however, he missed Adam. What Erika had been to him, he was to little Adam. At night he dreamed that Adam was sitting on the floor, smiling and stretching out a tiny hand with a small ball grasped in it. Night after night the same image came back; just as he was about to touch Adam's hand and take the ball, he would wake up and desolation would flood over him.

One day, at recess, Emma came up to him as he was morosely eating an apple. "What's the matter?"

"Nuthin'. "

"Oh." Then, tentatively, she went on, "I guess you miss Erika."

"Yes. I do. It was bad enough when she went to Mahone Bay, but now she's gone for good. Maybe she's dead."

"I expect she's fine." Emma thought it was her duty to put a good face on events.

Then Nathan burst out, "If she's not, it's your Papa's fault!"

"Papa's!" Emma was stunned. Aaron and even Agnes had taken care not to let the children hear any hint of the gossip that swirled around them.

Now that he had started, Nathan felt the need to go on. "Yes, because Adam is your Papa's baby. That's why she had to go away. He made her have a baby." Now Nathan could feel the tears coming.

"How could he do that?"

"I'm not sure. It happened back in the woods, in the lumber camp. Everyone says so."

"No. No! He's a good man, Papa. He would never do anything bad to anyone." Now Emma was crying too. "You're horrible, and you're a liar. I know Papa didn't drive Erika away. He thought she was really good cooking at the mill. I know he did. He said so a lot."

And then, in a dramatic afterthought, she added, "Don't ever speak to me again."

"Maybe I won't. I'm leavin' school this summer."

"What?"

"I said I got to leave school."

"But why?"

"Because my father says so. Me and Obadiah both. We got to go to work in the woods this winter."

"For my father?"

"Yeah. Who else?" And he walked away.

Emma stood dumbfounded. What was it Nathan had said about her father? That he had "made Erika have a baby." How did you do that? She imagined her father standing over Erika with his shooting rifle: "Have a baby, Erika, or I'll kill you." How did you have a baby? Her mother had had so many and had not complained, as far as she knew. But then, her mother was married. The framed certificate in the parlour with the cherubs on it attested to the fact. Having a baby when you were not married was a sin, a sin against God. She knew that. But Erika didn't seem particularly sinful, and the baby had been sweet.

All afternoon, through the dreary mathematics lesson, she agonized. Sometimes she looked furtively across the aisle at Nathan, as if he might somehow transmit more knowledge to inform this mystery. Nathan was completely absorbed and refused to return her stare. But he was, she saw, not concentrating on the math lesson anymore than she was. Instead, he was drawing. What was it? She, Emma, filled her art book with carefully copied pictures of chickens and flowers, but Nathan drew things that weren't there in front of him – things he just saw in his head, he had said once. And now – what was it? She craned her head. It was a baby, a baby sitting on the floor with a ball in its hand. It looked rather sweet; it looked like Adam.

She said nothing to Virtue on the way home from school, but as soon as she reached the house she confronted Agnes. "Mama, Nathan says that Papa made Erika have a baby, and that's why she had to go away. He said everyone knows it."

Agnes had been dreading this moment. "What everyone says, and what they know can be different." This, as a general statement, was not a lie.

Emma was not satisfied. "But did he make her have a baby or not?"

"Men don't make women have babies, Emma. At least, not decent men. And your father, you can be sure, is a decent man."

"So Papa didn't make Erika have a baby."

"No, of course not." (With the "make" italicized, she was fairly confident this could just about pass for truth as well.) "People can be jealous of Papa, and then sometimes they say mean things. I expect Nathan heard it from someone else and just repeated it."

But Emma knew, from the way he had said it, that Nathan at least believed it was true.

ॐ

Nathan walked disconsolately home. Why had he said that to Emma? Of course, she wouldn't believe him. And even if she had, what good could it have done to tell her? And why did he have to leave school? Emma didn't.

That evening he pleaded with Jacob. "But Papa, I don't want to go to work yet. Just another year, please. Obadiah is two years older than I am. Let me stay here a bit longer."

"No, it's better if you go together. You can use a two-handed saw and look out for one another."

"I won't work for Aaron. He made Erika go away."

Jacob flushed. "And who else will you work for back here? Just who else? There's things people like us just have to put up with around here. We ain't got much choice."

But isn't it good to have lots of education? Emma is goin' to school until she's done grade ten, she says."

"It's all right for some – Aaron's got the money. We don't. And as for education – well, there's two ways of lookin' at it. There's education that'll get you a good job and lots of money and a nice suit of clothes. But then there's education that'll lead you to think you know ev'rything. Smarter'n God some o' these educated fellers think they are. Smarter'n God!" And with that pronouncement, he sat down on the kitchen bench and took a long draw on his pipe.

So that was it; Nathan had no choice, it seemed. He thought back to all the times he'd been happy – the summer picnics at the lake, even the one when his head was so sore from his accident and he felt dizzy all the time; the hours when he was drawing, oblivious of time or anything else; the times outside church when he watched Aaron's white-clad daughters jumping gracefully down from the wagon, Emma the most graceful among them. She would still be going to school. He would know nothing, and she would get to know everything.

🐦

There was another, less likely, person who missed Erika. Her loss had penetrated the cotton batten cocoon in which Muriel and Zachariah had kept Rose encased. They were two years apart in age, but given the scarcity of young women in Waldenstein, this had not seemed a large gap. It was Erika's sheer vibrancy that had struck Rose. Erika was always busy doing something, even before she had a baby to look after. "Come, let's go find some wild mushrooms," she would say.

But when Rose told Muriel what they were going to do, she would refuse to let her go. "Mushrooms! Half of them are poisonous, and you won't know which are which. Anyway, it's full of flies back there in them woods. You'll get bitten to death."

Or Erika would come to the door in the winter with her sled and ask Rose to go sledding with her. But again, Muriel would usually intervene. "It's bitter out, and you still have a cough from that cold you got before Christmas."

But after Adam was born, and Rose had actually helped in the birth, Erika would bring him up to Muriel and Zachariah's place, and she and Rose would play with him together. Even the ever-vigilant Muriel couldn't object to that. Sometimes Rose was even allowed to go down to Erika's house to help look after Adam.

Now both friend and baby were gone, and Rose was walking alone in the old orchard, much as her mother had walked twenty-three years before. Unlike her mother, however, there was no young man to come and rescue her. This was a pity, because she was rather pretty – not ostentatiously beautiful, too thin and pale for the taste of some – but with fine features, a perfectly formed nose, tiny ears and long, chestnut hair. She was wearing a simple long white dress with a wide black belt at the waist, which accentuated her slenderness. She seemed to be waiting for something, but what on earth was likely to happen here? If her mother had been overworked in her childhood, with a household of noisy brothers, she was bored in the same house with only her grandparents for company. But Erika was gone, "a terrible lesson to us all" her grandmother said, and there was no one to replace her.

So she walked in the orchard and thought about what she might do in life. This wasn't a subject she could discuss with other people in Waldenstein. She couldn't think of anyone else who had decided to do anything. Unless you counted Erika. But even Erika had not "decided" to go to England – if that's what she had done. Things had happened to her, and little by little she got pushed – first to Mahone Bay, then to Halifax, then to who knew where. Maybe that was how most people lived in Waldenstein, she thought. Life nudged you, and you quietly acquiesced. Or maybe it wasn't a nudge but a huge shove, as it had been with Erika. A woman was supposed to find a young man and settle down and have children, who would in turn grow up to do the same thing. In between having children the wife helped her husband in the field and garden; together they survived. Was that what life was about? Surviving?

Thus, she talked to herself, walking among the blossoming trees. There was never anyone else to talk to, so she had developed the art of self-dialogue to a high degree. Where were her sisters? Living their own sociable lives two miles away along a path through the woods that she was rarely allowed to walk alone. Too dangerous. She didn't feel part of their family at all; she didn't feel part of any family. Muriel and Zachariah "rubbed along together," as the saying went. Like sandpaper, Rose thought. This meant they occupied the same dwelling, ate meals together at the same table and rarely spoke except to arrange practicalities or grumble about the weather. Or to reveal subtle hostilities.

Zachariah: "Boiled cabbage and salt meat for dinner again, I see."

Muriel: "You didn't bring in enough wood to make a fire that would last long enough to roast anything in the oven."

Of course, they never fought, did they? – appealing to Rose to testify publicly to their forty years of wedded bliss.

So what could she do for herself? Becoming a schoolteacher was out, because she had so little schooling. Every winter she missed large chunks of school because her grandparents thought the two-mile walk every day too much for her. And it was true that she usually had a cold and cough. Even now, in the May sunshine, she stopped to cough every few minutes. Perhaps she could become a nurse, or at least look after people in some practical way. You didn't need a lot of book learning to do that, she believed.

Then a new and practical idea struck her. Maybe she could practise to see if she'd be any good at nursing. Sophia just down the road – she needed looking after if ever anyone did. Ben tried to do everything, but he couldn't, really. The house was a mess; Sophia and everyone around her was dirty and unkempt, and now there were days when she didn't even get out of bed at all – just lay there, staring at the ceiling.

She walked back to her grandparents' house with a new sense of purpose. At supper that evening she would talk to them, and this time she wouldn't be easily put off.

Once the main meal was cleared away and the fruit preserves and tea had arrived, she said, "I've thought of a plan."

"A plan?" Muriel was incredulous.

"A plan for me, I mean. You don't want me hanging around here forever, now that I'm grown up."

Actually, that was exactly what Muriel and Zachariah did want. Conversation between just the two of them grated on the ear. The voice of the other was an irritant, the body of the other an inconvenience; Rose provided a neutral buffer.

"Where are you plannin' to go? Erika went away, and look what happened to her!" Zachariah sounded very doubtful.

"I don't plan to go away, actually. Not to stay. Or not at first. I just thought if I could go and look after Sophia by day that would make life easier for everyone." She said this with a direct simplicity that she hoped would reassure them.

"Well…Sophia could certainly do with some help, though whether you're the one to give it or not – I'm not sure. You know you're not strong."

"There won't be that much to do once I get the place sorted out. Ben isn't much trouble, and young Benjamin is almost grown up. I'll just try to cheer her up a bit and maybe get her to do some things herself. No one goes to see her anymore."

So the next morning Rose walked the quarter mile down the road to confront the extremity of human grief. Sophia, lying in a rather dirty bed, simply rolled over and refused to speak to her. Undeterred, Rose spent the day sorting out the kitchen. First she washed every pot and pan in sight. Then she wiped down the shelves before she put them back. She threw out the oilcloth covering on the kitchen table, scrubbed down the wood, and told Ben when he came in to lunch that if he wanted a tablecloth he'd have to buy a new one. On the scale of tragedy in Ben's life, this was less than cataclysmic. By afternoon she was heroically tackling the floor, first sweeping, then washing it with a brush and five successive buckets of water. The Benjamins, father and son, were given to understand that boots were no longer acceptable on this pristine floor.

The next day, apart from feeding the menfolk and Sophia, she tackled the sitting room in the same manner as the kitchen and with the same satisfactory results. The parlour posed a particular problem, as it was piled up with all the detritus that was wanted nowhere else. But Rose was nothing if not decisive. Some things that seemed worth keeping she put in a wooden chest that stood under a window, and the rest, with terrible finality, she burned in the stove.

After a week she was ready for the main challenge. She marched brightly into Sophia's bedroom and said, "Wouldn't you like to see what I've done to the downstairs?"

"No. Makes no difference to me." Sophia barely moved her head.

"But it's all bright and shining, just like you used to keep it."

"Huh. Much good all that work did me. Got nothin' left to show for it. No daughter, no son."

At least this was a response with a bit of feeling in it, but the dismissal of young Benjamin seemed particularly hard to Rose. "What about Benjamin?"

"Oh, yes, I guess there's Benjamin," as if this were a concession that scarcely mattered.

And she turned over once again to leave Rose looking at her lumpy back, wrapped up in the wool-bed.

This was discouraging, but Rose went downstairs and prepared lunch as usual. After a while, there was the scraping sound of slippers on the stairs, then soft padding across the sitting room. "Why you done all this?" the wild-haired apparition at the kitchen door demanded.

"Because it needed to be done, and you couldn't do it." Rose was polite, but firm.

Sophia sat down in her rocking chair the better to contemplate the transformation. Dimly, she remembered a time when her house had looked like this, when Ophelia sang in the kitchen and danced in the sitting room, when Dilphin stole cookies and cakes from the pantry between mealtimes. She began to cry. It was as if the normalcy of the house brought back the sting of the other changes more sharply. Rose might have knelt down beside her and embraced her, but she didn't. Instead she seized her chance and went up to the bedroom, stripped the bed, made it again with clean sheets, dusted, scrubbed and tidied. Now only one project remained: the person of Sophia herself.

Another week went by before she dared approach the subject. But in that week Sophia got in the habit of coming downstairs for part of the day to sit in the rocking chair and watch Rose cook dinner. Gradually she even began to talk. "What are they sayin' about me round here?" she asked one day. Rose took this concern about what other people thought as a sign of returning sanity.

"Not much. They're just sorry for everything that's gone wrong for you, that's all."

"They don't say I'm lazy?" This would be the ultimate insult.

"Well, no. Not that exactly. They say it's a shame you can't look after things anymore, but they don't really blame you."

"Huh. I bet they do, inside."

"Well, they don't say it." Rose refused to feed self-pity.

"Huh." Said in a tone of skeptical resignation.

Rose took a deep breath. "Don't you think it would be nice if you matched the house, now that it's tidy and shining?" She expected an explosion, or an immediate retreat to bed. Instead Sophia just rocked. Twenty minutes went by. Then she got up and said, "All right."

And so it was that Rose washed Sophia's hair, drew a bath for the rest of her person, put out fresh clothes, and finally brushed her shining hair – still dark brown, not a grey hair in sight – and did it up expertly in two braids around her face as she had worn it before. She brought a mirror; Sophia looked at herself in amazement. When the two Bens came in for supper, she actually smiled.

Rose had cured Sophia – a miracle. She must be an angel. For a month after she got Sophia out of bed, cleaned and dressed, she continued to go down to the house just as she had before. Only now she was not working alone, nor was she confined to cooking and cleaning. One day they actually made a trip to New Germany where Sophia took an active part in selecting material for a new dress. When they went home, the two of them devised a pattern, cut it out and began sewing. Sophia even started to show some interest in the lives of her neglected child and husband. No one spoke of the past.

Then one day Rose could not come. Muriel went down to the house to tell Sophia that she had a severe cold and needed some rest. It was a week before she returned. To her delight, things had not deteriorated. The house was clean and tidy, Sophia was washed and dressed and busy cooking chicken stew with dumplings for dinner. That day, as she left, Rose said, "Maybe you only need me three days a week from now on." There was a certain sadness in this, but she could see that her very success had made her redundant. Anyway, it was November now, becoming winter, and she was very tired.

It was a particularly awful winter in Waldenstein. Snow made everything invisible. The houses were banked to the rafters on the windward side; you had to shovel your way out of your back door. The roads themselves disappeared in huge white drifts that swirled and moved constantly. No feature of the landscape remained the same. There was a terrifying isolation in this whiteness – nothing beyond the wood fire, the small circle of chairs, the root vegetables in the cellar. For days on end, neither Emma nor Virtue could go to school. Nothing was heard of Aaron at his logging camp across the lake; nothing was heard either of Jacob, Nathan, or Obadiah and the others camped out with him. Would any of them even get back for Christmas?

Then came a lull. Not a thaw, but a week of sharp cold when the snow ceased to fall and lay instead sparkling and crusted over. Two days before Christmas all the men came back, walking web-footed on snowshoes that slid over the crust like a charm. Nathan in particular was glad to be home. The first few nights in the woods he had cried softly into his pillow, hoping Obadiah would not hear. He wanted home, he wanted his mother, large and warm. Then he got used to it, as everyone said he would. At least he had Obadiah, who didn't seem to mind leaving school or working in the woods at all. Day after day they stood, one on either end of the huge double saw, moving it back and forth against the tree trunks until, with a final crackling rush, the trees fell heavily in the white snow.

The men would stay home for a week. Then, with the New Year, they would return to work. Two days after Christmas the weather was still crisp and cold but clear, and Nathan decided to visit Emma. He couldn't have said exactly why, or what he hoped for. She had said she would never speak to him again, but she had – within minutes. He might hate Aaron who had robbed him of his sister and nephew, but despite this, something was drawing him towards Aaron's house. Perhaps he wanted to recapture something of the child's life he had been forced to leave; perhaps he wanted to see what it was Emma was now learning from which he had been excluded; perhaps he just wanted to see her.

He wrapped up warmly, tied on his snowshoes and put on the new red scarf his mother had knit him for Christmas. An hour later, cold but exultant, he reached the porch of the Millers' house. It was two o'clock, and he could see through the window that no one was in the kitchen. Only then did he hesitate. It occurred to him that he must be prepared to give some reason for this visit, and he couldn't think of an acceptable one. So he waited on the doorstep, and then, determined now that he had come this far to persevere, he gave a loud knock. It was Virtue who came to the door, dressed demurely in a dark green dress. She looked in some astonishment at Nathan, and then, out of habit, said, "Oh. Do come in. Mama and Papa are in the parlour."

Indeed, they were all in the parlour; the little cast iron stove was burning with a fierce heat. In one corner stood the tree, with real candles on it. And they had actually burned the candles; you could see the dark ends of wick. In his home there were candles on the tree, but they were never lit. When the tree was taken down they were packed away carefully with the ornaments to be re-used the following year. The Millers must really have lots of money, like people said.

Emma was sitting on a straight-backed chair with a book in her hand. She was wearing a dress of the same cut as Virtue's, but made out of a soft blue material. Somehow it looked completely different on her, Nathan thought. Flora was sitting on the floor cutting up wrapping paper; Joan, Hannah and Harry were playing with some new toys and, yes, there was a new baby, Agnes' capitulation to Aaron after the business with Erika – another girl, little Rachel.

Nathan stood awkwardly in the doorway, holding his cap, taking in the scene. "Come in, come in," said Aaron. "Come in and sit down." Somehow a chair was found for him in the crowded room. He knew they were wondering why he had come, waiting for him to explain himself. What could he say? Hardly that he had come to see Emma. Why, they would think, why would he do that?

What he actually said was even more preposterous. "I was passing by." No one ever "passed by" the Miller's house, which was as far from anywhere else one might be going as it could be. They let it go. He had come, and he must be welcomed.

He turned to Emma. "What are you reading?"

"Just a story. I got it for Christmas." She didn't say novel. She knew that would sound pretentious to Nathan.

"Is it good?" Nathan was genuinely curious. What would it be like to sit on a chair with a velvet cushion and read a storybook?

"Yes. It's very interesting."

Now she was the one who felt awkward. Had this silly boy who now worked for her father and, furthermore, thought he was a bad

138

man, really walked more than two miles in the freezing cold on snow-shoes to ask her what she was reading?

Nathan felt more and more uncomfortable. He should have felt at home. This house was laid out exactly like his own home. Their parlour was more or less the same – maybe a foot narrower, but otherwise identical in plan. There was a reed organ in each, some family photos, lace curtains from the mail order catalogue, a small sofa and chairs covered in something scratchy. But it was different. He couldn't have said exactly how, but it was. First of all, it was more crowded. Secondly, there were books. And thirdly – but thirdly escaped him, even though he knew it was there, lurking in the burned candle ends, the kind of music propped up on the organ, the dresses the girls were wearing.

He got down on the floor and began to help Harry build a house with a complicated, and doubtless new, construction set. But Harry rebuffed him. "Go 'way. I can do it self. You don't understand it. It's vewy complicated."

"Harry! That's not nice. Nathan is only trying to help." It was Emma who rose to his defence.

"Don't need help."

So Nathan sat back on his chair. Then Aaron suggested they all have a cup of tea and went to fetch it himself. They drank tea and ate some cakes that Virtue had made, and since Flora did not wish to be outdone, some cookies that she had baked.

After the tea he managed to extricate himself, saying that he must get home before dark, a reason that no one would ever contradict. They said "Come again," and Aaron added, "See you on Monday."

Then he was out in the cold of the winter dusk, strapping on his snowshoes. It had not been quite as he had imagined. He hadn't really managed to talk to Emma at all. He hadn't asked her about school and what they were learning. He hadn't asked her anything. She had joined in the chorus of "Come again." But so had Virtue. So even had Flora. So what did it mean? They had been nice to him. He was a neighbour; he belonged to a family they had wronged – yet there had been no sense of false humility. They were different. He let it go at that.

※

Erika stood in a drawing room in Leicestershire. It was a large room with a carved limestone fireplace ablaze with heat and light. Outside the light was fading; the hazy view over the orchard down to the river would soon vanish completely. She closed the heavy velvet curtains across the bay window. Inside there was a Christmas tree decorated with more candles than Nathan or Aaron had ever seen in their lives. They had all been lit. Erika poured tea for Reverend and Mrs. Manley from a gleaming solid silver teapot polished to perfection. Adam sat on the floor, playing with two little girls. One of them bent over and kissed him on the cheek.

A Shaking of Certainties

Rose

1920

Rose sat shivering in the rocking chair in front of the sitting room fire, her tiny figure wrapped in a dark wool shawl. She was the one member of the family who had not been present when Nathan came to visit the day after Christmas. She had come over for Christmas dinner, but then retreated to her grandparents. Every evening now she sat thus, rocking gently and coughing and saying it was nothing. It was just winter, didn't she always have a cold in winter? Muriel ran about applying home remedies: hot poultices on the chest, Vick's vapour rub, and, gradually as she became more desperate, salt herring tied to the soles of Rose's feet – superstition mingled with a certain canny practical wisdom. But none of it did Rose any good. Taking her to a doctor did not occur seriously to anyone. You didn't go to a doctor unless you had a broken bone or were dying. And Rose wasn't dying! Muriel didn't even contemplate the possibility. She was a young woman, it was winter, and she had always been delicate. She had a cold. To think of death, she unconsciously felt, was to assent to its possibility.

One day in late January when the weather had turned a bit milder and the snow was sinking into slush, Virtue went over to see Rose. Her boots were not designed for this kind of weather, and her feet were getting wet. Still she plodded on. Why? What did she really know of Rose, a sister who had never lived with her, who was six years older than herself? Yet there was something about Rose that tugged at you. And Virtue sensed that now something more than usual was wrong

142

with Rose, and she was the sister nearest in age to her if you discounted Flora – and Flora was always discounted.

Rose was sitting in her usual pose by the fire. Muriel, surprised to see Virtue, fussed around both of them offering tea, homemade molasses cookies, raisin cake.

Virtue was shocked by what she saw. Rose was not just thin, she seemed to have grown transparent. You could see through her – veins, arteries, bones. It was rather horrible as well as frightening. She couldn't even bring herself to ask Rose how she was. It seemed a pointless question. One could see how Rose was. "Mama couldn't come," was what she said instead. "She couldn't leave Flora." And indeed it was now Flora, more often than the infant Rachel, who kept Agnes at home. But if she knew how things were, maybe, just maybe, she could have come this time, Virtue thought. Rose simply nodded. "Well, I'm glad you came, anyway."

"I didn't know you were really sick, or I'd've come before."

"I'm not really sick," panted Rose. "Just have a cough – and tired."

"But look," said Virtue, newly alarmed, "isn't that blood on your handkerchief?"

"Maybe a little. Not much, not often." She rolled the handkerchief up into a ball and made a fist over it.

For a while they talked about Christmas and presents, and even Nathan's visit. "He just turned up. It was the oddest thing. We didn't know what to say. Nor did he!" She giggled. "He looked all around as if he were memorizing the parlour. And especially he looked at Emma. I think he's sweet on her. Maybe that's why he came."

"He didn't want to talk to Papa about work?"

"No, not a word. We gave him tea and cake and then he left."

"How odd."

And then Rose said, wistfully, "I don't think anyone will ever be sweet on me."

"Of course they will. When you get better and can go out again, there will be lots of young men." What else could she say?

"Most of them are dead. In the war, or in accidents." She didn't say accidents at the mill, but they both knew what she meant.

Virtue bristled with optimism. She believed that when you went to visit the sick it was your duty to cheer them up, and Rose's thoughts did seem to have taken a decidedly gloomy turn. "You'll be about soon, and it will be spring, and then you'll see."

Rose sat for a few minutes trying to suppress a cough. Then she whispered confidentially, "Virtue…do you have your periods yet?"

Virtue was rather insulted by the question. Of course she had periods; she was sixteen.

Rose continued, "I used to. But now they've stopped. I don't know why."

"Oh." Virtue knew of only one reason why periods stopped, and that was impossible in Rose's case.

"Have you told Grandma?"

"No." Rose sighed. "She'd only have some remedy worse than the salt herring on my feet. And it wouldn't work. Her remedies never do."

"Maybe you should go to the doctor." Here was a desperate suggestion, but Virtue was running out of ideas.

"Pa would never take me. Twelve miles each way, tires out the horses, costs the earth. And, anyway, I'm too tired to go all that way. It would be cold and horrid and when I got there I'd have to take all my clothes off probably." Virtue couldn't decide whether this last objection was due to the cold or modesty.

"Maybe you should have the doctor come here."

Rose was appalled. "That would cost even more."

"But if you need it, I'm sure Papa would pay. He doesn't know how sick you are." Virtue was coming to feel the strain of responsibility; she was the only one who was there, who could make a difference.

"Nobody cares, do they." It was a statement, not a question.

"I care. We all do. We just didn't know. We should have seen at Christmas, but I guess we were just all so busy, particularly with the new baby and all."

At once Rose was contrite. "I'm sorry. I shouldn't have said that."

Virtue squirmed. Now she felt guilty. They were all guilty.

"I've got to go now. But I'll come again soon. Promise. And…and I'll get Mama to come too."

☿

Virtue reached home feeling cold and frightened. "Did you see Rose?" Mama asked. And then, in a perfunctory way, "How is she?"

If it had been Emma, not Virtue, she would have said, "She's dying." Virtue said, "I don't think she's well at all. I think she's really very sick." And then, when Agnes did not respond: "I think you and Papa should go and see her. I'm sure she'd like that."

Agnes half turned from the stove where she was busy cooking supper: "Well, of course, we were planning to go, but the weather's been so awful…"

"I think you should go soon." From Virtue, this was practically an order.

Still Agnes was not really alarmed. "Maybe we could harness Josh up to the sleigh and go around by the road." She had become used to Rose being "delicate," being cosseted by Muriel, her mother, and rather despising her for it. Rose was always ill; there was no reason this should ever change. Rose was the child of whom she had been robbed, the first-born that, in reality, none of the others had ever quite replaced. She had coped with this fact largely by cutting Rose out of her life. If she were not to have her wholly, well then, she would not have her by halves.

She stirred the beef hash for those under her own roof, all of whom were well and hearty.

Virtue went up to her bedroom. She felt she had discharged her duty, and, as far as she was concerned, there was nothing more to do other than to make sure she went to visit Rose much more often, until…well, until. Emma, as usual, was lying on the bed reading.

Virtue felt the force of her name more than usual. "I've been out to see Rose."

"Oh, good," Emma responded offhandedly.

"Maybe it wouldn't hurt you to get off your backside once in a while and do something other than read."

"What's wrong with reading? I like it more than anything else."

"We can all see that. But it might be good if you did something for someone else occasionally." This time Virtue was sure she had right on her side.

Emma sat up. "Fine. So you've been to see Rose and you've come home all self-righteous about it. Why get mad at me?"

"Because she's really sick, and she thinks no one cares."

"Well, you didn't seem to care until a few hours ago. Anyway, she's always sick. It's part of the way she is." Emma had absorbed her mother's attitude to Rose without really thinking about it.

"But this time she's *really* sick. Truly. I don't think she'll get better." Virtue's face, which was contorted as if she might cry, suddenly brought Emma to her senses.

"You mean you think she's going to die?"

It was Emma who had uttered the taboo word, so Virtue could concur without being the bringer of bad luck. "Yes, I do."

Emma was sitting bolt upright now, the book dropped on the bedclothes beside her. "Oh Virtue. I'm so sorry; I had no idea."

"Neither did Mama or Papa. I've just talked to Mama, but she didn't seem to believe me. Not that I quite said that to her."

"That's really awful."

ॐ

Emma lay back on the pillow and thought about death. Death and the Maiden. Images of Death from Victorian readers, themselves imitations of medieval images. Skeletal death, with long bony fingers, reaching where no man dared reach before on the maiden. Death grinning a gumless grin: "Methinks Death like one laughing lies/Shewing his teeth, shutting his eyes."

Then the scene changed. The maiden was in a pure white satin-lined coffin, surrounded by lilies. She carried one lily in her stiff hand, itself as white as the flower. Now there was music – the singing of a German chorale in a minor key. Everyone was weeping, although in some way this did not diminish the splendour of the singing. Beautiful words: "I am the Resurrection and the Life." There was no actual graveyard in this vision; there was no earth in which the fair maiden would decay. She remained caught in an eternal stasis, forever beautiful, forever surrounded by mourners, forever lamented. Curiously enough, God did not feature in this scenario. God was something else – judgment and the possibility of hell fire.

Virtue, too, thought of death. She knew what the church taught, and that must be the right thing to think. When you died and the last breath left your body, God would take your soul with him up to Heaven, unless, of course, you had been wicked, in which case devils came for you and took you to Hell. But Rose had led a good life. She was helpful to Muriel, and look at what she had done for Sophia! She practically brought her back from the dead! So Rose would be all right. Except that dying was frightening all the same because you couldn't know. What could you not know? Well, you just couldn't know about anything for certain, not even when the Church had said it. But after a while she dragged her thoughts out of the land of uncertainty; it was not a comfortable place. Rose went to church and was a good person; that meant there was no need to worry.

When Rose thought of death (and she often did now) it was quite different from the meditations of her sisters. She looked at her body, and it frightened her. You could see the veins that held the blood, contained and restrained it. But now they were so close to the surface they seemed ready to pierce the skin. And when she coughed, there it was, more blood, now no longer confined to wherever it ought to be confined. Then she thought of the death of animals on the farm – the quick stroke on the head, the slice of the knife, the blood, the silence. The intestines of pigs laid out to be washed before they were stuffed with sausage meat were not pretty. That was death: the dissolving of form and flesh – or form abandoning flesh, leaving it to its own messy and rotting inclinations. She did not use the word "form," of course. She thought it all simply in pictures, and it was all the more terrifying for that.

Then she tried to think of death as she knew she was supposed to think of it – the end of the weary struggle of life, the repentant sinner's reward. "Oh come quickly, Glorious Lord, and take my soul to rest." But this rest would be in an unknown realm. And while her life had not been joyful, neither had it been a struggle. Only recently had it become weary. Besides, as long as one was alive something might change; something might happen. Other people got married and had children; was it so inconceivable that she might? Look at Erika. She thought often about Erika now. Surprisingly, she found herself almost envying her. At least something had happened in Erika's life. So she had made a mistake, but that mistake had ended in a lovely, cuddly baby that called her Mama. Rose remembered being allowed to cuddle Adam, his little fat fists reaching up to grasp her hair. It had been blissful. Erika could cuddle Adam whenever she wished.

And who knew what Erika might be doing now? Naturally, everyone in Waldenstein was convinced she was dead or on the streets, but knowing Erika, Rose doubted this. Erika would be making her way

148

and taking her baby with her on that way. She wished she could talk to Erika. She still believed that, despite what other people said, Erika was good.

She sighed and then, with the deep breath came the rattling cough. She shouldn't have said what she did to Virtue. It was self-pitying. Self-pity was a sin. She was full of sin. She had never loved her mother as she ought; she couldn't even love Muriel properly. As for Zachariah, he was a shadowy figure who sat on a bench and smoked his pipe, no longer pretending to keep up the farm. He rarely spoke.

People said how wonderful she had been to bring Sophia out of her long sulk, but she had done even that more for herself – to give her an occupation, get out from under Muriel's feet – than to help someone else. "There is no health in us." Well, that was true, she thought, in many senses. And for a moment she could almost stand back and laugh at herself. If she had been brought up with Aaron and her siblings she might have had the intelligence and wit of Emma. She envied Emma – always so certain, so full of crazy, wonderful ideas. But to think that would be a reproach to her mother and lead back again into the cavernous, echoing labyrinth of sin – sin lurking everywhere, but never able to be pinned down precisely so that one could do battle with it.

What would it be like to die? She had never seen a person die, only animals. Would it be different, somehow? Would angels really come and take your soul? "If I should die before I wake…." There was an angel in one of the church windows, but it looked to be a static, ineffectual angel, not one that could achieve the rescue of a soul.

She was very tired. She fell asleep in her chair.

🐎

When she woke up her mother and father were there. Agnes was speaking to her. "Rose dear, we should have come sooner. What can we do?"

Then Aaron burst in, all energy and activity: "You must see a doctor, of course. What has Muriel been thinking of?"

Muriel, who had just come into the room, was not willing to be wrong-footed so easily. "It's only the last few days she's seemed really sick. You yourselves saw her at Christmas. If she was so ill, why didn't you call the doctor then?"

Aaron took charge. "Come, let's not argue. Agnes will stay here, and I'll go off for the doctor. The horse and sleigh are right outside the door and ready to go."

So the three generations of women were left alone together. Each sat on a wooden chair, Rose on the rocking chair in the middle. They had no idea what to say to one another. Anything would sound like an accusation now. Gradually the afternoon wore on and the room grew dark. A tiny bit of firelight flickered through a crack in the iron stove. Muriel reflected that she had taken Rose off the hands of her two young and busy parents when they most needed it, had brought her up thinking of nothing but her good (that she would swear), cosseted her from drafts and germs – and now, at the end, it was she who would be to blame. Except that she still did not believe it was the end. How like Agnes and Aaron – to leave one well alone when one might have liked a little help and consideration, and then to turn up suddenly making a big fuss about nothing. It was all that Virtue. She had come over this morning just to make trouble. She was a troublemaker, that one, if ever Muriel had seen one. Cold and tight and pinched as they come – and she couldn't even get her grade eight, they said. Not that anyone needed a grade eight. Certainly Rose had never bothered, and look how well she had turned out. Except, of course, that she was ill now. But that had nothing to do with not getting her grade eight, and besides Rose had been ill before, and she always got better. At least she hadn't killed her by making her walk two miles each way to and from school. Yet she would be blamed, whatever happened; that was always the way of it.

Agnes finally got up to light a lamp. The matches were still in the same place they had been in her girlhood. The oil sprang into life with a small fizz, and she replaced the chimney. She sat down again and looked at Rose. Her head was thrown slightly back, and she was breathing rapidly. The child that had been stolen from her at one year old was now to be stolen permanently, she feared. Would this have happened had Rose lived at home? Surely not. She would have noticed earlier. Yet Muriel's reproach was true. She had seen Rose only a month ago and had not noticed. Well, at least she might have had a happier life with her sisters. She might have laughed sometimes. She realized she could not remember how Rose laughed. Maybe Rose didn't laugh. Was that possible? She should have insisted on not leaving Rose with Muriel. That was what Aaron had urged her to do, but she had said no, she couldn't defy her mother that way. So she had abandoned Rose and, because half measures were so painful, she had given her up wholly. She reproached Muriel, but even more she reproached herself.

Rose sat with her eyes closed between these two presences and tried not to think. At times she dozed off, then jerked back to consciousness. She had a vague sense that her mother and grandmother were sitting on either side of her hating one another and hating themselves. It did not bode well. Why, in addition to everything else, must she be a cause of dissention?

"Why don't you go to bed? The doctor can see you there just as well when he comes." Muriel roused herself from reverie at last.

"It's worse when I lie down; I can't breathe properly." And as soon as she talked, she began to cough again.

At last Dr. Beale arrived. He was new to New Germany, quite young and not at all like the sympathetic if old-fashioned medic who had coped with Flora's fits, set Jacob's leg and delivered Erika. At first he just stood and watched Rose as she sat struggling to breathe in the rocking chair. He could have produced his diagnosis based on this alone. But he did the professional thing, the thing everyone expected. He got out the magical stethoscope and listened to her chest. He knocked it with his knuckles; he had her bend forward so he could listen to it from behind. "How long have you had this cough?"

Muriel was quick off the mark. "Oh she's had this cough ever since late October, but she gets a cough every winter. Then in summer it gets a bit better. Of course we treat it with hot poultices and herrings and just everything."

"Herrings?"

"Oh yes. Don't you know 'bout herrings? Why you tie two salt herrings on your feet and it draws the fever right out of you," Muriel replied with as much authority as any doctor.

"I see. Well I'm afraid it's going to take more than herrings to cure you this time, Rose."

"What is it?" Rose wanted a name. All her life she had been kept from knowledge. Now that it could do neither good nor harm she still desired it.

"Well, of course I can't be sure without an X-ray, and you'd have to go to Halifax for that – a long hard trip and it wouldn't do you any good – but I'd say it's pretty advanced tuberculosis. You've probably had it in one form or another for years."

"So what can be done?" Aaron could not conceive of a situation where action was of no avail, and if Rose had had tuberculosis for years, surely it could not be so dire all at once.

Dr. Beale looked at Aaron and shook his head. Then he touched Rose's hands, folded in her lap, in a gesture of pity. "Nothing. There's nothing you can do. It's too late."

"But surely – I have a bit of money. We could hire a nurse, take her somewhere else, like Halifax, that you mentioned…"

"It would make no difference. Once the disease reaches a certain point – well, recovery is extremely unlikely. I'd say she has only about twenty-five percent lung function now, and that will decline fast. She probably wouldn't survive a trip to Halifax, particularly in winter."

"So…what will happen?" Aaron said, almost belligerently.

"You know." And Dr. Beale began to pack his bag.

Aaron seethed. Twenty-five percent something-or-other. This young whippersnapper then had come all the way out here just to impress him with his book-learning, and he could actually do nothing at all. A waste of time and money.

"Keep her warm and comfortable. Let her eat what she wants. Prop her up in bed on lots of pillows if she can't breathe."

Muriel was weeping softly. "Keep her warm and comfortable." As if she hadn't done that from the day she was born.

The door closed, and the doctor left.

"Let her come back with us, at least," Agnes pleaded. "Let her spend a bit of time now with her sisters."

"No. She belongs here with me. This is her home. They can come and visit her if they want to see her so much after all these years," Muriel said defensively.

Rose raised a hand as if seeking permission to speak.

"What would you like, Rose?" Agnes appealed finally to her daughter.

"I'd like to stay here. It's what I know."

ॐ

Now that she no longer cared, Rose did have visitors, lots of them. Young people didn't die this way in Waldenstein. They either died rapidly in epidemics of diphtheria or scarlet fever when they were very young, or they disappeared instantly in accidents like Dilphin and Ophelia. If you had survived the boat journey over and the first few winters in a new land, then you and your children were unlikely to succumb to slow, insidious diseases. Rose, dying gradually in their presence, was a novelty. So they came to pay homage, not just to her but to the strange thing she embodied – death living among them.

Naturally, Sophia came weeping with gratitude for what Rose had done for her. She really had nothing to say, except to thank her over and over and to speak the platitudes she had grown up on. "The good die young." "Death wants the beautiful for his own." "Life is a vale of tears." And so on. Some of these she actually believed to be Biblical. Certainly they must be true; Rose's condition proved it.

Virtue and Emma came together. Virtue still deemed it her duty to cheer Rose up. "You'll be fine in no time if you just have a good rest, like you're doing now."

"That's not what the doctor said." Rose didn't want false comfort; hope was too painful.

"Well, what does he know? Look, you did a miracle for Sophia, how come no one is going to do one for you? Me and Emma are praying as hard as we can."

Emma was more reticent, partly because she was less willing to spout the formulas than Virtue was. In part, she was just curious. She had never been really close to Rose, and now she was an interesting subject.

"What is it like?"

"Tiring and boring." Rose could no longer resent anything, not even being an object of research.

"Are you afraid?" Emma persisted as Virtue stepped on her toe.

"No. Why should I be?"

"Well, of dying."

Virtue, at this point, punched Emma very hard in the side and said loudly, "She's not dying. Not if she doesn't think about it."

But Emma merely replied, "How can thinking make a difference?"

Virtue stood her ground with determination. "It just does. Everyone knows that."

Even Flora was allowed to come. She looked at Rose, and then, with an intuitive sympathy, curled up beside her on top of the covers, her wig askew. "We've always been outside it, ain't we Rose? You and me. Now soon it'll be just me. I'm sorry, Rose"

The last day came. How did they know it was the last day? They just knew, as their animals knew when it was time to die. For finalities you sent not for the doctor but for the minister. A blizzard was raging outside, but Josh the horse was harnessed, and Aaron set off for Reverend Rasmussen. The great thing about a horse, Aaron thought, was that he knew the way even when you could barely see the road. The sleigh moved swiftly against the sharp crystals of snow that blew in Aaron's face. He remembered his crossing of the lake two winters ago when he had thought he would not survive. Now it was one of his children who would not make it.

Josh kept up a steady trot, probably hoping to arrive at some destination that was less hostile than the open road. When they got to the corner he turned right for New Germany, the cemetery to one side, overhanging spruce trees bowed low with the snow on the other. The cemetery! This business was a punishment; God was taking away his oldest daughter because he had defiled the oldest daughter of another man. The justice was there for all to see. But was it just that Rose, who was innocent, must suffer for his sin? These things were difficult. Would Reverend Rasmussen have an explanation, even if he dared to ask him?

At length he reached the tiny village, almost invisible under its white covering. He turned in at the large snowy hump beside the church, which was the parsonage. Reverend Rasmussen sighed, did himself up in his coat with the huge fur collar, and soon they were out in the icy blast again. The road twisted and turned, but in every direction the gusts of wind were against them. Daylight was fading, and with it the familiar landmarks, but Josh was going home now and navigated by some kind of inner radar.

When they reached Muriel and Zachariah's house at the very end of the road, everything was still. For a moment Aaron was disinclined to get down and go in. As long as nothing moved, nothing would change. Life would be caught in this moment, which was agony, but not as great an agony as what was to come if time moved on.

Nevertheless, he got down and went around the sleigh to help Reverend Rasmussen on the other side. As he clambered out he fell heavily against Aaron for a moment, then straightened quickly and brushed the ice from his beard.

In the bedroom the oil lamps had been lit and cast a dull glow over the pale birds on the wallpaper of the spare room where Rose had been moved for her final days. Her breathing was the one sound in the room. Everyone moved aside as the priest approached the bed and began the prayers for the dying: "Confirm, we beseech Thee, Almighty God, Thine unworthy servants in Thy grace; that in the hour of our death the adversary may not prevail against us, but that we may be found worthy of everlasting life; through Jesus Christ, Thy Son, our Lord. Amen."

Then at last they all – Muriel, Zachariah, Aaron, Agnes, Flora, Virtue and Emma – believed that she really was going to die and that this was really what death was – the laboured breathing, the lamp shadows flickering on the wall, their adversary, the devil, hiding in a corner, the clergyman holding him off with the promise of eternal life for the faithful. It was grave and ceremonial; it was suffocating and frightening.

Rose opened her lips to receive the host but could not swallow it. In the end, Reverend Rasmussen had to remove it lest she choke. Then he wet her tongue with the wine, and she died.

They all waited, watching Reverend Rasmussen for a sign as to what they should do next. He began to read a psalm – and what a psalm:

Lord, Thou hast been our dwelling-place: In all generations....
Thou carriest them away as with a flood, they are as a sleep:
In the morning they are like grass that groweth up.
In the morning it flourisheth, and groweth up:
In the evening it is cut down, and withereth.
For we are consumed by Thine anger:

And by Thy wrath are we troubled.
Thou hast set our iniquities before Thee:
Our secret sins in the light of Thy countenance.

"Our secret sins." Rose had no secret sins, Aaron thought. She was good. It was he who had the secret sins. He began to hate Reverend Rasmussen and glared at him through his tears. He could barely stop himself from crying out: "It is I; I have done it all!"

There were more prayers. Then, eventually, it was over and Reverend Rasmussen turned to go. Aaron prepared himself once more for the twenty-four mile round trip through the snowy night. He would use the time to confess to the priest, to ask him about sin and punishment and what, if anything, one could do to atone. And he would repent, repent, repent.

But as they opened the door and stepped out into the night, Reverend Rasmussen dropped down suddenly in the deep snow. At first Aaron thought it was a simple stumble – pray God no bones were broken. He tried to pull him up, but the clergyman sank back into the snow, absolutely motionless. Then, as he neither stirred nor uttered a sound, a fear as cold as the weather came over Aaron, and he cried out to the others in the house.

They carried him back into the kitchen and stood baffled as he lay on the rug by the stove, a look of sheer surprise on his face. They rubbed his hands and his feet; they loosened his clothing, lifted him up and tried to force some water down his throat. The vial of sacred wine had fallen out of his pocket and lay on the floor. "Perhaps some of this…?" But nothing, not even the holy wine could recover him. He too was dead.

By this time the commotion in the kitchen had led everyone to abandon Rose and gather around the recumbent form of Reverend Rasmussen. Only Agnes stayed with her daughter, oblivious of all other activity. She rehearsed yet again leaving Rose with Muriel that day twenty years ago. She saw Rose's little hand waving good-bye. She never should have done that, left her for her grandmother to bring up. It was never likely to come to good.

Out in the kitchen all was confusion. What should they do next? They had to send for the doctor to make sure – and they had to tell his wife. Aaron set out again for New Germany, but without even the comfort of confession.

The only relief in the dark night came from a few lamps still burning inside the widely separated houses he passed. What was going on in those houses? Most of the families he knew or thought he knew, but now, as he saw them from the distance of the road, enclosed in their own little worlds, it occurred to him how little anyone knew, really knew, anyone else. Himself, for example. People thought him lucky – possibly, by the standards of the area, rich. But one daughter was simple, and now another was dead. And there was still the deed that he had confessed openly to no one.

Seeing Aaron, Dr. Beale stiffened. Stupid, arrogant man, expecting him to cure his daughter when he had neglected her condition for years. And at this time of night! And in this weather!

"I explained that there's really nothing…" he began.

"No." Aaron cut him off quickly with a wave of his hand. "It's not Rose. Rose died earlier today. But Reverend Rasmussen came to give her the last rites, and…and…."

"And?"

"As he was leaving the house – I was going to drive him back here – he fell, and we thought – well, we thought it was just a fall, but we can't seem to bring him round."

"I'll come with you." And he gathered up his bag and the warmest clothing he could find.

After a mile of silence, Dr. Beale said, "Probably a stroke." Another mile and he added, "He's old, and going out in cold weather can often be dangerous – brings it on. The blood seems to freeze in the arteries." And he gave a short laugh.

The laugh disconcerted Aaron. He kept Josh to the road and said nothing. How could he respond with laughter? And at a time like this?

Reverend Rasmussen was indeed dead. By morning the whole community knew and gathered silently outside their houses in front of the banks of drifting snow as Josh, after a short rest, once again made the weary journey to New Germany bearing Reverend Rasmussen's body on the sleigh. They felt that, as a priest's body, some special respect ought to be shown to it, and to this end someone had gone into the church and removed an altar frontal and draped it over the corpse. In New Germany, word seemed to have preceded them, and again there were the silent groups of people standing motionless, huddled against the cold.

As Agnes sat in her house, numb with grief and remorse, it occurred to her that by the strange coincidence of Reverend Rasmussen's passing, Rose had been deprived of her death as she had been deprived of her life.

Who would even bury her?

This, at least, Aaron felt he could deal with. He went to Mahone Bay and arranged for the minister there to come up and take the service. Pastor Heinz was less than eager since he had already been engaged to take Reverend Rasmussen's funeral, which, he judged, would be a taxing occasion. But what could one do? The father was obviously distressed, and the young girl, by all accounts, had been devout.

Rose had died on a Thursday, and funerals normally took place rigidly on the third day, thereby commemorating in a rather bizarre way Christ's resurrection. The weather remained bitterly cold, and Nathan was delegated to go to the church hours before the service to get a fire going in the cast iron stove. He, too, was bewildered by events. It had not really occurred to him that a girl only a few years older than he was – only a few years older than Emma and Virtue – could die except in an accident. And the old pastor as well! What had they done that God was so angry with them?

The whole community struggled through the snow to pay their respects to Rose. They sang "Abide with Me" – but Rose had never reached a proper eventide. They sang "Rock of Ages," but the references to blood were too reminiscent of Rose's horribly stained handkerchiefs, and Agnes and Muriel could not continue. Finally they sang the chorale "Jesu Meine Freude" in German, and that alone seemed right.

On the way home in the sleigh, Emma asked her mother, "Why did Rose die?"

"Because she caught TB, and no one noticed in time." A practical answer to what seemed a practical question. But it was not what Emma meant at all.

"No, no, no! That's not what I mean." She was shouting now. "I mean why did she die, why did Flora have fits, why did Dilphin drown in the lake, why, why, why?"

"You mustn't think like that, Emma." Agnes was shocked. "You mustn't question the will of God. Things happen, and we can't understand them, but God knows and understands. Questioning His will is very wrong."

Another Country

1920

A Tuesday morning in May: Erika dusted the drawing room, moving carefully from one precious object to another on the stone mantel – a silver spoon-warmer shaped like a nautilus, two Meissen candle holders encrusted with tiny porcelain flowers, a silver christening cup engraved on three sides, given to someone long dead. These relic objects gave her a sense of calm and permanence as she fleetingly touched them. It was hard to imagine grief or passion in such a setting, when even death, that final grief and passion, transmuted itself into such wonderful objects left behind.

Outside, the pear and peach trees were just coming into blossom, and the river below the orchard seemed frosted with their petals as you looked down through the trees. She thought for a moment of the apple blossoms in her father's orchard in Waldenstein, and from there she was soon in her parents' parlour, with its distinctive, musty smell – last autumn's rose petals fallen from a flower, dead in a tall glass vase, a few scattered sheets of music on the reed organ bench, dust on the picture frames that lined the walls. The parlour in Waldenstein was not on the regular cleaning schedule at all, since it was opened up only at Christmas, Easter, funerals, and when the minister came to call. She had always been rather afraid of the parlour, but here, in its elaborate equivalent, she felt a certain peace, a desire to sit down and pretend it was her very own.

From the moment she stepped on the boat, her life had become in-substantial. No longer connected to anyone she had ever known or loved, except for Adam, she floated in an ether-like space, devoid of reality. At one level, of course, there was lots of reality – cooking for the men on shipboard, looking after Adam who was at first upset, not unreasonably, by this strange change in his circumstances, and then gradually, as the men on shipboard came to like and trust her, be-coming the confidant of some of them, doing odd jobs like sewing on buttons, repairing seams in shirts, and so on. They, in turn, took delight in amusing Adam, showing him the engine room, watching him care-fully as he crawled around the deck, putting him in the lifeboats and pretending to row with him.

She valued these little kindnesses from the men more than she would, in her former life, have thought possible. Yet this was an in-terlude, a hiatus in which life paused, not knowing which direction to take. She waited, fearfully, for the time when she would have to take control and make decisions again.

When the boat finally docked in Liverpool, she was seized by sheer terror. The captain would have been happy to keep her on board for the return journey – possibly for many return journeys. But that was unthinkable; it was no life for a baby like Adam. So on the dockside she bade goodbye to them all, her friends of two weeks, gathered her possessions including the pram she had brought all this way and sat down on a bench in a small park by the quayside to think. In front of her, in the pram, Adam sat bolt upright, expectant.

It was October then, and in Waldenstein the leaves would have been gleaming yellow and scarlet against the morning frost, but here the air was balmy, though the sky was dull and there seemed to be a smoky haze over everything. In front of her a gentleman – yes, defi-nitely a gentleman – in a funny coat that came down to his knees, walked past. He glanced her way, continued for about ten paces, then, as if he had forgotten something, turned and came back. He went a bit farther in the opposite direction, then repeated the process and came back again.

This time he stopped, tipped his hat and addressed her. "Excuse me, Ma'am, but can I be of any assistance to you?"

"Not really, I'm afraid." And then, because Adam was smiling beatifically at him and because she really did need to trust someone, she added, "Except…I've just come off shipboard and am looking for lodgings. I suppose, if you knew somewhere you could recommend…."

He thought for a minute, "Are you perhaps looking for work as well? Some sort of position?"

"Well, yes. Though I'm not really qualified to do a lot." Fear overwhelmed her again, but she forced herself to go on. "I was the cook on board a ship on the way over here, and I've done general housework."

"You're Canadian, aren't you?" He was good at discerning accents, even the subtle differences of Canadian and American.

"Yes, from Nova Scotia."

"Ah yes, where they've had that awful tragedy, the explosion. Of course you wanted to get out."

Erika decided that if he wanted to provide her with a plausible excuse for leaving home and country she would not undeceive him. Naturally he must be making other assumptions as well. Here she was with a child. Where was the husband? He might, of course, have been killed in the explosion. She could make up stories as well as he.

"Our parlour maid was called up to work with the wounded when they came back from France. And then she met someone and got married – as is the way with young women – so my wife and I are in a bit of a problem."

"In a bit of a problem." Erika had never in her life heard anyone speak like this.

"May I sit down?" He was nothing if not courteous.

"Yes, of course."

Adam was squirming and wanting to get out of the pram. "He's a very handsome boy. Looks strong and healthy as well." He paused.

"My wife and I never had a son, just two girls." Erika sensed that this was a major disappointment.

"We couldn't offer you a lot, but we have a lovely house on a river, and if you'd like to come and see it, we might be able to find an arrangement that would suit all of us. The child, of course, could live with us as well. There is a cook and a housemaid, so you would only have some housekeeping duties and a bit of looking after the girls. They're eight and ten now, but they won't be going away to school until they're thirteen."

Erika could not take in all the strange ideas (perfectly common-place to her companion) that were being presented to her – a large house on a river, a cook, a housemaid, two girls that needed someone other than their mother to look after them, two girls who would be sent away to school at thirteen. Yet the overwhelming question had nothing to do with any of this. It was, quite simply, could she trust this man.

"I'm a clergyman," he added, almost as an afterthought.

This should have inspired confidence. But anyone could say they were anything in this strange world where there were no anchors to reality, past or present. And yet, just because of that, she decided to float, to let the current take her where it would.

She sat quietly for a few minutes, and he waited for her. Then she said, "Yes, I'll come and work for you – at least, that is, if you really want me."

And so it was that, two hours after landing in Liverpool, Erika and Adam were flying along a road in a motorcar, the speed of which certainly put her ride to Halifax into perspective. They drove for several hours, mostly through countryside and small villages that were unlike anything she had seen in Nova Scotia. The houses were compact, close together, and some had roofs made out of the most curious thing – it looked like straw. She gave Adam some milk she had brought from the ship, and after a while he fell asleep on her lap. There was little conversation between her and her new employer. At one point he said suddenly, "By the way, I haven't told you my name. I'm the Reverend Austen Manley."

"I'm Erika," she replied. "Erika Wentzell."

"German?"

For a moment she thought he might stop the car and throw her out. "Yes, but way back. My ancestors went to Nova Scotia in the eighteenth century."

"When, of course, Germany didn't really exist."

Erika didn't know about this, but kept quiet since it seemed to please him that this should be the case.

He could be taking her anywhere. He could be a murderer, a rapist or a complete fraud. But eventually, to her relief, just after they had passed through a village with an old stone church, he turned off the main road and down a long drive lined with overarching elm trees, still mostly green. The road ended in a circular garden with a fountain in the centre. And there, behind the fountain, was the stone house, glowing cream in the low sunlight. Behind it were long fields and an orchard stretching down to something she could not see clearly, but assumed to be the river. Reverend Manley helped her and the still-sleeping Adam out of the car and then went ahead to alert the household to developments.

Erika stood uncertainly on the driveway, still holding Adam, who got heavier and heavier. Suppose Mrs. Manley did not share her husband's enthusiasm for picking up parlour maids just off shipboard? She was very tired, tired with anxiety as much as anything else.

Then a small woman, with light brown hair done up in a roll at the back and wearing a wool skirt and silk blouse, came out of the house. She looked even more tired than Erika felt. Had she been crying? "This is Erika," said Mr. Manley. "And this is Adam," pointing to the sleeping baby. "Erika, this is my wife, Mrs. Manley. We are both very happy to welcome you to the Rectory." Mrs. Manley managed a faint smile, shook her hand, and they went into the house together.

In the large front hall stood two other people, a man and a woman. "This is Jack and Millie," Mrs. Manley said to Erika. "Millie cooks

165

delicious food and Jack – well Jack does just about everything else. Millie and Jack, this is Erika, our new parlour maid – and Adam."

Millie gave a small curtsey; she was fortyish, plump, smiling and dressed in a printed cotton dress that bunched around her waist, the bunching somewhat concealed by a large apron. Jack was slightly older – probably fifty – fine-featured and tall, with dark eyes and hair. He was wearing black trousers and a white shirt with rolled-up sleeves, and of course, an apron on top. They greeted her with small bobs of the head and "pleased to meet you." Then Millie disappeared somewhere into the back part of the house, and Jack carried Erika's meagre belongings up to the top floor. There he left her, saying, "I do hope you'll be happy here."

Her new room was modest but pleasing. The wallpaper had sprigged blue flowers. There was a blue and white bowl and jug on a small washstand, a writing desk in the opposite corner and a bed fresh and clean with white linen. Through the partly opened window, its white muslin curtains floating in the breeze, she could see the garden and river. There was also, she noticed, room for a crib for Adam. Mrs. Manley, who had accompanied them up to the bedroom, anticipated her needs here as well. "Jack will bring in a cot shortly for the baby."

"A cot? But he still needs a crib with sides."

"Yes, that's what we call a cot in this country." She made no further attempt at intimacy.

Erika was given leave to wash Adam in the family bath, and soon Millie brought, on request, some mashed baby food. By the time all this had taken place Adam, despite his sleep in the car, was ready for bed. She sang him to sleep, closed the window (who would leave a window open at night in October?) and tiptoed out of the room.

Reverend and Mrs. Manley seemed to have disappeared. Erika walked down the rather narrow carpeted staircase to the landing of what she would have called the second floor. Silence. She then descended the grand staircase with its elaborate banister and turned spindles to the main hallway. Rich carpeting lay on top of large flat stones, polished to a fine sheen. And she had thought Mrs. Meisner's house in Mahone Bay was the height of grandeur and luxury!

She stood for a few minutes, wondering what was expected of her now. Would there be an evening meal? Was she supposed to be working straight away? Then from behind the closed door to the left of the stone entrance she detected the sound of muffled voices. Sound did not travel well in this stone house, she realized. In Waldenstein the wood houses projected every sound from one room to another in a communal buzz. Here all was quiet, separate. Would she even hear Adam if he woke up and cried? She was about to knock on the door from where the sounds came when Millie appeared, coming through a large door covered in green felt-like material just down the hall.

"Oh there you are. Baby gone to sleep? I'm just getting the family their dinner, and then we can eat ourselves. You can go down there to the kitchen to wait for us."

So she would not eat with the family. Everything was so strange that this could scarcely have been described as a surprise, but it would have been unthinkable in Nova Scotia, where the hired hands and all the help always ate with the family.

Erika moved down the hallway towards the green door as Jack, now dressed in a formal black jacket that matched his trousers and without the apron, came out of it, went down to the door on the left, knocked on it and said, "Dinner is served, Ma'am." Then, fascinated by this spectacle, she watched Reverend and Mrs. Manley and two girls walk across the corridor to the room opposite, through the door that Jack held open for them, and disappear. Jack and Millie then busied themselves pushing trolleys and generally moving food from kitchen to dining room. Eventually Millie went back to the kitchen to get ready to serve the next course, and Jack stayed in the dining room. Empty dishes came out; new, full dishes went in. Erika, meanwhile, sat at the large wooden kitchen table and drank a cup of tea and ate a cookie (biscuit, Millie called it) that she was given. After an hour and a half, the family went in solemn procession back to the drawing room, and soon the girls could be heard going upstairs.

At last Millie, Erika, Jack and a young girl called Fanny sat down to eat. Jack said grace and served each of them – chicken, carrots, potatoes, gravy and some leftover pudding from the Manleys' table. The food was good, and Millie and the others were clearly trying to be kind and helpful. To Erika's relief, they did not inquire too much about her past or how she came to be there. In fact she was the one who asked the one question that seemed to embarrass everyone.

"I wonder why Reverend Manley happened to be in Liverpool. Does he go there often, or was it just chance?"

There was an awkward pause. Then Jack said, "We don't inquire into the Rector's doings. He comes and goes without asking us." A significant glance passed between him and Millie.

She felt his reply a rebuke and concluded that the ways of the English were past understanding. She had known clergy in her time, but none of them lived in grand houses like this; none of them had servants. They seemed mostly poor, except that they had horses – but then they had to have horses to get around to take services. They were respected not because they were wealthy, but because they were men of God who held the power of life and death – eternal death – over you. They were obliged always to be there when you needed them, because that was part of their calling.

When they had finished eating, Millie took her back up to her room.

"I sleep just over here," Millie said, pointing to a room across the hall. "So if you need anything for yourself or the baby, you can just call me." Fanny, too, lived up here, but Jack had a room downstairs at the back of the house, off the kitchen. She was to be up by seven o'clock the following morning. They would eat breakfast together before the family had theirs.

"Do the girls go to school?"

"No, not yet. Mrs. Manley teaches them at home. If she likes you, I expect that when he's older she may teach Adam as well."

"Might she...might she not like me?" Erika asked tentatively.

Millie gave a look that Erika could not interpret. Then she looked at Adam, curled up on his front, with one fist stuck out through the bars of the cot. "He's a handsome one." And she said goodnight.

ॐ

Gradually the days began to assume a shape. She knew what was expected of her, and as she always had done, she found she could fulfill the expectations. The house itself and everyone in it fell into place. There were four large main rooms downstairs, two on each side of the central corridor. The drawing room and dining room were in front, the study and morning room in the back. Behind these, in an addition that in Waldenstein would have been called an "ell", were the kitchen, scullery, larder and Jack's bedroom. Millie was in charge of the kitchen, and Jack was in charge of everything else, including polishing the family silver. Fanny laid the fires in the morning, helped Millie and did most of the rough housework. Erika was expected to do dusting and tidying and ironing, and when the girls were not occupied with schoolwork, she was to play with them, accompany them on shopping expeditions to Leicester or Loughborough, take them boating on the river and generally entertain them. She was a kind of parlour maid-nanny. Adam was allowed the run of most of the house except the drawing room, dining room and study. He toddled around with Erika as she did the housework, and was a joyfully welcomed addition to the girls' entertainments and expeditions. In fact, Ella and Alice treated him like a large teddy bear that could walk and was quickly learning to talk as well. As for Adam himself, he took naturally to this life, running around the big house as if he had been born to possess it.

Erika remained slightly in awe of Mrs. Manley. She was not particularly demanding and certainly didn't indulge in temper even if things were not done quite right or on time. But there was a reserve, an aloofness about her that made Erika uncomfortable. Sometimes she looked at her strangely. Occasionally she would play with Adam, but in a curiously stiff fashion as if she had learned it all out of a book. To be fair, she played with her own daughters in the same way; it was not discrimination. It was as if everything real or spontaneous within her had disappeared years ago to be replaced by form and custom. She never did anything wrong nor spoke anything out of place. Erika found this in itself unnerving.

Once she asked Millie, "Does Mrs. Manley not like me?"

Millie gazed at her intently. Then she said slowly, "No, I think she does like you. But her life has not been easy." So – still nothing but mystery.

Up until lunchtime, Mrs. Manley taught the girls in the morning room while Reverend Manley worked or read in the study. After lunch she might go out visiting, or she might retire again to the morning room to read or embroider. Erika thought of the schedule of her own mother – cooking, baking, scrubbing floors, knitting and sewing not because they were ladylike occupations but because without them her family would be cold and hungry. Mrs. Manley had to do nothing except discuss menus with Millie and the day's schedule with Fanny and herself. Was this good or bad?

Reverend Manley was an enigma as well. He was less reserved than his wife and could be heard laughing and joking outside with the squire and other country friends. But when Mrs. Manley was around, he almost never spoke to Erika or even looked at her. Then one day, when she was dusting his study, he said abruptly that she could borrow some books to read if she wished, provided she recorded what she took in a little book on his desk. She thanked him and kept on dusting. He continued to look at her – look at her in a way she knew all too well. A few days later, again in the study, he complimented her on the elegance with which she had arranged some flowers and put his arm lightly around her shoulder. Erika recoiled. "No," she said softly. It didn't happen again.

He had had the house built for himself, it emerged. His older brother was a baronet, whatever that meant, and he had obviously inherited quite a lot of family money. Clergy were supposed to be poor, Erika had thought. Like Christ. Not here, it seemed. The other clergy and friends that were entertained from time to time seemed as wealthy as he.

Every Sunday they all went to church. The family had their own pew, but Millie, Fanny and Jack sat some way farther back. The liturgy was slightly familiar to Erika, based, like the Lutheran service, on the Roman mass, but the hymns were mostly foreign to her. Still, the most peculiar thing was Reverend Manley's sermons. They had little to do with how one should live or with Christian teaching in any broad sense. Instead he would take a tiny snippet of text, as it might be "In the beginning..." and wring every possible ounce of meaning out of it. First, what did the Hebrew mean? Then, how had it been translated into Greek, and why had someone called Erasmus used that particular Greek word? Then he would move on to the Latin, until finally he arrived at the English word "beginning," which by now had so many possible meanings that no one could be sure what it really meant, if anything. Erika watched the eyes of her companions glaze over. At least he never quizzed them on what they had heard afterwards.

At first Erika was impressed by the straight erudition displayed. Later, she saw that it was a smokescreen to prevent him from having to talk about anything real or relevant. What did he believe, if anything? How could one possibly guess?

In the winter they hunted. Erika knew that you could subdue the countryside (the Bible even said you could) so that it gave you a meagre subsistence. But here it was a giant playground, or so it seemed. People went to expensive schools and university and then spent their lives playing. They played at being parents, at keeping up a house and estate, while other people, employed by them, did the real thing, put in the hard hours required to make their lives possible. So in winter they played at being providers. But what they hunted wasn't even fit to eat! Whoever heard of eating stringy fox meat? Nathan and Obadiah would go out and catch rabbits, and they would have a tasty stew with carrots and turnips. Sometimes Jacob would shoot a deer. But here they only pretended to hunt. They set dogs to chase the foxes and galloped with horns and halloos after them. They didn't even kill the fox themselves; the dogs did that. The thought of the dogs mangling the fox to death made Erika sick. She kept Adam away while they were gathering outside the house, sitting on horseback, drinking small glasses of sherry that Jack passed up to them on a silver tray. This, she was led to believe, was civilization. And, against her will, it fascinated her.

Sometimes in the evening they had music. Mrs. Manley played the piano, Ella the violin and Alice the cello. One spring day, Mrs. Manley had found her listening outside the door. She was covered in confusion. "I'm so sorry; I didn't mean…I was just listening to the music."

"Well, Erika, would you like to come inside so you can hear it better?" Gradually this sad woman was becoming less hostile towards her. So Erika found herself standing against a wall in the drawing room, listening to the most exquisite sounds she had ever heard. There seemed to be three different parts, taken by the three different instruments that came in after one another and made a complicated pattern that she couldn't quite decipher except that it was wondrous beyond any music she had ever heard before. She stood rapt until it ended, and she expressed her thanks and left.

Now this was civilization. She felt her own ignorance and wished to do something about it. Sometimes when she was dusting she would cautiously touch the keys of the grand piano. Once, as she was doing this, she saw Mrs. Manley standing in the doorway. She started guiltily, but Mrs. Manley simply said, "Would you like to learn to play, Erika?"

And so it was arranged. She was to take lessons from another woman in the village and was given an hour a day to practise. Millie and Jack gave her to understand that this was completely unprecedented. "You really must have charmed her."

"No, it's not me, I'm sure; it's Adam they like." Often Adam would come and curl up in a chair to listen, and this was allowed because his mother was present and, as they all said in wonderment, "He never touched anything."

One Saturday morning, when the girls were out riding with some friends from an adjoining farm, Erika heard what were unmistakably sobs coming from behind the closed morning room door. What should she do? She knew that to go in or even knock, in these circumstances, would be an unpardonable breach of protocol. She decided to go to the kitchen and seek the advice of Millie. "Someone's crying in the morning room; I think it's Mrs. Manley. Should we be doing anything?"

Jack, who overheard from the pantry, came in. "No, there's nothing to be done. It's just that the master's gone on a trip to Liverpool again."

A trip to Liverpool! That was where he had gone the day he met her and brought her home. "Do they need another servant then?" Though she knew this was a stupid question.

This time Millie was more forthcoming than she had been on Erika's first evening. "No, the master has a friend there that he goes to see sometimes."

"A friend." Erika was no longer the naïve country girl she had been when she conceived Adam; she understood. But a clergyman! How could he? And what had been the real reason he had brought her here?

By dinnertime he was back, and the civilities of normal life resumed. Mrs. Manley gave no hint of distress nor any remonstration that reached the servants' ears.

ॐ

Now that she had been here for more than a year and a half, a kind of tranquility had settled on her. Adam was happy, and Mrs. Manley agreed to teach him, as she did her daughters, when he got a bit older. Erika no longer saw the curve of her life as an individual narrative, with herself the heroine of a small drama spun out of courtship and marriage and children. The space she occupied was at the side of the stage, adjusting a few props here, adding a line or two there, and waiting for the grand epic of her son's life to begin.

She would never hear from anyone in Waldenstein again, she believed, which meant that she was at least spared its accidents and horrors. There would be no more Sophias or Dilphins, no more whispered remarks from her neighbours, no more danger from Aaron. If her new life still seemed quite unreal, at least it was secure and coherent, impervious, she believed, to shock. As she put back the silver nautilus on the mantel, she breathed a small sigh of relief.

Enlightenment

1920

He came on a black horse. Everyone in Waldenstein remembered this much later and embroidered it with his or her varied interpretations. Yet if you had asked them what their first impressions were, they wouldn't have given you a description of what he looked like or what he said. They would simply have reverted to their own feeling: "He was strange; something was going to happen."

The summer before he arrived, even Sunday was a day of freedom; there was no church.

"Do you suppose we'll be punished for not going to church?" Virtue worried.

"Of course not. God couldn't be that unreasonable. He took away our minister and hasn't given us another one yet. So how can we go to church?" Emma's God was nothing if not reasonable.

"That's true. And at least no one's died. Maybe God knows there'd be no one here to bury them if they did." Virtue was coming to see it all as fortuitous after all. God would not let anyone die until there was a minister present and they could die in a state of grace. The grown-ups had doubtless worked that out already; that was why they were not more worried about the situation.

Eventually there was a rumour. A clergyman had been found for them. Not someone from Canada or even the United States, but from the "Old Country." The very words filled the community with a vague nostalgia. For despite the fact that they had come to the Promised Land, and that a village not twenty miles away was called Paradise and another thirty miles in the other direction Eden, they still clung to a deep-seated feeling that maybe "old" was better than "new." Perhaps they were simply imitators, not really authentic – even though they no longer had a clear idea of what the authentic that they were imitating might have been. Was New Germany, for example, merely a weak copy of the Old? They never said this sort of thing openly to one another, but the suggestion lurked under most of the attitudes they held. And now it found expression in their inability to understand why such a minister from across the sea would want to come to New Germany – or to Waldenstein. They whispered about it together in hushed tones when they met on the road, or in the store in Barss Corner, or in the evening in the privacy of their families. And if the authentic arrived, would they even recognize it?

☙

Emma walked to school purposefully through the crisp autumn air, swinging her book bag and scuffling the dry fallen leaves with her feet.

"It's the very best time of year, I think. Everything is starting again. New books, new teachers, new stuff to learn."

Virtue, walking rather sullenly beside her, remained silent. Had Emma really forgotten that she wasn't learning anything new this year but repeating a grade that she had failed? Or was she just rubbing it in?

"I think I'm really going to like geometry. It's so logical, and you can figure it out. The problems, for example. You say that because this is like this, and that is like that, then something else must follow. Kind of like life."

"You mean like people saying that because Papa got Erika pregnant and followed her to Mahone Bay, then she had to go to Halifax and disappear." Virtue was feeling the bitterness of her situation.

"That wasn't quite what I meant, but you have to admit it's logical."

"You're horrible." And Virtue stomped on ahead.

"Now what's wrong?" Then Emma remembered that geometry was one of the subjects Virtue had flunked. Oh well, perhaps she had been tactless, but really she just felt so happy to be going back to spending all day sitting at a wooden desk scratched with the initials of her predecessors, thinking new and interesting things, reading exciting stories and plays. How could Virtue not feel the same way?

This year they were going to start Shakespeare. Virtue had already read *Romeo and Juliet* last year and had said it was a pile of nonsense. But Emma had taken Virtue's copy and read it and thought it wonderful. "Gallop apace, you fiery-footed steeds,/ Towards Phoebus' lodging." One summer evening she had quoted this back to Virtue while standing at the bedroom window.

"What on earth are you talking about?"

"It's from your play, it's Shakespeare."

"Oh. Who's Phoebus?" Virtue looked bored rather than interested.

"I don't have any idea, but it sounds nice. You can just see the horses galloping through the sky."

"Horses don't fly through the sky."

"But the point is, they seem to be pulling the day along with them so that it will quickly become night. At least, that's what I think it means."

"Why are they on fire?" If Emma thought she could explain the passage, then let her do so thoroughly.

"Oh Virtue, I think it just means they look red in the setting sun – or maybe their feet are fiery because they're running so fast. You just have to see the picture." Virtue had sniffed.

When Emma reached school, Virtue was already sitting at a double desk in the second row. Emma joined her; they had always shared a desk, just as at home they shared a bed. Virtue pushed her with her elbow, "Go away and find someone your own silly age to sit with."

"What's wrong with you?"

"You know perfectly well what's wrong with me. Now go away."

So Emma got up and sat two aisles over with Violet Sparrow, who happened to be the only girl in the school apart from the Millers without a German surname. She was pale and listless and didn't have the energy to tell Emma to go away, even though she rather wished she would.

෨

A few days later a strange young man arrived – dark-haired, dark-suited, perfectly chiseled nose, high cheekbones, six foot tall, and sitting proudly on his horse. He stopped outside the schoolyard and tied his horse to a tree. Then he went inside and introduced himself to the teacher and students. Mrs. Oliphant, normally very self-assured, was flustered by this good-looking young man with a decided air of authority. Thank goodness the children seemed quite as overcome as she was and were behaving themselves.

"I have come to greet you the very first, because you are the church of the future. It is here that the work of God must first be carried out, or the rest will be in vain."

Suddenly, they all realized who this stranger must be. He was their new minister from the Old Country; he was the "authentic" for which they had longed, in living flesh. He spoke to them for about fifteen minutes, then made his farewell and left the stunned class behind. So this was the new minister!

"What did you think?" Virtue pressed Emma after school.

"He's very handsome, and he speaks very well even if sometimes he puts his words in a funny order."

They ran home quickly, dragging Joan and Hannah after them to spread the news, but when they arrived the minister's black horse was munching grass in the pasture in front of the house.

"He's here." (Emma, excitedly.)

"I can see." (Virtue, nonchalant.)

He must be in the parlour talking earnestly to their parents. The four girls rushed through the back door. There they found Flora, exiled to the kitchen, where she was supposed to be looking after Rachel. In fact she was having a small pique and sulking on the bench under the window, while Rachel crawled recklessly around the room eating crumbs and bits of dust. Hannah, always hungry after school, set about sampling some icing from a cake left on the kitchen table.

"Stop that at once, Hannah." Virtue immediately took charge. Then she picked up Rachel and began to rock her.

"Who's in there?" Flora wanted to know from what she had been excluded.

Virtue was quick to answer: "The new minister. At least that's his horse outside."

"How do you know?"

"He came to school to visit us first. We saw him and his horse." Virtue did not disguise a sense of superior knowledge.

"I want to go to school," Flora moaned plaintively.

"You're too big. Anyway, you can't learn much." This was from Emma, direct and brutal.

Flora retreated again to the window bench, looked out and began to chew her thumb.

"Oh do stop that, Flora! You know Mama doesn't like you doing it."

At this Flora screamed loudly and went clomping up the stairs (next to the parlour) to her room.

"Now look what you've done," Virtue scolded Emma.

"Look, she wasn't doing what she was supposed to be doing – looking after Rachel – anyway." Though Emma did feel perhaps she had gone too far.

"Yes, but she wasn't making a huge racket and screaming so that the minister would hear. Now he'll think we're all barbarians.".

"Oh, let him think!"

They sat in subdued silence for some time, Virtue rocking Rachel who was sucking on a piece of muslin. At last there was the sound of footsteps, voices. The front door opened and closed again. Now foot-steps were moving from the front hall through the sitting room to the kitchen.

"What's the matter with you girls? And where's Flora?" Aaron made no attempt to hide his anger.

"Flora's gone upstairs to sulk. She wasn't looking after Rachel and when we scolded her she got mad and ran away." This was the most benign explanation Virtue could think of.

"Well, you could have chosen your time better, I must say. The new minister comes to visit and what does he see or hear of our family? Anger and shouting. First impressions are lasting."

"It's not his first impression of us. We've met him already." Emma couldn't resist this. "He came to the school because he said we were the church of the future and therefore we were the most important part."

"Some church it'll be if it's in the hands of girls who can't even get along with their sister. Go up to your room and stay there."

"It was all your fault, you know," Virtue insisted, as they mounted the stairs. "Why didn't you say so?"

"Because it wasn't. You were just as cross at Flora; it's just that you always leave it up to me to say things you don't dare say. Why should I take the blame if I only say the things you think?"

Virtue could not come up with a quick answer to this, and so they went together to their room where Emma read a book and Virtue sat silently contemplating the injustice of the universe.

Everyone, absolutely everyone, turned out for Reverend Selig's first Sunday service. It was held at three in the afternoon, since New Germany, as befitted its status with all of five hundred inhabitants, got the eleven o'clock morning service.

It was a beautiful autumn afternoon, sunny, with the sky a clear, translucent blue. He strode into the church in a black Geneva gown, confident but slightly diffident at the same time. Tall, slender, with wavy black hair and eyes the colour of the autumn sky outside – who could not be taken with him?

When he began the sermon, Aaron listened intently. This was how the new man would most clearly reveal himself. Reverend Selig began confidently, speaking about Abraham leaving Ur of the Chaldees for the Promised Land. "By faith Abraham…." All this was rather familiar, orthodox stuff, though he did manage to insert some disconcerting asides into it. "So here we are," he said, "all of us, in this strange land." Aaron thought it odd that it did not occur to the pastor that to him and all the others in Waldenstein, who were five or six generations away from the original settlers, this land was no longer "strange." It was all they knew.

And then he quoted from someone Aaron had never heard of, someone he called a "great philosopher, Kierkegaard," who had said, "Who is so great as Abraham, and who can understand him?" Reverend Rasmussen had never talked like this. He would have praised Abraham, but he would have seen no mystery. God had commanded him to leave Ur, and so he did. God had commanded him to kill his son, so he had prepared to do it.

"A strange land," Aaron thought. Indeed it must seem so to this man. Why had he come here? Now that was a mystery, surpassing Abraham. Then he thought of Erika who had probably crossed the Atlantic in the other direction. He knew all too well why she had done so. But he put the thought of any similarity in the cases out of his head as unworthy, sacrilegious. This was a man of God.

ॐ

In keeping with his initial statement that the young people must be at the heart of the church, Reverend Selig soon broached the matter of a confirmation class. For the last few years of his ministry, Reverend Rasmussen had been delinquent in this matter, so now there was a substantial group of children who were not full members of the church. Of Aaron's children, only Rose had been confirmed; of Jacob's, only Erika and Hibbert. Nor was this matter of confirmation to be taken lightly; only once confirmed could you take the bread and wine of the sacrament. Now Reverend Rasmussen, when he had confirmed young people, usually thought a twelve week course of talks after the Sunday service was good enough, so it came as something of a shock when Reverend Selig made it clear that two hours a week for two years would be required. "What in heaven's name is he goin' to teach them in all that time? They're not studyin' to be ministers like him!" Ben Wentzell exclaimed.

But their new pastor was not to be deterred. Furthermore, to their astonishment, he invited any adults who might be interested to join the classes, to brush up what they had forgotten. Some found the suggestion insulting, but others, like Aaron, decided to take up the offer. They would meet alternately on Sundays after the service and on Saturday mornings. The subject matter alternated as well. On Saturdays, it was Luther's Small Catechism; on Sundays, it was the Bible itself.

The students and the adults who decided to join sat in two rows of church pews, while Reverend Selig perched on the back of the pew two rows in front and faced them with his feet up on the seat of the pew immediately in front of them. If he was uncomfortable he gave no sign of it. He rested the text on his knees, leaned forward and spoke with intensity.

There should have been little problem with the catechism. It was sacrosanct. You memorized it, and then you discussed what it meant. So far, so straightforward. "We should so fear and love God…" Yet even here there were doubts and ambiguities that had never been raised in Waldenstein before. What did it mean to "put the most charitable construction" on your neighbour's actions? Suppose he had done something really wrong, should you just let him get away with it? Jacob was not attending these classes, but Nathan and Obadiah were. They looked at Aaron, who coloured.

"But how can you be certain that what you believed he did, he really did," Reverend Selig probed.

"You just know."

"Well, you may think you know, but have you never thought you were right about something and then found out, years later, that you were wrong?"

Obadiah shuffled uneasily. He had blamed Nathan for years for breaking a wind-up car he had been given one Christmas – the only wind-up toy he had ever had as a boy – but then, unexpectedly, Hibbert had come to him and said, "I broke the car. I couldn't tell you before; I was afraid."

Week after week certainties fell away like small grains of granite from the tombstones of their faith. The young were untroubled, but among the adults who had signed up there were serious conversations. First it was just, "Did you ever think of that before?" Then, "Did you ever hear the like?" But he must be right, because he was the minister.

If the classes on the catechism were worrying, those on the Bible were downright startling. He used words they had never heard before, like "myth" and "allegory." The Creation myth, he said, was a kind of poetry.

"But God created the world," an adult voice from the back protested.

"Yes, indeed, but not necessarily in exactly the way the book of Genesis tells us. Read the first chapter of Genesis. Aaron, you aloud read."

So Aaron proclaimed the Creation of something out of nothing and the infinite goodness of this creation.

"Now, Emma, you the second chapter read, from verse four."

So Emma read.

"What do you think of that, Emma?"

"It's sort of the same, but different," was all even she could manage.

"How different?"

She thought again. "Well, it's not so much about the plants and animals, but more about Adam and Eve and the garden of Eden and how they sinned."

"So we don't have six days and nights here at all, do we?"

"No, it doesn't say how long it took," she conceded.

"Would you be surprised then, if I told you that these are two different accounts of Creation, written at two quite different times?"

The adults gasped. But Emma, unperturbed, said simply, "That would make sense."

"Hold on a minute." Ebenezer Conrad was becoming quite upset. "I mean, no disrespect to you, but are you sayin' that two different people put down their ideas about this? If God wrote it all, how can that be? You can't have a God who changes his mind, can you?"

"God may not change his mind, but the people who wrote the Bible sometimes understood things differently, or sometimes remembered things that happened differently, just as we might today."

And then Johannes Selig proceeded to give them a lesson on the two accounts of the feeding of the five thousand. "So you see, not everything completely accurate in its detail is."

"Are you tellin' us that the Bible ain't true?" Ebenezer could not believe what he was hearing.

Everyone was aghast now. You didn't argue with the preacher. You couldn't say he didn't believe the Bible. You couldn't even say it in the form of a question.

Emma squirmed. She thought that Reverend Selig was wonderful. He knew so much, and he thought they were worth telling everything he knew. Most adults weren't like that; they only told you what they thought was good for you. But she could see her father's face tightening, fearing for her and for Virtue. If he exploded, it would be far worse than anything Ebenezer could say.

Reverend Selig was unworried. "Of course I'm not saying the Bible isn't true about the things that matter. Remember what Luther says, 'The Bible is the inspired and unerring record of what God has revealed concerning Himself and the way of Salvation.' The Bible isn't a textbook about scientific things or about trivial things like exactly how many people were fed on a particular day. It's about things that are more important than that – the nature of God and how we can reach Him."

Emma breathed a sigh of relief. She didn't need to fear for him; he could answer anything. But why should she fear for him anyway? Why should she care?

She and Virtue walked back with their father through the late autumn afternoon. Most of the leaves had fallen, and they made small scuffling sounds as they walked the woodland path, the shortest way back to their house. Aaron was silent for much of the distance. At last he said, "I just don't know."

"What don't you know?" Emma jumped in quickly.

"I just don't know how to take what he says. He knows a lot, that's for sure."

"He knows everything." She was excited, full of enthusiasm. A new world was opening up.

Virtue was doubtful: "He doesn't know everything. He doesn't know as much as God."

"Maybe not, but he knows more than anyone else in Waldenstein. And wasn't old Ebenezer awful, telling him that he didn't believe the Bible." Emma could not contain herself.

But Virtue came back in her matter-of-fact way, "It did sound a bit like that."

"No, it didn't. He was just explaining how to read the Bible."

"As if we didn't know."

"But maybe we don't."

Aaron intervened. "That's enough, girls. We'll just wait and see how it goes."

That night Virtue and Emma talked late, after the oil lamp had been put out, after the first frost had formed in lacy patterns on the window pane.

"Don't you think it's exciting?" Emma needed someone off whom to bounce her exhilaration.

"No, not particularly." Virtue felt her responsibility as older sister. "I think it's upsetting. What's he doing coming here and telling us all this stuff we don't need to know?"

"How do we know what we need to know? That's just so like you! I want to know everything I can."

The vast abyss of possible knowledge opened up in front of Virtue, a huge dark pit full of intricate passages like the picture of a coal mine in her geography book. You could get lost in there, she feared.

Then she said, "It scares me."

"How can just learning something be scary?"

"Well, it can. Look at the stories of lepers with their huge sores and no fingers or toes that we learned in Sunday School. That's scary."

"But that isn't knowledge. That's just information." Emma felt rather pleased with herself.

Emma continued to circle around the question. Sleep was out of the question now. Even Mrs. Oliphant, her teacher, seemed to think knowledge could hurt you. Take Hamlet, for example. Mrs. Oliphant said the reason Hamlet couldn't make up his mind about anything, like ghosts, was because he thought too much and asked too many questions, and the reason he did this was because he had gone to university in Wittenberg and had too much education. Better not to wonder or think too much about things, she seemed to feel. But Reverend Selig seemed to think it was impossible to know too much or think too much.

In geography, also, Mrs. Oliphant seemed to feel you could know too much. They were now studying the formation of the land features of Nova Scotia. The textbook they were using taught about Ice Ages, with artists' impressions of huge glaciers that had covered the whole province. Grinding along, they pushed massive mounds of earth and rock with them. Then, when it became warmer, the glaciers melted leaving behind these huge piles of gravel and earth that were the hills in the landscape today. The peculiar thing about these hills was that because the ice sheet advanced and retreated in one particular direction, all the hills sloped in that direction and each was steep on one side and more gradual on the other. The hills were called drumlins. The rocks too had scratches, all running in the same direction. Emma went around Waldenstein examining the hills, and yes, it was true. They did all slope in one direction and one side of each of them was steep and one gradual. This was quite exciting.

But Mrs. Oliphant had a peculiarly equivocal attitude to these glaciers. In fact, she stated outright that she did not believe in them because, according to the geography book, they had happened much too long ago, long before, as anyone who read the Bible knew, God had made the earth. Naturally, as a loyal servant of the Provincial Department of Education, she had to teach these things, but no one could make her believe them, and as a loyal Christian she felt it her duty to save the souls of the young by expressing her scepticism. If the hills all sloped in one direction, then it was probably because God had the good aesthetic sense to see they would look nicer that way. What she actually said was, "Well, class, you must know these things for your exams but…well, I'm not at all certain about them. I know they're in the book, but…" and her voice floated away in a querulous high-pitched sigh that did not invite further questions.

"So what do you think about the glaciers?" Emma persisted with her nocturnal catechism.

"I believe what Mrs. Oliphant says; it all sounds pretty impossible." Inwardly, Virtue groaned. She could tell that Emma was going to go on and on.

"But what about the scratches on the rocks, all going the same way? How do you explain that?" Emma's mind was racing ahead at full speed.

"It's just the way it is. I guess it was made that way," Virtue replied in a bored and sleepy tone, hoping to discourage her.

"But how? Why?" The insistent questioning continued.

"Stop thinking things like that, Emma; it won't do you any good." All she wanted was for Emma to shut up and go to sleep. But this wasn't going to happen anytime soon.

"How can you stop thinking things like that?" Emma's mind was a kind of mad railroad; once on the track she lost control and just kept going

"Don't be silly. I believe the Bible." That should have been final, Virtue thought.

"But maybe the Bible doesn't mean quite what we think it means in every way."

"Now you sound like Reverend Selig."

"And what's wrong with that? I'd sooner sound like him than Mrs. Oliphant."

"A lot. I still think learning all this stuff is scary, and if you're so struck on this new minister, good luck to you. Papa isn't going to be pleased, I can tell you."

"I'm not struck on him, just on his ideas. And how do you know what Papa thinks?"

"Because I heard him talking to Mama after we got back. And he said, 'I'm afraid there may be trouble if our young minister keeps on as he has begun. People aren't going to like it.' So there." Then, for good measure, she added, "I read the Bible and I know what it says. It says what it says."

This display of tautology was too much even for Emma. She rolled over towards the edge of the bed, pulling as much of the covers with her as she could.

A few weeks passed. People were beginning to think about Christmas and do extra baking. One Sunday afternoon after confirmation class, some of the adults produced tea and cakes, and they all had a little party. In this social setting, Reverend Selig seemed unusually relaxed and content. Gradually he was learning how to talk crops and harvest and wood lore. "All this wood you have," he was saying to Aaron, "Has anyone ever thought about making carvings from any of it?"

"Depends on what you mean. Little things – Jacob's boys are always whittling away making oxen or birds or something. Passes the time in the woods."

"I was thinking – where I come from, in southern Germany, men do that small sort of thing, of course, but they also do big carvings, and some of them they give to churches. For example, there are large carvings of Mary and Joseph with the Christ Child in the manger. And then, behind them, the shepherds, with their crooks and maybe carrying a lamb, all looking in surprise and wonder at the child."

Part of Aaron wanted to say, "No, we don't do that in Waldenstein; we have to work for a living." But the other half was intrigued, wanting to know more. So he did not object when Reverend Selig went on, "Look here, I have a picture." And there, in the dim light of the December afternoon, Aaron could see the peering shepherds, the kneeling mother, Joseph shadowy in the background, a perfect grouping. "Jacob, come here," he called. Jacob turned back from the window where he was watching the first snowflakes descend.

"There's gonna be a blizzard tonight, mark my words," he said.

"Look at this." Jacob too seemed astonished. "It's all carved out of wood," Aaron added. "Back in the old country, they do stuff like that, men and boys, and give it to the church."

"Well, I never!"

"Do you suppose that Nathan or Obadiah could do something like that?"

"Mebbe, I don't know. They never tried anythin' like it."

"I'd find them a nice piece of wood. What do you think? Birch? Or maple?" Aaron was already caught up in the project.

"Maple. Has a nicer grain," Jacob said. "And try Nathan. He was always the one who was good at drawin' in school."

So Aaron resolved to talk to Nathan about it. Reverend Selig, when he told him what he planned, seemed well pleased. "Nathan, yes. Doesn't talk a lot, but takes it all in. Yes, try him."

Yet as Aaron walked home with his family through the developing blizzard Jacob had prophesied, one huge question remained. Of course things were better, more beautiful, more "civilized" in the old country. Everyone knew that even if they didn't admit it. That was all very well. But then, what was Reverend Selig doing here?

🐦

In his small study in New Germany, Reverend Johannes Selig carefully spread out some writing paper he had brought with him. There was a letter as well, its elaborate handwriting crumpled and shadowy in the light of the oil lamp. He glanced at the letter, and began to write:

My Dear Sister,

I do understand why you are anxious about this new endeavour of mine, but I assure you, you do not need to worry. At first the people were, naturally, somewhat surprised to find someone from Germany, but now, I think, we are getting on quite well together. Of course they are mostly rather uneducated with quite unsophisticated ideas, both theological and scientific, but they are not unfriendly. In general, they seem to have an extraordinary respect for a minister. I think I would have to do something quite awful to shake that respect – and that, I am sure, you know I would never do.

The thing that strikes me most is what hard workers they are. The women especially not only have to cook all the meals for their very large families (ten or twelve children are not unusual) but, with no modern conveniences, they must make clothes for them, knit and darn socks, keep them neat and tidy, and then, when they have got the family in order, they have to clean and tidy the house. The young ones cope pretty well, but women who have been worn out by a dozen children at age forty look old – tired and exhausted, automatons going through the motions of the daily round. They are like sixty-year-olds at home. And the men farm all summer and then, in the winter, go back to a lumber camp owned by the one man of some substance in the village and cut trees in the freezing cold all winter.

Recreation? They don't seem to have any; there simply is no time. Except that some evenings, it seems, the men get together and sing – the legacy of some itinerant man who taught them sight-singing years ago. In fact, they are quite musical and can sing well in church even without accompaniment.

My own recreation is chiefly walking. There are exquisite paths through the woods and beside running streams, bird song everywhere, and on these little treks I feel such peace and tranquility as you can hardly imagine. I am better than I have been in a long time.
So do not worry, dearest sister,
Your loving brother,
Johannes

He began to write a PS: "And in all the hardship of their lives, sometimes there springs up...I don't know how to say this...but there is the most remarkable girl..."

He thought better of it, scratched it out, and sent off the letter.

ॐ

Aaron took the nativity scene project in hand at once. He found a huge trunk of maple, one that had been growing before he or anyone else had come to strip the woods for timber. He cut it off just above the roots and then again about seven feet higher up. That would make a background board and a crib in front. Then he cut five other strips six feet in length, but of ever-diminishing diameter for Joseph, Mary, an angel, and three shepherds. There were smaller pieces as well that could be turned into sheep or other animals.

Nathan had not been so happy since he left school. He began first to draw the outline of what he wanted to carve; then he tried to make this three dimensional in his head and move the idea onto the piece of wood. He lay awake at night planning exactly how he should cut it so as to make the most of its irregularities. Finally he began to carve. First he used an axe to rough-shape the trunk to the size he wanted. Then he began more carefully with chisel and hammer. At first he was afraid; any slip and a piece of wood necessary to the design might be lost. But gradually he gained in confidence. At the back stood three Gothic arches, shaped like the stained glass windows at the front of the church. In front of them, and much lower, the tree trunk curved out to form the manger, hollowed out and with a tiny figure lying in it. Every spare moment he worked. Sometimes Aaron gave him special permission to take half a day off to work on the sculpture. Then the other men grumbled, but not too loudly, for was this not a work for the Lord, and must it not be completed to stand in the church by Christmas?

After the background and crib were complete, he took one of the other pieces of wood and began on Mary. The folds of her gown as she knelt were not too difficult, but the face and hands proved quite tricky. He knew what it should look like – and that picture was not unlike Erika – but achieving it was another matter. Eventually he settled for less than perfection when it became clear that, if he kept on chiselling, Mary would have no features at all. After Mary, Joseph was easier. The features needed to be coarser, and anyway he had had some practice now. The first shepherd he decided to carve carrying a lamb draped around his neck. He had seen such a picture in one of the large Bibles in the church. But this took so long that it was the week before Christmas when he finished it, despite the fact that Aaron had practically stopped asking him to work in the woods at all. But even without more shepherds (they could be carved later) it was an impressive manger. When the men left camp, they put the wooden figures on a large flat sled and got the horse to haul them across the ice.

The final week Nathan spent at home sanding, polishing and oiling the figures. At last they were taken to the church and set to the front and right of the altar, where they could be seen by everyone. Who had known Nathan could do such a thing? Not even Nathan himself. Reverend Selig had an oil light specially mounted on the wall where it cast a dull glow down on the carving.

Emma looked at it in amazement and not without a pang of jealousy. Nathan had been singled out by Reverend Selig to do this special thing, and it was wonderful, but what could she do? She was nothing, abandoned by everyone, useless. All she was good at was schoolwork. She never had been able to draw like Nathan even when they were both in the same class. Now everyone could talk of nothing but the wonderful thing Jacob's boy had done. She moped and sulked and knew that moping and sulking were childish and unchristian.

But when Christmas Eve came, her evil mood vanished. Walking with all her family through the snow to the midnight service she forgave Nathan for being gifted and the centre of attention and was swept up in the wonder of the occasion itself. And strange and wonderful it

Rosalie Osmond

was. Not only did the carved crib focus everyone's thoughts on the supernatural reality that the night celebrated, but when Reverend Selig entered the church, he was not dressed in his usual black Geneva gown but in a wonderful white creation that flowed down front and back and had gold embroidered crosses on it. He said it was called a chasuble and was a special robe for a very special occasion. They even sang a new hymn that he had taught them in confirmation class: "Creator of the starry night," followed by all the old favourites – "O Little Town of Bethlehem," "Silent Night," "O Come all ye Faithful." Then out again into the cold of the real starry night. Everyone agreed it was the best Christmas service they had ever had.

Madness

1921

One Saturday after the morning class Reverend Selig asked Aaron to stay behind. When the church was empty except for the two of them he said, "Emma is a very exceptional girl. All your children are interesting, but she seems particularly gifted."

"Yes, we've always been proud of Emma." Aaron wondered what was coming next.

"I doubt that her schoolwork challenges her greatly."

"That's true. She finds it all very easy except for some parts of science, and that, she says, is only because she doesn't have the equipment to do the experiments. We don't have the money to buy those things for the school in Waldenstein."

"Naturally. I wondered, therefore, whether she would like, and you would permit me, to teach her Latin. It would just mean that she would stay after the others have left confirmation class for a short time – maybe half an hour – and we together could work."

Now Aaron had only the vaguest idea what Latin was or why one might want to learn it. It was a foreign language, he believed, and a very old one at that. But what possible use might it be? And, apart from all this, was it a good idea to have Emma staying behind alone with Reverend Selig? What would people say? What would they think?

"Latin," he began. "No one here knows Latin."

"I know that. So I am the only person who can teach her."

"Yes, but...."

"Why would one want to learn Latin? Well, it helps you to understand the structure of a large number of other languages that are still spoken today, because they all came from Latin, but most of all, it opens up a whole new world of reading and knowledge to you. The Romans" (ah yes, Aaron remembered, it was the Romans who had spoken Latin) "were good authors; they left us many excellent books. And while some of them have been translated, by no means all of them have been and, anyway, you can get something out of the original that you can't from the translation. Think about it. And talk to Emma. She'll know what she wants to do."

Aaron was only too aware that Emma would know what she wanted to do. Her excitement knew no bounds. "He wants to teach me Latin! How absolutely wonderful!" Now Emma didn't really know much more about why it might be a good idea to have a knowledge of Latin than her father did, but what she did know was that Reverend Selig had singled her out, had offered to teach her something special, had felt that she was worth teaching Latin to, and that was all that mattered.

So Emma regularly stayed behind, and Virtue was left to shepherd Flora, Hannah and Joan home. Aaron was away in the woods until spring now, so he no longer attended. Most of the other adults had dropped out as well, to Reverend Selig's disappointment. Reverend Rasmussen had never felt that all this knowledge would make you a better person or more acceptable to God, they muttered. Anyway, how did he know these things? Were half of them true? He had suggested that men were related to the animals, monkeys in particular. Could this possibly be right? Should they even be letting their children hear such ridiculous things? Fine services and fancy gowns were all very well, but the fact was that they wanted a minister to get them into Heaven, and they weren't sure that Reverend Selig knew the way himself.

Emma, meanwhile, was oblivious to all this. She looked with wonder at the small Latin grammar he gave her. They began with first declension nouns and first conjugation verbs: *puella, puellae; amo, amas, amat. Puella amat.* Who is the girl and whom does she love? One day in late March when she had been studying for nearly two months he said, just as she was leaving, "What are you going to do, Emma?"

"Do?"

"I mean when you grow up."

"I expect I'll be a school teacher. That's what most girls who finish school do – unless they want to do nursing."

"And you don't want to do nursing?"

"No."

"Why?"

"I don't like people's bodies." Emma never intended to shock people; it just came out like that. But Reverend Selig seemed impervious to shock.

"An excellent reason, if an unusual one. Do you really want to teach?"

Emma thought, and then she said, "Yes, I do. Because learning things is exciting, and I want to make it exciting for others."

"Again, an excellent reason."

As she walked home through the slush and mud of the late March thaw, she pondered what had just happened. Why had he asked her these things? Did he think she didn't know what she was going to do? Did he think her choices were good or bad? What did he mean by "an excellent reason"? Was he sincere, or was he laughing at her?

And what did Reverend Selig do when Emma had left him and gone home? He went home himself and shut himself up in his study and read. When it grew dark, he lit the oil lamp and began to write. First he replied to letters – so many letters, the man in the post office assured everyone – mostly in German, mostly from across the Atlantic. Their very smell took Johannes back to a land he could conjure up all too vividly: his family in the Schwarzenwald, his university days in Heidelberg, long nights spent in argument with friends or writing essays. The smell of learning and of antiquity; the smell of Luther himself writing away at night, translating the Bible. The letters from his university friends and colleagues kept asking the same questions that worried his sister. Was he unhappy here? Was he homesick? He replied that, on the whole, he was not unhappy. Solitude suited him, and Heidelberg was not a place of solitude. He loved the very emptiness of the New World, its sense of possibility. They logged, he observed, in much the same manner as they did in the Old Country, but here the spaces over which they could range were limitless. Sometimes when he was not preaching or reading or writing he simply went out and walked towards the horizon, exulting in the sheer immensity of it all.

But, for his parishioners, he confided, the open spaces did not seem to have produced open minds. It wasn't that they didn't know much that worried him; that could be remedied. It was that they resisted knowledge, found it threatening. Yes, he supposed he could understand even that, remembering his own early encounters with the Encyclopaedists, with Darwin, even with Pascal. Perhaps he could still bring them gently to explore new ideas with him. But then, was he right to do so? They understood life and death – or rather they accepted it in a way that precluded understanding. Was this so bad?

One Sunday night in January he replied to Hermann, a particularly close friend with whom he had read Kierkegaard:

> *The people here have no knowledge of anything since the mid-eighteenth century except for a hazy recollection of the Great War and a rather more vivid impression of the Halifax Explosion. Certainly, they are untouched by any of the discoveries of modern science or by Enlightenment thought. Yet they are not unhappy, because they accept everything as God's will and therefore to be endured rather than questioned or resisted. Their children die; their animals fall sick; they suffer appalling accidents while cutting trees in the woods – which is what they do all winter, frozen and isolated in a 'camp' a hundred miles from nowhere. But this is what life is like; they know nothing else. And they trust implicitly in an eternal reward, and far be it from me to cast doubts on that certain and touching hope.*

He leaned back in his chair and re-read it. It sounded like the report of an anthropologist, and a condescending one at that. He crumpled it up and threw it on the floor.

In fact, that air of detachment and cool observation was not all he felt by any means. He had seen into some of these people's lives with an intensity that his cool writing did not convey. There were secrets here that he longed to uncover. Something about Aaron. He was hiding part of himself, Johannes could feel it. He talked a lot about guilt, and how it could be expiated. Why? And what about the young people? What an extraordinary work Nathan had produced with only the barest hint of what he should do! When he had asked him how he had known what the Virgin should look like, he had said simply, "I thought of Erika." Who was Erika? "She's my sister, but she's gone away." He hadn't felt it right to press him further.

And there had been another girl who was no longer here, he had heard – the eldest in the Miller family. She had died, but no one seemed to care much or talk about her except old Mrs. Ben Wentzell, who called her a saint. If she had been a saint, why had no one else noticed, and why was she forgotten so quickly?

And last of all, there was Emma. He could not pretend to be indifferent to Emma, pretty and headstrong and gifted. Something good should happen to her in life, something wonderful. Then he told himself he must not think this way. He ceased writing and began to read again until he was tired enough that he knew he would sleep.

Spring came at last and then, scarcely without a pause, full-blown summer. The air was thick with the buzz of cicadas; the ground was pinky-purple with pale laurel. Emma could hear the buzzing and smell the flowers through the open church windows on Trinity Sunday. She tried to concentrate on the sermon, but her thoughts kept drifting away. This was a pity, because the adults were obviously concentrating all too well. It was summer vacation and Reverend Selig had said there would be no more Confirmation classes until school resumed in the autumn.

"The Trinity," Reverend Selig was saying, "is three different manifestations of God, three different ways of looking at Him. This is how there can be three persons and yet one God. Think of water that can be frozen or turned into water vapour, a gas." They were fascinated by the science, but somewhere in the pits of their stomachs, fear churned. How could this God be real, a God who spoke to them, who saw the little sparrows fall, who was with them as they were dying? The Trinity was three people, and they had pictures of each in their mind: the Father sitting on a throne in Heaven, remote and judgmental; the Son, smiling benignly at mankind, pleading with the Father for weak humanity and asking him to put away his wrath; and finally the Holy Ghost who, admittedly, did not have a human form but was like a dove pointing downwards, giving them faith and courage. These three could talk to one another and come to decisions regarding human affairs, one moderating the views of the others, and if they were really all the same thing, how could they do this, how could you explain both judgment and mercy, anger and love? "So today," Reverend Selig was concluding, "we celebrate the reality of God in his three manifestations, yet one God, indivisible."

The people of Waldenstein had never contemplated anything so unreal. Real was concrete, something that you could picture, not an abstraction. Was this man a Christian at all? Should they be listening to this? Was it heresy? Who had sent this man, and why had he come?

Summer was busy, "not a good time of year" for extra commitments, but nevertheless, they decided to hold a meeting. It was not Aaron who initiated this, but Ebenezer Conrad. Since he lived on the very edge of Waldenstein, beyond even Aaron's house, they decided to meet at Jacob's.

The following Saturday morning all the men assembled – Zachariah, Ephraim, Ebenezer, Benjamin, Jacob, Aaron, Josiah – an Old Testament roll call of men. Women were not invited nor were boys like Nathan and Obadiah. Hibbert was included, but then everyone knew he would say nothing. Frederika had baked a fresh batch of molasses cookies, so there they all sat around the kitchen table eating the cookies, drinking black tea and contemplating God.

"It's the children I'm worried about," Ebenezer began. "You've been to some of the classes, Aaron, what does he teach them?"

"Nothing real bad, I don't think (if I did think, you can believe I'd take my girls out pretty quick), but some of it is – different."

"Different, yeah, that's what I'd call it too," Ben chimed in. "That's what most of his sermons are anyway."

Old Josiah Veinot added dryly, "Yeah, if by 'different' you mean 'heretical'."

"No, no, I wouldn't go that far." Aaron could see the alarm on the others' faces. This was the first time in their lives any of them had criticized a minister. "Look at what he said about the Trinity. He didn't deny it, he just explained it differently."

Jacob slowly put down his teacup and leaned forward. "But what about Creation? Nathan and Obadiah came home saying he had told them stuff that seemed real strange. Like there were two stories about Creation. Does he think God got things mixed up and wrote it out twice?"

"And he says it didn't happen in seven days after all! What about that?" Zachariah sounded personally affronted.

"He's an educated man. Maybe he's right." Of all of them, Aaron had the most touching faith in education.

"More educated than God?" This was Josiah again.

"We don't know the mind of God," Aaron pronounced solemnly.

"We got the Bible. All you need to know is how to read." Jacob felt that here he must be on firm ground.

"How to read! He's telling us we don't know how to read, we're readin' it wrong." Thus Ebenezer drew the controversy into even more dangerous waters.

Frederika came round with more molasses cookies. They each took another one, chewing nervously.

They were discussing things that were essential to their eternal happiness. To condemn a minister wrongly would be a terrible sin. But wasn't the devil always there, ready to tempt you; didn't Luther throw his inkpot at him once; didn't they pray every morning in Luther's morning prayer that the devil might have no power over them?

"Maybe he thinks the devil isn't real, just like he thinks the Trinity isn't real, it's just steam," Ebenezer concluded.

"Maybe he *is* the devil." Josiah Veinot, always giving voice to the unutterable, added.

"We mustn't say things like that; we mustn't even think them. They are wicked in themselves." Aaron felt things were getting out of hand.

"Well, he's not like us," Jacob concluded.

This was unanswerable because it was true.

"It's cloudin' over." Jacob pulled back the white curtain and squinted out at the sky.

"So what are we going to do?" Ebenezer felt that after an hour and a half things had to come to an end. He had hay to rake and stack before it rained.

"Nothing. Let's just wait and see." So Aaron had the last word, and they all went their separate ways.

Everything started up again in the autumn. Nathan began to carve a few more shepherds and animals for the Nativity scene. Emma resumed her study of Latin. By now she could translate some of the simpler passages from Caesar and could not resist showing off to Virtue. "You can say things so nicely in Latin, you have no idea, Virtue. It's just so concise. Like *Veni, vidi, vici.* That means, I came, I saw, I conquered. But doesn't it sound nicer in Latin? All the words begin with the same sound, and have the same rhythm."

"And does your minister whisper these lovely things into your ear, my little sister?" replied Virtue.

"You can be really horrid, Virtue. I'm only trying to teach you something!"

"Maybe I don't want to know."

One day after they had spent an hour reading and discussing Caesar and Emma was packing up her books to go, something strange happened. Reverend Selig, standing very straight and looking somewhat stern, said, "I would wait for you."

"I'll be finished putting my stuff away in a second and you can lock up."

"No, that's not what I meant."

"What then? Wait for what?"

"I meant until you have finished school and teacher training college." He stood impassive, holding himself still against any false move.

Only then did she grasp his meaning, or thought she grasped it.

She felt herself blushing. "Oh, I don't…know. I…."

"No, of course you don't." And he turned away, back towards the altar while she made her way towards the door.

She was trembling with joy, excitement and fear as she made her way home. It did not occur to her that this was perhaps the strangest proposal of marriage any girl had ever received. All she knew was that she must keep it secret. The consequences, otherwise, for him as well as for her, would be unthinkable.

❧

Both the confirmation class and Emma's Latin progressed apace. In Luther's Catechism they had completed the Ten Commandments and the Lord's Prayer and were now studying the creed. "I believe that Jesus Christ, true God, begotten by the Father before all worlds, and born of the Virgin Mary, is my Lord…"

"What does 'begotten' mean?" Emma blushed for Joan, who was always asking dumb questions.

"Begotten means that a Father makes a child."

"What about Mary? And what is a virgin?"

This time Virtue as well squirmed.

"A virgin is a woman who isn't married." (Obadiah sniggered.) Reverend Selig went on, "In this case, the fact that she wasn't married meant that Jesus could have no father other than God."

Towards Emma, either in company or when alone, he behaved with the utmost propriety – so much so that she began to think she had dreamt the conversation of a few weeks ago, that it had proceeded from her imagination alone.

Yet she could not stop imagining. Suppose she did become Mrs. Selig and was incorporated into the exotic mental world she was sure he inhabited. Perhaps he would return with her to the place they always called the "Old Country," and which, for Emma, held all the romanticism and excitement that the new lacked. She might see the originals of the carvings that Nathan had modeled his work on; indeed, Johannes (for she allowed herself to call him this in imagination) might have such a church himself. She envisioned herself, as in a Christmas card she had seen once, walking towards the stone porch of this church on a snowy Christmas Eve in a tight-bodiced and full-skirted coat, with the sound of bells bursting all about her.

All this imagining took up a lot of time, and Virtue found her remarkably uncommunicative during their usual chats in bed.

"What's wrong with you? You're wool-gathering."

"Sorry. What were you saying?"

"I said I'm going to New Germany to school. Papa's going to pay for me to board there. He says the school there is better."

Virtue had failed to get her grade nine, and this made sense, if only to enable her to avoid the humiliation of being in a class of girls, including Emma, who had now caught up with her.

"Why's he leaving me here then?" Was Emma, after all, number two in her father's affection?

Virtue had thought of this as well and rubbed it in. "Maybe he doesn't care as much about you."

"That's not true." Deep down, they both knew Emma was his favourite.

"Well, work it out for yourself then. I don't know."

So Virtue went away during the week, returning only on Friday night so that she would not miss Confirmation Class. If you missed more than two classes in a row without a good excuse you could not be confirmed in the spring. An exception was made for the boys who worked in the woods in winter; they had to make up classes at Christmas and at the very end, just before Easter, after the ice had melted. Emma missed Virtue, but, on the other hand, it was nice to have the bed to herself.

On the Saturday of the second week in October, when Johannes collected his pile of letters from the little post office and scanned through them he saw that one was from his old mentor in the philosophy department at Heidelburg. Doctor Gustafson had been very kind to Johannes, and, indeed, it had been he who had suggested he look for a placement abroad "just for a year or two, until you are fully rested." He must have had strange ideas of Canada if he had thought working here would rest anybody, Johannes had reflected after a month or two in Nova Scotia. Still, Johannes was glad to hear from him. He opened the letter as soon as he reached his house, but then there was a message to go and visit a Mrs. Ramey in New Germany who had fallen and might not last the night, and, when he got back from giving her the last rites, there was a sermon to write for the next day. So he stuffed the letter in his service book, thinking he might read it on the way to Waldenstein the next morning, if his horse behaved himself.

Unusually, he was giving Emma her Latin lesson on Sunday rather than Saturday this week, and now, Mrs. Ramey having died in the night, he was in a hurry to leave as soon as they had completed a reasonable amount of translation in order to visit the Ramey family. He explained this to Emma and, indeed, was out the church door before she was. As she bent down to pick up her book bag she saw a piece of paper under the pew ahead where he had been sitting and, curious, picked it up. It seemed to be the page of a letter written on a cream-coloured sheet in a fancy, curly hand. It must have fallen out of one of Reverend Selig's books. What should she do with it? She could save it and give it back to him, or she could leave it on the floor where it lay and where Ebenezer, who cleaned the church, would find it and throw it into the stove. She convinced herself that leaving it for Ebenezer would not be the best course, so she picked it up. Of course she would not read it.

As she walked home, the sheet of paper, ornamented with language, tormented her. Who had written to him? What might it say? She longed for some further glimpse into the hidden depths of his life. And since he had asked her to marry him, more or less, did she not have the right to get to know him in any way she could? She took the letter out and studied it. "Lieber Johannes," it began. Of course it was in German! How stupid of her to imagine she could read it. Anyway, should she read it? She knew, absolutely, that she should not. Why then had she stuffed it inside her catechism and taken it home?

What should she do next? She could not read it. But she believed her mother could. Agnes' parents had spoken German with some frequency in their home; Rose had understood German. So probably her mother did as well.

After dinner that evening when Agnes was sitting darning socks Emma approached her. No one else was in the sitting room.

"Mama, I found something today."

"What?"

"A letter – or part of a letter. It fell out of Reverend Selig's Bible."

"Well, keep it and give it to him next Saturday at class."

"But it might be important."

"What do you mean? Papa isn't going to saddle up Josh just to take a letter all the way to New Germany. If the minister needs it he can come to find it himself." Agnes was tired; she sighed.

"But if you looked at it, maybe you could tell whether it was important or not." She suddenly found herself capable of such wiles of self-justification.

"Why me?"

"Because it's in German. I can't read it but I thought maybe you could."

Now Agnes, even more than Emma, knew that the last thing one should do was to read someone else's correspondence. Yet she acquiesced and took the letter Emma held out to her. The mystery of this man held her in thrall as well – and she didn't even know he saw her daughter as a prospective wife. She began to peruse the fancy script. At first it seemed to defeat her; then she said, "It seems to be from a friend in Germany. He hopes Johannes is well, and that the period he spent in the sanatorium in Switzerland has done him good."

"What is a sanatorium?" Emma interrupted. Agnes ignored her.

"What a good idea it was to send him out to the wilderness to complete his cure. No stress, no theological arguments, no love to distract him – just beautiful landscape and docile people who must be glad to have such a gifted teacher. Surely there he is recovering the balance of his mind and the good humour for which he was always noted before his unfortunate breakdown. That's all. Then it goes on to another page. Maybe it's not from a friend but from a former teacher; I can't tell."

Agnes paraphrased the letter with some hesitancy, not only because of the difficult handwriting, but because some of the words were unfamiliar to her and had to be worked out from the context – and, also, as she continued, because she knew she never should have consented to read it. But she had read it. What to do now? Give it back to Emma, tell her to give it back to Reverend Selig and pretend no one knew what it said? Easier said than done. Emma herself began to ask insistent questions. What does it mean? Why does he need to "recover the balance of his mind," and what was his "unfortunate breakdown"?

"It would seem that he had mental difficulties."

"But he's so clever!"

"Not that sort of difficulty."

"You mean he was crazy?" The idea seemed preposterous to Emma even as she uttered it.

"Well, yes, possibly."

"No, no! He can't be!" And Emma began to cry.

By now Agnes had made a decision. "I must show the letter to Papa. It was very wrong of you to bring it here, but now that we've read it we must let him know what it contains."

Aaron looked grave when Agnes paraphrased the letter a second time for him. "So that explains it."

"What? What does it explain?" Emma was hovering, still tearful.

"Well, we thought he had some strange ideas – you know like double accounts of things in the Bible, creation, some of the parables and so on. We thought it was just that he knew too much. But now it seems it is because he's out of his mind."

"No, that's impossible. He's not out of his mind. Everything he says – both in Confirmation Class and when he's teaching me Latin – makes perfect sense. He makes more sense to me than any of you lot!" And she ran up the stairs to her room that, mercifully, was free of Virtue who had gone back to New Germany to be ready for school in the morning.

Madness. The very idea, with its suggestion of possession, lack of control, blasphemy – all those Biblical precedents – terrified the people of Waldenstein. When they thought of madness they thought of creatures that had nothing to do with them, beings far removed from God and man, hidden gibbering and salivating behind a curtain, running wildly out into the street cursing and killing. "Of course he was mad" they might say of a man who howled at the moon in the dead of night, ate his own offspring, burned down his house with his family in it. These things were never actually seen, but everyone knew they could and did happen – somewhere else. In their own community, of course, no one ever went mad. They might be "peculiar," or "queer," or "not quite like the rest of us," but they were never mad. Hibbert's hiding in a ditch by the road all day as a child rather than facing school, Sophia's refusal to get out of bed for a year, Josiah Veinot's erratic outbursts, Flora's fits of uncontrollable, smashing anger – all of these were domesticated by their very choice of words.

Aaron, too, held this deep, primitive fear of madness. However wrong Emma had been to take the letter and give it to her mother to read, he could not keep the knowledge that it contained secret. The greater wrong, he convinced himself, lay with the Synod or whoever had sent this lunatic to them, believing he would never be found out. Well, he had been found out, and something would have to be done.

Another meeting was called, this time at Ben Wentzell's house. Sophia hovered around providing tea and biscuits hot from the oven. Aaron told them what had been discovered.

"Well, I guess it all makes sense now, don't it?" Ebenezer Conrad leaned back in his chair as if calmly making a judicious observation.

"And what about all that Latin he was teachin' Emma?" Jacob added. "Nothin' good was ever goin' to come of that. She told Nathan some o' those words and they sounded like abracadabra to me. Spells, I tell you."

Aaron stiffened at this. "There's nothing wrong with Latin. It's an ancient language used by the Romans."

"Yeah, and they was heathens, I bet." Jacob spoke with venom, the new cause giving him the right to vent his old anger against Aaron.

"He's gotta go – and fast." Josiah Veinot was never one to think long about a problem. But in this case, they were all agreed in the space of half an hour. The leaders in the Church in New Germany were quickly informed and were as horrified as the people of Waldenstein. He had to be removed. The only question remaining was who was going to tell him.

This, the New Germany contingent insisted, must fall to Waldenstein since they had discovered the matter. They all felt that his closeness to Aaron's family ruled him out. And anyway, he declined, knowing that his own hands were not altogether clean in this matter. Similarly, after his kindness to Nathan, Jacob declined. So, in the end, it had to be Ebenezer. They agreed that the Saturday confirmation class would carry on as usual, and Ebenezer would tackle him after the Sunday service.

This left Emma in the awkward position of having both the confirmation class and her Latin lesson in the interim, when she knew her Johannes was going to be asked to leave, but he did not. She fidgeted; she could not answer the questions; she failed to recite the Bible passage assigned for memorization. Reverend Selig raised his eyebrows, but did not reproach her.

When they were alone for the Latin lesson, he asked her if she had seen a sheet of a letter that he might have dropped last week. Terrified, heart pounding, she replied that yes, she had found it and picked it up. Then, because she had feared such a thing might happen and had insisted on having the page returned to her, she added faintly, "Here it is."

"Thank you so much. If you had left it on the floor our friend Ebenezer might have found it and tidied it into the stove."

"Yes, I thought of that."

And so the lesson proceeded. At length it was over and she was free to run home, which she did.

The following morning the congregation emptied the church quickly after the service, while covertly watching Ebenezer sidle slowly up to Reverend Selig.

"Can I have a word?"

"Of course. Do you want to stay here or go into the vestry?"

"Here is fine." Ebenezer had the mad thought that if things went wrong he might need the support of the congregation now gathered watching from the church's front porch and lawn.

"It ain't that we don't like you," he began.

Reverend Selig stiffened, suddenly nosing what was coming. He knew that good news never began with someone telling you that, really, they did quite like you.

"But we've found somethin' out. Maybe we should've knowed sooner."

"What have you discovered?"

"There was a letter."

"A letter?"

"Yeah. A letter you dropped."

"Oh, you mean the page of the letter from my old mentor Gustav at Heidelberg. Yes, Emma gave that back to me yesterday morning." He sounded nonchalant, but the full truth of what had happened now dawned on him.

"Yeah, that letter." Ebenezer rested against the end of the pew for support.

"Well, what did it say then? I assume you must have read it," said Johannes icily.

"No, we didn't read it. Only a few of us like Agnes can read German, especially German like this."

"So this is hearsay."

"Not exactly. Agnes told Aaron, and he told the rest of us." Thus the whole truth tumbled out.

"Did you not feel that you should not be reading private correspondence?"

"Well, there's two ways of lookin' at that. You see, yes, we know we shouldn't read others' letters, but then when somethin' is deliberately kept from you and the wool is pulled over your eyes, perhaps you need to try to find out what you can when you have the chance." These country people could be wily, not so stupid after all, and strangely capable of finding moral justifications for what they had done when necessary, Johannes reflected. And maybe, just maybe, they did have some right on their side.

"So, to come to the point, what did you find out?"

"That you was mad." Blunt and to the point, definitely.

"Mad? How did you conclude that?"

"From the letter. It said that you was in a sanatorium and hoped that you would recover from your madness."

"I don't think that was the word the letter used. But in translation…"

"No, but we figured that's what it meant."

"You figured." A certain scorn crept in here.

"What else could it mean?"

"Naturally, if the people here no longer want me to minister to them, I shall go. You can be sure of that. You can tell your friends, whom I know are waiting for news outside, that there will be no difficulty about my leaving." And he rose and walked into the vestry.

Later that day, safe in his study, he re-read the first page of the letter. He read it with the eyes of Aaron and Ebenezer. He particularly noted the unflattering reference to the docile people he now worked among. Had he given Gustav that impression of the people here? He wrote to him very infrequently, but could there have been something in what he had said that led him to that conclusion? Docile! Ha!

Then he came back to Emma. Had he offended her? Why had she given the letter to Agnes to read? Or was she just curious, the curiosity of a young girl whom he had believed admired him. Yes, he could have loved her. Now even saying good-bye was impossible. He took out his pen and began to write – to the President of the Synod, tendering his resignation; to the shipping line that had brought him over, requesting a reservation, to a friend in Germany explaining that things had not worked out and that he would be returning. Could he try and find an academic post for him? It didn't matter whether it was particularly prestigious; he just needed something to enable him to live. Then at last he thought what he should – what he could – write to Emma. He simply wrote: "As you know, I am leaving. I have enjoyed teaching you. Keep up your Latin, and good luck."

The following Sunday there was no service. He had gone.

Only then did Waldenstein look at itself in consternation and under-stand what it had done. "We *fired* a minister," Jacob said to Frederika over dinner one evening, incredulity in his voice. Technically Rever-end Selig had submitted his resignation, but that was not how it would be seen and reported in the outside world. And it *would* be seen and reported.

One week later, to Jacob's consternation, a strange man turned up at his house. He wanted to see the person who was "in charge" of the Lutheran congregation in Waldenstein. Now who might that be? Whatever else, Jacob was certain it was not himself. Aaron seemed as good a candidate as any. At least he had the gift of the gab.

So later that afternoon, just as Aaron was beginning to pack pro-visions for the winter stay at the logging camp, he was confronted by the said person who, of course, turned out to be a Halifax newspa-per reporter. What could Aaron tell him about the decision to dismiss Reverend Selig?

"Well…it was just that he didn't seem suitable for us," Aaron re-plied with studied casualness.

"Not suitable? In what particular way?"

"Hard to say exactly." Aaron had never before felt himself at such a loss for words. It was dawning on him that what they had done could have consequences beyond his imagining.

"Did he behave…unsuitably…with the young people?" The re-porter clearly hoped for a gem of real scandal.

"No, no. Nothing like that. It was more…more the way he talked."

"You mean you didn't like the fact he spoke with a German ac-cent?"

"No, no. Not the way he talked so much as what he said." Aaron was not used to having to clarify everything in this maddening way.

"But he was very well educated, was he not?"

"Oh, indeed, that he was."

"Could you not understand what he said?"

"Oh I think we understood him, all right. It was just…different… from what we'd been used to."

"In what way?" This man would not give up. He came for a story, and he was going to have one.

"Well, he talked about different stories of Creation, and different versions of parables, and it got sort of confusing for us. He even talked about something called 'evolution', I think that's what he called it, once – an idea that, as I understood it, said we didn't come straight from God but were related to monkeys. At least that's what we thought he was saying. He didn't really make much of that, because we told him to stop since there were impressionable young people listening."

After this and a bit more of the same the reporter thought he understood what all the fuss was about. "**Ignorant Country Folk Expel Pastor**" the headline to the article read a few days later. Since no one in Waldenstein got a daily paper, this did not greatly disturb its people.

Quite apart from the scandal of having got rid of a minister, something much deeper began to trouble Aaron. A small nagging doubt haunted his days and nights. The reporter had seemed to laugh when he had told him about the different accounts of miracles and about Creation not being true. Aaron was always seeking to know new things. Suppose Reverend Selig was right? Suppose the Bible wasn't true. Or at least not true as Aaron had always believed it to be true. Suppose Job was just a made-up story – one of the other heresies Reverend Selig had let slip. Suppose….

෨

Aaron's distress was as nothing to that which engulfed Emma. She was angry – a bitter anger mingled with guilt. It was all her fault. If she had not picked up the letter, if she had not shown it to her mother, if she had not been so curious, none of this would have happened.

She had read some of the classical myths with him, and she recalled Pandora.

His note to her – it read so coldly. There was no reproach, though he must know how the letter had reached all of Waldenstein. But neither was there any affection, any forgiveness, any thought that he might see her again. And why should she expect that? He would *not* see her again. This seemed impossible, and she wept inconsolably in her room.

But things like this did happen, she reflected. Look at Erika. None of them would ever see her again, even if she were alive. Maybe that was what life was like; the cast kept changing, and unlike plays you read in books, some people you knew just walked off stage left and vanished. Or perhaps, from their perspective, it was you who vanished. There was no continuing plot, just bits of stuff that happened without an overriding story. What had been the story of Rose's life? She had only bit parts in the life of her parents and siblings from the age of one. She had a moment of fame when she resurrected Sophia from her torpor, but then she simply slid into sickness and oblivion. It didn't make a great story.

That weekend she tried to talk some of this through with Virtue.

"Do you ever think how odd some of the things that happen are?"

"Like what?"

"Like Erika and her baby just disappearing."

"Well, that was probably all for the best." Virtue took a practical view of this, as of most things.

"Or like Rose hardly having a life at all and then just dying."

"I was sorry about Rose, but I'm sure she's with God now."

"But I mean, all this stuff happens to people, and it doesn't make sense. It's not even a good story."

"Whatever happens must happen for a purpose because God does it all."

Virtue's God needed simply to know what He was doing; Emma's needed some literary acumen. "Well then he's not very good at working out plots. He should take some lessons from Shakespeare."

215

Virtue was genuinely shocked. "Emma!" She thought a moment. "Is this really all about *your minister* and the fact that he's had to leave?"

"He didn't *have to leave*. He resigned; he left." Emma stamped her foot, near tears.

"Everybody knows he was forced out because he was crazy and preaching heresy."

"That's not true." And then she did really begin to cry, and Virtue went in disgust down to Agnes in the kitchen.

Left alone, Emma thought about the rocks that had scratches all going in the same direction. She remembered Mrs. Oliphant, no longer in Waldenstein, who had doubted the textbooks, saying that it couldn't be true because God had done it all. Now Mrs. Oliphant, who had defied the textbooks in defense of her faith, was teaching in New Germany, a promotion. Reverend Selig had given a rational interpretation of the creation story in the Bible and was exiled to the old Germany.

A New Generation

Skirting Sex

1923

Aaron felt the community hardening against him. Why always him? Because he was the person who took the lead in doing things, he told himself. It was he who had told them about the letter, he whose daughter had been singled out by the minister to learn goodness-knew-what inscrutable language.

At first they had been glad Reverend Selig was gone. But then as the months went by and no one replaced him, they began to turn. Who would bury them if they died? Or come to visit them before they died? Already there were unbaptized babies, and while they had persuaded the Mahone Bay minister to confirm those whom Johannes had instructed, that had been an act of generosity on his part, not to be repeated. He had made that perfectly clear.

"Well, you got rid of one for us, now how about using your cleverness to find us another!" Ebenezer, of course.

What could he do? He turned inward, to his family, and, in particular, to that part of his family upon whom his hopes rested. Harry, his one and only son, was nine, a large healthy boy with his father's piercing blue eyes and dark hair. He had already developed a high opinion of himself matched in intensity only by his contempt for the female half of the human race. From infancy he had been served by women, so naturally he imagined that this was the designated order of things. Aaron did nothing to deflate his hubris. Now he singled Harry out to be instructed in wood lore.

In March, when he came back from the logging camp, he made it a daily practice, as soon as Harry was back from school, to take him out into the woods and teach him about trees – good trees and bad trees, trees ripe for cutting, and trees that should be left for a few more years, trees that were diseased and what, if anything, you could do about it, trees that were good for lumber and trees that could only be used for firewood. In this Harry was an apt pupil. School did not interest him. Despite Aaron's love of books, Harry perceived that reading was something girls did. He spent most of his time in the classroom flicking bits of his slate pencil at any girl within range or carving intricate patterns on the underside of his desk with a penknife. Trees and woodlands were a great relief.

"So what about that spruce tree there? Should we cut it down or let it grow a bit more?"

"Cut it down, because look – the little branches are bunching together at the top. That means it won't grow much at all anymore; it's getting ready to die."

"And what do you use spruce wood for, my boy?"

"It's good for framing houses, or even for floors and trim inside, but it's not as pretty for that as pine, and if you use it for a floor it will dent very easily."

"What would be a better kind of wood for a floor?"

"A hardwood like oak or maple or birch or ash."

"And what is the chief difference you can see between hardwood and softwood trees when they're growing in the woods?"

"Hardwood trees have leaves that die and fall off in the autumn, while softwood trees have needles that don't drop – except for hackmatack."

Gradually Aaron taught him how to cut a tree, how to assess in which direction it should fall, and then how to make the notch in that side of the trunk and saw from the opposite side.

Aaron swelled with pride in his son; but others noticed things that Aaron didn't. Emma watched him puff himself up like his namesake of old. And the way he addressed her and his other sisters was simply astonishing! "Do get my slippers from by my bed, Emma. My feet are all hot and tired from walking in these boots." Or "Can you find my penknife? I don't remember where I put it." It was infuriating or funny depending on your mood at the time.

Agnes tried to intervene. "I know he's a good lad, and he deserves to be praised for what he has learned in the forest with you, but look… his school report is not good at all. And he treats all the rest of us as if we were his servants. He needs to be taken down a peg or two."

Aaron refused to listen. "Oh the girls enjoy looking after him, playing mother."

She wanted to say, "Look how he treats me, his *real* mother." But she saw there was no point. And if she rebuked Harry himself, he would only appeal to Aaron, who would back him up. He strode around the house like a little prince with his sisters and mother as courtiers.

The one person who refused to defer to him was Flora. He rarely asked Flora to do things for him, probably because he thought anything she did would not be up to his requirements. But on the odd occasions when he did ask, she generally refused, not with an excuse, but just with an abrupt "No." And then Harry would make a face behind her back, but usually he let her alone.

One day in early May, Harry and Flora were alone in the house together. The girls were at school. Harry should have been, but had pleaded a sore throat, and Agnes and Aaron had gone to visit Zachariah and Muriel who were now less and less able to look after themselves.

Harry was lolling on the sofa as befitted his supposed invalid status. Flora was darning socks (she was very good at this sort of domestic task) in the rocking chair by the window. Harry was bored. His sisters would have been reading a book or playing the reed organ or helping Agnes in the kitchen. But indoors Harry could discover no occupation. So he said to Flora, "Can you get me a glass of water. I'm thirsty."

Flora refused. "Get it yourself. You know you're not *really* sick."

"I am so. Anyway, how would you know?" There was a casual contempt in his tone.

"Why shouldn't I know?"

"Because you're stupid." And then, warming to his subject, he went on, "And you look funny. Your eyes are crossed, your lip hangs down, and that wig doesn't look like real hair at all."

No one in the house had ever spoken to Flora like this before. Flora was "different"; she might be a little slow, but there was nothing too much wrong, really. She had a good, kind heart; she would do anything for you.

The younger members of the family knew nothing of her before that terrible night when she was eleven. To them she simply was what she was – a part of their lives, even if defective, rather like a piece of furniture with a missing arm or leg. After a while you scarcely noticed. She had never had a fit since that time, but the results of that one were permanent.

But never had Flora been spoken to by her own flesh and blood like this. She rose out of her chair and in an instant transformed herself into something wild and vicious – a cat, a tiger, strong and feline. Harry barely had time to raise his hands to his face before she was upon him on the sofa biting and scratching, flailing, and hurling herself at him with an animal ferocity. Now Harry, apart from the odd scuffle in the playground, had no idea about defending himself. He protected his face and other delicate bits of his anatomy as best he could, but he was pinned down on the sofa. Flora was large and surprisingly strong. And she was furious. She cried as she pummelled him, "You spoiled brat, you stuck-up pig, you wicked, wicked boy!"

"Stop, stop, you're hurting me!"

Flora was beyond stopping. She began to tear his shirt, pull his hair (unlike her own, rooted) and pull off his clothes.

Neither of them heard the door open, but Harry, face upwards on the sofa, was first to see his parents entering the room. "Mama, Papa, help, help!"

Aaron pulled Flora off Harry with one huge lunge. Flora flew sprawling on the carpet, and Harry became a crumpled, wailing ball.

"What do you think you're doing?" Aaron was furious.

Agnes, totally stunned, turned to Flora. "Flora, how could you!"

"He was calling me names." And Flora began to cry.

"What names?" This from Aaron.

"I didn't call her names. I just told her what she looks like. It was the truth. You said I should always tell the truth!"

"He said I was stupid and that my lip hung down and my eyes were crossed," blurted Flora through her tears.

"Did you say that, Harry?" Agnes knew Aaron would not ask, would not want to know.

"Something like that, maybe. But it's true, look at her, it's true!" It was almost a crow of triumph.

Then Aaron did take charge. "Both of you go to your rooms until Mama and I decide what to do."

Flora started away, but Harry stood, his scratches beginning to ooze blood, in the middle of the room.

"*Go!*" And Harry went, crying aloud as he did so.

"He's a monster." Agnes glared at Aaron. "You've raised a monster."

"And what about a girl who attacks a brother who is thirteen years younger than she is!" Aaron retorted.

"You always take his part. That's why he thinks he can speak to her as he has."

After a few minutes they both sat down out of sheer exhaustion – Agnes on the brown sofa, lately the scene of the battle, and Aaron in the window rocking chair.

"So what are we going to do?"

"Surely they must both be punished more or less equally." Agnes was trying to be conciliatory, because left to herself she would have smacked Harry thoroughly and let Flora off with a talking to.

"I had no idea Flora could be violent. I didn't know she had it in her. This could be serious, particularly if she attacked someone outside the family."

"Why should that happen? No one outside the family would be so cruel to her – no one inside the family except Harry. What would happen if he were to insult people outside the family as he has Flora? Have you ever thought of that?"

Aaron considered. What might happen if any of this spilled outside the home? Suppose Martha Conrad from across the lake had come over for a chat, as she sometimes did, and found Harry and Flora in a pile on the sofa; what would she have thought? And said? Suffering began in earnest, as Aaron knew all too well, when what was done in darkness was exposed to the light of public scrutiny.

Eventually, as the time for the girls to come home from school approached, Aaron and Agnes reached an agreement. Flora and Harry were each to have extra chores assigned for two weeks, after which they would apologize to one another and the matter would be forgotten. Harry would be forbidden to tell even his sisters what had happened to his face.

ॐ

What neither of them knew was that in that moment of biting and scratching, Flora had experienced something forbidden and wonderful. She could not have described what had happened but it had felt *good* to be writhing, screaming, pummelling another body. She woke at night with a strange beating in her forbidden regions. She knew they were forbidden because she had been told never to touch them from early childhood. She slept alone now in a single bed. One night when she could bear it no longer; she reached down and began to scratch. How could it be wrong to scratch yourself, she reasoned. Except even she could see that what she was doing was not quite scratching. It was rubbing, and rubbing as the pleasure grew more intense and finally something happened; she knew not what, but she knew it was over and she felt peaceful and sleepy.

The next night it happened again, with the same result. Now she longed to go to bed, and leapt in with expectation, not waiting for the inevitable throbbing invitation but actively soliciting it with her own hands. She had no idea why this might be wrong, but she was, nevertheless, convinced it was, so no one must know she was doing it. It became her secret life, a place where she was free from taunts and feeling that she was no good and less desirable than all her sisters. As the moist darkness enfolded her, she became one with something that made all the slights of the day irrelevant.

One warm June afternoon when the girls and Harry were still in school and her mother and father out haying, she felt she could not wait until nightfall. Left alone in the house to prepare supper for the family, she hastily washed some early lettuce, sliced some cold beef left over from the previous day and made sure there was lots of fresh white bread in the bin. Then she crept upstairs to her room, and the secret joy enfolded her. The white curtains blew softly in the westerly breeze, and the room was surprisingly cool considering the strong spring sunshine. Smells of lilac and apple blossom wafted in through the window. Flora would never hear of Zephyrus, but what she felt was the pure anticipation of pleasure. She lay down on the white bedspread and raised her skirt.

Time passed. She was in no hurry; the afternoon lengthened out to the slow plodding of the team of oxen whose tinkling bells sounded through the open window. Pleasure came in waves, rising and falling. Things grew dim. Then suddenly her mother's voice: "Flora, what are you doing?"

"I think I must have fallen asleep."

"And what were you doing before that?" Agnes had arrived at the bedroom door in time to take in the scene – Flora lying on her back, her panties in a dishevelled pile on the floor, her skirt drawn up.

"Were you playing with yourself, Flora?"

"Maybe a little." Even the way her mother described it sounded so innocent. "Playing with yourself." Why was it so wrong? But she knew better than to ask.

"A little! If you weren't so big I'd whip you, yes I would. You're turning into a thoroughly wicked girl."

Flora began to sob into the pillow. How could the one thing she had found that gave her life any pleasure be so wrong? It didn't hurt anyone else. Yes, maybe she should have made something more for supper – a cake for dessert. But her mother was not scolding her for being lazy. It was much deeper than that, she could tell. As she had suspected, what she was doing was very, very bad. Or was it bad only because she liked to do it?

"Come down and set the table when you're ready." And her mother was gone.

꙰

Agnes did not know whether she should tell Aaron or not. It was so private – a woman's secret. And how would she describe it? She didn't even know the proper word. Such things were never talked about, and quite right too. They weren't talked about because there was no need. They never happened! Thank goodness it had been she who found Flora, not Aaron. No, she wouldn't tell him.

But the matter of Flora nagged at her. What would become of her? She would never get married, that was certain. The other girls probably would, or they would become schoolteachers or nurses or *something*. But Flora – what of her? That she should have to go out and keep house for some old lady was inconceivable. The Millers didn't do other people's housework; the others worked for them.

So that evening, after everyone else had gone to bed, Agnes spoke to Aaron not of what had really upset her but in generalities that would arouse no suspicion. "You know we're not going to be around here forever."

"What now?" Aaron, after a hard day in the fields, was in no mood to contemplate his mortality.

"I was just thinking of Flora."

225

A certain impatience sharpened Aaron's reply. "You're always thinking of Flora, and it does no good. Flora is as she is, and we can't change her. Maybe God has a purpose for her we don't understand."

In the light of the direction Agnes saw Flora tending, she doubted this last.

"I was thinking about who would look after her when we're gone," she said carefully.

"Come on, there's lots of time for that yet." Why should he die? He, Aaron Miller, the richest man in Waldenstein and one who could still put in a good day's work haying.

But Agnes persisted. "Who knows? Do you even have a will?"

"You know I don't, and you know why. It's precisely because I don't know what to do about your precious Flora that I don't have a will. I don't have a will because I don't know how to make one, and I'm not deciding tonight."

And with that Aaron went upstairs.

Agnes sat for half an hour more, thinking about the future, a future that, for reasons she didn't wish to disclose to Aaron, she saw without herself in it. Everyone was sleeping now, quiet breaths drawn in each bedroom as if they were at one – but Agnes knew that each, in sleep, was living a completely separate life, private in dreams. Flora, what was she dreaming? Or doing? And the other girls, growing up so fast. Emma was now washing monthly the red cloths that marked her womanhood. Virtue had been doing the same for three years. Soon it would be the turn of Hannah and Joan. All these lives she had tried to nurture were unfathomable; they were stretching out, reaching for something she could not even imagine.

Moving On

1923–1924

Emma and Virtue were in a flurry of excitement. *Normal* College – why was it called that? For someone from Waldenstein there was nothing normal about going to any college – certainly not one that was as far away as Truro and trained you to be a teacher.

They pored over the Eaton's catalogue every evening discussing just which dresses, coats and hats would be most desirable. "One dress, one coat and hat, and two blouses and skirts each," Aaron dictated. Even this was extravagant by Waldenstein standards, but his pride meant that his girls must be equipped to meet the outside world – such as he knew of it. Thus restricted, it was even more important to make the right choices. The dresses would be of navy blue crepe with large lace collars; fortunately, there were two such dresses in subtly differing styles in the catalogue so they could be the same but different. Their coats would, of course, be wool against the bitter winds that everyone knew swept down the Minas Basin, through Cobequid Bay and up the valley to Truro. Virtue chose dark green, but Emma ordered a rich magenta. "You'll get tired of that," Virtue advised in a tone that spoke of the school teacher already.

"Well, at least I won't start out tired of it as I would if I got one like yours!"

The skirts would be dark brown and navy – serviceable colours but not so grim as black.

So they were fitted out, and the order was about to be placed when Emma was struck by a thought. All these clothes for classes and church on Sunday were very well, but might there not – oh hope against hope – be some evening parties at Normal College? Emma didn't really know about such things, but she had seen pictures in magazines that Frederika (once-pretty Frederika, who still set her hair weekly and got Jacob to buy the latest fabric from the store in New Germany) possessed that showed such events, glamorous women in long dresses inclining ever so slightly and modestly towards men in tightly cut suits. So where were their party dresses?

Here were two whole pages of them in the catalogue. Virtue, too, had seen them and had had much the same thoughts but considered it unseemly to mention it to Papa. It would look frivolous, and he always complimented her on her good sense. However, if Emma was prepared to take the risk (Emma's credit depending more on brains than good sense), she was prepared to go along with it.

"Look, Papa," said Emma, spreading the glories of the catalogue out before him, "here are dresses for going to parties. Don't you think we might need one of these at college?"

Aaron looked at the dresses and found them beyond comprehension. Little skimpy sleeveless things falling more or less straight down from the shoulder straps, festooned with diagonal frills or bows and made out of something called taffeta. But then, his girls were going out into a world of which he knew nothing, and he was proud of them. Perhaps in that world taffeta party dresses were indeed a necessity.

"We could order them and send them back if they weren't nice," Emma reasoned.

"It wouldn't hurt to have them to try on," even Virtue now chimed in.

And so, in the end, Virtue ordered a pale green dress with a bow modestly concealing what lay below the scooped neckline, and Emma ordered one in flaming red with diagonal frills wrapping round its straight lines from waist to hem. Strangely, once they arrived and had been admired, there was little talk of sending them back.

One glorious morning in early September, Aaron took the girls and their trunks with the horse and wagon to New Germany, where they would get the train. Indeed, he was so anxious about their safety that he ended up taking the train himself with them as far as Bridge-water so that he could supervise their change for the train to Halifax and thence to Truro. But that was a mistake. Because there, on the station platform of the small town, any illusion that he had done well by them was dispelled. His girls stood, huddled together in their new wool coats, their small trunks beside them, while round them swirled a company of bright young things with opulent mink collars, or with dead foxes hung around their necks, shiny high heels on their feet and stockings not of heavy lisle but of the finest silk. He was mortified. At least, he consoled himself, his girls had a party dress each.

For Emma and Virtue, as well, the comparison between them-selves and their contemporaries was not reassuring. How could they ever speak to these creatures from another planet? Where were they going? They overheard some of them talking loudly and confidently about "Dal" or "Acadia." Emma and Virtue dimly recognized them as universities they had heard of. These wondrous beings were clearly on their way to do something quite spectacular. Yet, they couldn't help noticing, they were really rather silly, talking about boys in terms that would have been strictly off-limits in the Miller family. "So I decided to scare him and not turn up. Make him jealous."

"And was he?"

"Oh yes, he sent me flowers the next day with the sweetest note. He thought I must be ill. Of course I never let on." Giggles all around.

At Halifax they had to change trains again for the line to Truro. Most of the giggling fashionable girls disappeared, leaving Virtue and Emma feeling very vulnerable as they tried to understand the signs that were everywhere in the cavernous station building and so con-fusing. "You girls looking for something?" A young man in a station attendant uniform approached them.

"Yes, please, where is the train to Truro?"

"It hasn't come in yet; but it'll be on platform two when it does. Why don't you sit down and wait?" And off he went, whistling non-chalantly.

So they sat and waited while the other seats filled up with girls from the city done up even more elaborately than those they had seen in Bridgewater.

"What do they need all that stuff for – muffs and fancy handbags – and look, there's one that I do believe is wearing rouge." Virtue was determined to retain some vestige of superiority. Emma meanwhile was quietly deciding that to look like these girls was definitely something to which she aspired – but not here, not yet. Still the sight of them was like a vision that might someday be realized.

They reached Truro at last. And there, as promised, was a generously-sized woman waving a large card that had "MILLER GIRLS" written in capitals. She ushered them into a car, black and shiny, and off they drove with their trunks strapped on the back. What a place Truro was! So large – streets and streets of houses, shops that sold clothes, restaurants with gaudy signs, a hardware store – how could one take it all in? At length they stopped outside a large white house with a veranda on the front, a bay window on the side and *three stories* in height. They crossed the veranda and went through a small vestibule with stained glass in the inner window ("It's like a church," Emma whispered to Virtue), and then straight into a large hallway with a heavy oak staircase ascending on the right. A young man who seemed to be standing there for the purpose lifted up one of the trunks, which had been deposited in the hallway, and started up the stairs. "Jim will show you your rooms straight away, and you can wash and unpack. Dinner will be in the dining room at six."

Up they went, up and up. On the landing they caught sight of lace-curtained windows, large plants growing in pots in front of them, a polished table with curved legs and a small lamp on top. There was a smell of – lavender? – something strange and mysterious. They continued on up a further flight of stairs, somewhat narrower and with thinner carpeting. The walls here were dark paneled wood, and when the upstairs hallway opened out it was not as wide or as well lit as the one below. But it was still amazing to the two girls. And they were to have *separate* rooms. Emma's was at the back and looked out over a small garden still blooming with dahlias and late roses. Virtue was at the front of the house, which had the noise of cars and horse carts passing by, but was also more interesting for people-gazing. In each room there was a single bed with a white bedspread, a washstand with a bowl and pitcher, and a small desk and chair. Virtue's room had a soft easy chair as well.

"Will this suit you then?" Mrs. Eagles asked.

"Oh yes," Emma gasped.

"Indeed," Virtue echoed.

This was luxury such as they had never seen at home.

"There'll be two other girls as well. They should be here any time now. I must go back in the taxi to collect them." So the car wasn't hers after all. But even so! What must Papa be paying for a place like this? He had said, "I want you somewhere respectable, somewhere you'll be safe." And so he had produced Mrs. Eagles, who was a relative of someone he sold lumber to in Mahone Bay.

As soon as the second trunk had been brought up and Mrs. Eagles had gone out for her further charges, the girls began to exclaim. And what struck them both was exactly what had struck Erika when she first went to Mahone Bay: most of the things in this house were not *necessary*. The deep carpets, the stained glass, the lace curtains, the lamps secreted in dark corners everywhere – they were all strictly unnecessary to the pursuit of life as the girls knew it.

"And what is all that carved stuff hanging down from the eaves on the outside of the house?" Virtue demanded.

"I have no idea. Maybe it's just decoration."

"*Just decoration.*" Virtue was outraged by the very idea. "No one would spend money on carving like that just to make something look nice."

"You never know." Emma was beginning dimly to apprehend a world whose values were different from those she had known, a world of wonderful possibility where dresses did not have to come from the catalogue and where one might even have more than just one party dress.

Soon the two other girls arrived. Violet and Amy appeared to be somewhere on the fashion spectrum between the stuck-up fashion plates they had seen at the Halifax station and themselves, Emma decided. Their coats were thicker and better cut than Virtue and Emma's, but they were not made ostentatious by fur or other elaborate trim. The two looked like what Agnes would have called "nice girls," and Emma and Virtue relaxed a little. Violet came from Windsor in the Valley where she said her father was a schoolteacher; Amy was from Antigonish; her father's occupation was not divulged.

At six o'clock, they all trooped down to dinner. It was growing dark now, but when they opened the door of the dining room they were overcome by a blaze of light. They had never seen electric lights before. The white tablecloth glistened, and the display of plates and cutlery was awesome. Emma and Virtue sat down with lowered heads beside one another. For once, even Emma was cowed. Food was put before them; they ate it, looking round furtively to see what the others were doing. Violet seemed wholly at ease, picking up the right knife and fork and wielding them simultaneously with practised skill. Emma and Virtue did as they had always done; they cut the meat up and then ate the whole meal with their forks. To their relief, Amy did the same, but Mrs. Eagles seemed to be operating on the same occult system as Violet. There was steak, potatoes, green beans and a little salad of lettuce and tomatoes on a side plate shaped like a half moon. Violet treated this salad as a separate course and ate it after everything else with a stubby fork that was simply left over in Emma's and Virtue's economy. Dessert was apple pie *with ice cream*. The girls had never had ice cream except at the Wentzell's Lake Picnic.

The other girls talked while Emma and Virtue mutely stared at the cutlery. Violet, it emerged, had done her grade twelve and would therefore be qualified as an 'A' grade teacher. Amy had grade eleven, which would entitle her to a 'B' licence. Poor Emma, then, was forced to admit that she, with her grade ten, was only eligible for a 'C.' Then it was Virtue's turn. "She's been ill a lot," Emma suddenly heard herself saying. Everyone looked with commiseration at Virtue, and the conversation moved on.

"Why did you say that? It was a lie," Virtue confronted Emma afterwards.

"I know. And you know why I said it."

"Did you see Violet smoking?"

"Yes. She got her packet of cigarettes out as soon as the coffee came." Emma was happy to be complicit in this joint bolstering of egos. There were, after all, some things *nice* girls didn't do.

"Did you like the coffee?"

"No. It's bitter and horrible. But the food is great," Emma replied. Then she went on, "Did you notice that string of beads that Amy carries around with her?"

"Yes, very odd. She seems to keep feeling them. Why doesn't she put them around her neck?"

"They're not very pretty." And for Emma, that settled it.

All this was whispered in Virtue's room after they went up for the night. Then they had to part as Emma went back to her bedroom over the garden. A cacophony of cats began to wail. Even when she switched off the light (and how odd was that, *switching off a light?*) the room still seemed luminous. Yes, there was a light that she could just see leaning out the window on a pole beside the road. It must be even lighter in Virtue's room. She thought of home. The dishes would have been done by now, and Mama, Hannah and Papa would be in the sitting room, Mama sewing, Hannah studying and Papa reading. The little ones would be in bed. And Flora? Flora would be sitting there too, maybe doing a little darning, maybe just sitting. Still, it all seemed very attractive. Emma got in bed and pulled up the soft duvet. She fell asleep almost at once.

Two hours later, she woke up. What time was it? Where was she? Then she remembered and began to cry. After a while she got up very cautiously so as not to wake anyone and tiptoed towards the front of the house. Slowly she opened the door of Virtue's room. She could see Virtue's face by the light of the streetlamp. It was smooth and relaxed in slumber, but when she came nearer she could see a wet trickle on her cheek. She pushed Virtue over as of old and crawled in beside her for the night.

ঌ

The next morning classes began in an imposing red brick building; its massive permanency struck terror into the girls' hearts. Silently they filed through the huge doors, the vast hallway open to the second floor, the miles of corridors, and at length found the room to which they were assigned for their first class. C's and D's were taught together in one group, and A's and B's in another. The desks at least were familiar – wooden and with the writing surface of each attached to the back of the seat in front. Virtue and Emma squeezed into one together, then noticed that, in contrast to the Waldenstein school, everyone else was sitting at a desk alone. Hastily Emma moved out to the desk behind. These girls did not have fancy dresses or coats; some were visibly poorer than Emma and Virtue. Like them, they were mostly country stock who had had no chance to get a higher grade. Of course both Violet and Amy were in the other section for their classes.

Mr. McKittrick entered – a short man with ginger hair, a ginger moustache, a Scottish accent, and a decidedly sadistic bent.

"Well, here we are again, a nice room full of country lasses, eager to save the world from ignorance. So how do we begin? Well, it seems we must actually learn something ourselves before we can impart it to others. So we begin with classes in math, in history, geography and literature, and then we go out into the wilderness of the Truro schools and practise teaching these things. Today we shall do math. We'll begin with a few simultaneous equations."

Emma crouched behind Virtue. Poor Virtue had nowhere to hide. "You, with the dark hair back in a bun, you *look* like a schoolteacher already. Come up here to the blackboard and see how you get on with this charming example." Now Virtue would not have known a

simultaneous equation if she had met it walking in the meadow behind her father's house. But what could she do? She got up, flushed
red, and walked to the blackboard on which Mr. McKittrick was
writing some incomprehensible figures with brackets and equal signs
randomly distributed through a maze of numbers and letters.

"I...I don't think I've been taught to do this before," murmured
Virtue.

"Well, see if you can figure it out now," was the helpful reply. "It's
perfectly logical."

Virtue stood, ungainly, a piece of chalk in her hand, head bowed.
Mr. McKittrick waited.

"You really have no idea how to do this at all?"

"No, Sir."

"You're even more ignorant than I thought. You, in the dark
green skirt, you come and try." And another hapless soul made her
way towards the blackboard.

As Virtue retreated, Emma could see the tears beginning to flow.
This man was a monster! But she would show him, if she could.

The class continued in much the same unproductive way until
at least half the girls were reduced to tears. At this point his mission
seemed to be accomplished for the day, and he said, "Now tomorrow
we shall plumb the depths of your knowledge of history. Could you
each please come prepared to talk about a Roman you particularly
admire?"

There was a mad rush to the tiny library in an adjoining building. Of course there were not nearly enough books to go around, and
those who failed in the book stakes went back to their lodging houses
contemplating suicide. But Emma had a plan. She had forgotten most
of the finer points of Latin case endings and conjugations, but she still
recalled a great deal of what Reverend Selig had told her about Roman history. She wouldn't talk about Caesar; everyone else would do
that – though she generously told Virtue enough about Caesar so that
she couldn't be humiliated again. She would talk about Cicero and
the Ciceronian style. She wrote it all out carefully before she went to

bed and found that instead of dreading the next day, she was actually looking forward to it. She didn't have time to cry that night, nor did she wish to go to Virtue.

She let some other girls bear the full brunt of Mr. McKittrick's sarcasm ("Well, you are a citizen of the world, aren't you. One whole fact about Caesar."), and then she put up her hand.

"A volunteer! A very Daniel! So, Miss, whom do you wish to tell us about?"

"Cicero, Sir."

"Cicero. An excellent choice. So what do you know about Cicero?"

And Emma poured out everything she knew about Cicero – his relationship to Caesar, his oratorical style, still known as the Ciceronian style, and concluded with a list of English writers of the Renaissance who had imitated this style in their own writing.

"And is there another style of Latin writing that contrasts with this and has also been imitated by English writers?"

"Yes, the Senecan style," said Emma without hesitation.

"Have you read Cicero?" Mr. McKittrick was genuinely amazed.

"No, Sir, I never got far enough with my teacher to read Cicero. We stopped with Caesar."

Mr. McKittrick was not precisely struck dumb, but he did seem to waver slightly as he said, "Thank you very much, Miss…?"

"Miller."

"Miss Miller."

That evening Violet and Amy crowded excitedly around her. "We hear that you really put Mr. McKittrick in his place today."

"How did you hear that?" Emma did not know about academic grapevines or the gossip of girls.

"From the other girls in your class. It's all over the college. We all hate Mr. McKittrick. He doesn't teach you anything, just tries to show you that you don't know anything."

On Sunday the girls were all expected to go to church. There was no Lutheran church in Truro, so Virtue and Emma went to the Church of England, a tiny congregation with less people than attended the church in Waldenstein. Violet went to the Methodist church. But Amy – *Amy was a Roman Catholic!* They discovered this when Emma finally asked her about the beads she carried with her. At first, "They're coral" was all she would say.

"They're lovely," said Emma, though she didn't think so really; they were a dirty orange colour. "But why do you always have them with you?"

"They're a rosary."

"A what?"

"A rosary. You use them for saying prayers. Like, 'Hail Mary mother of God...'." And suddenly Amy was rattling off something so quickly that Emma could barely follow it.

"I still don't understand. How do they help you to pray?"

"They help you to know how many times you've said the prayer, like the 'Hail Mary.' You move along one bead each time you say it and you know how many beads are on the string, so that way you can keep count."

"But why would you want to say the same prayer over and over?"

Now it was Amy's turn to be amazed. Why would you *not* want to say the same prayer over and over? She replied, "Because sometimes when you've done something wrong the priest tells you to say one hundred 'Hail Marys' or something like that."

"I see," said Emma. But she didn't at all. Perhaps the Catholic God was inattentive so you had to repeat things a lot to be sure he heard them. It still didn't make sense.

One Saturday Amy said, "Why don't you and Virtue come to church with me tomorrow."

Emma hesitated. "I'm not sure if we should."

"But why not? You'd be interested to see what it's like."

Now how could Emma reply, "Because we've been told you don't worship the real God and that the Pope is the AntiChrist."? Even Emma's candour stopped short of this. So it came about that the next Sunday she and Virtue rose early to be introduced to the worship of the Great Satan.

They dressed for church as usual – navy blue dresses with lace collars, hats, coats, gloves – and trotted off meekly behind Amy. The church was built of stone, not wood, because, as Amy explained, stone reminds one more of the eternal. They went in under an arch and past a small stone basin filled with water. Amy dipped a finger into the water and crossed herself. The symbolism escaped both Virtue and Emma, and from that moment on they were both struggling with a desire to giggle. People were kneeling in front of their seats. Amy led them to an empty pew and knelt down as well. When Emma and Virtue followed suit the wooden kneeler moved forward with an embarrassing squeak. They got out their handkerchiefs in an effort to suppress their mirth. Each wished the other was not there; alone their laughter could just about have been controlled; together it was irrepressible. At length the service began, but there were no hymns to sing. A church without hymns! Music was at the heart of their religion. Then the priest, dressed in elaborate robes of green and gold, began to sing out of key an indecipherable gibberish. It went on and on, rising tunelessly to the top of the mock stone buttresses and gables. At times in this long preamble, Amy and the others would bob down and up, quickly and inexplicably. At no time did they say anything. Then there was a sermon, short and perfunctory, but at least in English. After this the foreign gabble began again, and eventually they got to a stage where, after each name in an interminable list, everyone said something that sounded like "Orapronobis." Tiny bells rang; little boys in frilly white smocks pranced about solemnly carrying strange vessels; the priest came down the aisle with a large sugar-shaker on a chain and made everyone wet. Then they all knelt down again and the droning continued. Strangely, Emma did not recognize any of this as Latin, possibly because it was all done in a drone, possibly because much of the vocabulary was different from the classical writers, but most probably because she was concentrating all her effort on not laughing aloud. As everyone else went up to communion, Amy squashed her way past them saying, "You stay here!" They were mortified. Why had they come?

Finally it ended, and Emma and Virtue assured Amy that it had been "very interesting." Amy, head held high, walked home ahead of them. They knew they had done something awful – they had not only laughed in a church service, they had laughed *at* a church service. But it was only a Catholic church service, so maybe they wouldn't be damned for it.

After that, the weeks ran together, and before they knew it half the term had gone. Emma had earned the respect of Mr. McKittrick, and Virtue, as her sister, seemed able to shelter in the general aura of approval. Terrified, they went out to do practice-teaching. Reassured, they returned. Emma, in particular, found there was nothing more exciting than standing up on your hind legs before a captive audience and sharing with them something you really cared about. In math lessons the joy came from the clarity with which you could reach through the jumble of numbers and expose the basic logic, the elegant structure of it all. But in English it was far more than this – an opening out of the young lives before you to give them experience of others couched in the most eloquent of language. For Emma, contrary to all her expectations, teaching revealed itself as a romantic occupation.

But what of their party dresses, the red and green taffeta that still lay crushed and unworn at the bottom of their trunks? Some of the girls went out on Friday nights to dances organized by local charities. But they were "fast," Mrs. Eagles claimed; she did not encourage her girls to go. At the very end of term, however, there was to be a dance put on by the college itself, a Christmas ball, it was rather grandly called. Emma and Virtue got out their dresses and carefully ironed them. But how their glory had faded during three and a half months at the bottom of a trunk. What had seemed the height of fashion in Waldenstein looked skimpy and poor in Truro.

On the night of the party, Amy appeared in cream velvet, her sleeves caught up with little bows that ran down the sides of the dress as well and sprinkled themselves riotously at the hem. As for Violet, she was wearing *black*. But not just any black – a black broken and set off by flashing sequins that ran across the bodice, down a daringly abbreviated back and embellished the tight-wristed sleeves.

Emma and Virtue simply linked arms and walked together into the dimly lit dance hall, miserably aware that pale green and red skimpy taffeta just didn't make the grade at all. There were chairs down one side of the room and a band on a stage on the opposite side. Amy and Violet did not sit down but stood as near as possible to the floor where couples were already dancing, and conversed about nothing, simply making sure that their stance and faces were engaged and animated. Before long they were rewarded with a twosome of young men who swept them away to dance. Emma and Virtue, on the other hand, stood awkwardly beside the other two girls for a moment and then, realizing that they were not exactly welcome, slunk back and found themselves standing in front of two of the empty chairs. Then they were sitting in the chairs. This was all wrong, of course, and they knew it, but there they stayed, alongside other misfits, some even more embarrassingly out of fashion than they were. The evening wore on. Sometimes a handsome young man would appear to bound in their direction, but then he would fade away to the side, dimly visible out of the corner of an eye, flickering like a mirage.

Emma thought of Reverend Selig. How poor all these boys were anyway, compared with him! She retreated into her own private world. Then, strangely, Nathan was there with her. How funny he had been that Christmas when he came to see them all. But look at what he had done carving that manger scene! Now he worked for her father. Well, it wasn't his *fault* that he had had to leave school, was it?

Virtue roused her from her daydream. "They're going in to supper." Emma looked up. Other girls – gorgeous, sprightly, painted girls

240

– were taken in by equally handsome men whose hands circled their waists. They all seemed to be laughing at private jokes. So she and Virtue got up as well and slunk past the buffet tables, picking up a little food here and there, feeling they scarcely had permission to eat. Eventually they went home. They never spoke of it afterwards.

Another week and they were back in Waldenstein, fully qualified teachers, feted by their family and convinced of their utter insignificance in the grand scheme of things. Everything around them outside was white, and somehow that helped. It obliterated all significance in man or landscape and made a silent equality. Here they could stand again and plan for the future.

ᶘ

Nathan's future was less certain. The very day of Emma and Virtue's Christmas party, he had had a small adventure of his own. While moving logs out onto the lake, he had stepped on a patch of ice that was thinner than the rest. Perhaps someone had cut a hole out for fishing a day or two before, perhaps there was a peculiar current at that place, who knew? The ice cracked, and in he went, catching himself with his hands on one side of the ice that, miraculously, held. Stunned, he soon felt a long log pushed towards him. Already stiff with cold, he had just enough sense to hold fast to it so that he could be pulled out flat on the ice. Of course he was taken instantly to the camp for dry clothes, hot tea and general resuscitation. The following day he was back at work, reflecting that he was lucky not to have sunk beneath the ice without trace or fallen into more open water and drowned as his cousin, Dilphin, had. He had had a lucky escape.

Two days later, however, he felt very, very cold. It was not the coldness of the icy water but a shivery coldness that seemed to come from inside him. He couldn't breathe. After a bit he began to cough. Finally he put down the two-man crosscut saw that he was wielding with Obadiah and said, "I don't feel good. I'm goin' inside." Obadiah took this seriously. Men didn't just "not feel good" for nothing when the big winter cutting push was on. Obadiah went into the camp with him and then sought out Aaron. "Nathan's not so good t'day. Maybe you better go see him." So Aaron did. Half an hour later Nathan was making his way home. How he reached it he never knew. By the time he finally was at his front door he simply fell against it and waited for Frederika and Jacob to open it and carry him upstairs.

They brought the earthen crocks that served for hot water bottles and put them at his feet and side, but he was not warmed. Cold and thirst were the only things he knew. Discomfort was not localized, but everywhere. Soon he began to cry out in delirium. He was drowning; he was caught under the ice. Could they not see he was not a fish, he could not live there? "Cut me out," he cried. "Cut me out! I can't see down here, I can't swim, I can't breathe. For the love of God, cut me out." Because they were not privy to his nightmare, they could offer only general words of comfort. "It's all right. We're here. We'll see that nothing bad happens to you."

But still his imaginary struggle beneath the ice continued. The bedclothes writhed with his struggle. When they tried to hold him down, he only grew more frantic. "Let me out of the water, help me."

Jacob left for the doctor. He would know what to do. But alas, when Dr. Beale arrived, he didn't know. Of course he didn't tell Frederika and Jacob that. He used his stethoscope most impressively, muttered, "Looks like pneumonia," and poured some interesting red liquid into a bottle with instructions to take a spoonful every four hours. As a final gesture, he said, "Here's some pills. Give them a try. Three a day until they run out or...." He didn't finish, but they all knew what he meant.

ॐ

Emma felt this was impossible. Other people died – old people, of course, died. And young people like Ophelia or Dilphin died in terrible accidents. It was also true that her very own sister, Rose, had died of illness in her twenties. But all these cases, which might in their totality have made it seem very probable that Nathan – or, indeed, anyone in Waldenstein – might be marked for an early death, did not resonate in this way with Emma. Nathan was different. He could do things – carve the figures for the church Nativity, cut down more trees for her father than anyone else in a day, balance skillfully on the logs as he drove them down the river. Nathan was immortal, as she was. Or perhaps it was more complicated – her sense of her own immortality assured her of his. She couldn't bring herself to go and visit Nathan. She didn't want to see him like this. Later, when he was better….

Days passed. Christmas was only two days off, but Frederika thought it would be tempting fate to decorate a tree. Nathan raged and cried, gasped for breath and screamed. There was no escape for anyone in the small house. Obadiah, back from the woods for the holiday with all the men, took to doing large amounts of "barn work" where he could escape temporarily from the hell that home had become.

Then, on Christmas Eve, Nathan fell silent. He lay still looking up at the ceiling with glazed eyes. Privately, Frederika thought this was the end. In fact, Nathan was now enjoying a dream or vision as delightful as the others had been awful. He was back in the workshop again carving the Virgin for the Nativity set. The long folds of her robe were in place. Her hands were quiet in her lap. He reached up with his knife for a final adjustment to her smile. And then she looked directly at him. The smile he had created was just for him. "Don't worry, little boy," she said. (And it did not even seem odd that she addressed him as "little boy." It seemed just right.) "It's going to be fine for you, you'll see." She moved one hand from its resting place on her lap and brushed back his sticky hair. At that moment he saw that the Virgin was, in fact, Erika. Erika was soothing him. He shed a few quiet tears, and then he fell asleep.

It was Christmas afternoon when he woke up. The brightness in his room, sunlight reflected off the snow, seemed a portent. He felt cool and relaxed, sunk happily into the straw mattress as if nothing more might ever be required of him. He could hear distant voices downstairs. They must be in the parlour, he thought, since that was what was immediately under his room. Why were they in the parlour? Perhaps it was in anticipation of his funeral. But he didn't feel dead, just peaceful. He puzzled about this in a mild way, not really bothered, until Frederika put her head around his half-opened door.

"You're awake!" She came over to the bed and felt his forehead. "And I do believe you're on the mend." Then she went and called over the stair railing, "Come up everyone; Nathan is getting better!" And as they all – Jacob, Hibbert and Obadiah – streamed into the room, she began silently to cry. Nathan looked around for Erika; then he remembered. Erika was gone.

After a bit, Frederika recovered sufficiently to remember that there were a few Christmas presents for Nathan. She sent Obadiah downstairs to collect them, and Nathan suddenly understood why everyone had been in the parlour; of course, it was Christmas. How long had he been ill? More than a week must have passed.

He couldn't manage to open the gifts, so they were unwrapped and held up before him – nothing exciting, just a new pair of knit socks from Frederika, some sturdy boots from Jacob, a carved bird from Obadiah, which he presented hesitantly, knowing that Nathan could have done it better, and a large carved whistle on an elaborate braided leather band to go around his neck from Hibbert. "In case you fall into the lake again," Hibbert explained, and everyone laughed.

Some weeks later the doctor turned up, curious that he had not been summoned back to sign the death certificate. And there was Nathan, sitting up at the table, carving a piece of wood. "Well, so you didn't die after all."

"No, I did my best, but in the end I just couldn't bring it off." Nathan was not without his own wry sense of humour.

Dr. Beale examined him and declared he had made a most remarkable recovery. "Just take things easy for a few more weeks, and you'll soon be as fit as can be." Then he added, making sure that

Frederika and Jacob, who were hovering in the doorway heard, "Of course you can't go back to working in the woods."

"But why?"

"The cold, the damp – you'd be ill again in a year. And next time you wouldn't make it."

"But what can I do?"

"You'll just have to find something else. A job in a shop, maybe?"

What world did this man live in? The nearest shop was in Barss Corner; it was much too far to walk the journey every day, and no job in a shop paid enough to enable one to board.

Obadiah too was devastated. "If Nathan can't go back in the woods, I ain't goin' neither."

"Well you're not both sittin' around here eatin' me out of house and home." Jacob felt it was bad enough Hibbert had given up cutting wood and worked, or pretended to work, on the farm, which was barely a living for a couple, certainly not a family. Anyway, he couldn't leave the farm to all three of them.

For some days they pondered. The idea, when it came, seemed like a kind of accident. By this time, Nathan had not had his hair cut since three weeks before Christmas. It was the end of January, and the hair, falling down in wavy locks on both sides of his face, had passed all acceptable Waldenstein standards – though Frederika thought it quite endearing. He still wasn't strong enough to walk to the nearest barber in New Germany, however, so Obadiah said brightly, "Why don't I cut your hair?"

Was it a joke, or was he serious? Nathan decided he was game for it. So he sat on a high cushion on a wooden chair in the middle of the kitchen with two towels around his neck and over his shirt, and Obadiah began to snip. After a while, Nathan could see the floor was covered with little curls of dark hair. Obadiah could get it off at least! But what about the shape of that left on his head? "Just a bit more on this side so it's even." Obadiah was talking to himself as much as to Nathan. "Wait a minute, I need to take it a little higher on this side." And so it went. After half an hour, Nathan persuaded his brother to give him a mirror. Yes, there were a few "irregularities," but on the whole it was better than Nathan had feared.

And then the idea struck. "You know, we could learn to do this properly, I bet."

There had been an advertisement in an old farmers' paper: "Become a professional. Training in all aspects of haircutting, shampooing, shaving, head massage, moustache trimming, etc. Leave with highest certificated qualifications." The address was somewhere called Dorchester Street in Montreal. Where exactly was that? They searched a map. You could get there by train, it seemed. The excitement of the new took hold. They wrote a letter, and within two weeks, a reply came. They would be very welcome to enter the six-week course from the beginning of April. It would cost twenty-five dollars each plus room and board, but they could make a bit of money shaving in the school once they had mastered the basics. Each of them had a small nest of savings which, they thought, should be sufficient. That settled it.

And so it happened that on a late March day, when the slush was still on the ground, Nathan and Obadiah left Waldenstein. The night before they had gone to see Emma and Virtue, who had both decided the occasion demanded that they dress up in their red and green party dresses. It was certain that Obadiah and Nathan seemed to appreciate them more than the men in Truro. At the very end, when they were alone on the porch (Obadiah and Virtue having lingered in the sitting room) Nathan swiftly and unexpectedly, surprising even himself, kissed Emma. He really had no idea how to go about this, but she looked so sweet and pert standing there in the frilly red dress that he just did it. Then he disappeared into the night.

The next evening, they were rolling along in the train between Halifax and Montreal, having already negotiated the perilous passage via horse cart and three separate trains to board this one. They would sit up all night; the luxury of a sleeper was not for the likes of them. And they had brought some food along as well – fresh brown bread made by Frederika, molasses in a small jar to put on it, and pudding in its long gut case just waiting to be cut in delicious slices with a jack knife.

Across from them in the carriage were two other young men, possibly brothers as well. They were both deeply involved in a contraption the like of which Nathan and Obadiah had never seen before. It had a horn fixed on the top and a handle for winding on the side, and they had a black disk that went on the top of the box. They busied themselves winding up the handle on the side, then putting something on a lever down on the now rotating black disk, and suddenly the carriage was filled with music.

> *Hallelujah, I'm a bum*
> *Hallelujah, bum again.*
> *Hallelujah, give us a handout*
> *To revive us again.*

The boys across the aisle giggled. Nathan and Obadiah giggled as well, partly because it was funny, but also because it was kind of – well, embarrassing. Over and over the song went, and gradually they knew not only the refrain but all the verses as well. It was springtime, the singer said, so why should he work? His efforts at begging were rebuffed ("I went to a house / And I knocked on the door / And the woman said 'Bum-bum, / You've bummed here before.'"), but he kept up his merry round of travelling and begging, ending up with thirty days in jail after a minor drunken brawl. He didn't want to work! He drank! He seemed happy! Nathan and Obadiah had clearly strayed into a parallel universe where the values of Waldenstein were set on their head. This was not something they could talk about together; indeed, they had not quite articulated any of it even to themselves. But they knew somehow that they were not prepared for Montreal.

They fell asleep; they roused; the music still went on, seeping into their dreams and unconscious. Once Nathan opened his eyes and saw that the two young men with the record player were drinking something pale brown from a bottle. This seemed to make them laugh even more. Could they be – *drinking?* No one in Waldenstein drank. At least not in public, though there was a rumour that old Josiah Veinot had taken to making his own moonshine out of no one knew quite what after his son was killed. Drinking was *dissolute*. Not working was sinning against God's injunction that man should earn his bread by the sweat of his brow. This song glorified a life of ease. And yet something in Nathan still thought it funny; deep down, he wanted to laugh. He didn't dare ask Obadiah what he thought.

Their journey ended in an enclosed space vaster than any they had ever seen before – a huge, arched temple to travelling. People were rushing about purposefully, some of them jabbering in an unintelligible language. A few of them were dark-skinned and had noses the like of which they had never encountered. And their hair? Now how would you cut hair like that? They knew vaguely that there were different kinds of people out there; the Old Testament story of Noah explained how they had become that way, but they had never seen any before. All this flashed through their minds, but chiefly they felt afraid. The brothers walked close to one another, hauling their old strung-together suitcases until they saw a poorly penciled sign that said "Wentzell brothers." The man holding it was old and wizened and had lost most of his teeth. He smelled of tobacco. But he was there to guide them, and for that they were grateful.

"The barbering school sent me; they've got a place for you to stay."

Nathan and Obadiah followed this decrepit piece of humanity out of the station to a noisy, busy street with cars whizzing in all directions. He led them, terrified, across to the other side where a parking lot – a desolate piece of tarmac with a few cars parked higgledy-piggledy – stretched out before them. They went to one of the oldest cars with a taxi sign on its top, strapped their suitcases to the back and off they went. Soon they were hurtling through the streets of the city, narrowly missing death every second. Their knuckles were white from holding on to the seats. Ox carts, even horse carriages, did not move at this speed. Trains, though they moved fast, were at least predictable; they ran on rails. Sometimes the car stopped – abruptly. "Are we there yet?"

"Nope. Red light," their driver retorted.

What was a red light? *Where* was a red light?

At length they pulled up before a large ramshackle house on a noisy road. They paid the fifty cents the driver demanded (a fortune, it seemed; at least they didn't know about tipping) and knocked on the door of the house where they had been deposited. A woman in a dirty apron opened the door. "Vous de Wentzell boys?" This was an unpromising beginning. They nodded, and she led them up and up stairs with ever more frayed and dirty carpeting as they ascended, until they reached a large room with no furniture except two beds, a wash stand and a wardrobe with no door. They had not expected anything fancy, but home in Waldenstein was at least *clean*. "Filthy buggers," Josiah Veinot had said when he heard the boys were going to Montreal. "Filthy buggers."

"Toilet," the lady of the house said to them, pointing down the corridor. Then she disappeared and left them to it.

Well, what choice did they have? They were there for six weeks and had better make the best of it.

That evening, their supplies of bread, molasses and pudding exhausted, they went out to find somewhere to eat. "Try Bens," the taxi driver had said. At last they found a shop on a corner of St Laurent Street that proclaimed itself to be "Ben's." They looked through the window. It was all yellow and green and shiny chrome, with many stools arranged around a large counter and little tables in the large open space behind. Lots of men, and some women, were cavorting noisily, while others got on with the serious business of eating. They all looked foreign – not foreign-foreign, just different, with large noses and slicked-back black hair and loud voices that penetrated the thin glass, babbling in an incomprehensible language. Did they dare? Timidly they went in and found two empty stools side by side; clearly the tables were not for the likes of them. They looked at the menu with apprehension. It was all in French. When the waitress came, Obadiah pointed to the plate the man next to him was eating and said, "Two."

"Deux," the waitress corrected him.

The food was dark bread filled with mounds of thinly-sliced beef that tasted vaguely like their salt beef but with a new and delicious twist that they couldn't quite identify. The pickles, however, were a great disappointment – not like those Frederika made but sour, tasting of some shrill substance that assaulted the tongue with a bitter tang.

One of the young women, dressed in silk, with a dead fox around her neck, came up to Nathan and put her hand on his shoulder. She was holding a cigarette in a long tube-like thing. "Très beau," she remarked through swirls of smoke. Nathan stared in amazement, his mouth hanging open gracelessly. Emma had never worn a slinky dress with a fur animal around her neck. The young lady retreated.

Then the bill came. They could not have imagined that a mere sandwich could cost so much! Luckily, they had brought all their spare money with them for security. They paid up and escaped, vowing never to set foot in a restaurant like that again.

They had a map, and next morning they easily found the barbering school on Dorchester Street, a busy jangling thoroughfare with cars that ran on rails and had set places to pick people up and let them off. This transport looked dangerous, they decided, and besides it cost money. Better to walk.

At the school, they began with easy things like washing hair and wrapping the toweling professionally around the neck. Then there was the actual cutting – manipulating the clippers in one hand and the comb in the other, snaking the curve of the hair carefully up the back and sides, making sure it was even all the way around. They learned to tickle the hair away from the neck gently with a soft brush, then to take the sheet off and give it a sharp crack to dislodge all the remaining hair. Finally, there was shaving with the straight razor. They began by practising on balloons. If the balloon burst, that was a bad sign. Soon they progressed to human beings.

This was downright terrifying. Nathan could not understand why a French-Canadian, no matter how poor and in need of a shave, would come in and volunteer his throat for this experiment. You had to get the beard soft; that was the first thing. To do this you whipped a wet brush around and around a mug with shaving soap in the bottom and covered the face thoroughly – the neck, behind the ears, up to the top of the cheek. And then you took the razor, which you had already made certain was absolutely sharp by rubbing it continuously on the leather strap that hung by the side of the chair, and, adjusting the angle carefully, oh so carefully, you began to scrape it over the tender skin so that roads appeared in the froth of lather. Down you went, down to the collar line, up and back around the ears, and a final straight cut across the bottom of the sideburns. Then you put sweet-smelling liquid on the face and rubbed it with a clean towel. In the unfortunate event that your customer began to bleed from a pore or two, you had something called a styptic pencil that you rubbed on the wound to stop the blood. In case of major disaster, presumably you just ran!

Both the brothers were rather adept at using their hands, and they progressed well. The intervals at night that they spent in the unsavoury boarding house began to seem insignificant. They learned little French other than *coupe de cheveux, raser,* and *faire la barbe*. Why should they? They had no intention of staying in this bewildering place. They were used to surviving, but they found life in the noisy, dirty city, bumping against "foreigners" all the time, much harder than life in a remote lumber camp where you were at least among friends and even the dirt seemed familiar, friendly dirt. They persevered, however, and soon they were qualified barbers, ready to take on the world – or at least Lunenburg County.

A barber needed a place to ply his trade. The world was unlikely to beat a path to Waldenstein for even the most exquisite haircut and shave imaginable. So they began to look for a place to set up shop. First they looked at Mahone Bay – the only town of any size that either of them had ever seen. A pretty place, they decided, and Erika had lived there for a time, which recommended it to Nathan at least. But after a day of searching and asking, they discovered that the town was full-up with barbers, and there was no spare shop or custom to be had. Having already decided that New Germany was too small, they thought they might as well try Bridgewater, a market centre and the largest town in the county. Here they found a small decrepit shop down near the river that could be had cheaply. Its situation, however, was not promising, and there would be a lot of work fixing it up. It was a possibility, but first they would check out Lunenburg.

Now Lunenburg had the advantage of being a thriving fishing town, and the first thing any fisherman wanted when he got ashore – well, no, the second thing, a bottle of rum was the first – was a shampoo, haircut and shave, the works. As luck would have it, there was a small shop for sale on the lower street, just where these fishermen would find it when they first got off the boat. The liquor store was on the corner, so they wouldn't have to travel far to satisfy both of their pressing needs. And, in a further stroke of good fortune, there was a small Cape house beside the shop that was for sale with it. This meant that they would not have to board but could set up housekeeping on their own, with their own friendly dirt.

But the decisive factor was, indeed, none of this but the sign from heaven – or so Nathan believed – that appeared, not in the sky, but on the road before him. Walking from the site of the shop and house up to Main Street, where they had seen a small restaurant, Nathan suddenly saw, lying on the sidewalk, a five dollar bill. He picked it up – a small fortune! It didn't occur to him to find the owner or to turn it in at the police station, if there was one, because anyone could claim the bill was his; it wouldn't be fair. Anyway, Nathan was convinced that this was a sign from God. This was a fortunate town. Here he would stay.

Absence

1924

"They've all gone," Aaron remarked one September evening. He and Agnes were sitting together, she mending, he with a book in his hand that he read in spurts and starts. Now the book was in his lap, and he was looking out over the fading landscape. He was thinking of Emma and Virtue, both of whom were out teaching, and Hannah, who had followed her sisters to Normal College. These were the ones – apart from Harry – to whom he could talk; these were the ones that mattered.

Agnes countered, "Not all. Joan and Harry and Rachel are still here – and Flora." Ah yes, Flora. Surely Agnes wasn't going to ruin the evening by bringing that up again.

There was a silence. At length Agnes ventured, tentatively, "Have you thought about what we discussed a year ago?"

"What, what thing? How can I remember everything we talked about a year ago?"

"You *do* remember. Flora. A will."

Oh yes, here it all came again. Aaron stiffened. "I don't know what to do. Harry must have the business, but I suppose Flora must be looked after somehow."

"Somehow? Is that what you want for her? Somehow?"

"You know what I mean. Don't twist things."

"I'm not twisting. I'm just repeating your own words back to you."

"Yes, yes." He thought for a while. "Maybe one of the girls, Virtue or Emma, will take her in when they get married."

Agnes bit her tongue and was silent.

But after ten minutes she looked up once more. "There's something else – my parents. I can't see them managing on their own much longer."

This even Aaron had to concede was true.

Ever since Rose had died Muriel had withdrawn into herself, rarely going out to visit and hardly attempting to talk to those who came to visit her. "She's gettin' on," Sophia observed.

Zachariah had begun to forget things. At first he forgot little things, like where he'd put his pipe and whether he had fed the chickens. Then he began to forget bigger things, like how many pairs of underpants to put on and whether he himself had eaten supper or not. Agnes and Aaron went over as often as they could, taking food, cleaning, looking after such few animals as remained, but it was a two mile journey. They could not do it every day, and anyway, in the winter, Aaron was away in the woods. Ben and Sophia, who lived much nearer, also gave what help they could, but it was still not enough.

"I guess we'll have to have them come and live with us," Agnes finally said. Neither she nor Aaron wanted this; the rupture that occurred when Muriel had insisted on keeping Rose had been exacerbated by her death. "If she had lived with us, she might not have died. We would have noticed something was wrong sooner," had been Aaron's final verdict.

Now he quizzed Agnes about her precise intentions. "And where will they sleep?" he asked. He wanted them in his house even less than Agnes did.

But Agnes had a ready reply: "Now that Virtue and Emma have gone, they can have their old room. Joan and Rachel can share as they always have."

"And when Virtue and Emma come back to visit?"

"We'll just have to work something out," said Agnes with resignation.

Aaron sighed his acquiescence. He knew it was not just the right thing but the only possible thing to do.

Still, he was spared; it never happened. Something worse did.

Towards the end of September, when everyone had finished haying and was digging the fall potatoes, pulling carrots and turnips, and thinking about which pig they should sacrifice against the winter, Zachariah did his final forgetting.

It was a warm evening, and all the doors and windows in the house were open. A light breeze stirred the white kitchen curtains, blowing them in and out, in and out. Muriel had gone to bed early, tired with the heat, tired with making supper, and above all, tired of Zachariah who sat now on the kitchen bench watching the curtains. The more he watched, the more they looked to him like Muriel had when he first went out with her and she wore long, flowing dresses. All the distance and acrimony that had sprung up in later years disappeared as he watched the rippling curtains. "Darling," he murmured. He touched the piece of muslin. It felt gentle and beguiling in his hands. Then he took it down and began to dance with it. Round and round he went, the piece of muslin obligingly pliant, floating around the kitchen. When he was tired he escorted the muslin to what looked like a seat along one side of the room, where he patted it and left it. A few minutes later he followed Muriel upstairs.

The maiden muslin sat for a while comfortably on the stove, which was no longer particularly hot, since it had only been used to boil water and fry potatoes for supper and had been dying down since then. All might have been well had not Zachariah also forgotten to put the lid back on the front left-hand burner when he had emptied his pipe into the stove. Another gust of wind, stronger than any before, and a corner of the muslin moved towards the opening. Yet another gust, and the corner fell down into the stove. From then on the rest was inevitable.

ॐ

Ben Wentzell was up later than usual that evening. He had a sick calf that he was feeding with milk at least four times a day. Tonight he was feeling rather pleased with himself because the little animal had looked up after the last feeding and licked his hand. He swore the creature almost smiled at him. Maybe she would make it after all.

As he walked up to the house with the empty milk pail swinging in his hand, he became aware of a strange light in the sky up on the hill to his left. He turned to look more closely and saw, to his horror, that the light was flames coming out of the kitchen window of the Kraus' house. Immediately he screamed for Sophia and began to run up the hill. By the time he reached the house the kitchen ell was a mass of flames, and the main part of the house was beginning to catch. There was no way he could enter through the kitchen door, and the front door would be locked. The front doors of all houses in Waldenstein were always locked except for funerals and weddings. He ran to it, nevertheless, and after a few minutes managed somehow to break through one of the door panels. It was not large enough to allow him to enter. Why hadn't he stopped to grab an axe? He watched with horror through the broken slit as first a small flame licked the bottom of the stairs, then greedily ate a bit higher. Suddenly, as he yelled at the top of his voice, the whole staircase became a mass of flames. Nothing could be heard against the whoosh of the wind rushing through the broken panel to drive the fire.

Next Sophia was beside him, screaming hysterically. What a fool he had been to rouse and bring her to this sight, so reminiscent of the way that Ophelia had died. They stood embracing one another helplessly as the whole house went up in flames. There was no sound except for the crackling of the fire. No distraught figures appeared at the bedroom window calling for help, nothing. Then part of the upper floor collapsed and fell with a crash and a flare of sparks into the downstairs. There was nothing more they could do.

"You go back home, and I'll go get Aaron. There's no good we can do by standin' here. At least I don't expect they suffered much."

Ben went off across the fields and down the woodland path to the Millers' house. It was a beautiful night, with a moon two days past full just coming up. A rabbit scurried through the grass getting out of his way as he walked. High in a spruce tree, an owl hooted. He was alive, he was alive! Poor Zachariah. He had said little while he lived, and then that little he knew and said deserted him. And Muriel. People claimed that she wouldn't let Rose go all those years ago, and that was why Agnes never was – well, as a daughter should be to her mother. But this would set them all back.

Everything was silent when he reached the Miller house. No lights, no one stirring. Should he rouse them or go home and wait until morning? For a while he stood on the porch hesitating. What he was about to do seemed brutal. There was nothing anyone could do for Muriel and Zachariah. Yet something told him Aaron and Agnes would want to know at once, even as they would also long to go back to that state of ignorant slumber just before they knew.

He knocked on the door and called out. "It's Ben."

After a short time, Aaron appeared in a long nightshirt. "What's the matter; what's happened?"

"There's been a fire."

"Where?"

"Zachariah and Muriel."

"Did they get out? Are they all right?"

"No."

The two men stood facing one another in the moonlight, dumb and motionless.

‍🌀

In the morning the whole community turned out, grief and curiosity blended. Houses built of wood and heated by more wood were a hazard. You just had to be careful, that was all. But as you got older, being careful became more difficult. They all guessed that it had been Zachariah who had been at fault, but no one would ever know for certain. And absolutely no one would ever know that it was a last ecstatic dance with his imaginary bride that had led him to his end.

Later, when the debris had cooled, they found the charred bodies. The bed and floor of the bedroom had been demolished so that everything had fallen through into the parlour, but it was noted that Zachariah was still curled up as if he had not stirred from his sleep. Muriel had her arms outstretched over her head. She had seen the horror and tried too late to escape.

❧

All this time Waldenstein had been without a minister. There had been no regular church services, and only dire emergencies such as a burial brought a clergyman all the way up from Mahone Bay. On special occasions, such as Christmas and Easter, Aaron or even Ebenezer might read the service, and they would sing the old hymns. But who would have the audacity to preach to his neighbours, and who had the right to administer the sacrament? "They've just abandoned us," Ben Wentzell had said to Jacob early that summer as he was walking out to plant the first crop of beans.

"Looks like it," Jacob replied, leaning on his hoe on the other side of the fence that separated their farms.

"I blame Aaron. Mebbe I shouldn't, he couldn't know how it would all turn out, and that Reverend Selig was sure odd, but he was better than nothin', which is what we got now."

"Still," Jacob consoled himself, "I guess God's still up there. What difference does a minister make anyway, unless you need to get buried?" And he had laughed at his black joke.

But then, as if in answer to Jacob, one had arrived, just a few weeks before the fire. He came from Ontario, which was superficially reassuring. Good things came from Ontario – mostly the tax dollars that kept Nova Scotia afloat. But a good clergyman might be another possibility.

When they saw him, they were instantly disillusioned. Just out of college, Reverend Herzel was tall and thin like his predecessor but without his easy elegance. Too many bones stuck out in too many places; in fact, there were protuberances everywhere – large nose, jutting jaw, sticking-out ears – a cartoon Ichabod Crane. Among his other deficiencies, he could barely ride a horse. Apparently he had been taking lessons before he arrived, but the smooth Ontario trails did not prepare him to coax a nag over the rough dirt roads of the countryside.

Alas, his preaching was no more polished than his appearance. He spoke with a literal earnestness, explaining the readings of the day in painful detail. After one sermon on the parable of the sower and the seed, Aaron felt he would have been prepared to write an exam on the topography of Palestine. Reverend Herzel was trying so hard. His every gesture said, "Like me, welcome me, I am at your mercy."

"I think they're still punishin' us," a grim Ebenezer said after his third service.

"Well, at least we don't need to ask why he came here, do we?" Ephraim Zwicker rejoined. "He couldn't get a job anywhere else!"

ஃ

Now it was this apparition to whom Aaron had to appeal to take the funeral of his parents-in-law. He did so with trepidation.

Reverend Herzel conducted the service with due solemnity, but when it came to the address he trod on dangerous ground. "You know not the day nor the hour when the Son of Man cometh" was his text. And, with his usual literalness, he translated this into a horror story of how poor Muriel and Zachariah had gone to bed having no inkling that their souls were to be required of them. How terrible to be summoned by the Lord unprepared! And what a fearful end to make, smothered in a fire that he somehow managed to suggest was the fire of damnation, a foretaste of the everlasting fire. They all left stunned. Yes, there were warnings against the wicked in the Bible; they all knew that, but the wicked were always others, those who plowed on Sunday, those who swore and drank, those who never went near the church. The idea that a couple living among them, *just like them,* might have been visited by the Lord's judgment was unprecedented.

"How can you say things like that? How *dare* you say things like that!" Aaron let fly at the church door once the coffins had been taken out.

Reverend Herzel had heard that Aaron was a troublemaker. He replied mildly, "I was merely preaching the word of the Lord."

And, of course, he was. What did they want, these people? They had kicked out the last minister because he was too "advanced," too "modern." Now they rebuked him because he preached the unvarnished scriptural truth. A hard-hearted people indeed! The Israelites had nothing on them.

With these thoughts, he deposited Zachariah and Muriel in the small graveyard with the appropriate words, got on his nag and rode away.

❧

Autumn passed. The charcoal remains of Zachariah and Muriel's lives were picked over bit by bit by Aaron and Agnes – a small comb here, a blackened piece of jewellery there, tin pots swollen and misshapen by flame – and then, miraculously, unharmed, a picture of Agnes holding Rose when she was only six months old. Agnes took the picture and felt, in a curious way, that at last she owned her child once more.

Knowledge

Adam

1925

Adam rode his pony proudly around the fenced paddock. Yes, *his* pony. The girls had gone away to a place called Roedean to be properly educated, and what could be more natural than that he should inherit the pony? So now, released from his morning lessons with Mrs. Manley, he decided to spend the fine spring afternoon jouncing up and down on Percy. Perhaps in a little while, if he were allowed, he would ride across the fields to visit his friend, Daniel. That should be alright, since he had already done his piano practice, and he could study his lessons after supper before he went to bed.

Erika looked out the window at him astride the pony. What a proper little English gentleman he was in his riding coat and boots. Then she thought what a joke it would be if his father could see him now. She thought she knew Aaron well enough to judge his reaction; he might pretend to be horrified, but he would be secretly pleased. She had heard Adam spoken of in the parish as "the Rector's boy." Maybe, given Reverend Manley's predilections, they thought he genuinely was. And indeed, as time went by, he was treated more and more as if this were so. He no longer slept in the same room with Erika but had his own room, decorated to his taste, on the top floor. That location, and the fact that he still ate in the kitchen with Erika, Millie and the other servants, marked out his official status, but his *de facto* status was quite other.

Erika could not help but rejoice at the advantages that were being lavished on her son. But that was exactly the problem – for how long would he remain her son?

A few days later, the dreaded confrontation that she had always known must come, took place.

"Mama, where is home?"

"What do you mean? We live here; this is your home."

"Yes, I know, but Daniel says I came from Liverpool."

"Well, he's wrong. You didn't come from Liverpool."

"But was I born here?"

There was no way out. "No, you were born in a different country a long, long way off."

"But where?"

"In a little rural place called Waldenstein in Nova Scotia, which is part of Canada."

"Oh yes, I can find Nova Scotia on a map. Mrs. Manley showed me."

"Well, that's where you were born."

"So how did I get here?"

"I was very unhappy there, so I went to Halifax and got on board a big ship and we travelled together across the Atlantic Ocean and landed at Liverpool. Reverend Manley met us there by accident and gave me this job, so we came to live here with him and his family."

Adam thought for a minute and then went on, "Daniel says Mr. Manley goes to Liverpool a lot. He says he has a bad woman he keeps there. But you weren't a bad woman, were you?"

Was she a bad woman? Well, certainly not in the sense Daniel meant. Erika gathered up her courage and went on. "Daniel knows nothing about those things and should be quiet about them. But you can be certain I was never a woman Mr. Manley set out to meet. We met quite by chance as I came off the boat and he was walking near the pier. Now that's enough questions for today."

"But why were you unhappy before you came here?" There could never be enough questions.

"Maybe I'll tell you another time, but not now."

"I'll go and tell Daniel I didn't come from Liverpool." Adam was already out of his chair.

"No, you'll do nothing of the sort. These are not things to be discussed with Daniel," said Erika with finality.

Erika knew this was not the end but the beginning of an endless catechism, and she had better work out the answers to the questions.

Six days later, a Sunday, it began again. "Is Reverend Manley my father?"

"No, he is not your father, though he treats you very well."

"I'm glad he's not my father, because I think his sermons are altogether dreadful. But who is my father?" The perpetual question of the child.

"Does it really matter? You have a good home, every opportunity in life, and I love you very much." Thus Erika attempted to deflect him.

"Well, yes, it *does* matter. Because Daniel says that what you do in life and how far you can go depends on who your father is." This kind of determinism was a new idea to Erika even after all these years in England.

"Well, I'm sorry, but Daniel is wrong about that also. How far you can go depends on whether you have the chance to get a good education, but even more on how ambitious you are and how hard you work."

"I think I work pretty hard. But *who is my father? Why can't you tell me?*" And Adam was on the verge of tears.

There was no escape; she must tell him. "He was a very clever man who had a good business with lots of men working for him cutting down trees and turning them into lumber."

"What was his name?"

By now Erika was trembling. "Aaron Miller."

"Hmm. Aaron is all right, but Miller is a bit common, don't you think?" Thus spoke the English child. "Did he have a lot of money?"

"No, but he had more money than anyone else in Waldenstein."

"I guess that's all right, then. Was he your husband? Did he die and that's why you were sad and wanted to come away?"

Oh how easy it would be to say "yes"; Adam himself had provided her with the perfect alibi. And here, so cut off, how could anyone ever discover the truth? She had confided it to no one, not Reverend or Mrs. Manley, not Millie – no one. And such was their discretion, no one asked. But somehow she couldn't do that. She had been brought up a Lutheran; she couldn't tell the easy lie.

"No, he didn't die."

"Is he still living in Waldenstein then?"

"I believe so."

"Why isn't he here with us? Why didn't he come over with you?"

Truth was a hard road. "Look Adam, you're a clever boy, but there are some things you won't understand until you're older."

"You're just trying to get out of telling me." This, of course, was also true. What a strong, hard-edged child he could be sometimes, sitting there at the table, his hands folded tightly in front of him, persisting, persisting. Like Aaron. Except that in the end, Aaron did not have the courage to face what he had done. He cared too much about what people would say.

"All right then, I'll tell you, but you may not understand everything about it just now."

"I understand everything. Mrs. Manley says I catch on to maths much quicker than Ella or Alice did."

"Yes," Erika conceded, "but this is a little different from maths."

So she began her story. Almost as if it were a fairy story, she found herself distancing it, using the past tense. "Your father was married to a nice woman called Agnes, and they had eight children. In the winter, when your father and the men who worked for him went to cut down trees (it's best to cut trees in winter when the sap isn't running under the bark), he and the men all lived together in a remote place on the opposite side of a big lake – a bigger lake than you've ever seen in this country – and they needed someone to cook for them there. One year they couldn't find anyone to do the cooking, so I went and did it for them. We all had beds around the edge of the room, just curtained off from one another."

"Like in the hospital when I had my tonsils out?"

"Well, yes, a little bit like that. Anyway, most of the men weren't interested in reading. In the evening, when they had finished working and eaten the supper I made for them, they sat around the table and played cards and smoked until they went to bed. But your father was different; he liked books very much indeed, just like you do. And since both he and I liked books, and there weren't many books around in those days back there, we would share books by reading them together and talking about them. So we became good friends.

"Now one night, I guess we both must have been feeling lonely, and it was very cold, so after we had finished reading he came and asked if he could share my bed with me." Then, as she spoke, Erika felt the shock of a new realization. She had just said he had *asked* if he could come to her bed. Was this true? Or had she just added it because it seemed the right thing to say to Adam? *Had* he asked? She had not remembered this before. What she had acknowledged to herself was that he had simply touched her and led her to the bed. There was no sound track to this scene. But now she could hear his voice, as he gently moved the curtain aside and stood over her, murmuring, "Do you mind?" And she had nodded acquiescence. The whole scene came back with a clarity it had never possessed in those early days, those days in which she was wholly the innocent victim, denying any complicity on her part. A new wave of guilt swept over her. Perhaps she was accomplice, as well as victim.

Adam noticed the narrative had stopped. "So what took place next?" he demanded.

"I should have said 'No,' but I liked him very much, so I didn't. That night he held me close and kissed me, and you came into being. So while letting him hold me that way wasn't really right when he was married to Agnes, something wonderful, nevertheless, came out of it – you."

266

"Was I born that night, in the camp, like Jesus in the stable?" Adam could see that this story had romantic possibilities.

"No, you weren't born in the camp, because it takes nine months for a baby to grow inside its mother's tummy. You were born at my home, and my mother and father and my brothers loved you very much."

"And my father. Was he there? Did he love me very much?"

"It was very difficult for your father because you see his wife was very unhappy that he had held another woman that close."

"Was she angry?" New possibilities were opening up before Adam.

"Yes, she was angry."

"Did he ever come to see me?"

"Yes, he did, and he thought you were a fine boy. Boys were special to him because of his eight children only one was a boy. All the others were girls."

"But he didn't want me, even so." This was still the brutal fact, so hard to take in.

"He *couldn't* want you because he was married to someone other than me. But *I* wanted you, very much."

"Would you have married him if Agnes had died?"

"I don't know." This was as honest as everything else.

"So I don't have a father, not a proper one."

"You can see it that way. Or you can say that you have two fathers – Aaron back in Waldenstein and Reverend Manley here, who gives you opportunities you could never have had if we had stayed in Waldenstein."

"What do you mean by 'opportunities'?"

"Well, for example, you are getting a good education, and I think that when you are a bit older Reverend Manley may send you to a first-rate boarding school, just like he did his daughters. You live in a lovely house, you have a pony to ride; in fact, you are a very lucky boy."

"Weren't there ponies in Waldenstein?" How could Adam conceive of a place like Waldenstein?

"There were a few horses, but mostly there were just oxen that they used to pull plows and cows, who gave them milk. And you couldn't ride the horses just for fun like Reverend Manley and his friends do. If you had a horse it had to work, pulling you in a cart from place to place, or moving logs, or plowing like the oxen."

"So what did people do for fun?"

Erika was tempted to laugh hysterically and say they went to church for fun – which, in a sense was true, it being the one regular social gathering. But she must remember that, clever as he was, Adam was still a child. "Well, there wasn't a lot of fun, but sometimes people did get together and have a sing-song, or even a square dance."

"What's a sing-song?"

"Oh you know, you just get together and sing a lot of the songs you've known since you were young. Some of the people were very good singers. Your grandfather, my father, took sight-singing classes for a time until the teacher moved away. That meant that he could sing something he had never heard before just by looking at the page." Erika, who had not been taught to read music until she reached the Manleys, had always thought this amazing.

At last Adam was impressed. "Wow!" He thought a moment. "I bet I could learn to do that too."

"I'm sure you could. Now it's time for you to go and practise the piano, and I must take tea in to Reverend and Mrs. Manley."

But his last words were disquieting: "So I really don't have a father at all…."

It had happened. She always had known there would come a time – how could there not – when this conversation would have to be had. She just wished it had not been so soon.

She took the tea in to the Manleys scarcely aware of her surroundings or what she did. She was back again in Waldenstein, and it was so painful she simply wanted to go away and weep. What had become of them all? She thought of Rose, who had been her best friend and who had never said an unkind word when she had – well, made her "mistake." What was Rose doing? Had she found someone to marry? Did she have children? The idea that she might be dead never occurred to her. And what about Obadiah and Nathan – particularly Nathan, who was the favourite among her siblings? He would be eighteen now, out working. She hoped he wasn't working for Aaron; she hoped Jacob had let him stay on in school longer so that he could do something better than cut down trees. And of course she thought about Aaron. Did it give her satisfaction to know that he could never be perfectly happy again? She knew it shouldn't, but neither should Adam have to believe he had no father. Who felt the loss more keenly, father or son? As for herself, it was her burden as well. She had nodded; she had nodded assent.

Much of her spare time now she spent reading, taking full advantage of Reverend Manley's library. She particularly enjoyed books that asked questions about how the world worked. She found a strange man called Darwin who claimed that all higher kinds of life came (or evolved, a new word she had mastered) from lower forms, so that the world was not created in seven days as the Bible said but over millions of years. She longed to ask Reverend Manley what he thought of this, but somehow she couldn't. It seemed he probably didn't think of it at all, even though the book was in his library. Insofar as Erika could tell, he thought of the following things, and in this order: Liverpool (and all its associations), fox hunting, his family pedigree (of which he was inordinately proud and possessive), Greek words and their meaning, his daughters, Mrs. Manley, Adam, and finally things necessary to the running of his estate, like herself. And then, as she thought further about these things, she realized there was one great common thread between life in Waldenstein and life in this Leicestershire rectory – it was unquestioned. Breakfast was served on the sideboard from eight; dinner was at seven; one's children went to public schools; fox hunting was the sport of gentlemen; servants were a necessary part of life; men could be unfaithful with impunity, women couldn't; everyone went to church on Sunday; everyone believed in God – or at least didn't make a fuss if they didn't; life in general was quite comfortable, except for the odd war or other setback, which must be accepted with equanimity as part of the general scheme of things.

But now Erika was beginning to question life – life in Waldenstein, life in Leicestershire, because, unlike the others, she had lived in both and could see that the ordering of life was not an inevitable, single pattern. So then she asked not how does one live, but how ought one to live. And then there were no answers, because no one else in Erika's worlds had ever asked these questions seriously. Clearly, one ought not to have sex with someone else's husband; that caused too much misery whether it happened here or in Waldenstein. But whereas you became a social pariah in Waldenstein if you did such a thing, in Leicestershire, it seemed, you could get away with it – a knowing nod or wink, a slight tut-tutting, but unless, like Mrs. Manley, you were directly involved, you let it pass as a small indiscretion. Certainly you didn't attempt suicide, even if you were directly involved. How could you commit suicide in a house where the tea tray would be coming in at four o'clock and there would be sherry at six-thirty? It would be in such extremely bad taste.

Somehow, she must try to bring Adam up to see that it was fine to ask questions, but not always to expect answers. Already she could see that he accepted life as it was going on around him. What you could do, what you became, depended on who your father was. He said he had no father. She must try to let him see that this was an opportunity, a blank slate on which he could write what he would.

Search for a Father

1930–1935

One day when Adam was twelve, Reverend Manley called Erika into his study. She stood obediently, like the servant she still was, in front of his desk. Since that day in her first year there, he had never tried to touch her.

"Do sit down," he began. So she found a chair.

"I'm very fond of Adam, as you know," he said.

She waited. What was coming next? A "but"? Some misdemeanor?

"I really think of him almost as my own son. I never had any sons, despite...." He trailed off, and looked up at her expectantly.

Still she waited.

Then it came. "I'd like to send him to my old school, if you don't object. He's a bright lad, and I think he'd do well there. I can afford it, and it would give me pleasure. I'm sure he'll be a credit to all of us." He leaned back in his chair, looking intently at her, waiting for her reaction.

She was surprised, and yet not surprised. Millie and Jack had suggested to her that something of this nature might happen. So she was ready to say, with equanimity, "That's very good of you, Sir. I'm sure Adam will be delighted. He's been talking about which schools his friends are going to, and of course he has had no idea where he might go – or even if he would be able to go to a proper school at all. As for me, I couldn't possibly object." Though in her heart she could object, because it would mean Adam would grow ever more distant from her and closer to this strange new society in which they lived.

"Well, Adam will have no cause to be ashamed among his friends of where he's going. He will go to the best school of them all – Eton."

She had heard of Eton, a fabled place where people like Reverend Manley had been educated. But did she really want Adam to turn out like Reverend Manley? Maybe not, but she couldn't turn down a generous offer like this. What could there be even to discuss? So she said, "I can't thank you enough, Sir. May I tell Adam, or do you want to do that yourself?"

Reverend Manley was not without some human sensitivity. "You may tell him yourself, if you wish."

And again she said, "Thank you very much," and turned to go. But then he said, "Erika. I've never asked you about your past, why you came to England, or who Adam's father was. You've been a boon to all of us here, and we value you and Adam very much. But now... if you didn't mind telling us a bit about your background and circumstances, who his father was, for example, it might be helpful."

She was overcome with fear, but in the circumstances, how could she object? So she began, "I came from a poor country community in Nova Scotia. Everyone worked from dawn to dusk to stay alive – and many did not manage to stay alive even so. I don't mind who knows that. But as for Adam's father – all I can say is that he was the cleverest man in the community and the one who employed almost everyone else. I'd sooner not say more, Sir."

Reverend Manley was scarcely a man with the right to pry into the darker corners of the lives of others. And he knew that, to begin with, his own motives in bringing her home with him had been less than pure. "That's fine then. I'll put myself down as his guardian."

Now there were certain social niceties to be resolved. Up to this point, Erika had been unambiguously a servant. Valued and trusted she might be, but she ate in the servant's quarters and slept in the attic. Adam's status was a bit more ambiguous. Formally, it was the same as his mother's, but the private tuition, the pony and the friends that were children of the Manleys' friends all conspired to break down the class partitions. Since he was going to Eton it was deemed that he should eat with the family to acquire the manners and social graces he would need in his new life. But how could a son eat a world away from his mother? So, somewhat to her own discomfiture, Erika found that she, too, was to take her meals in the dining room, served by Jack and Millie. She also found that for this she was provided with a new wardrobe – dresses of fine wool and silk rather than gingham that looked best when covered by an apron.

English life was peculiar enough viewed from the vantage point of a servant, but now that she was actually being incorporated into it, the strangeness intensified. Adam, of course, felt none of this. His mother might be a servant, but she wasn't *treated* as a servant – at least not anymore. She was introduced as a friend of the Manleys; people no doubt assumed – if they assumed anything – that she was a rich widow or a lonely relative. And she played the part for Adam's sake. She did not want him to be ashamed of her.

When the September day on which he was to leave the Rectory came, she was filled with an overwhelming desire to say "No," to pull him back into her world. He had been her only connection with home, and she knew that when he came back from Eton he would be changed beyond recognition.

Adam, too, felt a sense of loss as he was driven out of the Rectory gates, past the fields where his pony and later his horse had grazed, away from the river and the pastoral landscapes of Leicestershire. All the boys at this new school would be like Daniel, he feared. They would want to know who his father was because that determined who you were, and how could they be your friend if they didn't know who you were?

When he arrived at his "House" the Dame there took charge of him and his trunks and showed him to his room – small, with one window looking out over a narrow lane, but quite adequate except that there appeared to be no bed. Then, with an expert flourish, the Dame released the bed, which folded up into the wall like a closet by day and came down at night. Adam was pleased with the ingeniousness of it all and set about arranging his possessions with enthusiasm, his earlier nervousness forgotten.

Later in the afternoon they had tea in the House garden and were introduced to the other boys. The first year boys all huddled in a group trying to sort one another out, except for one who stood apart and was deferred to by the others as Lord Thornbury. He looked a rather sad little boy, with remarkably thick blond hair and features refined almost to extinction. His father was dead (hence his title), and his mother had married again, to his great distress. He looked so lonely that Adam was drawn to him but didn't dare approach him. He, Adam, was universally introduced as "Wentzell".

"That's a funny name," Cranley, a large dark-haired boy with an already broken voice, observed, smiling. "Where does it come from?"

What could he say? Germany? Still, in 1929, this was not a particularly fortunate choice of origin. So he said simply, "Canada." And then, to prevent further questioning along these lines he added, "My father lives in Canada, but Reverend Manley is my guardian in this country."

That seemed to satisfy Cranley and the others, at least for the time being.

Then they were each introduced to the prefects for whom they were to "fag." Adam had drawn the Head of House, one Worcester. Worcester took him up to his room, where Adam was intrigued by the huge number of history books. When he commented on these, Worcester condescended to say that he was going to "read" history at Oxford. Then he moved the conversation to matters that ought to be of more concern to Adam – the way he liked to have his shoes polished, the precise temperature of the water to be brought to him for shaving in the morning, and the terrible nature of the punishments he would suffer should he fail in any of these tasks. Adam tried to take in all the details of his duties, but so alien was the idea of physical punishment to him that he couldn't move his mind from the horrible possibility that such might fall upon him.

Then there was dinner, and after it an interval that would subsequently be filled with school homework, so they were assured. Finally there were prayers at which genuine praying occupied only about three minutes. Here the Housemaster appeared in all his tail-coated glory. He was, Adam decided, about forty-five – definitely younger than Reverend Manley, but with an air of authority that even the Rector never quite achieved. He too was ordained, but unmarried, devoted, so he assured them, totally to their well-being and progress through the school. Boys must be industrious, fair-minded, honest in everything they did. They must be considerate of those less fortunate than themselves – a category which, in his opinion (though he did not quite say this), included just about all the rest of the world that did not have the glorious opportunity of studying at Eton. Here too there was the veiled threat of terrible punishment should they fail to live up to any of these ideals.

At last the day was over, and Adam could retreat to his room, pull down the bed and lie there thinking about the home he had just left and his mother. He wasn't really sad, he decided; this was going to be a great adventure. But he did feel sorry that Erika couldn't share it with him.

The next morning he woke up with a sense of panic. In what order was he supposed to do things? Did he dress first and then go up to Worcester's room to minister to his needs, or were Worcester's needs so pressing that he should attend to them before putting on his extraordinary costume of tail coat and striped trousers? He decided Worcester would be offended to see him in anything but school uniform; it might show disrespect. So he rushed through his toilet and then bounded up the stairs to polish the Head of House's shoes, make his bed and generally attend to any other of the great man's needs. In the midst of all this, it suddenly occurred to him that he now was a servant and that, as such, he was closer to the world of his mother than he ever had been before.

He had been well prepared for school by Reverend and Mrs. Manley, and lessons were no problem. Greek and Latin, maths and history – they all came to him easily so that he was the envy of many of his classmates. Cranley, in particular, who was at the bottom of almost every set, eyed him after homework books were passed back with nothing short of contempt. As long as it remained a look or a gesture, Adam didn't mind; he could ignore it. Then one November day all this changed.

ॐ

When he returned to the house after games and before late afternoon lessons, a group of boys from his year, Cranley among them, were standing at the bottom of the stairs blocking his way. When he tried to push past, he was stopped. "No you don't!"

And then Cranley said, "Where did you say your father lived?"

"Canada, I told you."

"But," and Cranley leaned forward suggestively, "what part of Canada?"

"Nova Scotia."

"And where exactly in Canada is that?" asked Cranley, who had only heard of Ontario and Quebec.

"It's on the east coast, a peninsula, next to New Brunswick." By now Adam was beginning to panic. Where was this going to end?

"Nova Scotia. So, what's it like? Ever been there?"

"Uh…" What should he say? But he had been to Nova Scotia; he had been born there. So he replied, "Yes."

"When?"

"A long time ago."

"So what's it like there?" Cranley was pushing his advantage for all it was worth.

What could Adam reply but, tentatively, "I don't remember."

"Your father lives there, and you haven't been there since 'a long time ago'; you 'don't remember' what it is like," laughed Cranley derisively. "We don't believe a word of this, do we fellows?" And he appealed to the rest of the group. "This boy has no father."

"That's not true." Adam was struggling not to cry. "I do have a father; he just doesn't live in England."

"He doesn't live in England so we can't see him; we can't see him so he doesn't exist. Case proven." For Cranley, this was quite a flight of logic.

"Case *not* proven," yelled Adam. "All kinds of things exist that you can't see."

"Like what?" Cranley yelled.

"Like…God!" Adam brought this out triumphantly; surely they could not deny the existence of God.

Cranley was momentarily flummoxed. But then he called in the reserves. "What do we do to little boys who have no father? What do we do with little boys who only have fathers like God?"

And in a moment the pack of them were on him, scratching, punching, kicking him. Then the bell for classes rang, and they scattered.

Slowly Adam picked himself up and climbed the stairs to his first floor room. He took off his games clothes, washed himself and dressed for class. There was a large scratch beneath his right eye and a growing bruise on his cheek. Nevertheless, he must present himself for lessons. Of course he would be late for the first one. What would happen as a result of that?

"Wentzell, see me after class," bellowed Mr. Pankhurst as he stole quietly into maths class. Cranley and some others exchanged glances. But when he saw him later, Mr. Pankhurst was inclined to be lenient. Adam was, after all, a favourite. "Do this set of extra problems and bring them to me at break tomorrow. And don't let it happen again."

"Yes Sir; no, Sir." Adam was relieved beyond all measure.

"I see you've been in a bit of a scrap as well," he said, eyeing Adam's wounds.

"Yes, Sir," said Adam, expecting some further enquiry. But none came. Boys got into small fights; it was to be expected. And they mustn't be encouraged to "tell" on their fellows.

After dinner that evening, however, a remarkable thing happened. Lord Thornbury came quietly up to him and said, "I saw what happened; I was watching from the stairs above. I don't have any father either; he's dead."

Part of Adam wanted to protest, "But I really do have a father, and he's alive," but he thought better of it and accepted the gesture of sympathy. From then on the two were fast friends.

☙

Gradually life at Eton assumed a routine. Lessons, games, music practice (for now Adam had taken up the clarinet), choir, chapel, evening prayers and, finally, exams.

The first exams, just before Christmas, had been dreadful – all the boys in his year, sitting in rows, scratching away furiously with their pens while several beaks paced up and down constantly to make sure no one had any concealed notes or managed to look at his neighbour's script. But even more dreadful was the day of judgment when the grades were given out – all the boys again, but this time gathered together, sitting in a large lecture room where the results were read out in order from the bottom up. Cranley did not have long to wait. His name was number five out of the two hundred boys in the year. Adam sat with his hands clasped tightly in front of him, his head down. Gradually, as more and more names were read out and he did not hear his own he began to relax. Then a new fear struck him. Suppose his name *had* already been read out and he had simply failed to hear it? He glanced up. Some boys were still sitting tensely, others were looking relieved, still others (a very few) had their hands up to their faces and appeared to be weeping silently. Finally, at number one hundred ninety-five, he heard "Wentzell, Adam." The relief was indescribable.

He wanted to stand up and shout. "I did it, I did it! You may say I have no father but I beat the whole pack of you!" The four remaining names were those of the acknowledged geniuses in the school, one of whom rejoiced in the name of Darwin, and another who was a Trevelyan. They definitely had fathers – and grandfathers too.

In general, he managed his duties as a fag with credit. He satisfied his prefect, and when the general cry "boy" went up (at which all the fags in the house were to run instantly to satisfy the needs of whichever prefect had called), he was among the first to respond.

His one defect was that he didn't really enjoy games. You got wet and cold and muddy, and running around a field kicking a ball seemed completely pointless. After all, he had not been inducted into these sports at a prep school as many of the other boys had. Once compulsory games were over, he managed to forget them instantly. Worcester, however, was one of the star senior players for the school, and an important game against Harrow was coming up on Saturday. One of a fag's duties was to see that his prefect's games clothes were in order. Usually this merely consisted of picking them up from the floor of the changing room, shaking them out and leaving them on a hook to dry, except on the day once a week when they went to the laundry. But if your prefect was playing a game against another school, then it was the fag's responsibility to make sure the clothes were washed especially for the occasion. And on this occasion, Adam forgot.

He was far away in the world of ancient Athens when a tornado hit his room. "Boy!" This was Worcester's voice as he had never heard it before. Indeed, he normally addressed him by name, not as "boy" at all. The shouting continued in a torrent. "My games clothes, they're filthy, and we leave for Harrow in half an hour. What have you been thinking of, you insignificant little idiot!"

Adam stood up to face the fury; sheer terror seized him. "I…I guess I forgot, Sir. Oh I'm so sorry, what can I do?"

And Adam would have flown off, defying the laws of gravity, grabbing the clothes to have them washed and dried in an instant if he could. But, in fact, he just stood there, aghast and trembling.

"I'll just have to borrow someone else's, I guess, and they won't fit properly. I'll look a mess and play badly as well. As for you, I'll deal with you tomorrow morning when I'm back." And he was gone.

Adam sat down again, speechless, miserable beyond words. How could he have forgotten something so essential? He spent the night in great fear, and his legs barely carried him up to Worcester's room in the morning. Worcester let him perform his usual duties, and then he slowly and deliberately drew a cane out from under his bed. "Sorry, Boy, there's nothing else for what you did but this." Then he added, as if it were a direct consequence of Adam's negligence, "We lost the game."

Adam bent over with his hands on the chair back in the approved manner, and the cane came down. One, two, three (a pause); then four, five, six. At length Worcester stopped and said, "You can go now." But then, as he stumbled towards the door, Worcester said something that was worse than the beating. "I should have known I couldn't trust a boy who has come from nowhere, who has no father."

He would never tell anyone what had happened – not his mother, not Reverend Manley, not even Lord Thornbury – but, of course, there is always gossip, and the triumphant smile Cranley gave him at dinner that night left him in no doubt that he, at least, did know.

To his surprise, as they were leaving for the summer break, Lord Thornbury (Edward by first name) asked him tentatively whether he would like to spend a week with him at his home. There was no difficulty in getting permission from the Manleys or his mother, so on the first week of August he was off to the West Country by train. Edward and a driver met him at the station. "This is Tom," said Edward to Adam, and then lapsed into silence as they drove through a pretty village and out the other side. "We're nearly in Wales," he finally volunteered. And then he continued, almost in a whisper, "My family's a bit funny, you know."

Adam reflected that the same could be said of his own, but said nothing. Edward went on, still in a whisper, "My mother probably won't pay much attention to us at all – which is good, because we can do what we like – but it's so different from your mother, when she came on the fourth of June. She's lovely, isn't she?" And Adam remembered his mother, slim and pretty in her new silk dress, talking animatedly with the other parents as if she had been born to this life. Yes, she was lovely.

Edward went on, "I mean, mine didn't come at all, because Philip, her new husband, had a race on. He races horses you know. All he cares about are the horses, and all she cares about is pleasing him." He paused a bit and continued, "The estate's going to rack and ruin the servants say. They want me to finish school and then take it over before my mother and Philip have spent everything." Another pause. "But I don't really want to; I'd like to go to university first and maybe become a Professor."

Just then they turned and began to drive up a gravelled path between two rows of elm trees. In the distance a large Georgian stone mansion came into view. Now Adam had an idea that a lord must be quite grand, but this had not yet translated itself into the specifics of house and manner of living. "Goodness, is that really your house?" he exclaimed.

"Yes. Well, officially it's mine, but you'd never know it. Philip acts as if he owns it most of the time."

"It's amazing."

Then they were at the foot of the wide flight of stairs going up to massive front doors. Servants descended on them, taking Adam's bags. He felt deficient in not having enough baggage to satisfy all of them.

The front door opened onto a vast hallway with stairs going up from two sides and meeting at the back of the floor above. The ceiling ascended to a large dome, with small coloured windows letting in a flood of light to everything below. Up they went, bags and servants following.

His room was large, with three tall windows overlooking gardens the like of which Adam had never seen before. There were patterns of little hedges, tidy and clipped short, radiating out from a small fountain in the centre; within each of the enclosures formed by the hedges were rather miniature plants, some with purple flowers, others with yellow.

"The herb garden," Edward explained nonchalantly. "It was planted in the fifteenth century, we think, before this present house was built."

There were other similarly patterned gardens to the right and left filled with roses, delphiniums, columbines and many other colorful plants that Adam couldn't precisely identify. Beyond the formal garden were long arched pathways loaded overhead with laburnum or wisteria that led away to something Edward called "the wilderness." And Adam had thought the gardens running down to the river at the Rectory were extensive!

"My room's just next door," Edward said reassuringly. "Do you want to see?"

All this time the nameless servant had been waiting patiently, trying to disappear into the wallpaper. Now, as they were about to leave the room, he spoke: "Would you like me to unpack for you, Sir."

"Oh no, I can do it myself," said Adam, casually.

"He's *meant* to do it," Edward said.

"Oh, in that case, of course." – though he was disturbed at the idea of a servant rifling through all his belongings. Who knew? He might read the diary he had recently taken to keeping.

After the tour of the house and garden it was time to dress for dinner. They descended the formal staircase together, and only then did Adam meet Edward's mother. She was tall (which was surprising since Edward himself was quite small), slender, with tight dark waves of hair fixed to her head, crimson lips and fingernails, and a long cigarette holder and cigarette in her hand. "*Darling*," she gushed and kissed Edward on the forehead. "And this is your little friend?"

"Yes, this is Adam, Mother."

"How wonderful to have a friend of Edward's with us." And Adam was the recipient of a kiss as well. He could see that Edward's kiss had left a lipstick stain, and he wanted desperately to see if his had done the same and to wipe it off, but naturally this was not possible.

They went in to dinner where Mr. Williams, Edward's stepfather, was waiting near the head of the table. He, too, greeted both boys, but without the kiss. He had thick blond hair not unlike Edward's and a ruddy complexion. His features, however, were coarse and dominated by large protruding lips so that the total effect was less than wholly pleasant. They sat down to a formal dinner at a table so vast (though there were only four of them) that each place had its own miniature salt and pepper. Mr. Williams sat at the head of the table; after all, Edward was only a child. Conversation was strained. Adam was asked politely about school and his home and then, not maliciously by any means, about his parentage. "Who did you say your father was? I don't think we quite caught that from what Edward told us about you?"

But Edward put in quickly, "His father is in Canada; Reverend Manley is his guardian in this country." They were too polite to pry further, but for Adam the question cast a shadow over the rest of the evening.

After dinner, when the two boys were back upstairs, Edward burst out in indignation, "He has some right to ask you who your father is! He lies about fathers. Do you know what he says to me?" Edward rushed on, unstoppable. "He says that he is my father. He says my mother knew him, in all senses I suppose, before my father died, and that I am his son. 'Look,' he says, 'at your hair? Where does that hair come from?' "

"But he doesn't really look like you – nothing except the hair – and he doesn't seem to care much for you."

"No, he doesn't care for me at all. What he does care about is the title. Because if I'm his son, then, you see, I'm not Lord Thornbury, I'm not the heir. And there are hardly any other relatives, so he thinks, in that case, he just might get his hands on the whole estate for himself. He hasn't gone public with this yet, but he threatens to."

"But your mother. She wouldn't let him do that, would she? What about her good name?" Adam was appalled.

"As it happens, her name isn't that good anyway, and she's so besotted with him she might let him do anything. But it's not true, you know. My father had that kind of thick blond hair as well. I know that awful man you saw at dinner tonight is just not my father!" By now there were tears in Edward's eyes, and Adam began to understand many things about him – his lack of confidence, his general reticence among the other boys at school, and why Adam's own lack of a father should have become such a bond between them.

After this the week passed pleasantly enough with riding and walking through the hilly countryside, listening to music on Edward's wind-up gramophone and talking, talking, talking. They only saw Edward's mother and Mr. Williams at meals. 'Babs,' as his mother was called, was always out visiting friends or going in her capacity as Lady of the Manor to take part in some official function. Mr. Williams ('Dodo' to Babs) spent most of his time in the company of the horses.

As Adam was being driven back to the train station at the end of his visit, Edward said, "Well, now you see how it is."

"Yes, yes I do." And Adam had a sudden impulse to share everything that he knew of his history with Edward there and then. But there was the driver, who might overhear – and there was something else as well; he wanted to know more before he shared anything.

By the second year at Eton, Adam no longer had to do fag duty, and, more importantly, he was secure in his place at the school, having been awarded an Oppidan scholarship on the basis of his high marks. Cranley and others vanished into the background hum of school life.

He played in the school orchestra, took vignette parts in school plays and continued to excel academically. In his last year it was decided he would go to King's College, Cambridge, to read classics, that being one of the few places one would choose to go if one had been at Eton.

Reverend Manley showed no sign of regretting the role he played in Adam's life. In truth, he had never quite forgiven Mrs. Manley for having only girls. His dalliance in Liverpool had begun directly after the birth of Alice, when Sarah was told it would be too dangerous for her to have more children. (Ah yes, women were delicate here, Erika reflected on being told this. They were delicate and they paid the price. In Waldenstein, they just got on with the business of raising a family, and died or lived, as fate decreed.) So both the Manleys looked upon Adam as a real stroke of good luck. Whether or not Reverend Manley believed in divine providence was never completely clear, but if he did, the arrival of Adam would have been seen as evidence for it.

At home Adam rarely asked to know more about his father or about Waldenstein. Sometimes Erika tried to talk to him about the life she had lived before coming to England, but he seemed not to want to know. If she would not tell him the central facts, he didn't want to be bothered with the details. Erika was hurt by this; she needed to talk about Waldenstein to confirm that it had been real – or maybe to confirm that the life she was living now was real. The two halves were so cut off from one another, so completely separate not just in time and space but in character that she could not connect them. She had been one person there, and she was someone else here. Only Adam provided a tenuous link between the two, and he now refused to function in this role.

One of these lives must be a dream from which she would wake to find herself exclusively in the other, but which was the dream and which the reality? At first she would have said England was the dream, but now, after seventeen years, she was not so sure. Soon she would have lived half her life in this country. Reverend Manley had asked her on numerous occasions since her elevation in status from servant to companion whether she would like to go back for a visit. She knew he would have been only too willing to pay for this, and perhaps to pay for Adam as well. He felt completely unthreatened by her past. It was right that she should be able to see her parents again before they died, and he could not conceive of losing her. Why would anyone elect to stay in the country she had described to him over the life he was providing for her here? But Erika had no desire to return. There was no connection; there could be no connection. She was afraid to return.

෴

Ella, the elder daughter, was getting married in early July of the summer Adam finished school. It was a highly proper county wedding. Her fiancé was the elder brother of the Daniel who had been Adam's best friend as a boy, and the lands of the two families adjoined. It was, nevertheless, so everyone insisted, a love match. Erika did not understand why this needed to be stated and restated; she had no concept of what an age-old pattern of betrothal and marriage the two young people were fulfilling.

It was to be an elaborate affair with a marquee in the garden near the river and a band playing well into the evening. Jack polished all the silver and brass; extra knives and forks were brought in from the groom's family, so Jack polished those also because he was convinced Rupert, his counterpart in the other household, would not do it as well as he. Erika was involved in a sub-organizational capacity, just one step below Mrs. Manley. Millie cooked and baked. The cake was ordered from Fortnums; the dress came from Fenwicks. The veil came out of the tissue paper in the drawer where it had rested between weddings for generations. Adam was especially favoured by being asked to be best man, while Daniel was to be an usher.

The morning of the great day arrived, and, yes, the sun was shining. Ella was beautiful as she processed into the old church where her father had presided for thirty years. Adam performed his role with distinction.

Back at the house, there was much eating, drinking and laughter. Then, in the late afternoon, Alice looked around and said, "Where's Adam?"

"Don't know. He was here earlier playing his clarinet with the band. Maybe he went into the house for a rest," Daniel said. All at once everyone realized that, in the midst of the festivity, they had not noticed Adam for quite some time – hours, in fact. He was not in the house or the garden either, for that matter. His room was empty, and a suitcase, some of his casual clothes and other personal belongings were missing.

Erika was doubly distressed, both for herself and for the Manleys. And guilty as well. Who ought to have foreseen this and prevented it if not she? At a subterranean level she felt that this had happened because of what she had done all those years ago, as if the propensity to run away were genetic. "Now you know what it feels like," she could hear judgmental voices crowing. "Now you know. You've been paid back at last."

In Waldenstein the wedding celebrations would have been suspended while the runaway was searched for. But this was not Waldenstein. After the initial consternation, the family put on a brave face and continued as if nothing had happened. Young people danced in the marquee and some launched boats and rowed on the river. The food and wine continued to be excellent and abundant. Erika carried on with her role as part servant, part hostess. By nightfall, everyone agreed it had been a splendid wedding.

Only on the next day were the police informed and a search begun. But Adam was nowhere to be found.

"Do you have any idea where he might have gone?" Reverend Manley questioned Erika, not harshly, but with an intimation that she ought to have some idea of what went on in the head of her own son.

"No. He said nothing to me. Never."

"Was he unhappy? Did he not want to go to Kings?"

"I'm sure it's not that. Only…"

"Only what?"

287

"Only...he just might have tried to go back to Nova Scotia."

"What makes you think so?"

"It's just a hunch. He always wanted to know who his father was."

"But surely I have been a father to him. Was that not enough?"

Erika felt a terrible guilt, as if she had been subversive in even telling Adam he had a father, who would of necessity became a mysterious figure endowed with who knew what qualities. Could this man standing accusingly before her not see that this was likely to happen, that it was almost inevitable?

"Yes, you have been as good as any father to him, of course," she said, not daring to look up at him, wringing her hands quietly in her lap.

He saw she had nothing more to offer, so he left her alone and set out for Liverpool. Erika ran to her old room in the attic and wept.

There was nothing definite to be discovered in Liverpool. Yes, a boat had left for Halifax the day before, but that was not extraordinary. Yes, such freighters sometimes took passengers, but how would any of the men loafing around the wharf know whom or whether? He returned to his estate defeated. By now nearly forty-eight hours had elapsed. It occurred to Reverend Manley (as it had already occurred to Erika) that Adam had not chosen Ella's wedding day to disappear out of malice or spite. He had chosen it because he knew that on that day he would not be pursued.

Erika felt a sense of déjà vu. Seventeen years ago a young girl had left her parents' home intending never to be found again. Now a young man had done the same thing. Adam had gone. Who could be certain where?

Coming Home

1934–1935

All that winter it snowed. Sometimes the flakes fell down slowly like large balls of cotton batting, covering the earth with a soft down. At other times the snow came in tiny, pellet-like fragments that blew fiercely and stung like needles, piercing the tender skin.

The family of Aaron and Agnes had diminished. Hannah and Joan had followed their elder sisters to Normal College and now, like them, were out teaching in tiny one-room schools. The weather was such that only rarely could any of them come back for a weekend. So only Rachel, who was finishing school, and Harry, who worked with his father, remained – and, of course, Flora, who would never leave.

"How quiet it is now," Rachel said one night to her mother. She missed her sisters and their boisterous, argumentative chatter. Flora rarely spoke, and even Agnes seemed to have taken a vow of silence. She came to depend more and more on Flora for household tasks. There were fewer of them than there had been in earlier years, and Flora now did most of the cleaning and baking, while Agnes spent most of her time in the rocking chair in the sitting room knitting and sewing. Only Harry's room Flora refused to enter – not to take back clean laundry or even to pick up a single sock from the floor. So Agnes herself had to do this; obviously Harry could not be expected to.

In late November Aaron and Harry went off to the lumber camp with their men. They had a male cook now, as they had had every year since Erika left. He was efficient and made their simple fare with gusto, but Aaron sometimes thought back to that winter when, after the day's work was done, he could read books with Erika. That had been the real pleasure, not the momentary madness that had altered both their lives forever. Perhaps it could have been different if he....

Harry was a great help now, but he did not share his father's love of books. He had left school at thirteen and had been working with his father ever since. He was industrious and intelligent about the things a woodsman needed to be intelligent about – though sometimes Aaron wondered how he would manage the business side of things on his own – finding buyers for the lumber, negotiating a good price, keeping up repairs to the mill, looking after the men. It was the latter that worried Aaron most. The men who had worked happily with him for twenty, thirty years did not like Harry. He was abrupt and domineering with them.

"Get out there and do an honest day's work – if you know how." This to Ephraim Zwicker, as he drew a last comforting suck on his morning pipe while pulling his boots on.

"Stuck up slave-driver," Ephraim muttered as he emptied the pipe and went out the door.

As November moved into December, Aaron found himself more and more exhausted, so that he ended up spending some days doing nothing but lying on his bunk. Still, it was with some misgivings that he finally decided to go home and leave the operation to Harry. Naturally, this was temporary. He'd just go home and have a little rest – maybe until after Christmas – and then he'd be back again, good as new.

When Christmas came Aaron was no better, but at least his girls had all come home, bringing presents for everyone with them.

"Oh it's really good to be back here again," and Hannah flung herself down on the old sofa beside Emma and Virtue.

"That's no reason to be throwing yourself around and destroying the furniture." Emma looked up from her book.

"But that's precisely the point of home. You can fling yourself around and destroy the furniture if you want to."

Aaron sat in the rocking chair, smiling at his schoolteacher daughters. They were smart and good-looking, and confident in the outside world – even if none of them had got a man yet. Flora was grinning from ear to ear as she brought in some biscuits she had just baked. She had a responsible position, and her sisters deferred to her in domestic matters and helped her in the household work. Only Harry stood in the corner, refusing the biscuits, chewing on a piece of spruce gum. "Barn chores need doing; I'm off." And he was gone.

That night Emma and Virtue again slept together in the old bed. "Have you noticed how Papa looks?" Emma whispered.

"Yes, he's positively grey – grey everywhere, not just his hair."

"And Mama. She hardly moves at all anymore. She pretends to be busy, standing by the stove, wiping her hands on her apron, and then she just sits down on a chair again, breathing fast and heavy. It's Flora who does it all now."

"Do you think we could get them to go to a doctor?"

"No!" And Emma turned over on her side as she always had done when the night-time conversation was over.

But Virtue had something more to say: "Emma…"

"Umm…what?"

"Nathan. Has he spoken to you?"

"Maybe."

"Oh don't be coy with me. Has he or hasn't he? Because Obadiah has, and he said Nathan was going to and that they were both coming over on Christmas Day to tell our parents."

"Well, well. He seems pretty certain of what we'll say, doesn't he, if he's arranged all that." And Emma turned over again, decisively. Virtue felt she had her answer.

🌱

Christmas Day: The parlour was filled with presents spilling out from under the tree over the carpet in a riot of colourful wrapping and ribbon. Emma brought silk scarves for Agnes and Flora; Virtue gave each of her sisters leather gloves lined with silk. They clubbed together and gave Aaron and Harry wristwatches. Agnes got a brown velvet dress, a luxury undreamt of in the girls' childhood. "Look what we've got you!" And Agnes smiled and put on the dress, which (bought to fit the size she had been a year ago) now hung in folds around her. But no one mentioned this. Virtue merely insisted that she have second helpings of everything because the food, for which Flora took all the credit, was more wonderful than ever before. There was a real turkey, not just a large chicken, stuffed with a summer savoury and onion dressing, and all the old favourites as well – mashed turnip, carrots, parsnips, roast potatoes, pickled green beans, and for dessert a choice of pumpkin pie, mincemeat pie or curd pie. Agnes did not refuse the second helpings, but they were still on her plate when it was cleared away.

Afterwards they gathered around the reed organ and sang Christmas carols, while Rachel, who had been practising especially for the occasion, pumped and played.

"I shall remember this always," thought Rachel as she listened to all the voices behind her singing in unison. "We must do this every Christmas to the end of time."

Suddenly there were two more voices, one of them singing a strong bass line. Nathan and Obadiah had arrived and, when no one heard their knocking, walked in and joined the chorus.

After they sat down, the chairs were pulled about and they chattered in groups, the sound rising and falling, a loud laugh breaking out here, an exclamation ("No, you didn't!") there. Eventually Obadiah stood up, and with a self-important air declared, "I have something to say."

There was a hush. Virtue blushed; Emma didn't. "We've fixed up the house in Lunenburg. It's got two kitchens now, all the latest stuff in them, and two living rooms. And, of course, there's the bedrooms upstairs. And we've even put in a bathroom." Here he seemed ready to stop, but then, in a rush, he added, "Virtue and I are going to get married." A great clapping of hands. "And (he paused and nodded to his younger brother) Emma and Nathan are going to get married too." More applause.

Then Emma jumped up, pulling Nathan up with her: "I just want to say…to say that we are not 'too'; we are getting married first, foremost, and because we wish to."

Obadiah looked abashed; Nathan stared at the carpet. Everyone clapped a bit more to fill up the hole that had opened.

"Why did you have to do that?" Nathan whispered.

"Why did you let Obadiah announce *our* engagement?"

"Because he wanted to; he said it was best if just one of us did it, and he was older."

"Well, Virtue's older than me, but she's never tried to pull anything like that."

That night in bed, Virtue chastised Emma. "Why did you have to ruin it all?"

"I didn't ruin it all. When you said Obadiah was going to announce your engagement you didn't mention that he was going to announce mine as well."

"You always have to be first, don't you?"

Then they lapsed into silence, each lost in her own reverie. Marriage, Virtue thought. She and Obadiah eating an eternity of blissful meals together, going for long walks in the evening after he had finished work, lying together at night in the same bed – though her thoughts did not stray as far as sex itself. On the other hand, she did imagine children, not conceived by any natural means, but perfect little beings, receptive, quiet, attentive, loving – unlike the children she taught.

Emma, to her consternation, found herself thinking not of Nathan at all but of Johannes, Johannes Selig. It was all so long ago now. She knew what married life with Nathan would be. She would be secure and warm; she would be loved; Nathan would be faithful, of that she was sure. But that was just it – deep down she longed for a life that was not secure but enchanted. The word came to her and slid into her fading consciousness like a jewel – deep blue, many-faceted, refracting light in all directions. Enchanted. Each day would open on new prospects; life would be a landscape of verdant, flowering arches of greenery, flowing from one scene to another. It would be abuzz with ideas, with patterns forming and reforming, a kaleidoscope of dazzling configurations. As she was falling asleep, Johannes came and kissed her. She shuddered; she was engaged to be married. This lover was a fiction. Nathan was real; that was both his strength and his weakness.

ᴓ

As Agnes climbed slowly up the stairs that night she heard weeping. It was coming from Flora's room, so she went in.

"What's the matter, Flora?"

"I want to get married too."

"Ah, yes." She sighed. After such an eventful and tiring day, now this. "Well, that may not happen. But you are so important to all of us. We couldn't have managed Christmas at all without you. And as for being married…well, it's not everything."

ᴓ

Nathan and Obadiah went back to Lunenburg, quite pleased with themselves.

"That went pretty well, I think," Obadiah observed complacently. Nathan kept any reservations to himself. The girls must have known they planned to marry them for ages; perhaps they even wondered why they had to wait so long to be asked. Virtue would be nearly thirty-one and Emma twenty-nine. But you couldn't ask a woman to marry until you had a house to put her in and a secure income to keep her there. They now had both. The Cape Cod house had a central hall with four rooms downstairs and four upstairs. Originally these had been a kitchen, dining room, living room and spare bedroom downstairs and four bedrooms upstairs. Obadiah and Nathan had converted the downstairs into two living rooms and two kitchens, one set of each on either side of the central hall. Upstairs, the bedrooms were fine as they were, and they turned a large five-sided bay on the front of the house into a bathroom. So far, so good.

Still, and particularly after Emma's outburst that very afternoon, Nathan had some misgivings. The central hall, or, for that matter, the bathroom, to whom did they belong? The hall clearly was shared territory. It had to be. The only form of heating – a furnace in the basement – had its one and only register in the centre of the hallway, and the steps to the upper floor went up from the hall as well. It also meant that there was no way that doors to kitchens or living rooms could be shut in winter, unless one wanted to freeze to death. And the bathroom also must be shared because there was no space for a second one.

When he had mentioned how they planned to live to some of his customers in the barbershop, they had implied that it was an odd way to begin married life. But Obadiah didn't think so. And Emma and Virtue didn't seem to think so either. Each of them, the brothers and the sisters, had shared a bed with the other in childhood, so nothing could seem more natural to them than that, in marriage, they should merely change the pairings. Life would be shared; the takings of the barber shop would be divided strictly in half, the cleaning of the common spaces would alternate week by week, and their children, double cousins, would play happily together. Nathan sighed gently, and let it go.

Spring came, and the men, including Harry, returned from the woods. Aaron had never managed to go back after Christmas. He pottered around the house and the farm a bit, but mostly he just sat on the sofa. Agnes remarked that now they really needed two rocking chairs! Aaron was sixty, Agnes only in her mid-fifties. But they felt old; they looked old. The life one led in Waldenstein did not, in most cases, lead to an active and blissful old age.

One evening, Agnes looked up from her knitting. Rachel and Flora had already gone to bed and Harry was out. "We need to talk."

Aaron was in industrial England with the Gradgrinds, congratulating himself that he had never treated his men as brutally as it seemed Bounderby did. "About what?"

"Flora."

"I don't know what to do about Flora. You *know* that. I've told you over and over." Aaron had reasoned long ago that Flora couldn't be his fault, his punishment from a just God, because her tragedy had happened before his "mistake." And if he was not guilty, why should he worry? Why did he need to take responsibility?

"Because whether you like it or not, she's your daughter. What is going to happen to her when we're gone? You ought to make some provision for her. Do you really think she'll go and live with one of her sister's families?"

"Well, why not?"

"Because they won't want her, that's why not. Your daughter will find herself out doing housework for any family that will give her room and board. You've got to make a will, I tell you."

"I'll get around to it. Just give me time, will you?" He put his head down in the book again. Agnes sighed.

So things went on, until one morning Aaron stepped out of bed and fell heavily to the floor. Agnes heard the thud from the kitchen and ran upstairs. By this time he was holding on to the edge of the bed, trying to get up. He was just a bit dizzy, he said.

Agnes called Harry, who was out doing the barn chores. "Your father's fallen and needs the doctor. Go."

When Dr. Beale arrived he looked at Aaron and questioned him. Had he been dizzy before? Was he tired a lot of the time? Breathless? Then he stuck a large needle into a vein in his arm and fed the blood into a little vial. He said he'd get it sent to Halifax for them to test. Meanwhile Aaron had better just take it easy and try not to worry. Also, he should eat lots of red meat and spinach; spinach should be coming along in the garden fairly soon.

They decided not to call the girls home; it would only worry them unnecessarily. Between them, Flora and Agnes toiled up and down the stairs attending to Aaron's needs. Rachel helped as well, but she had her final school exams in a few weeks and so must be protected. Sometimes Agnes herself was so tired that she had to sit down part way up the stairs to rest.

Two weeks later Dr. Beale returned. "It's not good news, I'm afraid. It looks like pernicious anaemia."

"What's that?" So Dr. Beale explained that "pernicious" meant very bad, not able to be wiped out, and "anaemia" was a lack of iron in the blood, which made one very tired and not able to think or work properly. Usually when one had just ordinary anaemia, one could get better by eating the right kind of things, like liver and spinach, but if one had "pernicious" anaemia, then the body had a problem; it couldn't convert the iron in the food one ate into the right kind of red blood cells.

"So," Agnes began tentatively, "what happens then?"

"Then..." Dr Beale seemed lost in thought. A minute later, he turned and looked hard at Aaron, who seemed to have no will of his own at all anymore. "I'll tell you what we can do. We can try to give you a blood transfusion." Then he added, "Of course the blood type must match his, so we will need to test the children to see who is a good match. Turning to Agnes, as if Aaron had already departed this earth, he continued, "He's AB negative, which is quite rare, but one or more of the children might have the same type."

Most of this made no sense to Agnes, but at least one thing was clear: the children had to be told and called home for testing.

No one matched. Not one of his children! How could this be? Was he not their father? But this he put out of his head. Agnes was incapable of deceit. He lay back on his bed. Then, faintly, he allowed himself to remember that he had another son – a dim, ghostly figure that he had never known. He would be eighteen now – a man. Perhaps… but he was in England, as far as he knew, unreachable, and anyway….

What had Dr. Beale said before coming up with the transfusion idea? Agnes had asked him what would happen. What had he replied? Aaron tried desperately to remember. Maybe he hadn't replied. Aaron could see him turning slightly away, looking out the window. But he couldn't remember any words. Perhaps, just perhaps, there had been no words. Then he had turned back and mentioned a transfusion, and everyone felt better; something could be done. But now the transfusion wasn't happening; it couldn't because not one of his children was, in some way he didn't quite understand, "right." Not even Harry. A certain bitterness crept into his thinking; it seemed there had been a failure – his, or his children's? He was very tired; the wind coming in through the white curtains was pleasantly cool. He slept.

Days passed like this. Meals were brought, and he ate some of them; he was moved and sat up in a chair while Flora and Agnes changed the bed linen; sometimes he propped himself up and tried to read a book. Then he fell asleep again.

After the school year ended, the girls returned home. They came up to his room and tried to "cheer him up." He was glad to see them, of course, but all emotion, all life, seemed to be viewed through a gauze wrapping. Everything was flimsy, insubstantial. He rather wished they would go away and let him sleep.

᚛

Monday of the third week of July: Emma was making bread, and Virtue was cooking a stew for dinner. Hannah was out doing the barn work. Well, someone had to do it, and Harry was running the sawmill.

Joan was cleaning in the sitting room, talking to Agnes who sat knitting in her chair, when a strange noise from outside attracted their attention. It sounded like a motor, but the only motor in Waldenstein was a small tractor Ebenezer Conrad had bought the previous spring. Looking out, what Emma saw was a cloud of dust coming across the field towards them, a small whirlwind, like something apocalyptic. As she watched, transfixed, she saw there was a vehicle, a car, a rather large and grand car inside the cloud. It whirled closer and closer; it was coming to them, stopping at their very door.

A young man got out of the passenger seat. He had dark hair and piercing grey-blue eyes. The eyes looked vaguely familiar. What was not at all familiar was what he was wearing. This person (or scarcely person, more god) was dressed in a suit and waistcoat; his black shoes glistened in the early afternoon sunlight. Not that Emma took in all this detail at once; in fact, all she really took in was that something strange and marvellous was happening.

"Virtue!"

"What?"

"Someone's coming."

"Who?"

"I...I don't know. I've never seen him before in my life. A stranger."

Now Virtue came to the window as well. But the young man was too close to the door to be viewed clearly anymore.

Emma remembered that night so long ago that Flora had her "fits." She and Virtue had been tumbled out of a warm bed by the noise, catapulted down the stairs and out into a strange, cold world. They had been in a shell, a small, protected place, and then the shell had broken, and they had fallen out into a frightening new space where no one, least of all Flora, was the same.

The young man knocked, and Emma opened the door.

"Excuse me, but I'm looking for Mr. Aaron Miller. Do I have the right house?"

"Yes," Emma replied faintly, holding on to the doorpost. As soon as he spoke, she knew, beyond any doubt, who this young man was. After an awkward pause, he said, "I'm Adam. I've come to see my father."

Another pause, and Emma replied, "Yes, I know." Then she managed to add, "Come in."

By this time Joan was standing in the kitchen door, open-mouthed. Virtue had not moved from the window. Everything seemed to have frozen, and just one movement, one gesture even, would break the fragile equilibrium and shatter it all. Emma steeled herself to make that movement. "I'll tell my Mother," she said.

Adam looked down at Aaron, gaunt and shrunken under the bed-clothes. Was this what he had come three thousand miles to see? This abject figure on the bed?

He looked around the room with its faded wallpaper, some-what tatty lace curtains moving languidly against the open window, the crudely fashioned pine dresser, the linoleum with a worn flower pattern on the floor, the hooked rug by the bed. This was the richest house in Waldenstein, his mother had said. But he had lived all his life among polished eighteenth-century mahogany and William Morris wallpaper. How could he have imagined this?

Still, he had come. The figure on the bed seemed not to have noticed him, so he bent down and spoke softly. "I'm Adam, your son," he said.

Aaron stirred; his eyes gazed up blankly at the young man standing over him. "My son...." His gaze fixed on the clean-cut features, the tidily parted hair, then down to the shirt and waistcoat. "My son is Harry," he said, decisively.

"I think there were two sons," Adam said gently. "I'm Erika's boy, Adam."

Then fear and joy passed in quick succession over Aaron's features. He shuddered slightly. "Erika's boy...*my* boy." He raised himself slowly up in the bed and asked, "Do you like to read?"

"Yes, of course I like to read."

"Your mother...she and I...we read together."

"I know. She has told me."

By now Aaron had come fully to consciousness. "Sit down. Talk to me."

ﺑ

Downstairs, all was confusion. While Agnes wept silently, Emma and Virtue scurried around, making her a cup of tea. Joan sat beside her, holding her hand.

"I never thought...," Agnes sobbed.

"Shh...Neither did any of us."

Virtue was concentrating on the practical. "Where will he stay?" she whispered to Emma.

"Well, not here." Emma was certain of that. Then, with genuine fear in her voice, she continued, "What will Harry do when he comes home?" Even Virtue had no answer to this.

"Maybe Adam could go to stay with Erika's family. After all, they're his grandparents."

"Who will take him all the way over there. Or...wait...his car's still here." Virtue looked out the window, and sure enough, there it was in all its gleaming splendour. The driver was reading a newspaper.

The afternoon lengthened. Eventually they heard Adam's footsteps on the stairs. He came in to the sitting room and addressed Agnes.

"I'm so sorry. I know this must be very upsetting for you. But surely you understand why I needed to come. And I'm so glad I arrived before...."

Just then something occurred to Emma. Here was another child whose blood had not been tested. Just perhaps....

"Mama...I've just thought...maybe Adam...if he really is Papa's child as well...maybe he could help Papa."

"Help Papa?"

"Yes, have his blood tested to see if it matches."

Adam stood confused, so Emma explained. "You see, Adam, (how strange to be addressing this young man, her half-brother, in this familiar way), it seems that if Papa could have a blood transfusion, it might make him better. None of us has the right kind of blood, but you...well, you just might."

At this moment, the back door swung open, and there was Harry, large and sweaty from his day working at the mill. "What in the name of...what's goin' on here?" For a moment, when he saw the large black car beside the house, he had thought, irrationally, that it was a hearse that had come to take his father away. But, of course, the car wasn't a hearse; he could see that. Now he stood in the kitchen, demanding answers.

Virtue met him. "Hush. Go and wash, Harry. We have company."

"What company? What stuck-up city slicker comes in a car like that?"

By now Emma was there as well. "Your brother, Harry. Adam has come back."

"Go and wash," Virtue insisted.

For a moment Harry stood, motionless. Then he shouted at Virtue, "Wash, woman! Wash! When this guy has come back now just to take my inheritance?" He moved towards the sitting room, where

Adam was saying that yes, of course, he would have his blood tested if that might help.

"So what have you come for? Timing's good, what?" Harry leaned menacingly against the door post, blocking any exit.

"Excuse me? You're...?" Adam got up from where he had been kneeling beside Agnes' chair.

"I'm Harry."

Adam moved towards him offering his hand. But Harry flailed out at him. "Don't think I don't know why you've come back. I don't know where from and I don't care. You have no business here."

"I came to find my father."

It was then that Harry struck him.

Suddenly everyone was in the room together in total confusion. Emma and Virtue dragged Harry away. "Behave yourself, Harry. This is no way to treat a guest."

"He's no guest. He's a trouble-maker, a fortune-hunter." And then, to Adam, "Get out!"

Adam thought of Cranley. But Cranley had no cause to hate him. Perhaps Harry did. He said, "Yes, of course, I'll go. My car is waiting." And he moved towards the door.

All this time Agnes sat transfixed. She had known, of course, had known from the beginning, even though Aaron could never bring himself to admit it. But knowing was one thing; having the living proof, the knowledge made physical – that was another. Such a fine young man! All that time upstairs with Aaron – what had passed between them? Then Harry had hit him, hit him right in front of her. It was unbearable; there must be some escape. Instinctively, she tried to rise from the chair. She had no idea what she was going to do. She just knew that she must do something; there must be some redress, some way out. Her whole life had been a trap, and now she must finally break free. So she rose, but as she did so everything seemed to recede and grow dim. She was in a vast, dark space, frighteningly empty. No sound, no colour. Still, there was freedom; the constraints, like everything else, had vanished.

As everyone moved towards the door with Adam, Agnes sank to the sitting room floor.

"Mama? Mama!"

"She's fainted; get some water."

Harry ignored this new confusion and slipped away. Adam stood apart, in consternation.

They rubbed her temples, offered her water, tried every remedy, weeping as they worked on her still body. At last Virtue said, falteringly, "She's not dead, is she?"

There was a pause. Then Emma said, "Send someone for the doctor."

"I can send my car, if someone can come with the driver to show him the way." So Emma got into the car with Adam and began the drive to New Germany. But not before Flora ran up to Adam, beat him on the chest, and screamed, "You've killed Mama!"

"No, Flora, Adam hasn't killed her." But deep down, it was what they all were thinking.

⚞

Driving to New Germany with Adam, Emma felt a strange sense of reprieve. She was no longer in a world of events and consequences, but suspended, cushioned by the large automobile from anything real. So she concentrated on Adam, this strange being who had dropped from nowhere and was yet so intimately entangled with all of them.

"How did you know?" was her first question, and "How did you get here?" her second.

Over the course of the journey to the doctor and back they exchanged stories. She told him about how she had said he looked like Harry when he was in his pram, and everyone had seemed appalled by the idea. And when she mentioned that she was engaged to be married to one Nathan, he exclaimed, "Not my mother's little brother! She has told me all about him, and I've even brought back the little carved bird he made for me when I was a baby."

"You will see him soon," Emma promised. "He and Obadiah come up to visit every weekend."

The idea that she was having this conversation while her mother lay at home, probably dead, seemed bizarre and natural at the same time. Again she returned to that night of crisis, when she and Virtue had gone through the snow to fetch Ebenezer Conrad, and that journey also had given a reprieve from what was actually happening. Now, coming back to the house with Adam and the doctor, she felt the old sensation of sick fear embrace her. As she entered, she saw that the worst she feared was true. Agnes had been laid out on a makeshift bed on the floor, and all her sisters were in tears around her. Dr. Beale could only confirm what they already knew.

Adam did not come back into the house. Emma had told him where to find his grandparents, and the car and driver whisked him away.

All this time no one had dared to go upstairs to tell Aaron, who had fallen asleep after his long talk with Adam. Now he was awake and calling out querulously, "Where is everyone? I'm thirsty."

Who would go? In the end it was Virtue. She walked up the stairs slowly and quietly. When she entered the room she could not think of what to say, so she blurted out, "Papa, Mama has died."

At first he seemed not to understand. "Died? But she's not sick."

"Maybe we just didn't know she was sick. Anyway, I'm afraid it's true. The doctor's downstairs now."

He fell back on the pillows and covered his face with his hands. For several minutes, Virtue waited. Then Aaron removed his hands, looked up at his weeping daughter and said a most peculiar thing: "I want Adam. Send Adam up to me." But, of course, Adam was not there.

ॐ

Adam approached the house of Jacob and Frederika with trepidation. Everything was happening too fast – the landscape, the people who spoke with a strange accent, the death of Agnes (*had* he killed her?), the rage of Harry.

So now, as his car pulled up before his grandparents' white house, he was afraid. Again, he knocked on a strange door. But here there was no confusion. Intuitively, Frederika knew at once who he was. "Adam, you've come back." And she drew him inside and kissed him. "Jacob, it's Adam." The driver and the car were dismissed, and Adam was taken into his family.

Erika, how was she? And so he began the fantastic tale of Erika, the daughter who was supposed to marry her cousin Dilphin and live a comfortable life in Waldenstein. Erika, who now played the piano, who went to concerts and plays with the Manleys, who lived in a house they could not begin to imagine. He showed them pictures; they gaped in disbelief. Erika, who had shown signs of plumpness in her youth, was now slim and chic, a proper lady. They were amazed, their darker imaginings confounded by this manifest reality.

Then there was supper. Frederika couldn't stop apologizing for the homely fare – fresh bread, cold meat, some tomatoes just ripened in the garden, freshly picked berries. But Adam ate with gusto. The food was good and served with love. Had he ever eaten a meal before prepared by people who loved him?

Only after they had eaten did he tell them about Agnes. "Poor Agnes," Frederika said. "She had a hard life. You might not think so, because Aaron could give her more than most husbands could, but he expected an awful lot back. She had a hard life…and, I guess," she added, "if I'm honest, Erika made it harder."

"And my coming back was the final blow," Adam said.

"No, you mustn't think that. Everyone but Aaron has known she wasn't well for ages. She wasn't goin' to last, no matter what."

"She was the best of that couple, believe me," was Jacob's verdict.

That night Adam slept in his mother's bed, the bed in which he had been born. In spite of the traumas of the day, he fell asleep quickly and did not wake up until morning.

Endings and Beginnings

Summer, 1935

Agnes' funeral was held on Wednesday. Somehow, Aaron managed to attend. A car and a wheelchair were procured, and Aaron was moved carefully from one to the other and wheeled into the church. Adam too went to the funeral, though he carefully stayed with Jacob and Frederika. The entire community was there, whether chiefly to honour Agnes or to see the illegitimate son was unclear. Naturally, they all knew, despite Frederika's denial, that it was Adam's return that had killed her. Poor Agnes, confronted by the sins of her husband even in her last hour!

Reverend Herzel spoke glowingly of Agnes – devoted wife, exemplary mother, bearing and caring for her large family with exquisite devotion, never thinking of herself, and so on and on. Remarkably, for a eulogy, most of this was true. What was not true was his assertion that she had borne it cheerfully.

At the graveside, Aaron finally wept. She had been so small, so lovely. He had destroyed her.

When the service was over, Adam went up to the two young men he had seen sitting with Emma and Virtue. "You must be Nathan and Obadiah." And he presented, like a talisman, the little bird that Nathan had carved for him when he was a baby. That evening, the entire Wentzell family, except for Erika, ate together.

Two days after Agnes' funeral, Dr. Beale turned up at the Miller's house. Aaron had declined notably. Getting out of bed was no longer possible; the girls took turns carrying up meals and carrying them down again, largely uneaten. They sat beside his bed and read to him – though much of the time he simply slept. He seemed too tired even to grieve.

Twice, Adam came to visit him, selecting his times carefully so that Harry was sure to be away at the mill. But what did father and son have to say to one another after all these years? What *could* they say? Aaron could not acknowledge guilt; he believed he had done all he could do – slip Erika a bit of money and leave her to work out her own destiny. Could Adam blame him? *Did* Adam blame him? Even Adam himself was not sure. Certainly, from his own perspective, his life had turned out better than if he had stayed in Waldenstein. But there was that primal need, the need for the father. Aaron, who had had no father of his own for most of his childhood, had dismissed that need with scarcely a thought.

Now here was Dr. Beale telling Aaron that, amazingly, he could have a blood transfusion after all. His one remaining child, his hitherto unacknowledged child, had the magic blood that could save him. To Adam, it was the final seal on his paternity. No one could deny it now, not even Harry. Or so he thought.

Harry was predictably outraged – so outraged that he went straight out to Dr. Beale's house that very evening and made a terrible scene. "How do you know that the blood is right? And my blood is wrong? You show me!" Here he seized Dr. Beale by the collar, so that Mrs. Beale, standing in the doorway, wondered if she should call for help. "You show me! Show me right now!"

"If you let go, I can show you the results of the test," said Dr. Beale. He went to his filing cabinet and, from Aaron's file, pulled out two small pieces of paper with the blood test results scratched in black ink. "Here, you see, most of you, including yourself, are A positive, which was your mother's blood type. A few, like Emma, are AB but positive, not negative. Now here, more recently, is Adam's result: he does turn out to be AB negative, just like your father. That's why he can donate blood to your father and none of the rest of you can." Dr. Beale was shaking before this madman, but he managed to put the case with remarkable lucidity, he thought.

Harry was not appeased. "I don't believe you can do that to blood. You and all them people – what you call them, lab technicians – they're all in this together. You side with Adam just because you and him got some education. But I tell you, I can do as much or more than you guys. Just you wait and see."

"This has nothing to do with ability. It is just about trying to give your father a transfusion that will help him, not kill him. If you care for your father, you should be glad that a donor has been found."

"Well, even if he does have the right kind of blood, that don't prove he's his son."

"No, of course it doesn't *prove* it, but given the rareness of the blood type, it is a reasonable indication."

"Go ahead, then. But, believe me, this better cure him."

"It won't cure him, you must understand that. But it may give him some more time." And with that, Dr. Beale suggestively opened the door and stood beside it. Harry left; Dr. Beale poured himself a large Scotch.

ᛒ

The transfusion could only take place in a hospital.

"A hospital," Rachel said softly. Everyone in Waldenstein knew that to go to a hospital was the next thing to going to a morgue.

Nevertheless, an ambulance was arranged, and Aaron, with Emma, Virtue and, necessarily, Adam, travelled to Bridgewater. There everything became surreal. For a start, everything smelled funny.

Even Adam, who had little experience of hospitals, noticed it. Then there was the strange, calm efficiency about the place that took no account of the drama of life and death constantly unfolding there. Dr. Beale supervised everything. Needles were procured; blood oozed into a bag; then Aaron was on a white bed in a white room, where the dripping blood stood out, flamboyant, against everything else.

Aaron stayed in hospital and, for a few days, he rallied. "I'm glad you're having a good life," he said to Adam one day. "I'm glad you've got a good education. And I'm glad Erika...she's happy too?"

"I don't know," said Adam. And this was the truth.

Then Aaron went on, "Don't stay here. It wouldn't work out. You see, Harry...." He couldn't finish. But Adam understood. Did he at last see in Harry what he had created?

"No, I didn't come expecting to stay," Adam assured him. "I just wanted to meet you and my grandparents, and see the place my mother talks about."

"She still talks about here, does she?" Aaron seemed surprised. Then he added, hesitantly, "Does she ever talk about me?"

"Not really. Not much. That's why I needed to find you for myself."

"Ah." He lapsed into silence, drawing his own conclusions. They seemed to be unsatisfactory, because Adam saw a tear on his lined face. Then he fell asleep once more.

❧

Harry came as well. "I'm glad you're looking so much better, Papa." But he could not help himself; soon he was delving into the storm of resentment he felt towards Adam. "That fellow, well, he may have given you his blood, but he's not really anything to do with us, is he?"

Now, what could Aaron say? "You're my son, Harry, and I've given you all I have. Isn't that enough?"

"But this Adam, he's not really your son, is he?"

Then Aaron sighed and said nothing. Harry had to draw his own conclusions.

"You…you…No wonder Mama died!" He strode out of the hospital room.

Aaron lay back, and a kaleidoscope of pictures moved before him. He was standing alone in the orchard with a map; everything was possible. Then, what he had not thought of as possible happened: Agnes – tiny, beautiful Agnes had come and given herself to him. Next he was struggling to hold down a screaming Flora, his lovely, gifted Flora. He sighed. "Everything all right, Mr. Miller?" A starched nurse passed the foot of his bed.

"Yes. Everything fine."

The mill. Reading with Erika. Holding Erika. Then he could bear to remember nothing more. Agnes, the blood, Erika's disappearance – it seared the edges of his brain; he would not let it enter into full consciousness. And after that? After that, what? Harry, promising Harry, who had somehow turned into a monster. Was this really his fault, as Agnes had claimed? And Reverend Selig. Here Aaron tried to sit up to think better until a nurse restrained him. "We're restless today, Mr. Miller. I'm sure one of your lovely daughters will be down to see you this afternoon." The nurse discerned that Harry's visit had not led to peace of mind.

Reverend Selig: Of course he had to be wrong. He was crazy, wasn't he? But maybe not. Emma said she had found the hills did all slope in one direction. Emma was a smart girl. Maybe…maybe… A whole edifice of certainty began to crumble. "Let Thy holy angel have charge concerning me, that the wicked one may have no power over me." It was all too difficult. He couldn't struggle with it now. Gradually the white walls around him faded.

When he woke up, Adam was there once more. "How are you feeling, Father?"

"I think I'm some better. Can't be sure unless I try to get up, and they won't let me do that yet." Then he added, "I'm glad you've come."

They talked for an hour – about Erika, about life in England, life at Eton, what Adam's life would be like at Cambridge. For Aaron, this was a reality that he never even had had the imagination to dream. His son! So clever, knowing so much. Then he took courage and asked him what he thought about, insofar as he could explain it, creation and evolution. "We had a minister here, a bit ago, a real clever fellow, but then he turned out to be crazy as well. Had some strange ideas...."

And gently, Adam revealed that he too believed these strange ideas, that in the world he lived in they were common knowledge. Aaron was stunned. "So maybe he wasn't crazy after all?"

"Well, not just because he believed those things, certainly," Adam replied.

"Emma...he liked Emma. Might have been a match if we hadn't sent him packing. But...but Nathan's a good man; he'll look after her."

"Yes, Nathan is indeed a good man. The very best." Adam put his hand on Aaron's shoulder and said good-bye.

Two days later, Aaron suffered a stroke and died. And he had *not* given Harry all he had, despite what he had said.

🐦

All of Waldenstein turned out for the funeral, and Reverend Herzel again tried to rise to the occasion. Aaron, he asserted, had been an exemplary man. He had built up the community single-handed, bought land, built a mill, generously (he seemed to imply) allowed all the able-bodied men in Waldenstein to work for him, all this while being also mindful of his duties to his wife and family. Often on winter weekends he would come home to visit them, sometimes at the risk of his life. He taught his children to read, sitting them on his knee and gently cajoling them; he taught his only son all the lore of the woods that he himself had mastered. The "only son" jarred a bit, though Adam was sitting tactfully two rows behind the rest of the family. And, withal, he was humble, working and suffering alongside his men and his family, sharing and trying to alleviate the vicissitudes of others. It was when he got to the word "vicissitudes" that old Josiah Veinot could not suppress a chuckle. "And he was never one of the frivolous time-wasters and nay-sayers, some of whom, alas, it was his lot to live among." So there was a sting in the tail. Eventually he ended, and they all paraded out of the little wooden church to the cemetery on the corner one hundred feet away, where a newly dug mound of earth stood to mark the grave. A few more words, then the coffin was lowered, and the life of Aaron Miller was covered with dust.

Jacob stood with Frederika, watching the coffin going down. "So that's that, then." He looked at Frederika. "What are you cryin' for? He's brought us nothin' but misery."

"He's brought us Adam."

"Not for long, I bet. He'll be gone in the wink of an eye. And he's lost us Erika forever. I know, just by the way Adam's talkin', she'll never come back."

Suddenly, they were very old. Slowly, they walked back the two miles from the cemetery side by side, saying nothing.

The Miller family went home to find that Martha Conrad was already there, making sandwiches and pouring cups of tea. Flora and Hannah began to help, passing around the sandwiches, while Emma and Virtue bustled about with the tea.

Harry stood propped up in a corner munching a sandwich. Everywhere he looked he saw nothing but pathetic weeping women – except for those two stuck-up brothers from the town. City-slickers, in their new suits and shiny shoes. What were they doing here anyway? His sisters hadn't actually married them yet, and if it were up to him he wouldn't let them contemplate it. Lily-livered no-goods they were, who couldn't hack the tough life in the woods. They looked just like the sort who would let their women walk all over them – which, given half a chance, Emma and Virtue most certainly would. When he got married he would have a wife who would do what he wanted her to do, and no mistake. Meanwhile, he was now the man of the family. He must sort out what to do with this collection of women that fate had dumped on him.

Then there was Adam, standing there in the corner, bending over Emma in her chair and saying goodness knows what to her. He glowered. Finally he could stand it no longer and went over to him: "Don't you make trouble!"

"Of course not. I'll be leaving in a few days."

And Adam tactfully said his good-byes and went back to his grandparents' house.

§

At last all the sandwiches had been eaten, the tea drunk. The girls sat around the parlour, their faces blank as school slates, finished even with tears.

At length Flora piped up, "Where will I live now? Will I stay here? Or where can I go?"

"*I'm* going to live here," said Harry, who had also remained unusually quiet until now. He knew that meant Flora neither could nor would.

Flora looked around the room in panic at her sisters, all of them with jobs except Rachel, and she was going to Normal College in September and would have a job after that. Emma and Virtue looked at one another helplessly. They would soon have a house. But Flora....

Nathan and Obadiah were lurking in the background, and Virtue saw Obadiah mouth, "No." This wasn't the time for *saying* "no," however, so they remained silent, hands clasped tightly together. Upstairs they could hear Martha beginning to clean the house.

Then Harry spoke again. "I shall have to find the will."

315

"There is no will. Mama told me." Virtue asserted her knowledge as the eldest alive and possessed of all her faculties.

"She must have been wrong. Papa couldn't have been so ill without making a will. He was a responsible person." A small arrow of fear shot through Harry. Suppose he didn't get it all, as he had assumed he would from childhood?

"No, Virtue is right," Emma asserted. "There is no will. Mama told me as well, and I remember Papa and Mama quarrelling, well not really quarrelling, but discussing, about a will a long time ago, and Papa just never got around to it. I don't think he knew how ill he was."

"Why? It's impossible! And besides…besides, he told me he had given me everything, *everything!* How can there be no will?"

"If you thought for a moment you'd know how, Harry, so just shut up and try." Emma had never spoken to her brother like this before. Harry turned around abruptly and raised his arm. For a moment Emma thought he might hit her. Then Rachel suddenly burst into uncontrollable sobs. "It's not real," she screamed, "I won't believe it's real!"

The long day wore on. At six o'clock Martha invited them all to come and eat the supper she had laid out in the dining room. After that there was more emptiness, more time. The days were so long in late July; they were a burden – just endless monotonous hours of sunlight, Emma thought. The slanting rays streaming through the window burned on the grief-stricken girls.

Finally, there was an interruption. Nathan and Obadiah said they must leave; they had to go back to Lunenburg to work the following day. Work, the sequence of days – it all seemed strange to Emma. Life going on as usual. How odd. She remembered that she was supposed to be getting married. In fact she was supposed to be getting married in two weeks' time. It was impossible. The world she was now in was one of timeless, static misery where nothing was ever going to happen again – certainly nothing good. Once more, she thought of Johannes. What might he have said to her now to console her? Nathan had simply held her and wiped her tears. Was this all anyone could do?

At last the day ended, and they could go to bed and cease feeling awkward that they had nothing to say to one another. As Virtue and Emma went up the stairs they heard weeping coming from Flora's room. They did not go in.

☙

"I must leave in six days," Adam said. "My passage back is for the last day of July."

Six more days – after seventeen years. It seemed very little. But then, it was more than they had expected. They had never expected to see him again at all.

So he stayed with them, sleeping on a straw mattress, eating their food, pumping cold water for himself with the kitchen pump, going to the outhouse, watching as Frederika washed his shirt on a scrubbing board, then starched and ironed it. He heard about the sad fate of Rose (how could he tell his mother this?) and saw the burnt-out house where her grandparents had died. He took flowers to the little cemetery – wild flowers that sprang up everywhere – and tried to comprehend what he had only known as a story.

Nathan and Obadiah managed to get up to visit him once more on Wednesday, their half day off, so they made an expedition to the other side of the Nine Mile Lake to see the logging camp where Erika had cooked. It was little changed from that time, and Adam found himself looking at the bunks lined up against the walls and trying to decide which had been his mother's. The curtain that Aaron had put up to shield his mother's privacy had long gone, but the bed that had been Aaron's was clearly discernible, since it was on the end and had no upper bunk. And next to it was another single bed. "Where does the cook sleep?" he asked innocently.

"There, just beside what was Aaron's bunk."

He knew he was looking at the bed in which he had been conceived. Not quite a stable, as he had visualized it in his childhood, but pretty close.

❧

Each night Adam lay awake in his mother's hard bed trying to make sense of life in this strange place. There was real warmth here, demonstrative love such as even Erika, living in England, had seemed afraid to give him since he was out of short trousers. Yet there was so much he could not fathom. What did they live for? What did they value? They had to work unstintingly just to stay alive. Jacob still went out to tend the cattle, though now in advancing age his once-broken leg gave him excruciating pain. But many of them did far more than they needed just to live. Frederika cooked and baked not only the essentials, but cakes and pastries as well, and these, as he learned when he asked Nathan, were not just being made now especially in his honour. She baked on this scale all the time.

When she knit socks, unless the need for them was urgent, she would incorporate an elaborate diamond pattern. Yet she seemed to have no idea why she did these things. She would never have said, "To make them beautiful" or "So that I can be proud of them." Even if he had asked her why it was important for her to go on living, he imagined she would only say something like, "Because I knew you'd come back some day" or "In order to see Erika once more" or even "To look after Jacob," but the truth was in none of these.

One night as he was sitting in the parlour (yes, the parlour had been opened up for him as if it were Christmas), he tried to explore this with them, delicately, he hoped. "What do you still hope to do with the time you have left?" he asked tentatively.

At this Jacob drew hard on his pipe and said, "Well, I'd like to see one more field cleared so that Hibbert can stock it with a few more cattle when I'm gone."

Frederika looked surprised at the very question. "I don't have big plans," she said, "particularly now Erika's not here. I just do what needs to be done when it needs to be done."

What he could not speak to them about at all was his father; that would be a liberty too far.

On Adam's last evening in Waldenstein he went out and stood on the Wentzells' porch for a long time, watching the sun move down the sky, changing from orange ball to a diffuse pale pink among the few scattered clouds. Then it turned deeper, and the black tops of the spruce trees on the ridge opposite stood silhouetted against a purple-red backdrop. Astonishing. But did Frederika and Jacob see it? He could not tell.

When it was time to leave, his grandparents stood holding hands in the doorway. People left, and you never saw them again; they all knew that. And what Jacob and Frederika longed for above all was to see Erika once more. They stood there before him, the old woman with her stooping shoulders, in whom he could still just discern faint traces of his mother's beauty, the old man with his stark blue eyes and troublesome limp. Their eyes were full of tears. "If only…" Jacob began. He saw Erika again as a small child under an apple tree, her curls blown back by the strong wind, her face turned up in glee with the exhilaration of the breeze that swept her. Such a small mistake… and maybe not really hers at all. "Tell her to come to see us before…." Adam knew what they meant. Perhaps she might even do so, he reflected, now that Aaron was dead. He said simply, "I'll tell her."

Then the taxi arrived, and he was gone.

༺

All the children remained in the Miller home after the funeral. It was not a happy place, but the school year had ended, and Emma and Virtue had not yet married, so they had little choice. Harry spent as much time at the mill as he could, returning only for a late supper. But after dark, when the sisters were in bed, they heard faint scufflings, scratching of paper, drawers being opened and closed.

"He's looking for a will," Emma whispered to Virtue as they lay beside one another in the old bed.

"But there isn't one; we told him," Virtue replied.

"And when did he ever believe anything we said?"

"He'll want everything, of course."

"Yes, of course. And he won't want to have anything to do with Flora either."

"Well he can't have the property without Flora. They must go together."

"That's what you think. He'll find some devious way of unloading her on one of us." In their planned living arrangements, each realized that having Flora unloaded on one of them would be having Flora unloaded on both.

"Look, I'm fond of Flora," Virtue protested. "And I feel awfully sorry for her. I can just about remember what she used to be like before…well, before. But I'm not having her as a life sentence, and that's an end of it." Virtue also knew that Obadiah would rebel at such an arrangement.

"This shouldn't have been left to us. It's not fair." And that appeared to be Emma's final word on the subject.

They lay silent, each staring up into the darkness with her own troubled thoughts. Then Emma said, "Well I'll tell you one thing. I'm getting married as soon as I can. I don't want anything big, I don't even want the honeymoon in Halifax we'd planned. I just want to be married and out of here."

For once, Virtue did not argue with her sister. "I don't think Mama and Papa would want us to postpone things."

ॐ

The following Sunday, when Nathan and Obadiah arrived as usual, Harry was ready for a showdown. After the noontime meal, he pushed back his chair and said, "I think we need to talk." Instinctively, they all adjourned to the parlour.

They entered the room with trepidation. Nothing here seemed to have changed. Why should it have changed in two weeks? Yet so great had been the upheaval in their own lives that the sameness of the room seemed incongruous.

Harry sat against the middle of the wall facing the door. He had some papers in his hand that gave him a look of being in charge. Flora sat in a corner opposite, as self-effacing as possible. Joan also had chosen a corner and disappeared into it as best she could. Rachel, already weeping, sat near the door. Only Hannah sat bolt upright, opposite Harry, spoiling for a fight.

Harry began to speak, "I have discovered that Virtue was right; there is no will. I have also found out that what would naturally happen in such a case is that everything gets divided evenly among all of us. Now that's crazy; you can all see that's *crazy*. Everything would need to be sold off. You can't divide hundreds of acres of woodland into seven bits, and even if you could, it would be pointless. None of the bits would be worth anything. And the house – well, how can you divide that around seven people? It's ridiculous. You all know that Papa wanted me to carry on the business. And he said to me, I swear he said to me, that he had given me everything. Why he didn't write it down I don't know, but I'm absolutely sure that's what he wanted."

He stopped. There was silence, so he went on, "I would absolutely need the whole of the estate, particularly the mill and the woodland, in order to do this. I know this may seem unfair to you girls, but two of you will have husbands soon who are doing well and will support you, and I have no doubt that the other three will be just as successful." He smiled rather snidely at Hannah, Rachel and Joan.

321

There was a moment's pause. Even Harry must have realized that what he was proposing was audacious, outrageous even. More silence. Then Hannah piped up, "What about Flora?"

This was the bit Harry was least prepared for. "Well, Flora...I...I thought one of you girls would be glad to give Flora a home. Maybe... maybe several of you could have her for part of each year or something like that."

"Play pass the parcel with her, you mean." Hannah was furious.

Then Flora herself spoke. "I want a home of my own. I've worked harder around here than any of you. I deserve as much as anyone else." And she began to cry.

"Look, what you'll each get if we divide it up won't amount to a hill of beans. If the property stays in one piece I can actually do something with it." There was an edge of desperation in Harry's voice. What was he himself trained to do if he lost the mill and woodland?

"Here's what I say." Emma finally raised her voice. "Maybe we girls can give it all away, but if you take the property you've got to take responsibility for Flora as well."

"But I won't, *won't* live with him – or anywhere near him. I hate him." Flora shouted this in an extremity of fear.

"You see? She doesn't *want* help from me." Harry sat back, looking justified.

"That doesn't matter." Emma had the bit between her teeth now. "There are other ways of doing this. Flora can look after herself if we all look in just now and again. You can build her a house all her own, a *nice* house. There's plenty of land here and she doesn't need to be anywhere near you." Emma was amazed at the speed with which she was improvising this.

She looked around at her sisters. They were all slumped in various poses of dejection. They (apart, possibly, from Hannah) would give it all up; she knew they would. And what would they do then? The world was a fine place for men to make their way, but women needed to be sheltered in houses. For all this time, Joan had said nothing. Just maybe.... "Joan?" Emma asked.

"I don't care what happens. I just don't care at all." And she put her head in her hands and disappeared farther into the shadow of her corner.

Then Harry roared out, "All or nothing! I must have all or nothing!"

For a moment they were stunned. The cry came again, "All or nothing!" There was something primal about it, an animal cornered and baring its teeth.

Finally, Virtue spoke: "Fine. I guess you can have whatever you want, Harry. You seem prepared to stop at nothing to get it. It's not worth it; nothing is worth this. Just make sure Flora is looked after."

Emma sat with her head bowed. It all went back to that night, that amazing, terrible night when she and Virtue had been wakened by Flora screaming and had walked through the beautiful snow to the Conrads' house and had watched the red flames dance on the kitchen wall as Flora was immersed in the water. That was why there was no will; that was why they were all sitting here hating Harry, who had not even been born at the time of Flora's illness. Dimly, she heard Harry saying, "I suppose I could build her a house. Something simple. She wouldn't need anything too big or elaborate." If Harry saw all women's needs as modest, he considered those of Flora as completely negligible.

"I want a house like my sisters." And Flora actually stamped her foot.

"You don't need anything of the sort. You'll never get married."

"I will too get married. And I'll have ten babies, one more than Mama. You wait and see." Flora burst into tears.

"You!"

"Harry, I'm not listening to anymore of this." Emma again asserted herself. "If you want anything from us you must look after Flora, and in a proper way. That's settled." For a time there was silence, each absorbed in his or her own thoughts:

"What would Obadiah want me to do?" [Virtue]

"Harry is a pig. Spoiled rotten from the day he was born. Mamma saw that ages ago." [Hannah]

"I have to make sure Flora gets what she deserves. Harry can't be trusted to do the right thing on his own." [Emma]

"No one cares what happens to me. I hate teaching. I can't go on." [Joan]

"What an idiot my father was not to make a will. I know he wanted me to carry on the business. He trained me up for it." [Harry]

"What will I do? What will I do? I shall be stranded in school boarding houses forever. None of this can be happening." [Rachel]

"I hate Harry. I want my mother." [Flora]

"I must do the barn chores." And Harry swaggered out, looking at none of them.

※

The following weekend Emma and Virtue, Hannah and Flora, Joan and Rachel all went quietly to the church where Nathan and Obadiah were waiting. The ceremony was performed simply and quickly. Joan had arranged bouquets of wildflowers for the brides and even made a small coronet of flowers for their hair. Then they walked back as they had come, to the old homestead.

When they got there, to their surprise, a wedding lunch had been prepared. Martha, who seemed to have foreknowledge of everything, had killed two of her own chickens and cooked them in celebration.

"I remember when you two were just little tykes. Do you know, that night you came over to get us when Flora was taken ill? I never understood how you made it through all that snow. But you did. And if you managed then, you'll manage now, believe me."

When the meal was over, the atmosphere changed. "I've got somethin' here," Harry said, "for you girls to sign." It was a legal agreement; he was to inherit everything, as he had wished. He would build Flora a house on the homestead on a piece of land of her own choosing. He would keep her there "in the manner to which she was accustomed."

The papers were laid out on the parlour table. There was no discussion this time. One by one the girls went into the room and signed, Virtue first, and so on down to Rachel. They did not look at one another. It was as if with the ink they negated themselves, wiped out their rightful patrimony, their possessions even down to their mother's wedding hat in the attic, the dolls they had played with as children. All were to be subsumed under the umbrella of male dominance. They were too numb even to cry.

ﺒ

Afterwards they went out into the fields around the house to pick blueberries together for the last time on the land that was no longer theirs. It was a glorious August day, and for a few moments here they could pretend they were still young girls. They would run home with the berries, and Mama would make a pie. Then when it came out of the oven Papa would put down his book or paper, and say how good it smelled, and Mama would offer him a piece with the warning that really it was better to wait until it had cooled. But he would eat it anyway, and the juice would run out into the cavity and pool in the plate. And she would laugh and say, "What a greedy man!"

ﺒ

Then it was time to leave. Nathan and Obadiah came out to the field to claim their brides, and the four of them climbed into the Chev, which was shared, as everything else in their lives was henceforth to be shared. For the first ten miles of the way home both women wept, their husbands silent beside them. It was all over; there was nothing more to be said or done.

But gradually Waldenstein receded like a dream in which they had been enmeshed for too long. As they approached Mahone Bay with its quiet harbour and white houses encircled by verandas, they began to speak. At first it was very mundane: Emma asked Nathan what she should buy at the butcher's for dinner tomorrow. "We could have pork chops, or maybe I'll see if there's some fresh mackerel come in down at the wharf."

Virtue wanted to know whether the new washing machine she and Obadiah had ordered had arrived. "No, but the man in Bridgewater phoned to say it would be here tomorrow."

He *phoned*. Now how amazing was that! Gradually they took hold on these tiny things that would anchor them in this new life that was beginning to seem just possible. They skirted the woods that ran between Mahone Bay and Lunenburg. Then, in a few more miles, they were rattling across the bridge above the railway cutting that separated their town from the surrounding countryside. *Their* town. Yes, that was what it could now be called. To the left they looked up and saw the imposing castle-like structure that was the school. Beside it was the Lutheran church spire, reaching up into the cloudless sky. Knowledge and truth set on a hill together.

They swept towards the lower street and smelled the sea, saw the gulls circling overhead. And here was the little house they were going to inhabit. There was more decorating to be done to it, new recipes to be tried out for their husbands, the whole world of the town to explore, babies to be born and loved. Anything might be possible here.

Words, unbidden, sang in Emma's mind. There was someone, some character in a book she had read once, who had gone running out into a new landscape shouting, "Life, life!" Yes, that was what she wanted to shout too: "Life!" But then she remembered that the line ended, "Eternal Life!" Ah, yes. Eternal Life.

There would be time enough to think about that later.

Acknowledgements

I owe a significant debt in the writing of this book to the late Pauline M. Veinotte whose local history, *Newburne Then and Now,* is one of the best I have ever encountered. I drew on this source for inspiration and incident as I invented the world of Waldenstein and the people who inhabit it.

I am also grateful to all those who have read the novel in manuscript and made suggestions, many of which have helped to shape the final version. In particular I wish to thank Jeannie Cohen, Leonard and Eleanor Jackson, David Monaghan, Christopher Feeney, Heather Veinotte, my husband Oliver and, at the U.K. Writers' Workshop, Eloise Millar, C. M. Taylor, and Harry Bingham. And to my tireless editor, Kathryn McKeen, many, many thanks.